D1045094

THIRD STRIKE

This Large Print Book carries the
Seal of Approval of N.A.V.H.

A CHARLIE FOX THRILLER

THIRD STRIKE

ZOË SHARP

THORNDIKE PRESS
A part of Gale, Cengage Learning

Detroit • New York • San Francisco • New Haven, Conn • Waterville, Maine • London

GALE
CENGAGE Learning™

LIBRARY OF CONGRESS CATALOGING-IN-PUBLICATION DATA

Sharp, Zoë, 1966–
  Third strike : a Charlie Fox thriller / by Zoë Sharp.
    p. cm. — (Thorndike Press large print thriller)
  ISBN-13: 978-1-4104-1308-6 (alk. paper)
  ISBN-10: 1-4104-1308-X (alk. paper)
  1. Fox, Charlie (Fictitious character)—Fiction. 2.
Bodyguards—Fiction. 3. Fathers and daughters—Fiction. 4.
Manhattan (New York, N.Y.)—Fiction. 5. Large type books. I.
Title.
PR6119.H376T48 2009
823'.92—dc22   2008047214

Published in 2009 by arrangement with St. Martin's Press, LLC.

Printed in the United States of America
1 2 3 4 5 6 7 13 12 11 10 09

This is a book about parents, and I shall always be profoundly grateful to mine. For Derek and Jill

ACKNOWLEDGMENTS

Writing a novel is supposed to be a solitary occupation, but we know it isn't. As always, many people came to my assistance with the writing of this book, generously providing encouragement, help, advice, and information. I'm humbly grateful, therefore, to — in no particular order — fellow mystery authors Reed Farrel Coleman, for details on the seedier areas of Brooklyn; Shane Gericke and Fred Rea, for firearms info; Libby Fischer Hellmann, for casting her eye over my accidental Britishisms; and D. P. Lyle, M.D., for his superb detailed medical input. If you want to know how to tie off an artery by the side of the road or break into a hospital, Doug Lyle's your man.

How can I not also mention other great writers who gave encouragement with this one — Ken Bruen, Lee Child, Jeffrey Deaver, and Stuart MacBride, as well as other enthusiasts within the industry — Jon and Ruth Jordan at *Crimespree* magazine and Ali Karim and Mike Stotter at Shots Ezine. Keep wiffling, boys.

McKenna Jordan and David Thompson, from the independent mystery bookstore, Murder by the Book in Houston, added geographical detail, as did Terry Farmer. Thank you to the staff at the Deerfield Pistol & Archery Center in Deerfield, Wisconsin, for letting me play with some cool stuff.

My test readers stood firm, as always — Peter Doleman, Claire Duplock, Sarah Harrison, Iris Rogers, Tim Winfield, and Shell Willbye (who also knows one end of a knitting needle from the other).

Of course, my biggest debts go to my agent, the incomparable Jane Gregory, her editor, Emma Dunford, and all the staff at Gregory & Company Authors' Agents, for their patience, faith, and understanding.

Also to my UK publisher, Susie Dunlop, and my editor, Lara Swift, and all the incredibly enthusiastic and hardworking staff at Allison & Busby. And to my U.S. publisher, St Martin's Minotaur — in particular my editor, Marcia Markland, who also provided New York info; Diana Szu; and all the sales and marketing people who work so hard to make this book a reality in the United States.

Of course, without the constant encouragement of my husband, Andy, nothing would ever get done. Again, thank you.

And finally, I'd like to mention Terry O'Loughlin, who made the winning bid at the charity auction at Bouchercon in Madison, Wisconsin, in 2006, in aid of the Wisconsin Literacy, Inc., charity, to become a character in this book and whom it was enormous fun to include.

ONE

I was running when I saw my father kill himself. Not that he jumped off a tall building or stepped in front of a truck but — professionally, personally — what I watched him do was suicide.

Although I hadn't been keeping a check of the distance, I reckoned I'd covered around eight miles at that point. Not fast, not slow. Just nicely settled into a rhythm where I could concentrate on working through the pain barrier. After six months' slog, it didn't seem to be getting any less solid, nor any further away. The doctors had told me I'd probably make a full recovery from the double-gunshot injury that had damn near been the end of me. They just hadn't said when.

But just as I thought I might finally reach the finish this time before I hit that particular wall, I ran headlong into something else entirely.

As soon as I saw him, my stride faltered, all coordination leaving me. I stumbled and fell against the guardrail of the treadmill, rebounding heavily. The heart rate monitor pads came away from my chest and the alarm began to screech.

"Charlie!" Nick, my personal trainer, reached out a steadying arm. "Are you all right? Your leg —"

I shook my head, shook him off. "Turn it up," I said, swiping the sweat out of my eyes. When Nick just gaped, I jerked my head towards the overhead TV. "The sound, Nick. Turn up the damn sound!"

I hadn't immediately recognized my father on the morning news program playing silently above me during this latest fitness test, but that was no great surprise. I was in New York City and he was safely back home in England — or so I'd thought. I hadn't spoken to him since I'd moved out here in the spring.

Not that relocating permanently to the States had greatly widened the rift that already existed between us. My parents had always disliked the career that had chosen me, almost as much as they'd disliked the man who'd helped make that choice: Sean Meyer.

Knowing the main reason I'd come here

was to be with Sean didn't exactly make them enthusiastic about the whole scheme. And the fact that the pair of us had been offered jobs with Parker Armstrong's exclusive close-protection agency working out of midtown Manhattan probably put the final seal of disapproval on it for them.

The Americans, I'd discovered, had a policy about persistent offenders — three strikes and you were out. As far as my parents were concerned I'd had my third strike and they were finished with me, and I'd done my best to put them out of my mind.

So, my father was the last person I'd expected to see on one of the news channels, but it was the scrolling headline across the bottom of the screen that identified him with the words DISGRACED BRITISH DOCTOR FACES QUESTIONS that really rocked me.

The "doctor" part was familiar, at least, although that was a little like describing Field Marshal Montgomery as a mere soldier. My father was a consultant orthopedic surgeon, brilliant, arrogant, at the top of his game.

But the rest of the caption — now that didn't square with the man I knew at all.

So, what the hell . . .

Nick, slow with sculpted muscle, had dropped the clipboard on which he'd been keeping a nitpicking note of my progress and had grabbed for the remote control, fumbling with the volume. He overdid the balance and suddenly my father's cool clipped tones cut across the gym, startling the handful of other occupants.

"Patients die," he said with a bluntness that would never win him the sympathy vote. "Sometimes it happens, despite one's best efforts."

"So tell me, Doctor," said the woman with the big hair and the microphone, "exactly how many patients would you *normally* expect to die in your care?" Her tone was snappy, verging on a gloat.

"I have been a surgeon for over thirty years," my father said, supercilious. He was holding his shoulders tightly bunched and the normal wealthy tan of his face was bleached out, the skin drum taut across his bones. "I don't expect to lose any."

"So you're claiming this is an isolated case?" the woman said blandly. "Surely, Doctor —"

"It's *Mister*, not *Doctor*," he cut in acidly over the top of his gold-framed glasses, the same way he would have castigated a junior trainee who bungled a simple diagnosis.

14

"Kindly make *some* attempt to get your facts correct, madam."

I sucked in a breath. I'd skirmished with the media myself in the past, enough to know that outright provocation was a grave mistake. They had the ultimate power, after the event, to maneuver you into the role of villain or fool, according to their whim. They'd played both ends of that game with me, and won with insolent ease.

Her eyes narrowed momentarily, but she was too much of a pro to let him rattle her. Instead, she tilted her head and smiled unpleasantly. "Oh, I think you'll find that I've done my research very carefully," she said. "Last week, for instance, I know that one of your patients died suddenly and unexpectedly in a hospital in Massachusetts."

He paused just a fraction too long before responding. "Yes, but no surgery had been performed —"

"And that your first reaction was to try and shift the blame for this away from yourself by claiming that the patient in question had deliberately been given an overdose of morphine. Despite the fact," she went on, steamrollering over any attempt at interruption, "that no evidence has been found to support this."

15

"I have withdrawn my comments," my father said stiffly, with such self-control that I could almost hear his teeth enamel breaking up under the strain. "And it would be unethical for me to discuss —"

" 'Unethical?' " She cut in, her voice cool even though her eyes betrayed the glitter. "Isn't it the case that the patient in question, Jeremy Lee, was an old friend of yours and was suffering from a painful degenerative disease? You were very . . . *close* to his wife, I understand," she murmured. Her voice was artfully casual, but the unspoken inference came across loud and clear. "You were staying with Mrs. Lee — alone, at her home — while you were treating her husband in the hospital. Isn't that somewhat . . . *unethical?*"

Walk away. I found myself willing him, hands clenched. *Why are you standing there like a bloody fool and letting her carve you up like this? Walk. Away.*

But he didn't.

"I've known both the Lees for many years," he said instead, keeping his impatience in check only with visible effort. "It's natural that I should stay with Miranda — Mrs. Lee — while I'm in America. It was Mrs. Lee herself who asked me to come and advise on her husband's condition. Nothing

16

more." I wondered if he knew that his uneasy denials only added weight to the reporter's snide insinuations.

"I see," she said, injecting an artful note of doubt into her voice. She frowned, as though considering his words and her own carefully, but underneath it I saw the triumph building, and realized that she'd been leading him to this point right from the start. "And is Mrs. Lee aware that you've been suspended from your duties for being drunk on the job?"

"I have never endangered a patient through alcohol," my father snapped, but as he spoke something flickered in his face. I saw it only because I was looking, but I knew others would be watching him just as closely and they would have seen it, too.

Guilt. Unmistakable.

Holy shit . . .

"But you don't deny that you've made life-and-death decisions after you've had a drink, Mr. Foxcroft?" She left a pause he didn't rush to fill and she allowed herself a small smile, as though politely acknowledging his admission. "Maybe even a couple of drinks." Smooth, smiling, she moved in for the kill. "Isn't it the case that your earlier allegation was simply an attempt to divert attention from your own transgressions?"

17

My father flushed, took a breath. "The hospital will no doubt hold some kind of internal inquiry. Until then, it would be improper to comment further," he said, struggling to regroup and only managing to sound pompous instead. "Not to mention unprofessional and unfair to the patient's family."

She didn't quite crow at this obvious retreat, but she allowed herself the luxury of another feline smile. "Oh, really, Mr. Foxcroft," she said. "I think it's a little late to worry about things like that, isn't it?"

He stiffened. "At this stage I have nothing further to add to my statement," he said. And then, just when I'd begun to think that the whole thing was some kind of gigantic mistake, he took my breath away by adding, "I — I've admitted that I have a problem with alcohol. I have agreed to withdraw from all surgical procedures and take an unpaid leave of absence until that problem is resolved."

What?

Finally — *finally* — he began to move away, but the reporter wasn't so easily shaken off. They were on a city street, I saw, with generic modern concrete buildings behind them and the sound of traffic in the background. My father was wearing an immaculate dark blue suit, white shirt, sober tie that reeked discreetly of old school, his thinning hair sleek to his scalp. An archetypal authority figure. The kind the media loved to see crash and burn.

"Mr. Foxcroft, numerous patients must have — perhaps misguidedly — placed their trust in you as a highly respected member of the medical profession," she persisted, thrusting the microphone into his face. "Have you *nothing* to say to them?"

"Charlie, what the —" Nick began, unconsciously echoing my earlier thought, as his brain finally caught up with what was happening.

"Ssh!" I braced my arms on the front of the stationary treadmill, suddenly far more badly winded than a mere eight-mile jog would ever justify.

My father paused and, possibly for the first time in my life, I saw uncertainty in him. Perhaps even the faintest suggestion of panic.

He glanced away from the woman's face and looked directly into the camera, as though he could see me staring back at him.

"I'm sorry," he said simply. Then he turned, ignoring the clamor the apparent admission caused, ducked into a waiting car, and was gone.

The reporter faced the camera, power suit, power makeup, scarlet nails clutched round her microphone as she delivered her gleeful wrap-up. Her words scalded me but afterwards I couldn't recall a single one of them.

It had finally dawned on me that the reporter was a regular on one of the local news channels. That the car my father had climbed into was a black Lincoln Town Car with no stretch, and the building he'd been standing outside was one of the big hotels less than a dozen blocks from where I stood.

He was right here. In New York. In trouble.

And I hadn't known a thing about it.

Nick still had hold of the remote control. He was big enough that it looked like a toy in his hands. As the reporter handed back to the studio, he thumbed the volume down again and eyed me with quizzical concern.

"So, that guy — someone you know?"

For a moment I didn't — couldn't — answer. My head was buzzing like I'd taken a blow. My leg ached fiercely, more of a burn. "I thought I knew him," I murmured at last, slowly. "But now I'm not so sure."

Nick frowned. "You okay to go on?" he said. "Or you wanna take five?"

That got my attention. I flicked him a fast glance. "Look, Nick, I need to leave. Now."

"You can't," he said. He picked up his clipboard, lifted a page, frowning harder. "You got maybe another twenty minutes, tops, then we're all done. Way you're going, you're gonna ace this. C'mon Charlie, what's so important that it can't wait twenty minutes?"

"That," I said, jerking my head towards the TV set. I scooped up my towel from the bench and started for the changing rooms, only to feel Nick's hand rough on my shoulder.

"Hey! You don't walk out on me, lady." His voice rose, harsh. "Mr. Armstrong pays me for results and I got a lotta time invested in you."

The only excuse I have for what happened next is that my mind was half in shock from the news report. It slackened the usual restraints that govern my behavior and my temper ignited to a white hot burn. I grabbed his imprisoning hand and stepped out from underneath it, jerking the heel of his palm upwards into a vicious lock.

Nick was around six foot one and more than two hundred pounds. He had six inches in height and maybe eighty pounds on me. Now, he tried to use that differential in resistance but his bulk was gym cultivated. Useful as a deterrent maybe, but clearly he had never been a fighter.

I tightened the lock and yanked him round like an Olympic hammer thrower going for gold. He sprawled into one of the racks of dumb-bells, sending half of them rebounding to the wooden floor, and thudded down heavily onto his knees. The noise was thunderous. Somebody nearby — a man — squealed.

I still had the lock on his wrist. Nick was grunting now, his substantial muscles trembling. In the right hands, pain compliance can be a wonderful thing. I leaned in close enough to smell the sweat.

"I'm in a hurry, so I'm willing to forget what just happened here," I said, my voice entirely reasonable. "But if you ever lay a hand on me again, *you're* the one who's going to need half a year of physio, okay?"

Two

Driving a car in Manhattan is madness, but reliably parking one there is worse. So, one of my first actions when we'd arrived was to buy another motorcycle. I'd left my Honda FireBlade in storage when I'd left the UK and missed it every day.

As soon as I'd felt physically capable of riding it, I'd succumbed and, in deference to my new adopted homeland, had bought a midnight black Buell XB12R Firebolt. It didn't have the outright speed of the 'Blade, but it was skinny and nimble enough to slice through the midtown crush. Most of the time, at any rate.

Usually, I can slip relatively unimpeded through the vast sea of yellow cabs that seem to outnumber the private cars on Manhattan Island by at least two to one. But today, because I was under pressure, because I was in a hurry, nobody wanted to give me mirror-width gaps. I'd cracked the

23

left-hand mirror less than a month after I'd bought the bike, and I didn't want to add to the bad luck.

So I sat, feeling the nagging pulse in my left leg, hemmed in by hot steel boxes vibrating gently as they scattered heat and fumes into the surrounding air, listening to the symphony of the city. Going nowhere. Ahead, Lexington Avenue ran arrow-straight south almost to vanishing point, like a taunt.

Around me, the monumental buildings of New York hummed and breathed. It was early September, balmy after the brutal summer just past, the temperature shedding its way gently into the time of year I still thought of as autumn rather than fall.

And all the while, I was running through scenarios of how on earth a man as coldly disciplined as my father could possibly have caused a patient to die under his hands through sheer bloody carelessness.

"Until that problem is resolved," he'd said, like being a possible alcoholic was a temporary, minor inconvenience.

I cast back through the empty rooms that held my childhood memories, but nothing clicked into place. There had been no unexplained clinking from the wastepaper basket in his study, no long periods he'd spent in the garden nursing a furtive hip flask, no telltale smear of peppermint across his breath. He liked the occasional single malt and drank it like a connoisseur, with due reverence and ceremony. No more than that.

But every time I thought I'd come up with some plausible excuse, his own words damned him all over again.

A long time ago, when I'd been up to my ears in scandal not entirely of my own making, I'd officially shortened my name from Foxcroft to Fox. At the time I'd explained my decision away to my half-offended, half-relieved parents by telling them I didn't want to drag their name through the mire along with my own.

I'd never considered for a moment that one day it might also work in reverse.

The hotel where I suspected my father was staying was Italian owned and run. Elevated in status more by its location than its own merits. Shabby chic. I took one look at the haughty doorman outside and knew I wasn't going to be able to charm or bribe my way through this one.

I found an alleyway where I could ditch the bike, and legged it two blocks south to the nearest booze store, where I bought a bottle of twenty-one-year-old Dalmore

Scotch. I had to show my driver's licence in order to prove I was older than the whisky, even though I was six years past that milestone birthday. Way I'd felt lately, it could have been sixty.

Outside, I flagged down a cab, my heart sinking a little when I saw the Pakistani driver. I worried that he might have an ethical problem with carrying alcohol, but as soon as I started explaining what I wanted, his face split into a toothy grin.

"No problem, love," he said.

I smiled back. "You don't sound like you're from the Bronx."

He laughed. "Just a bit further east, love," he said. His accent was Birmingham, West Midlands, rather than Birmingham, Alabama. "Us Brits should stick together, i'nt that right?"

I gave him the whisky, still in its embossed tube, with a hastily scrawled card stuck into the top, a twenty-dollar bill, and the delivery address. He took off into traffic and I jogged back to the hotel, loitering at a store window on the other side of the street. It took the cab a few minutes to circle back and I admit all kinds of thoughts passed through my mind about whether I'd just been conned.

A few moments later, I watched the reflection in the glass as the cabdriver pulled up

26

sharply by the curb. The hotel doorman reached automatically for the rear door handle until he saw the backseat was empty. By that time the driver was out, clutching my gift. A few explanatory words were exchanged. The doorman took the whisky, nodding, pursing his lips as he eyed the exclusive label.

The driver regained his seat just as a couple came out of the hotel, dragging luggage. I smiled. At least he'd picked up a genuine fare for his trouble.

I hurried across towards the entrance and walked inside without any hesitation. Look like you belong and most people don't question it. The lobby was dimly lit by comparison, all cracked tile floors and air-con chill. I went slowly across towards the elevators, digging in my rucksack, distracted, as though I was looking for my room key.

Out of the corner of my eye I saw the doorman hand the whisky to the concierge, who glanced at the card, tapped on his computer keyboard, then picked up the phone. From the way he peered at the box as he spoke, the brand was the deciding factor and I knew then that the Dalmore was worth the outrageous price I'd just paid for it. Despite the recent revelations, experience still told me that my father was a moderate drinker who went only for the good stuff when he did.

The concierge put the phone down and curtly flicked his fingers to a teenage bellhop, who took possession of my Trojan horse. I picked up my pace, timing it so the bellhop and I both arrived at a set of opening elevator doors together.

The elevator had mirrored walls. As I stepped in I made sure I moved to the side away from the control panel, forcing the bellhop to select his floor first. He pressed the button for twelve and glanced at me inquiringly.

"Oh," I said, feigning surprise, smiling. "Me, too."

According to the brass plaque on the control panel, the elevator was made by a company called Schindler, as they often were. Even after all this time the name still tickled me, but I'd soon learned that my amusement was not shared by anyone who didn't refer to an elevator as a lift.

We clanked upwards in silence, avoiding eye contact. The bellhop had dark hair and sallow skin and a pierced ear with the stud removed for work, I guessed. He fiddled with the whisky tube, smoothing out a crumpled area of the cardboard, like any damage might affect his tip.

At the twelfth floor I was hoping I could tag along unobtrusively, but he insisted that I get off the elevator first. *Damn these kids with manners.*

I took a couple of steps, then turned with a smile.

"Excuse me," I said, apologetic, playing up my British accent when I'd spent the last half a year toning it down. "I wonder, do you know anything about the times of the city tour buses that leave from the stop over the road?"

He was helpful, if not exactly chatty. I managed to fall into step alongside him and keep up the stream of brainless questions as we moved along the creaking corridor. The overhead lighting was just bright enough to make out the dusty pattern on the ancient custom-made carpet.

At last, just when I'm sure he thought I was trying to pick him up, the bellhop paused outside a room, giving me an apologetic shrug to indicate this was the end of his line.

I flicked my eyes over the number as I thanked him for his trouble and kept walking, making sure that when the door opened I was out of sight. There came the murmur of a familiar voice, then the sound of the door closing again. I gave it another ten seconds or so before I stuck my head back round the corner, just in time to see the bellhop disappearing. A moment later, I was knocking on the door to my father's room.

I was hoping that he wouldn't check the Judas glass again before he answered the door a second time, but I saw by the change in light behind it that he did. There was a long pause and I knocked again, hammered with my fist, staring straight at the little glass eye.

"You can have me thrown out if you want," I said, loud enough to be heard inside, "but you know I won't go quietly."

In my imagination, I heard an exasperated sigh. The locks were disengaged and the door opened to reveal my father standing square in the gap.

"Charlotte," he greeted me without warmth or enthusiasm. I tried briefly to remember if he'd ever smiled at me, his only child, for no better reason than because that's who I was. Maybe my memory didn't stretch back that far.

"Aren't you going to invite me in?" I asked, matching my tone to his. "Or are you . . . otherwise engaged?"

He stilled at the deliberate insult in my voice but didn't rise to it.

"Come in," he said calmly, stepping back

with an imperious jerk of his head.

Once inside I discovered that the room was more of a suite. Not that it was surprisingly generous with its floor space, just divided up more. The narrow two-pace hallway had a bathroom off to the left, then opened up into a small sitting area, hung with dull prints, where a stunted sofa vied for supremacy with a spindly looking desk.

Another door led from there into what I assumed was the bedroom, but it was firmly closed to my inquisitive eyes. The room décor, like the rest of the place, had once been quality but was now in dire need of a refurb.

I turned back just in time to see my father's eyes slide to the bottle of whisky sitting on the low table in front of the sofa, then back to me. "Your doing, I assume?"

I shrugged. "What good is knowing someone's weakness, if you don't exploit it?"

I hadn't intended to taunt him, but now I was here my anger rose up and roared in my ears.

"Ah, is that why you're here?" he asked. "To exploit my weakness?"

"Actually, no. I saw the news this morning," I said, and when he did no more than lift an eyebrow slightly, I added, "I was hoping for some kind of an explanation."

31

He was still wearing the suit I'd seen him in on the TV, the knot of his tie sitting up perfectly into the vee of the starched collar. God forbid he should ever loosen it in the presence of anyone except his wife of thirty-something years. And probably not even then.

"Ah," he said, the barest of smiles crossing his lips. He strolled over to the low table and picked up the Dalmore, studied the box with a vaguely disdainful air and put it down again. "And you think a bottle of cheap single malt buys you the right to one, hm?"

The "cheap" jibe surprised me. "For myself, no," I said coolly. "For my mother, I think it probably wasn't worth the price."

I didn't need to imagine his sigh this time. He made a show of pushing back a rigid shirt cuff to check the antique gold watch beneath it.

"Was there something specific you wanted to say?" he asked, sounding bored now. "I do have an appointment."

"Who with? Another reporter? The police?" I nodded to the bottle. "Or perhaps you just can't wait to open that?"

For the first time, I saw a flash of anger, quickly veiled, followed by something else. Something darker. Pain? He took a breath and was calm again.

"You've clearly made up your own mind without any input from me," he said. "But then, you always were a spoilt and willful child. Hardly surprising that you've made such a mess of your life."

The gasp rose like a bubble. I only just managed to smother it before it could break the surface.

" 'A mess'?" I repeated, the outrage setting up harmonic vibrations that rattled at the heart of me. "*I've* made a mess of *my* life? Oh, that's rich."

He made an annoyed gesture with those long surgeon's fingers of his, staring at me over the thin frames of his glasses. "Please don't go blaming anyone else for your mistakes, Charlotte. We both know you're over here solely because the people who have laughably employed you wanted the services of your semi-Neanderthal boyfriend enough to offer you some sinecure. And because he was too sentimental to leave you behind."

"They offered me a job alongside him," I managed. I was disappointed to note that gritting my teeth did nothing, it seemed, to prevent the slight tremor that had crept into my voice. "On my own merits."

"Ah, yes of course." He glanced upwards

for a moment, as if seeking heavenly intervention. When he looked back at me, his face was mocking. "Face it, my dear, you're little better than a cripple. A liability to those around you. You've already proved you can't be trusted to do a job without injuring yourself and others. What possible use could they have for you?"

"For your information, I've just been passed fit," I said, ignoring the fibrous tension burning up through the long muscles of my left thigh that made a lie of my words. I tried not to think of my abandoned fitness test, of what Nick was likely to put in his report. "I'll be back on —"

"Credit me with some experience in these matters, Charlotte, if nothing else," he interrupted, glacial now. "You may not approve of my ethics, but my surgical abilities are quite beyond question, and I've seen your records. You may be walking without that limp any longer, but your health will never be exactly what one might describe as robust again. A little light office work is about all you're fit for. You know as well as I do that they'll never quite trust you again."

The shock wave of his words pummeled into me, sent me reeling back before I could brace myself. It took everything I had not to let him see me stagger.

34

"Oh, that's right," I said, soft in my bitterness. "Your daughter — the disgrace. All your self-righteous lectures about the shame I've brought on you, on Mother, and for what? For being a victim. And then when I stop being a victim, still you damn me."

I paused. He said nothing and his silence only spurred me on. "You've never liked Sean — you've made that pretty bloody clear. But he's stood by me better than my own parents have ever done. And now I find you're nothing but a drunken butcher. How does that square with your sense of bloody superiority?"

"That's. Enough." It was almost a whisper. His face was bone white, his gaze everywhere but on me. When he put a hand up to his eyes I saw that it shook a little, and I was fiercely glad. But when he spoke again, his voice was neutral, almost dismissive. "I think you'd better leave, Charlotte. Throwing insults at each other is time-consuming and hardly productive, wouldn't you say?"

I whirled back towards the door and found I'd barely made it three strides into the room. I grabbed the handle and twisted, but found I couldn't leave it there.

" 'Surgical abilities beyond question.' Is that right?" I threw at him. "Well, at least whenever I've had cause to stick a knife into somebody I've always been stone-cold sober."

THREE

"You finally made it in, huh?" Bill Rendelson said. There was a row of clocks hanging on the glossy marble wall above the reception desk where he held court, and he pointedly twisted in his chair so he could check the one set to New York time. "The boss wants to see you — like, yesterday."

I'd barely stepped out of the elevator before Bill had delivered his ominous message. He heaved his blocky frame upright and stalked across the lobby to knock on the door to Parker Armstrong's office.

Bill could have buzzed through to let Parker know I was here, but he liked to rub it in. He'd been with the agency since the beginning, so the story went, and three years previously he'd lost his right arm at the shoulder in a parcel-bomb attack on the South African businessman he was protecting. His principal had survived unscathed, but Bill's active service career was over.

When Sean and I had first started working for Parker, I'd assumed from his abrupt manner that Bill had taken against us for some reason, but it was soon clear that he didn't like anyone very much. I often wondered if Parker's keeping Bill on — in a job so close to the heart of things but without actually being able to get out there anymore — was an act of kindness or cruelty. Sometimes I thought perhaps Bill had his doubts about that, too.

Now, he pushed open the door in response to his boss's summons, and jerked his head to me. I stiffened my spine and walked straight in without a pause, nodding to him as I went. He gave a kind of half sigh, half grunt by way of acknowledgment, and yanked the door shut behind me as though to prevent my premature escape.

Parker Armstrong's office was understated and discreet, like the man. Modern, pale wood furniture and abstract original canvases. Not for him the usual gaudy rake of signed photos showing chummy handshakes with the rich and famous.

The office occupied a corner of the building and was high enough not to be easily overlooked — no mean feat in any city. Parker's desk sat across the diagonal, so his chair was protected by the vee of the wall, his back to the windows, to allow potential clients to be slightly intimidated by the view.

He was on the phone when I walked in, and I expected to have to wait while he finished the call, but he wound up the conversation almost right away, stood and came round the desk to meet me.

Parker was a slim man, tall and serious. His hair had once been dark until hit by an early frost, and that made him difficult to put an age to. His face was handsome without being arresting, the kind that the eye would glance over, rather than rest on. Perfect for the line of work he'd chosen. And yet, if you looked closely enough, you saw something more in Parker, a depth, a strength, a watchfulness.

He was wearing a dark single-breasted suit with the jacket unbuttoned, and a narrow tie. I was glad I'd taken the time to put my business face on and change out of my scruffs. Wool trousers and a silk shirt in the obligatory New York black, the collar high enough to hide my more obvious scars.

"Charlie," Parker said, steering me towards one of the leather armchairs near the desk. "Take a seat. You want coffee?"

A gentle accent, not immediately placeable, the U.S. equivalent of classless. I'd heard him add twang or blur to it, depending on the company he was keeping. A natural chameleon. There was a lot about him that reminded me of an older Sean. Perhaps that was why Parker had offered him a partnership in the first place.

I shook my head and he moved across to the filter machine he had permanently on the go in the corner. "You sure? It's Jamaican Blue Mountain — just in."

His taste in expensive coffee was practically his only vice — or the only one I'd found out about, at any rate. He had fresh-roasted beans delivered by the pound from McNulty's aromatic old-fashioned store in Greenwich Village.

"So," I said, wanting to take the offensive rather than wait for him to do so, "you've spoken to Nick."

Lifting the coffee cup to his lips only partially obscured the quick grimace, his mouth twisting up at the corner.

"Yeah." He arched an eyebrow. "He's not a happy guy."

"He should have kept his hands to himself," I shot back.

"Maybe so," he allowed, "but you coulda been a little more, ah, diplomatic in giving him the brush-off."

I shrugged to cover the fact I'd already realized that. "Maybe."

Parker sighed and put the cup down, regaining his seat like a judge about to pass sentence.

"Close protection is all about attitude, Charlie," he said, sounding tired now. "Mind-set. You gotta see the big picture, weigh all the options. React to a high-threat situation — not just fast but smart, too."

Here it comes. . . .

There was a hollow panic rising under my rib cage. I swallowed it down along with my pride, and admitted, "I do recognize that what I did this morning probably didn't exactly qualify as smart."

For a moment Parker regarded me with eyes that seemed kindly, but missed nothing and forgave less.

"No," he said. "It wasn't."

I waited, heart rate beginning to pick up, for the blade to fall.

Then he smiled.

"But I'll bet it was damned funny," he said.

My shoulders dropped a fraction.

"Well . . . yes," I said faintly. "Yes, I suppose it was."

The smile broadened so that his whole face joined in, and slipped into a chuckle that he attempted to dilute with another mouthful of coffee.

"Nick's a nice guy, but he's a wanna-be," Parker said. "Always dropping hints about how he'd be a good guy for me to have on the team. I guess now he's seen what a real pro can do, he'll shut the hell up about it and I'll finally get some peace."

I sat there, blankly, wondering if I'd really just done what I thought I'd done. Got away with it.

"What about my assessment?" I said, still looking for the catch. "I didn't finish it and —"

"Charlie," Parker cut in, shaking his head. "Way I heard it, you just threw a guy nearly twice your size and weight halfway across a room. I think it's safe to say you're fit enough to get back to work, don't you?"

I still hadn't come up with a suitable reply when there was a perfunctory knock on the door. It opened without waiting for permission and I knew without turning around who'd just walked in.

Parker looked over my shoulder at the new visitor and his face lit up again.

"Hey, Sean," he said. "Come on in. I was just telling Charlie she's all out of excuses."

"Mm," Sean said, "I would have thought she is."

I turned then, alerted by the coolness in his tone, and found Sean watching me

42

closely. I knew him, on every kind of level, better than I'd known anyone, but at times like these I didn't know him at all. He was impossible to second-guess. I felt that near-black gaze like liquid on my skin.

Even years after he'd first terrified me as the toughest instructor on the Special Forces training course I'd crashed out of in such spectacular fashion, he still thoroughly unnerved and unsettled me.

Deliberately, I turned away, just in time to see Parker's eyes flicking speculatively between the two of us. He knew we had a relationship outside work — of course he did — but he'd never asked questions and we'd never given him cause to. A state of affairs I didn't intend to disturb.

"She needs a further assessment," Sean said now.

"Sean, I'm okay."

"Physically, yes," he agreed evenly.

"Yes," Parker said, regarding me carefully. "I get what you mean."

Sean crossed the office floor, making almost no noise on the tiles. He leaned his shoulder against the window reveal to Parker's left and folded his arms. Like Parker, he was wearing a dark suit and looked as at home in it as he once had in army camouflage. There was probably only ten years between them, but at that moment they could almost have been father and son. Both men eyed me silently, as though I was suddenly going to crack open for them to read.

"Well, would somebody mind spelling it out for me?" I said with a touch of bite. "What? You think I'm going to run away the next time someone points a gun at me?"

"No," Sean said. "I think you're more likely to make sure they don't get the chance."

"Overreact, you mean?"

"It's a possibility." He gave a negligent lift of one of those wide shoulders. Sometimes, for a thug, Sean could be very elegant. "We have to be sure — and so do you."

My father's words were suddenly loud and mocking inside my head. *You've already proved you can't be trusted to do a job without injuring yourself and others. What possible use could they have for you?*

"There's one way to find out," I said, as calmly as I could manage, chin rising to meet the challenge. "Put me back out there. You'll soon know if I'm up to it."

"Hey, whoa," Parker said, holding his right hand straight up, side on, and tapping his left flat across the top of it to form a T. "Time out, guys." He didn't raise his voice, but he rarely had to.

"For starters," he went on, glancing at me, "there's no way I'm going to use any of our clients to find out if you're gun-shy, Charlie. Not that I think for a moment that you are, but it would a real stupid move on my part, okay?"

I made a conscious effort to let my hackles subside.

"Okay," I agreed meekly.

"You've been doing great behind the scenes these last few months. Bill tells me the guys reckon nobody runs a team like you do. You're terrific on logistics. You don't sweat the small stuff, but you don't overlook anything, either. And you always remember to feed them."

The praise surprised me, not least because of its source. "But I don't want to be —"

"— stuck behind a desk all day," Parker finished for me. He indicated the office we were in with a sweep of his hand. "Trust me," he said wryly. "I know all about that one."

"There's a course coming up in Minneapolis next month," Sean said, drawing our eyes back to him. "Stress Under Fire. I've already booked you a place on it."

"You got her in?" Parker said. "Good work. They're usually pretty full."

Sean allowed himself a smile. "Ah well, I booked it a month or so ago."

"Stress Under Fire?" I queried, still processing the double-edged information of Sean's faith and lack of it.

"Does exactly what it says on the can," he said. "Checks out your reactions. What decisions you make and the way you make them when you're in the thick of it. It's tough. You pass that, nobody will question whether you're ready to get back out there."

"A liability to those around you," my father had said. *"You know as well as I do that they'll never quite trust you again."*

"And if I fail?"

Sean said nothing.

Parker smiled again, the action crinkling the corners of those watchful eyes.

"You won't," he said.

"So, do *you* think I'll fail?" I asked.

It was later. Much later. We were home in the apartment we'd rented on the Upper East Side. The minimal view of Central Park should have been enough to ensure the cost of it was stratospheric, but one of Parker's relations owned the building. Parker had abused the family connection to squeeze the rent down to a level that was merely exorbitant, as part of a tempting relocation package.

"Of course not," Sean said.

His face was in shadow, but in my mind he spoke too quick, too easy. I tried to acknowledge that I was just being touchy. That I would have taken any pause as a sign of hesitation rather than due consideration of the question.

As if he'd heard my thoughts, he sighed, his chest rising and falling beneath my cheekbone. I could hear his heart beating strong and steady under me. Incomplete assessment or no, we were both more than fit enough for our pulse rates to quickly drop back to a slow rhythm after exertion.

"If I thought that, I wouldn't send you," he said, his hand skimming lazily along my upper arm. "I trained you, after all. You cock it up and it makes me look bad."

It was dark outside, in as much as New York ever gets dark. The lights in the apartment were out but we hadn't drawn the window blinds and the rattle and glimmer of the city slipped in through the open glass like a slow-footed thief. For the first six weeks or so, the unaccustomed bursts of noise had woken me constantly during the night. Now I found it all vaguely soothing.

We hadn't had a chance to talk since our encounter in Parker's office earlier that day.

We'd spent the afternoon, and most of the evening, entertaining a group of high-ranking executives from a major banking corporation. The bank was trying to forge development links with certain South American countries, where its personnel would be prime targets for kidnap and extortion.

Parker had spent several months — not to mention a considerable amount of money — quietly trying to convince the bank the dangers were sufficient to subcontract all its safety precautions out to us. If tonight was anything to go by, it looked like he'd finally succeeded.

He'd taken a few of the top guys out on the town and had called in every spare operative on his books to provide a maximum force, minimum fuss, security detail for them. We'd gone to extraordinary lengths to be visible in the most unobtrusive manner possible.

Parker had put me working the inner ring, closest to the principals. Mostly, he'd done it because he was aware that women blended in much better in low-profile social situations than hulking great blokes. I'd certainly learned to dress like a young city exec since I'd been working for him. But it was also a good opportunity to show faith in me —

admittedly without much risk. Either way, I was profoundly grateful.

Parker had kept Sean at the forefront, too, and he knew how to play the game when it came to sweet-talking potential clients. We'd taken them to watch the sun go down over cocktails in a rooftop bar on Fifth Avenue that had a great view of the Empire State Building, then gone on to eat in one of the best restaurants in trendy TriBeCa.

It could have been romantic, had we not been working, and had we not been in a group whose main characteristic was an ego to match the size of the investment port-folios they handled, and the cocky self-assurance that went with it.

So, Sean and I had hardly exchanged a word all evening, and nothing in private. We hadn't even traveled home together. I'd changed at the office and taken the Buell, and Sean had stayed for the debrief with Parker and arrived by cab two hours later.

He'd got back to find me sitting curled up on the sofa in the airy living room, making a poor attempt to read a survival equipment catalog. I'd glanced up as he'd walked in stripping off his jacket and tie, unclipping the Kramer paddle-rig holster containing the .45-caliber Glock 21 he habitually car-ried. He was tall, deceptively wide across the shoulder without having the overdeveloped neck of a gorilla, and devastatingly but unself-consciously good-looking. My mouth had gone instantly dry at the sheer intensity of his face.

So it was only afterwards, as the cool air dusted the sweat from our bodies, that I finally had the chance to ask the question uppermost in my mind.

He shifted slightly and let his fingers drift along my spine, circling outwards to delicately trace the fading scar of the bullet wound in the back of my right shoulder.

"It's not that I don't have faith in you, Charlie, you know that," he said gently. "But what you've been through changes you. Christ Jesus, you nearly died. It can't not."

"It was probably worse from the outside, looking in," I said, knowing that was only partly true. "And anyway, I didn't die." *Hell, not long enough for it to count.*

But as I said it I tried not to think about the Vicodin I'd taken before the start of the evening. I was too scared of getting hooked to take the painkillers regularly, but they'd successfully taken the edge off the ache that had plagued me all day.

I blocked out my father's stinging comments. *You may be walking without a limp any longer, but your health will never be exactly what one might describe as robust again. A little light office work is about all you're fit for.*

Had Parker seen that? Is that why he'd made that comment about me being good at organization — because he wanted me to keep me reduced to nothing more?

Sean's fingers stilled a moment and I realized I'd braced myself against the memory. I took a quiet breath and let my limbs float heavy.

"Depends on what you classify as normal, I suppose," he said. "I've been there, too, don't forget. I know how it changes your perception of things — of how far you can go — because you know what the ultimate consequences are for failing."

"I know you've been hurt — shot, beaten, threatened with execution — but trust me, Sean, you have no idea," I said, hearing the rough note in my voice.

His hands stilled again, then tightened around me, cradling my head. I felt his lips brush my hair, then one of his fingers trailed delicately down the side of my neck and across the base of my throat, following the faint line of an old scar that was another constant reminder never to drop my guard. Shame it hadn't always worked.

"I'm sorry," he murmured. "That was crass."

"Yes it was. I can still function, you know," I said, unwilling to let him off lightly. "I'm not completely socially stunted. Didn't I prove that tonight?"

"You did," he said. "In fact, you were so successful in *not* looking like a bodyguard that one of the prats from the bank actually asked if you were, ahem, part of the entertainment package."

I stiffened for a moment, then a giggle escaped me and before I knew it we were both laughing.

"My God," I said. "What did you say to that?"

"I told him, only if he was likely to find it *entertaining* to be disemboweled slowly through his navel."

"I bet you didn't."

"You're right, I didn't," he admitted. "I smiled as though he'd said something witty and informed him with excruciating politeness that you were one of our top operatives and that, if he valued certain parts of his anatomy, perhaps he shouldn't repeat that kind of speculation within Parker's earshot — or yours, for that matter."

The amusement subsided and, just when I thought I'd got away with it, Sean asked quietly, "So, are you going to tell me what happened between you and Nick today?"

My turn to sigh. I rolled onto my back and stared up into the gloom while I recounted the news report I'd seen on TV, and the subsequent encounter with my father. I debated on editing the content slightly, but in the end it all came spilling out practically verbatim, until finally I talked myself to silence.

Somewhere in the grid of streets below us, a car cranked up and accelerated away. I listened to its blowing exhaust through two gear-changes before the noise was swallowed up by the background chatter of the city.

Sean still hadn't spoken. I listened to the tenor of his breathing and smiled at the ceiling

"Stop it," I said.

"What?"

"Gloating."

"I never said a word." He did injured innocence rather well. "Did I say a word?"

I rolled partway back so I could prop onto an elbow and look down at him. "You didn't have to. I can hear you cackling from here. It's very juvenile."

He grinned outright then, wholly unrepentant. "Well come on, Charlie," he said, not trying to hide the amusement that glistened in his voice. "Even you have to admit — after all that rampant disapproval — it's bloody funny to find out your old man's finally fallen off his high horse."

"No," I said slowly. "That's the trouble — it isn't funny. Even if I discounted half the things he said afterwards —"

"Which you can't."

I let my breath out fast, an annoyed gush. "Yeah, right, that's easy for you to say. You haven't spent half your life trying to get his attention and the other half wishing you hadn't succeeded."

"That's just it," he said, and he'd matched my tone. "I can view him as an outsider — God knows, he's always done his damnedest to make me feel that way. He's a cold-hearted bastard at times, but he doesn't have the emotional capacity to be vindictive. And he's not a drunk."

He tilted his head so I knew he was looking directly at me. I felt the prickle of it across my skin even though I couldn't see his eyes.

"Reasons?"

He crooked one arm behind his neck to support it. "You're physically fit. We both know that and, hell, he probably knew before we did. Calling you a cripple is gross exaggeration and he's not a man prone to flights of fancy. So why did he say it? What did he hope to achieve?"

"O–kay," I said, reluctantly absorbing his words. "But what about the drinking problem? How can you be so sure about that?"

He gave a soft, bitter laugh. "My father was a drinker, remember?"

I'd never met Sean's father. Long before Sean and I first met, the man had been killed in an inebriated car crash, which wrecked his ambition to die of liver failure at the earliest age possible. By all accounts, he had not been a happy drunk. I squeezed Sean's arm.

"I'm sorry."

"Forget it." I felt him shrug. "All I meant was, I know the signs and your old man doesn't have them. Besides, how long do you think he could keep the shakes quiet when he spends every day holding a scalpel?"

I sank back onto the sheets, frowning.

"But I heard him admit to it, completely unequivocally, on camera, and it's the kind of admission that will totally ruin his career — if it hasn't done already. Why the hell would he say that, if it's not true?"

"Seems like he said a lot of things today that weren't true," Sean said. "You either accept he's flipped his lid and we book him a nice padded room at Bellevue, or you go and bully the truth out of him."

He paused and, though I couldn't see his face clearly I could hear by his voice that the smile was back full strength. "After what you did to Nick today, I'd say you'll have no trouble on that score."

FOUR

One of the things I quickly learned to love about New York was Central Park early in the mornings. I ran there, and whenever I could find an excuse, I detoured through it using one of the numerous sunken roads.

It was extravagance on a grand scale to have such an expanse of carefully created countryside tumbling down the spine of one of the most expensive areas of real estate in the world. Early on, I'd been staggered to discover that the park covered more than eight hundred tranquil acres. Not just the lungs of Manhattan, but the heart of it, too. New York is never entirely still. There's always some part that twitches, shrieks or quivers. But Central Park is the closest thing to stillness that it has.

The leaves were just beginning to turn — losing their lushness and not yet fully ablaze — building up tension towards what I'd been promised would be a stunning autumn display.

I left behind the dog walkers and the power walkers and rode south down wide streets made narrower by the sheer height of the buildings on either flank. Brief flashes of sunlight splashed down between them as I wove through the spray of the sidewalk sweepers and the steam rising from the subway vents.

The Buell cantered lazily beneath me, all that bunched muscle constrained by no more than the slight rotation of my right wrist, bouncing gleefully over the generically appalling road surface. I eased back to let a stoplight drop from red straight to green at an intersection in front of me, then cranked on the power, feeling the shove in the small of my back as the rear tire bit deep. And it came to me, quite suddenly, that I was happy here. Content, even.

And I was *not* going to let my father's bitter spill of lies spoil it for me.

Because Sean was right — it was out of character. My father might well carry over the clinical detachment from his work into his family life, but he'd never been mean-spirited with it.

Until now.

■ ■ ■ ■

By the time I reached midtown, traffic was starting to herd towards the morning crush, jostling to the usual accompaniment of Morse code horns. I ignored the halfhearted bleat from a yellow cab I caught napping in the inside lane — if I didn't cause him to slam on the brakes, it didn't count as obstruction — and pulled up on the opposite side of the street from my father's hotel.

I let the bike idle by the curb for a moment, unzipping my sleeve to check with the Tag Heuer wristwatch Sean had bought me as a 'Welcome to America' present.

By it, I worked out I had roughly an hour before politics dictated I show my face in the office, even after a late-night assignment. Plenty of time for what I had to say.

I'd aimed to arrive at the hotel late enough not to rouse my father from his breakfast, but early enough to catch him before the most convenient and obvious of the morning flights to the UK, just in case he was planning to cut and run.

I eyed the same regal-looking doorman standing outside the front entrance and wondered if he'd still let me walk in unchallenged today, when I was in my motorcycle leathers.

Hm, probably not.

And just as I was debating my options, the mirrored glass doors to the hotel swung open and my father stepped out.

My first instinct was to abandon the bike and go to confront him right there. I'd got as far as reaching for the engine kill-switch when another man stepped out of the hotel alongside him, keeping close to his elbow. The second man was dressed like a cheap businessman — but a cheap businessman who has his hair cut by a military barber. My hand stilled.

As I watched, my father slowed to glance across at the man with the buzz-cut, frowning. Uncertainty oozed from every pore of his skin like a sickness.

Buzz-cut moved like someone bigger than his size, with an utter physical self-assurance that almost bordered on brash. He never broke stride, simply drew level and hooked his hand under my father's arm. Even from twenty meters away, I saw Buzz-cut's fingers pinch deep into the delicate pressure points on either side of the elbow joint.

My father stiffened, first with outrage, then with pain. The shock of it knocked the fight out of him and he allowed himself to be swept forwards.

My first thought, when I saw the way the guy carried himself, was that Buzz-cut must be a cop. He had a tense alertness, a slightly hunched stance, like he was constantly expecting someone to throw the first punch.

But I didn't think that even hardened NYPD detectives, would hustle someone of my father's standing out of his hotel in such a way. If they'd wanted to break him down before questioning, then marching him through the lobby in handcuffs would have done it nicely. For some people, humiliation works better than a beating, any day.

Just as Buzz-cut succeeded in propelling my father to the edge of the curb, a black Lincoln Town Car drew up smartly alongside them. It was identical to the vehicle my father had climbed into after his abrasive encounter with the news reporter only the day before, but they were too common in New York for me to read much into that.

The driver pulled in fast, braking hard so my father's companion had the rear door open almost before the car had come to a complete stop. It was smooth and precise and way too slick to be any kind of lucky coincidence. Buzz-cut must have called him in before they left the hotel lobby.

Their timing impressed me. I'd spent too

much time micromanaging exactly this kind of rapid inconspicuous exfil not to recognize expert work when I saw it.

After that one brief show of resistance, my father allowed himself to be ducked into the backseat without further demur. I read the tension in his neck and upper body only because I knew to look. The doorman gave them a bored salute, oblivious.

Buzz-cut took a moment to scan the street before he climbed in, and there was nothing casual about that highly proficient survey. I felt his gaze land on me and linger. Even though I knew the iridium coating on my visor meant he couldn't see my eyes, I had to fight the instinctive desire to break the contact too quickly.

Instead, I let my head turn away, nice and slow, and concentrated on my breathing, on relaxing my shoulders, letting my mind empty.

Not watching. Just waiting.

I was confident enough to know, as Parker had pointed out, that I was very good at blending into the scenery. The fact that this man took an extra second to check me out meant either I was losing my touch, or he was a real pro.

And — if he wasn't the police — what did that mean?

■ ■ ■ ■

I let the Lincoln get to the end of the street and make a left before I toed the bike into gear and followed. If the driver was as experienced as his companion, he'd spot a tail within a hundred meters.

As I shot through on a closing amber and launched into traffic, I flicked my headlights off. Usually, I never ride without them or most car drivers don't know you're there — right up to the point you go under their wheels.

But in this case, being seen was the last thing I wanted.

I kept half a dozen cars back from the black Lincoln, using the extra height the bike gave me to keep him in sight. The car had a cheap glass-mounted phone aerial, which had been stuck on haphazardly at the far right-hand side of the rear window. It was distinctive, and made them marginally easier to track.

Even so, I knew these guys were too good for me to stay undetected on their tail for long. I needed help and had no way to get it.

Sure, my mobile phone was tucked away in the inside pocket of my leather jacket, but it was no use to me there. I cursed the fact I hadn't bothered to fiddle around getting the Bluetooth headset that went with it to sit comfortably inside my helmet before I'd set off. That was still in my pocket, too.

I wasn't armed — unless you counted my habitual Swiss Army knife. Parker had enough clout to ensure both Sean and I received our coveted New York City concealed-carry licenses in very short order, but I didn't routinely carry unless I was working. Although I was now the fully licensed owner of several firearms, they were all locked away either at the office or the apartment. I had no choice but to stick with my father as long as I could, and ad-lib after that.

Where are they taking you? I wondered. *And — more to the point — why the* hell *are you letting them?*

We threaded our way downtown then, to my surprise, kept going. Over the Williamsburg Bridge and into Brooklyn. The Lincoln left the Brooklyn-Queens Expressway at the first exit and carried on down Broadway into Bushwick, the area dropping by stages. Fortunes change fast in New York. Things can go from safe to scary in the length of a city block.

Inevitably, by hanging back far enough

not to get made, eventually I got cut off at a light. I swore long and loud behind my visor as I watched the Lincoln disappearing into the blur of traffic ahead, wallowing over the ruts like an inflatable dinghy in a heavy swell. But, just when I thought I was going to lose them completely, the driver slowed up ahead and made a right. I pinpointed the location by the nearest signpost and dropped the clutch like a drag star the moment the light went green above me, forgetting for a moment how easily the sheer grunt of the Buell would whip up the rear tire.

Great, Fox. Draw attention to yourself, why don't you?

I almost missed the side street where the Lincoln had turned. It was little more than an alleyway, with the obligatory overflowing Dumpster partially blocking the entrance, and a network of zigzag fire escapes caging in the narrow slot to the sky. I slowed long enough to spot the Lincoln stopped about halfway along, but didn't follow.

Instead, I kept going, made two quick right turns to bring me out at the far side of the alley. It must have been a squeeze to get the fat Lincoln past the Dumpster in the first place and there was no way the driver would want to reverse out again so, logically, he'd exit here. After London's intestinal mass of side streets, the U.S. grid pattern was a breeze.

I cut the Buell's engine and was aware of the silence that rushed in to fill the vacuum as the throaty rumble died away. After a moment, somewhere behind me in one of the run-down warehouse buildings, something like a jackhammer was being put to work with enthusiasm. Other than that, the distant roar of traffic and the litter rolling gently across the cracked road surface, it was almost peaceful.

I paddled the bike backwards into a narrow gap between two huge boxy American cars, both of which had more rust than original paint. As I nudged the kickstand down and settled the bike onto it, I undid the strap on my helmet, reached for my phone. At least I'd remembered to charge it. Sports bikes are irritatingly short of cigarette lighter sockets when you get caught with a dead mobile.

Sean picked up on the second ring, as he nearly always did. I'd never yet seen him fumble for an awkward pocket.

"Meyer."

"It's me," I said. "Want to take a guess where I am?"

There was a slight pause, then he said,

"Well, I assume from the background noise that you aren't naked in bed and covered in half a pint of whipped cream."

"Yuck," I said. "If that's your fantasy, you can wash the sheets."

"I'll take that as a no, then."

"Besides," I went on, "you know full well where I was heading when I left home this morning. What kind of sick and twisted mind paints that kind of a scenario from a visit to my father?"

He laughed. "Hey, for all I know, your father has hidden depths."

I glanced across at the alleyway. "Yeah, I rather think he's plumbing new ones right now."

Sean's amusement snuffed out. "Tell me," he said.

I described the scene outside the hotel, giving him as clear a picture as I could manage of the man with the buzz-cut who'd put my father into the Lincoln. Out of habit, I'd kept a mental note of the number of turns and lights since we'd crossed the bridge, so I could direct Sean to my current location with some precision, even if I couldn't tell him exactly where *here* was.

"Well, if your old man has a self-destruct button, looks like somebody pressed it," he said when I was done. "And you've no idea who these guys are or what he's up to with them?"

"No," I said. "But the longer he's in there, the worse feeling I get about the whole thing."

"Okay, Charlie, listen to me. Sit tight and wait for backup. I'll be with you as fast as I can. Do *not* go in until I get there, all right?"

"All right," I agreed, but the reluctance must have shown.

"Promise me," he said, and I knew from his tone he'd hold me to it.

I glanced at the open mouth of the alley again, just as movement caught my eye. A shifty-looking guy walked out, turning up the collar of his cheap jacket. He glanced both ways when he reached the open street, furtive. There were no passing cars and I didn't think stepping out into traffic was what had him worried.

"I shouldn't have let them lift him in the first place," I said, hearing the stubborn note. "If he's not out in twenty minutes, I'm going in after him — alone if I have to."

"Don't worry," Sean said, his voice calm and steady. "You won't be alone."

FIVE

I didn't have to go in alone.

Sean arrived inside the time I'd allotted, riding the black Buell Ulysses he'd bought at the same time as my own bike. He'd left the office fast enough after my call that he hadn't even bothered to put on leathers. Instead, he was still in his suit. Apart from a helmet, his only nod to safety was some thin leather gloves that would have shredded in seconds if he'd hit the road surface in them.

He slotted his bike in alongside mine and flicked up the visor, his eyes hidden behind a pair of classic Ray-Ban Wayfarers with dark green lenses. His smile was all the more brilliant because I couldn't see his eyes.

"Status?" he said as he killed the engine.

"The Lincoln pulled out about five minutes ago."

Sean stilled, frowning as he slid off the shades and helmet and hung the lid over the Buell's bar end.

"And you're still here *because* . . ."

"My father wasn't in the car when it left," I said. I jerked my head towards the alley. "I hung around over there so if they made a move I could see which building they'd gone into. Got asked twice if I was 'working.' " My mouth twisted. "I think it must be the leathers. Anyway, two guys came out — Buzz-cut and the driver." The tension in my hands was somehow connected to my throat. "My father wasn't with them."

Sean touched my shoulder. "Thank you for waiting for me," he said. "I know what it cost you."

I swallowed. "Maybe I'm just too much of a coward to go in alone," I said stiffly. "At least if you're with me, then if it comes to it you can be the one to break all this to my mother."

Sean set the bike on its stand, climbed off. "What exactly are you expecting to find?"

I followed him, unzipping my jacket. "It's a brothel, Sean," I said. "And you knew that as soon as I told you where I was, didn't you?"

He'd already started across the road. I fell into step just quickly enough to catch the way the corner of his mouth quirked upwards, little more than a flicker. "I had a pretty good idea."

"So why didn't you say anything?"

He sighed, and the flicker became impatience. "What would that have achieved, Charlie? Your father's the most priggish, moral bastard I've ever come across. You said he didn't go entirely willingly. You're a bright girl. You put it together."

"They left him here," I murmured, feeling my eyes start to hollow out and burn. "He didn't want to come, but now he's stayed. He would only have done that if they'd . . . forced him."

I shouldn't have left him in there. I shouldn't have let them put him into that damned car in the first place. At the time, part of me had been still too angry with him to care. *And now . . .*

"Not necessarily," Sean said. He glimpsed my face and stopped, half turned towards me. "You know the real reason I'm here?"

I shook my head.

"The real reason," he said, "is how could I live with myself if I missed out on a chance to catch the great Richard Foxcroft with his pants down?"

I threw him a disgusted look and stalked on. We turned into the gloom of the alley

71

together, stepped apart and slowed slightly, wary. At the far end, past the Dumpster, I caught fast glimpses of passing cars, their paintwork glinting in the sunshine. Bright colors, movement. The alley felt stagnant by comparison, hushed and lonely as the grave.

We both did a casual sweep as we walked into that place, watching for watchers, even overhead. Either there weren't any, or they were better at concealment than we were at spotting them. Sean paused and reached inside his jacket. When his hand came out, it was holding a cheap Kel-Tec P-11 semi-automatic. He passed it over to me.

I turned the unfamiliar handgun over in my hands. It was old but serviced, the action well oiled when I worked it. The magazine was fully topped off with hollow-point nines.

"What's this?"

"Unregistered," he said, succinct. "So I'd leave your gloves on if I were you."

"Jesus, Sean! If I get caught with this —"

He flipped his jacket back to reveal what looked like a matching piece sitting just behind his right hip. The thought that he'd risked carrying two illegal guns through the middle of the city brought me out in a cold sweat. They'd throw away the key.

"Face it, Charlie," he said, "if we get

caught in a brothel, we're probably screwed anyway. Just remember the trigger's going to be a lot stiffer than your SIG, so watch you don't pull your first shot."

"I *have* fired one of these before, Sean."

He flashed me a fleeting smile. "Yeah, sorry."

He didn't need to ask which door my father had been taken through. There was a line of them, peeling and dirty, but only one had a clear path to the base of it to give away its regular use. The door was steel plate, if I was any judge, with a face-size inset panel at head height.

"I think I'm better suited for this, don't you?" he murmured.

Without argument, I backed round to the side of the Dumpster, out of sight of the doorway but only a couple of meters away. I held the gun down flat alongside my leg, where its outline wasn't obvious from the street, my trigger finger alongside the guard.

In the four or five paces it took Sean to reach the door, his whole demeanor changed. Suddenly, his shoulders had more of a bow to them and he'd added a slight shuffle to his gait. He was a big guy who usually moved with lightness and a lethal dexterity but now, with his collar and tie sloppily loosened, he just looked clumsy.

If Parker could see him now, he would have bitten off Bill's other arm rather than offer Sean a partnership. Mind you, if he really could see us now, we'd probably both get the sack.

Sean reached into his jacket pocket and brought out a sizable wedge of folded bills. He retrieved the Wayfarers, popped the lenses out carefully into a handkerchief and tucked it away, and slid the empty frames on. Not perfect, but convincing enough for now. The whole effect was the kind of tedious office nerd you'd run from the water cooler to avoid. He turned, saw my expression, and winked.

Then he banged on the steel and, after a long pause, I heard the grate of the panel sliding back.

"Yeah?" A man's voice, deep and rough, managing to inject a wealth of hostile suspicion into that single grunted syllable.

"Oh, er, yeah, hi," Sean said, his accent perfect New York yuppie. He'd allowed the glasses to slip down his nose a little and now he carefully used the hand that clutched the money to push them back up, like he was nervous. It was a beautifully weighted gesture that couldn't have failed to suck the man's attention to the folded bills.

"I was told I could, er, maybe *meet someone* here," Sean went on. He coughed, then turned it into an uncomfortable laugh as the man behind the door didn't immediately respond. "Er, have I got the wrong place? Only I —"

"Who sentcha'?" the doorman demanded.

"Oh, er, well, I don't know him that good. Guy called Harry. At the office." Sean waved the money again, jerking his thumb vaguely over his shoulder to indicate anywhere from Wall Street to Honolulu. "Well, he doesn't actually work *with* me, y'know? Ha-ha. No, comes in all the time, though. Deliveries. Harry said this was the place." He leaned closer, lowered his voice and wiped a leer across it. "Said the girls here were, uh, y'know, kinda *broad-minded.*"

There was another long pause, then the panel slammed shut. For a moment I thought his performance — authentically sleazy though it was — hadn't done the trick. Then we heard the bolts slide back.

Immediately, I came out from round the Dumpster bringing the Kel-Tec up in my right hand, steadied with my left. The money was gone and Sean's own gun was out though I hadn't seen him reach for it. As soon as the door began to open and we could tell there wasn't a secondary security chain, we both hit it. Hard. I was glad of the protective padding in the shoulder of my leather jacket.

I felt the hefty steel door kick as it connected with a body. One jolt as he rebounded backwards, then another as he cannoned off an inside wall and came crashing back for a rematch. The door won both rounds.

We charged through the gap to find a Goliath of a man struggling groggily to rise but his legs were trapped behind the vee of the open door. He wasn't tall so much as enormously wide, with a stained T-shirt stretched to the limit of the fabric's elasticity around his bulging gut. His physique might have been useful when he was upright, but floundering on the ground he was in serious danger of Greenpeace activists trying to roll him back into the sea.

Nevertheless, he made a reflexive grab for us. It was a valiant attempt but his coordination was gone. The best he could manage was to claw sluggishly at empty air as we passed. Sean merely swapped the gun into his left hand and, with almost casual violence, hammered the side of his fist into the man's exposed temple. The smack Goliath's skull made as it bounced off the brickwork behind him made me wince. When he went down for the second time, he was out cold.

We paused, tense, but nobody seemed to have overheard the doorman's rapid defeat. Nobody who cared enough to come and see, anyway.

I straightened slowly as Sean stepped back over the unconscious man and shoved the steel outer door closed again.

"Harry?" I said, keeping my voice no louder than a whisper. "Who the hell's Harry?"

He shrugged. "Oh, there's always a Harry."

Inside, the small bare entrance hall was only marginally less seedy than the exterior of the building had suggested. The doorman had a little recess at one side, with a folding card table and a chair with the stuffing leaking from the seat. The table contained a selection of dead beer bottles, some crumpled White Castle burger wrappings covered in ketchup, and a tiny portable TV tuned to one of the sports channels. It told me all I needed to know about Goliath's lifestyle and expectations.

Only one other door led off the hall and we took it, moving fast through the narrow opening and spreading out on the other side.

The next room was bigger, and empty. At least some attempt had been made at decoration here, with a couple of faded prints on the walls — illustrations out of the *Kama Sutra*. The positions didn't look anatomically possible, never mind fun.

A built-in couch had been fitted into the corner. It was covered in pink velour and had retained its original nasty hue by dint of the clear plastic cover that protected it — from what, I shuddered to imagine. The illumination had been kept low in a poor attempt to be seductive. A single bulb filtered through an upside-down dark red shade. The dull lino underfoot made faint sucking noises as we crossed it.

The far wall was covered by a thin curtain, that was suddenly pulled aside. Sean and I both reacted instantly, snapping the guns up. An Asian girl with long straight blond hair came through, wearing a smutty pale pink negligee. She froze for a second when she saw us, then started screaming.

I was closest. I reached her in one long stride and, following Sean's earlier example, hit her with my upswept elbow under the jaw, aiming for the sweet spot just to the side of her chin. The effect of the blow was magnified by the fact she had her mouth open when I delivered it.

Her teeth clacked shut as her eyes rolled back and she dropped, graceless enough that I didn't have to check if she was faking. She and the blond wig parted company, revealing short black hair, badly cut, beneath it. Close to, she was neither as young as she was supposed to be, nor as old as she had become.

I turned to find Sean watching me.

"What?" I said. "You think the 'Harry sent me' line would have worked on her?"

"Maybe not," he agreed, "but let's try and leave the next one awake enough to answer questions, shall we? Like — where's your father?"

I turned away without answering. As soon as we'd entered the place I'd been fighting the underlying sense of panic. My father might be many things, but indiscriminate was not one of them, and the last thing you could possibly be in a place like this was choosy. Surely, if he'd really wanted the services of a prostitute, he would have picked somewhere more upmarket than this. On sanitary grounds, if nothing else.

He's dead. My God, he has to be dead.

Shaking my head did little to dislodge the recreant idea of it. I flexed my fingers round the pistol grip of the illegal gun. If anything *had* happened to my father, I vowed I would find the men in the Lincoln, and I would watch their bodies fall.

My only disquiet was that it wouldn't be the first time.

"Let's find out, shall we?"

The brothel was laid out on five narrow floors that branched out from a musty central stairwell. Each floor had rows of doorways along a thin partition wall, leading to tiny, lightless cubicles. Sean and I swept the building from the ground up.

The occupants were nearly all female and mostly alone. The majority of the workforce looked Asian — possibly Korean or Vietnamese. The girls seemed to live in the rooms where they worked, their few shabby possessions hidden behind a curtain or in a flimsy plywood wardrobe.

The place had a smell all of its own. Old cooking fat that had been overheated one time too many, mingled with stale sweat and other, more earthy odors, all not quite masked by the false cheer of cheap fabric freshener and the thin reek of even cheaper perfume.

And desperation. The only locks we encountered were on the outside, which probably accounted for the browbeaten lack of reaction to our arrival. If any of the girls spoke English, they weren't making a big thing of it, but I suppose it was unlikely they were being paid — in any sense — for their sparkling conversational skills.

On the fourth floor up, we kicked the lock off the inside of a door this time and found a woman older than the others, a fact which was obvious even in the low light. Her larger living quarters spoke of middle management rather than labor.

We caught her bending over an old square sink in one corner of the room, and she straightened with an expletive that was pure homegrown Brooklyn. Statuesquely built, her most startling feature was a pair of massive breasts that, to my cynical eyes at least, were so clearly man-made they probably had a "Best Before" date stamped on them. Her dress was gaudy without even the excuse of being cheap.

Very recently, someone had caught her a belter across the left-hand side of her face and she'd been trying to negate the aftereffects with a cold wet cloth pressed against it. She went deathly pale at the sight of us, but stood her ground, putting the cloth down slowly.

"Who the fuck are you?" she demanded. Her eyes flicked to the doorway behind us a couple of times, waiting for Goliath's intervention. When it didn't come, she checked us out again and frowned. Her tone modified a little. "Whaddya want?"

"English guy," I said shortly. "Came in here about half an hour ago. Where is he?"

She heard my accent and her face grew calculating, but she didn't try to bluff us. By the look of the bruising, she'd tried that ploy once today already and it hadn't gone well for her.

"Upstairs," she said. The reluctant fear in her voice twisted in my belly, grabbed at my chest as I began to move. "Hey, I didn't have nothing —"

"Stow it," Sean said.

He was right behind me as I took the stairs to the final floor two at a time, was alongside me as we broke our way into each of the matted little rooms up there. He didn't speak, and I'm not sure I would have heard him over the raucous clamor inside my head even if he had.

It was the last room. It always is. We hit the door hard enough for the flimsy hardboard to rip out of the frame and sway drunkenly from one hinge before toppling to the floor.

Inside, we found my father standing centered under the dusty bulb. He was minus his suit jacket, with the buttons of his shirt halfway open, revealing a vee of pale hairless chest beneath, and he was just in the process of sliding his tie out from under his collar.

Or rather, the girl in front of him was taking care of that part.

She was young — much younger than just about any of the girls we'd seen so far in that place. Well under the age of any kind of informed consent, with taut skin the color of latte and glossy long dark hair. Her back had been to the doorway, presenting us with a perfect view of a slender body not yet entirely spoiled. She spun, gasping at the violence of our arrival, to reveal classic almond-shaped eyes.

Apart from too much makeup, she was completely naked.

Just for a moment, the side of my brain responsible for lucid thought and reasoned argument totally shut down. Instinct and training took me forwards, only peripherally aware of Sean moving to check and secure the room.

I closed in on my father, registered the absolute shock and the pure, undiluted shame that coated him like a layer of grime, moments before he covered it with a haughty mask. That was what did it. Another silent lie on top of all the others.

Blinded, I gave a howl of utter rage and backhanded him across the face with enough force to snap his head round. I was still wearing my bike gloves, which had tough carbon fiber protectors across the backs like lightweight knuckle dusters. My father staggered a pace from the blow, but made no attempt to block me or prevent another. That was enough to bring me up cold.

Raked with guilt and anger, I felt the blood drop out of my face so fast that my vision buckled and I nearly fell.

"You . . . *bastard,*" I said.

The certainty that he was dead, and all the emotions connected to that conviction, had set vicious barbed hooks deep into every part of me. The sudden discovery that he was very much alive ripped them out all at once, leaving behind a bloody mess of tattered thoughts and raw confusion.

He was alive, and I wanted to kill him for it.

"Charlie." It was Sean who spoke, gently, firmly, putting his hand onto my forearm to press it downwards. It was only then I realized I had the gun up, had been watching my father's reaction over the top of the sights and had seen nothing wrong with the picture that presented.

"Don't do this," he murmured. "I hate to

resort to cliché, but he genuinely isn't worth it."

I let my arm drop away, found it was trembling as badly as the rest of me.

"Don't worry," I said. "I wouldn't waste the round."

I lurched back as the adrenaline boost drained away, almost collapsed against the wall near the doorway to the corridor. My left thigh burned and I resisted the urge to grab at it. I was damned if I was going to show more weakness in front of him.

As soon as we'd burst in, the girl had scuttled onto the rumpled bed by the far wall and tucked her legs up close to her body, head buried against her knees and her arms wrapped tightly round them. If you look insignificant enough, and you can't see the monsters, maybe they will leave you alone.

No, they won't.

Her submissive posture angered as much as it disturbed me. There was a thin dark red robe on the floor that was trying to be silk but was as artificial as the madam's breasts downstairs. I leaned down, snatched it up and threw it across to her. She stopped rocking just long enough to clutch it in front of her body.

"Well, well, *Dick*," Sean said then, his

voice softly mocking. "This opens up a whole new side to you."

My father darted him a savage glance but didn't reply. The area around his cheekbone had already begun to swell, puffy. I hadn't broken the skin but he was going to have a hell of a bruise.

Still clinging to that brittle dignity, he retrieved his tie from where the girl had dropped it in her flight, fed it back through his collar, and began reknotting it. His movements were apparently calm and sedate, but it was little more than a thin veneer. I could see the shake of his hands, the pulse in his jaw.

"So, you still think you don't owe me any kind of explanation?" I said.

He refastened his cuff links and reached for the jacket he'd laid across the back of a narrow chair. The suit had been tailor-made for him by Gieves & Hawkes of Savile Row and fitted to perfection, in devastating contrast to the decayed dilapidation of that tawdry little room.

"I owe you nothing, Charlotte," he said then, and his arrogance was astounding. "I make my own choices. I won't ask how you found me — invading people's privacy seems to be second nature to you — but I most certainly do not need your approval for my actions." He allowed his lip to curl just slightly. "Nor do I require you to accompany me."

"*Approval?*" I said, aware my voice had become almost a squawk. I flung a hand towards the huddled creature on the bed. "She's young enough to be your *daughter,* for fuck's sake! Christ, she's practically young enough to be mine!"

He stilled. "Get out, Charlotte," he said coldly. His eyes skated over Sean, who'd been standing watchful and silent during the exchange. "And take your nasty little bully boy with you."

Sean shrugged off the insult and started for the door. As he passed, my father gestured to the gun Sean carried with an expressive flick of his fingers.

"Violence. Is that the only thing you people understand?"

We'd caught him in a run-down brothel with a naked teenage hooker and still he tried to take the high ground.

"Perhaps it is," I said, not moving. "So how's this for violence? If you don't walk out of here with us, right now, I'll knock you senseless and carry you out — and, believe me, it would be a pleasure. Either way, you're leaving."

His spine straightened. "You can't."

"Oh, don't tempt me."

"No, you *can't!*"

I registered the edge of panic in the rising tone with something akin to wonder. Of all the emotions he'd shown since we'd entered that room and exposed him, this was the first hint of fear.

"I can't leave you here," I said, without pity. "If my mother —"

"That's just it." He grasped the reference like a talisman. "Your mother. If you feel anything for your mother, Charlotte, then just leave me here and go before it's too late. Please."

"Too late? What the hell are you —"

Then, from underneath us, we heard crashing and high-pitched screaming and loud voices bellowing commands. Sean and I ran into the corridor. About halfway along was a narrow window with a view down into the alleyway. When we looked down, all we could see were the flashing lights on top of the squad cars.

"Oh. Shit," Sean muttered. His eyes met mine. There weren't any other exits or we would have found them on our way up. The management was clearly more anxious about customers trying to skip out without paying, than they were about the possibilities of escape from a fire.

Sean picked the illegal Kel-Tec out of my nerveless grasp. Without having to watch his hands, he stripped the gun down to its frame and dumped it out of the window, where it fell five stories, straight into the open Dumpster by the entrance. His own weapon quickly followed. Nobody on the ground heard or saw a thing. Even so, I knew we were headed for deep, deep trouble.

We went back. My father hadn't moved, but someone had hit fast-forward and he'd aged maybe twenty years. His face was gray in the dull light.

"It's the police," I said. "The place is being raided."

My father nodded, mildly resigned, as though I'd told him it looked likely to rain, and the sudden realization hit me that somehow he'd known this was going to happen. The girl continued to rock gently on the bed.

And we waited, the four of us, for the thunder of boots on the stairs.

Six

"Well, congratulations, guys. I do believe this will go down in history as a screwup of monumental proportions," Parker Armstrong said. He raised a tired smile that lost heart long before it reached his eyes. "As I understand it," he added with morose humor, "they can see it from space."

We were in the conference room at the agency. High-tech and spotless, it had been furnished with an eye to luxury and none at all to cost. The suspended ceiling seemed to hang in a cloud of ice blue neon, perfectly highlighting the swirling grain of the maple wall panels. At one end was a projector screen for presentations. It was rarely used, but I knew for a fact the sound system that went with it had cost more than my last house.

Parker was in the power seat at the top end of half an acre of mirror-polished table. Sean and I were shoulder-to-shoulder about halfway along, with Bill Rendelson scowling ferociously at us from the other side.

We'd been offered a seat but preferred to stand. I had to fight the urge to do so at attention. Back straight up, arms straight down so my thumbs were precisely in line with the seams of my leather jeans, knees just slightly bent so I could hold the position for hours if I had to. Only the lack of dress uniforms prevented this from being an action replay of the travesty that was my court-martial.

I felt thoroughly dirty. We were both still wearing the same clothes we'd been arrested in, roughly twenty-eight hours earlier. If it hadn't been for some fancy footwork on the part of Parker's legal team, we would probably still be in jail.

The last glimpse I'd had of my father was of him being bundled, handcuffed, into the back of a police cruiser. I'd asked the lawyer who'd got me out what had happened to him, but the man seemed to be billing by the word as well as the minute and my credit was obviously running short.

"I'm sorry," I said, aware that I was starting to sound like a scratch mix. "But don't blame Sean for any of this. I'm the one who dragged him into it."

"Aw, come on, Charlie." Parker sat back,

his voice almost gentle in its admonition, even if his body language betrayed his impatience. "You know as well as I do that Sean makes his own decisions."

"Of course," I agreed quickly, before Sean could jump in, "but nevertheless, this was — and should have remained — a family matter."

" 'Family matter' — is that so?" Parker echoed sharply. "You make it sound like some kind of sick tradition. Does your father always take you along when he goes visiting cheap hookers? 'Cause that's just plain wrong."

He waited to see if I had anything better to offer him. I did not. A few days ago I would have laughed at the idea of my father even looking at another woman, never mind paying her for sex. Now it was like dealing with a total stranger who'd somehow taken up residence behind his tight-lipped face.

"Or maybe he doesn't have time." Without taking his eyes off the pair of us, Parker reached out his hand and Bill hurried to smartly slap a folded newspaper into it, precise as a theater nurse handing over a pair of forceps. "Seeing as how he's so busy with his alcoholism and his euthanasia." With a contemptuous flick of his wrist, Parker sent the newspaper skidding across the tabletop towards us, adding grimly, "And there're one or two things here about *you* that weren't on your CV, that's for sure."

I reached out and stopped the paper sliding before it slipped over the edge onto the Italian tile, then unfolded it and scanned the story.

Somebody had been raking through the muck of my past history with a pretty fine mesh. They seemed to have caught just about all the most pungent bits of it, at any rate. My father's current fall from grace was recapped with salacious glee, and my own alongside it. They built me up first — my army commendations, marksman certificates, trophies, Special Forces selection and high hopes — all the better to knock me down again. Laid out in the most lurid terms was the story of the vicious attack by four of my fellow trainees, the revelation of my affair with Sean, my ignominious expulsion.

Journalistically speaking, they picked over the carcass of my career and whooped as they waved the bones in the air. In their eyes, their words, I was damaged goods. They hinted in their snide way that either I had been brutalized out of my humanity, or that I was simply a product of my upbringing. And then they started in on my father again.

Sickened, I let the paper drop back down onto the surface of the table and glanced up. I could tell from the angle of his head that Sean had been reading it, too, and I knew Bill must have done so before he'd brought the paper through to Parker. I felt the heat steal up into my face.

Sean knew what had happened to me that freezing winter night, but only secondhand and at a distance. He'd been posted a few weeks before and it wasn't until we'd met again, by chance, several years after the event that the truth had come out. And then he'd reacted both with anger and sorrow that had chilled me to the bone.

Now, he regarded Parker with a deadly gaze. "Do you think any less of Charlie because of what she went through?" he asked softly.

Parker shifted in his seat. "Hey, like I said, I'm not the issue here. But it looks like you and your dad are making headlines," he said, focusing back on me. "This business he's mixed up in with this dead doctor in New England is a hot story, and this just poured a truckload of gasoline right onto the flames. Nearly all the tabloids led with it."

I winced. Sensing I was about to launch into another — longer and more profuse — apology, Sean cut in again.

"How bad's the damage?"

"Bad enough," Parker said flatly. He rubbed a hand across his eyes, slowly, pausing to squeeze the bridge of his nose before allowing the hand to drop away.

Bill's face had darkened. "Besides all the questions about Fox's colorful past," he said, "we've been fielding accusations all day that we, as an agency, condone illegal activity by our clients and turn a blind eye to whatever they do while they're under our protection." He spoke without inflection, but the words were more than enough on their own.

Parker let out a breath, wry. "I think our legal bills this week will be enough to put both my lawyer's kids through college."

"I'm sorry," I said again, narrowly resisting the urge to hang my head. "Easy for me to say, Parker, I know, but I am. If I hadn't believed my father was in genuine danger, I never would have gone in there in the first place."

"Hell, I know that, Charlie," he said. That weary smile again. His disappointment was harder to take than his anger would have been. "I knew when I hired you — both of you — that you were not the type to walk away from a situation, and I wouldn't ask you to. I'm just having a real bad day."

Something in his tone alerted me and I was aware of a plummeting sensation in the pit of my stomach, like an express lift or the first long drop of a roller-coaster ride. And I knew.

"The banking people pulled out," Sean said suddenly, as though he'd been plugged straight into my central nervous system, too. It was not a question and I saw from both Parker's and Bill's faces that it didn't need to be.

Parker opened his mouth, frowning, then shut it again and shook his head a little.

"I had a call this morning," he admitted, "from the personal assistant to the personal assistant to the CEO — not the guy himself — informing me that they were reconsidering their options. Which is doublespeak for 'Thanks, but no thanks,' I guess."

"I'm —" I began.

"— sorry. Yeah, I know," he finished for me. "Question is, what do we do about it?"

"Well, can't you re-present to the bank?" I said. "Won't they let you explain the circumstances behind what happened and —"

"Do you want us to go?" Sean cut in, chopping me off in mid-breath as well as mid-sentence. "If it would cause you the least embarrassment to be seen to take decisive action, I won't hold you to the agreement we have." He paused, impassive, as though this didn't mean everything to him when I knew plainly that it did. I knew what it was costing to keep his voice so coolly polite, indifferent, and — from Parker's sudden immobility — he did, too.

For a moment neither man spoke. Bill twitched, as though desperate to put it to a vote and I knew which way he'd go. The silence stretched, gossamer thin in the over-dry, purified and conditioned air.

"For God's sake," Parker said at last, "will you take that damned stick out of your ass long enough to sit down? Both of you," he added. "No, I don't want you to go, okay? If you hadn't been on board, Sean, we wouldn't have stood a chance with the bank in the first place. This dies down fast, maybe they'll come around. And if not, fuck 'em. There'll be other clients." He gave a rueful little smile. "But not if we don't figure this out — pronto."

Parker rarely used bad language and, when he did, he sounded uncomfortable, as though it was something he felt was required of him rather than coming from the gut. There was more than a hint of bravado there, too. I knew what he'd put into trying to secure this contract and losing it would cost more than money. It was a question of face. In this game, reputation was everything.

I thought of the months of hard work, of the investment that had just been laid to waste and I wondered, had the positions been reversed, if I would have been so gracious. Probably not, I realized with a certain sense of shame. After all, my father had screwed up big-time as well, and look how I'd reacted to him. . . .

Without speaking, both Sean and I reached for the nearest chairs, slumping into them. As soon as I relaxed, my leg started muttering about being overworked and underpaid. Below the level of the tabletop, I surreptitiously jammed my thumb and forefinger hard into the muscle along the front of my thigh in an effort to persuade the nerves to gate.

Parker glanced at the pair of us, almost defiant, the hint of a smile lurking at the edge of his mouth. "So, Charlie, question is, what do we do about the situation with your dad?"

Across from us, Bill made a sound, like he was clearing his throat, but it could have been a growl. It was pretty clear that his choice of immediate action would have been to have both of us flayed alive and thrown off the roof of the building.

" 'We'?" I queried.

"I need this situation contained, and I need it contained fast," Parker said. "I thought your dad was a well-respected guy. When we hired you, our searches on your family" — and he smiled slightly in apology "— came up clean. What the hell happened over the last six months?"

"I'm as amazed by his behavior as anyone else," I said. "I dread to think how my mother's going to react when . . ."

My voice trailed off slowly before I could finish. I felt three pairs of eyes swivel in my direction but I didn't see them. My sight had turned inwards, riffling through the disordered filing cabinet of memories and senses.

"If you feel anything for your mother, Charlotte," my father had said, "then just leave me here and go before it's too late."

"Oh my God," I murmured. "My mother . . ."

"Do you think your mom even knows what's happening?" Parker asked, not quite catching it. "If she doesn't, then I don't envy you the task of telling her what her husband's been up to."

"No," I said, shaking my head. "He's trying to protect her."

"Oh, yeah, of course," Bill said, unable to maintain his silence any longer. He threw up his one remaining hand in frustration and I saw his other shoulder hunch as the ghost of his amputated arm tried to join the party. "Okay, so this guy got caught with his pants down, but, hey, that's okay because he's 'trying to protect her.' " The sarcasm overflowed to the point where it dripped. "How the hell do you figure that?"

"No matter what I, personally, might think of my father," I said, pinning him with a fierce gaze, "I happen to know he's a brilliant surgeon. And you know what makes him so bloody good at his job? It's because he's put whatever classifies as his heart and his soul into what he does for more than thirty years. I find it very hard — no, make that impossible — to believe he'd just throw all that away for the chance of a cut-price lay."

"People change," Parker pointed out. "They have . . . breakdowns, crises, or they simply burn out. Ever considered that?"

It was Sean who shook his head. "To burn out professionally you have to have some kind of emotional overinvestment in your work, and Richard Foxcroft's a very cold fish," he said. "But I would say that he does care about his wife — very much so." He glanced sideways at me. "And his daughter."

I gave a bitter, incredulous bark of laughter. "Well, he's got a bloody funny way of showing it."

"You didn't see how he was, Charlie," he said softly. "Back in February, when you were shot. He might have a bloody funny way of showing it, but he cares all right. I never thought I'd hear myself standing up for the bloke, considering he hates my guts, but don't kid yourself that he doesn't care about you."

"So much so that he tells me I'm a useless cripple," I shot back, disregarding our current audience, feeling my lip begin to curl. "Yeah, right, how stupid of me! How could I possibly have mistaken that for anything except paternal affection? And then we find him about to screw an underage prostitute. What are you saying — that perhaps my mother bought it for him as a wedding anniversary present?"

"Guys, guys," Parker murmured, eyes flitting from one to the other. "Uh, can we get back to the matter at hand here?"

"This *is* the matter at hand," Sean said, and his face was as cold as his tone now and his eyes were very dark, as close to

101

black as anyone I've ever met. All I could see in them was my own reflection and, from what I could read of it, I was flustered and angry and defensive. It wasn't a good look for me.

"The whole reason you went to see your father yesterday morning, Charlie, was because you knew he'd lied to you the day before," Sean said patiently, spelling it out. "But his behavior goes against everything you know of the man. Why are you so quick to believe the worst of him?"

The silence that followed his question lasted only around four seconds, but it passed like a slow decade.

"Maybe," I said, low, "it's because he's always been so quick to believe the worst of me."

"O-kay," Parker said, more of a drawl. "But if we disregard the possibility — for the moment, anyhow — that he's gone totally off the rails, what makes you think this would have anything to do with your mother?"

"Because, despite Bill's skepticism, he's always done everything he can to shelter her — from unpleasantness, from bad news, from blame. From life, come to that."

Parker frowned at the bitterness evident in my voice. "So, let me get this straight," he said. "He's confessed that he's a drunk and a liar. And now, from what you've said, he couldn't wait to get himself caught with a hooker. How is that protecting his wife?"

"It could only be," Sean murmured, "because he was afraid of something worse."

I snapped back into the here and now. "I need a phone," I said, aware of the hollowness in my voice.

Parker stared at me for a moment longer, then nodded to Bill, who sighed heavily but kept his continuing disgust to himself. He plugged a handset into the conference-call system that was a permanent fixture in the center of the table. It was clear from the way he practically threw the handset at me that he didn't think much of Parker humoring us like this.

I checked my watch and ran through the mental calculations. New York was five hours behind the UK. It was a little before one in the afternoon here, which meant it was nearly six in the evening back home.

I dialed the number. As I listened to the line play out at the other end, I realized, on how few occasions I'd bothered to phone home.

Sean leaned across and punched the button for the speaker. When I glanced at him, he merely said, "This I have to hear."

It took my mother a long time to answer. When she finally did, she gave her usual telephone greeting sounding strained to breaking point, as though under some unbearable pressure.

No change from normal there, then.

"Hello, Mother," I said. "It's me."

There was a long pause. Sean's eyes flicked to mine and I saw his eyebrow quirk. It shouldn't have been a trick question.

"Darling . . . how lovely to hear from you," she said at last, with that false brightness she always employed when speaking to her only daughter. "How are you? How's your poor leg coming along?"

The second bullet I'd taken had hit my back high up around my shoulder blade and had ended up planted somewhere in my right lung, which had then collapsed. My heart, so they'd told me, had temporarily stopped at the scene but I don't remember too much about that.

During the early stages of my recovery I'd had mobility problems with my right arm and hand. At the time, it had seemed that the through-and-through wound to my leg was minor by comparison, but it had proved to have longer-lasting effects, and now that was the part everyone focused on. My mother was no exception.

"The leg's fine," I said, which was mostly true. "*I'm* fine." I suppose that was mostly true, also.

"Oh. Good," she said. Another pause before a splintered little laugh. "Was there anything in particular you wanted, darling, only I'm rather in the middle of something right now. It's the church fête next week and I'm making a batch of treacle tarts."

I could picture her, a blur of high-tension activity, in the tall kitchen of their Georgian house in the expensive part of Cheshire. She'd cajoled and bullied and eventually worn down my father into having a Smallbone of Devizes custom kitchen installed about ten years previously. I'd been in my teens but I could still remember the chaos and excitement of the transformation from 1950s ugliness to an expanse of blue pearl granite worktops and limed-oak cabinets under an array of halogen spots.

She ruled her sparkling domain like the most temperamental celebrity chef, creating wonderful dishes that seemed to drive her so close to the brink of nervous exhaustion to produce, it took away the pleasure of actually eating them.

"Speaking of tarts," I said bluntly, ignoring the sudden consternation on Parker's face, "have you heard from my father today?"

"Your father?" my mother said vaguely, as if we were discussing a casual acquaintance. "I don't believe so, darling. He's, um, away at the moment."

I suppressed a sigh. Up until her retirement the previous year, my mother had been a local magistrate and, contrary to popular satire, she was far from the bumbling picture of the rural judiciary that was so often portrayed. Hard to believe now that she'd once been praised and feared for her incisive mind.

"Oh, yes?" I said. "Run away with a younger woman?"

"Well, *really*," my mother said, but there was more stiffness than heat. "He's attending a medical conference. You know how often he's called upon to lecture these days." She paused again, uncomfortable, but she'd always been a bad liar. "I — I spoke to him only yesterday. He sends his love."

I heard a slight sound in the background at her end of the line and said, "I'm sorry, I didn't know you had visitors."

"W— what? Oh, no — just the radio, darling. I was going to listen to the six o'clock news when you rang. Anyway, I must go. Things are starting to burn."

"I'll call you tomorrow," I said.

"No, don't do that," my mother said quickly. "I have people coming round for dinner and I shall need all day to prepare. I don't expect you remember the Hetheringtons, do you?"

"Yes . . . yes, I do," I said, and allowed my voice to take on a slightly disappointed tone. "Well, in that case, Mother, I'd best leave you to it."

"Yes, all right," my mother said faintly, her relief at my imminent departure evident. "Thank you for taking the trouble to call, Charlie. We don't see enough of you these days, you know."

"I know," I said, and ended the call. I stared for a moment at the surface of the table as though the future would eventually present itself in the pattern of the grain.

"Wow, she sounds like one tense lady," Parker said.

"I wouldn't read too much into that," Sean said. "She always sounds on the verge of a nervous breakdown."

I looked up. "She's in trouble."

Bill grunted. "How'd you work that one out from a conversation about baking?"

I turned to eye him coldly. "Because there's no way my mother would be making tarts a week before they were needed. She's a perfectionist, and they'd be stale."

Bill's grunt became a snort. He rammed his chair back and got to his feet as if he could no longer bring himself to sit through such crap. I let him take half a dozen paces.

"Quite apart from the fact that my father has never *sent me his love* in twenty-seven years, she called me Charlie," I said quietly. "She never does — absolutely hates it. They both do. I was always Charlotte at home, right up until I joined the army. She told me once that nothing reminds her of me as a soldier quite like hearing that name."

"So you think she might be trying to make some reference to your military career? Then the comment about not seeing enough of you," Parker said. He never took notes and his recall was practically recording quality. "You think it might indicate she needs that kind of help?"

"Maybe." I shrugged. "But the real clincher was the fact she mentioned the Hetheringtons," I said. Bill had stopped and turned back almost in spite of himself. "No way are the Hetheringtons going for dinner at my mother's tomorrow night."

"Right," Bill said. "Another cryptic clue?"

"Well, they certainly wouldn't be able to eat much," I said coldly. "Seeing as they've both been dead for five years." I looked from Bill to Parker to Sean. "They lived not far from my parents for years. Nice people. They were shot and killed by intruders who broke into the villa where they were staying on holiday in Turkey."

"So that wasn't the radio in the background," Parker said grimly.

I shook my head. "She never has the radio on when she's cooking — too distracting," I said. "There are people in the house with her, right now. And I can only imagine what they've threatened to do to her, but it's made my father prepared to ruin himself to prevent it."

SEVEN

"On behalf of your Delta crew we'd like to be the first to welcome you to Manchester and hope you have a safe and pleasant journey to your final destination today. Local time is eight-thirty."

The flight across the Atlantic had been uneventful. We'd left JFK at 8:30 in the evening, New York time, and landed apparently twelve hours later, after a seven-hour flight. I still had trouble sometimes getting my head round the mechanics of international time zones.

We'd had enough of a tailwind to arrive early and been forced to stack, the pilot spending twenty minutes or so giving us hard-banked alternate views of Cheshire countryside and the sprawling conurbation that makes up the Greater Manchester area. The fields below were muddy, and the houses seemed very small and very close together. None of them had a swimming pool in the back garden. I missed America already.

Bill Rendelson had taken care of our travel arrangements. He claimed he'd only been able to get us into Economy at such short notice, but when we boarded half the seats in Business Elite seemed to be empty and they wouldn't let us move forwards, despite our frequent-flyer status. As we trudged along the jet bridge into the terminal building, I felt gritty of eye and knotted of neck.

We trailed blearily through Immigration, collected our bags off the carousel and wheeled them out down the "Nothing to Declare" channel at Customs. It was a short walk across the Arrivals hall and then we were assaulted by the smell of diesel and cigarette smoke and the thin damp chill of a rapidly approaching British winter.

Sean had relinquished all day-to-day control of his own close-protection agency, based just outside London, in order to join Parker Armstrong's outfit, but he'd called in favors. Madeleine Rimmington had first become a partner and was now the boss, so I was surprised to find she was the one waiting for us at the curbside, looking as polished and poised as ever. The contrast with my own rumpled appearance was as stark and irritating as ever, too.

"I didn't expect the executive treatment," I said once we'd thrown our bags into the rear of one of the company Mitsubishi Shogun 4×4s and climbed in.

"You think I'd pass up the opportunity to see you both?" she said, smiling over her shoulder as she pulled out into traffic. She was wearing her long dark hair in a chic French pleat and had a thrown-together casual elegance that I reckoned probably took her several hours every morning to achieve. But it could just have been me acting bitchy. For some reason, I'd never quite liked Madeleine as much as she'd seemed to like me. "You're looking well, anyway — nights spent in police custody notwithstanding."

"Bad news travels fast," Sean said. He was in the front seat, so I couldn't see his face, but his voice was dry.

Madeleine grinned at him as she shot out onto a roundabout, cutting up a Skoda minicab with cheerful disregard. She had clearly taken advantage of her new position to book herself on all the latest defensive and offensive driving courses.

"Well, come *on,* Sean," she said as she sliced through the thickening morning traffic. "You get caught, with a principal, in a police raid on a house of negotiable affection, and you don't expect word to get round? It's the most exciting piece of industry gossip I've heard in ages."

"Some people need to get out more," Sean muttered. "And it wasn't a client." He glanced back at me. "It was Charlie's father."

"Oh my goodness," Madeleine said faintly, and laughed. "Oh, I'm sorry, Charlie, but I would never have thought he was the type to —"

"He isn't," I said shortly. "Where are we going, by the way?"

"I came up last night and stayed at the Radisson," she said, controlling her amusement to become brisk and businesslike again. "I got a room upgrade, so I don't have to check out until three. I thought you'd probably like to head back there and grab a shower and change before you get started."

"Ah, Madeleine, you are an absolute wonder," Sean said, with enough lazy affection to send my hackles rising unnoticed in the backseat.

She flushed, pleased. "The restaurant's not bad, either."

Considering Madeleine's long-term boyfriend was now a top chef in London, that was high praise.

"We don't have time to eat," I said, abrupt. The shower I could do with. Going into a situation tired was always bad practice, so anything we could do to freshen up was an operational necessity. I knew we should refuel, too, but the way my stomach was clenched tight, I didn't think I'd keep anything down. Eating could be done later, once the job was done.

We walked confidently through the hotel lobby without our presence being questioned, and took the lift to the ninth floor. Sean was enough of a gentleman to offer me first use of the shower and I stayed under it for as long as I dared, hands braced against the tiles, letting the stinging spray pound my neck and shoulders.

There had been a time, not so long ago, when I hadn't been able to stand having hot water played directly on the bullet wound in my back. Not having to think about being careful when I showered was still enough of a treat to be savored.

When I eventually emerged, scrubbed pink and dressed in a clean polo-neck sweater and jeans, it was to find Sean and Madeleine sitting at the low table by the window, heads bent close together as they pored over a pile of paperwork that no doubt related to the agency. Both glanced up at my reappearance and I could have sworn a flicker of annoyance passed across Madeleine's face at the interruption, but I recognized my bias against her.

"My turn, I think," Sean said, rising.

As the bathroom door closed behind him I hovered uncomfortably near the bed. My Vicodin was in my travel bag and my leg was complaining hard enough after the cramped flight to warrant taking a dose, but I didn't want to do so in front of anyone — least of all Madeleine.

"I realize you said no to a meal but can I at least make you some coffee?" she asked, gathering up her papers and sliding them into an attaché-case with neat, economical movements. "Or would you like me to order something from room service?"

I shook my head, shoved my hands into my pockets. "No — thank you. I just want to get this done," I said.

She nodded, sympathetic. "It must be hard — getting back out there, I mean — after . . ."

I bristled. "I'm fine," I said, with more snap than I'd been intending.

She regarded me for a moment and I painted pity into her eyes.

"I'm not trying to have a go at you, Charlie," she said, her voice mild. "Don't forget,

I've seen firsthand what you can do. You don't have to prove anything to me."

I forced my shoulders down, tried to let my guard go with them.

"I'm sorry," I said with a small smile. "I've been feeling a bit under pressure since . . . well, since we moved."

"Not from Sean, surely? You two look good together. Easy in one another's company." She smiled more fully than I had done, turning a pretty face beautiful. "It's nice to see him looking so happy."

"Happy?" I said blankly. There were many words I could have used to describe Sean, but that particular one hadn't been high on the list. "You think he looks happy?"

"There's a . . . lightness about him that wasn't there before," she said. "Oh, I can see he's worried about all this, but it's only surface worry, you know? Deep down, he knows he can face it. He can face anything, now that he's got you."

I shifted restlessly, uncomfortable with her frankness and her intrusive insights. And, if I'm honest, scared by the weight of the responsibility she'd just dumped on me.

"And Sean told you all this in the time I took to have a shower, did he?" I said, trying to hide behind a cynical edge. "Fast worker."

Madeleine smiled again, not fooled for a moment. "He didn't have to. He lights up when he's with you. It's awfully sweet, really."

"Oh God," I muttered. *Is that why Parker doesn't trust either of us to still have a clear mind?* "I'll have to get him fitted with a bloody dimmer switch."

The bathroom door opened and Sean came out with just a towel draped around his hips, totally unself-conscious. Most people do not look good without their clothes on. Sean was not most people. I found myself mesmerized by the way the muscles moved under his skin as he reached for his shaving kit and clean gear. The action accentuated the slightly reddened starburst of the old bullet wound high in his left shoulder. On him it was not so much a blemish as a badge of honor, although I knew he would never have seen it that way.

He sensed the atmosphere between us instantly, like we were putting it out as some kind of scent, and his eyes skimmed over us. And there was, I realized, a distinct twinkle lurking in those moody depths.

"Play nice, girls," he murmured, and disappeared again.

Madeleine grinned as though that proved her case. Her own overnight bag was lying open on the bed. She zipped it closed and set it down near the door.

A few moments later, we heard the water running in the bathroom.

"I really ought to take exception to that but somehow, from him, I don't," she commented with a small grimace. "Since I took over I've been constantly mistaken for the secretary. Old clients walk in and look round nervously for Sean, and new ones think I can't possibly know anything other than typing and filing. Drives me mad. It must be even worse for you — at the sharp end."

You don't know the half of it.

"I cope," I said.

"I'm sure you do," she agreed equably. "I seem to remember that run-in you had last year with one of our guys — Kelso, wasn't it? You broke his arm in two places, I believe."

"Three, actually," I said, my voice bland. "Whatever happened to him?"

"He left." She pulled a face. "As you found out, he had a problem working with — or in this case, *for* — a woman."

She smiled again, more ruefully this time. "I'm not wired the same way you are, Charlie. I can't offer to take on the guys in a fight and have a hope of winning. I don't have any combat experience. So I have to use a certain amount of psychological warfare to get my way instead."

"What — feminine wiles?" I suggested, a little stung by the inference — entirely conjured by my own insecurities — that she was too clever to need to beat anyone up. Whereas I . . .

She offered a censorious little sideways glance at the acidic flippancy, but was still showing a gentle amusement.

"Not quite," she said. The grin faded and a shadow of gravity crossed her features, revealing a steely core that belied her earlier good humor. Madeleine, I realized, would be a tough negotiator and no easy pushover as a boss.

"They know that if they keep me informed at every step, I'll back their actions if I have to." She shrugged, diffident. "I can't afford to be caught on the hop because, ultimately, if I don't give the guys the right information and they make a mistake, it's my neck on the block. Meantime, I have their trust and, I think, their respect." She glanced up, locked my gaze. "And that's what it's all about, isn't it, Charlie? Gaining respect?"

Respect. I seemed to have been reaching for that rainbow's end for half my life and never quite attained it. So, where did it all dawn? My childhood? My parents? Never delicate and feminine enough to satisfy my mother. Never the son my father so badly wanted, and had almost had. . . .

Just for a second I saw myself as a teenager again and imagined a different Tao line unfurling into the future like a high-speed link.

If I hadn't wanted to prove that I was as good as — better than — the boys, I would probably never have gone on the activities weekend that had revealed my latent ability to shoot. Would never have joined the army. Would never have applied for Special Forces, got through the selection process, or tried so hard on the training course that I came to such particular, unwelcome attention.

The line divided, split into a hundred different possibilities from that single strand. I'd been bright. Could have gone to university, a degree, a job in the City. Neat little skirted suits and high heels, like half the women we'd seen rushing through the airport. Tired and stressed and headachy from banging against the glass ceiling of the corporate world.

I'd been into my horse riding as a kid, too, almost obsessed with junior three-day eventing. I'd had a pony with heart and spring, and the nerve to ride him fast at big fixed timber. Could have pursued that as a career — people did — and moved up to horses. Might have been at international level by now. Could have had a dusty Land Rover with straw on the seats, a couple of black Labradors milling round my heels, and a flat-capped young farmer with wind-raw cheeks and gentle callused hands waiting by the Aga.

Instead, I had a fractured career dogged by scandal; an ability to kill without hesitation that even I shied away from exploring; no relationship with my parents to speak of; and a lover who'd been at least as damaged by this life as I had.

I gave myself a mental shake, hard enough to snap me out of it, and found Madeleine watching me carefully. She took a breath to speak, but at that moment the bathroom door opened, and I was saved from whatever homily she was about to deliver.

Sean emerged, damp-haired and dressed in jeans and a shirt, still buttoning the cuffs. He looked at my face and paused, frowning. I didn't give him chance to start an interrogation, either.

There was a hair dryer on the wall near the mirror and I grabbed it. I'd had my hair restyled into a kind of choppy bob since we'd moved out to New York. It was casual enough to survive being under a bike helmet, but the quality of the cut meant it fell back into some kind of order when I gave it a quick blast of hot air. I took my time over it now, while Sean gathered up our bags. By the time I was done, we were ready to go.

"I'm sorry I couldn't provide you with any artillery at such short notice," Madeleine said as the lift doors slid shut behind the three of us. "I'm sure you could pick up something easily enough in one of the dodgier areas of Manchester. Have you time for a detour into Moss Side before you head down to Charlie's parents'?"

Sean glanced at me. The police had not discovered the guns he'd jettisoned at the brothel, and before we left New York he'd made a trip back there to retrieve and dispose of them. Even so, the arrest meant our names would have been flagged and we couldn't afford to get caught with anything that wasn't strictly aboveboard, even on this side of the Atlantic.

"We'll improvise," Sean said now, as the lift doors opened and we stepped out into the lobby.

Outside, Madeleine handed him the keys to the Shogun. "I'll take care of checkout here and the hotel will drop me off for my shuttle flight back down to Heathrow." She checked her slim-line Cartier wristwatch. "I have a couple of hours before I need to check in."

"Thank you, Madeleine," Sean said. He set down his bag and put his hands on her shoulders, turning her slightly to face him and giving her one of those simmering smiles that tend to make women sigh a great deal and want to strip and lie down. She resisted the urge, confirming my earlier suspicion that she was made of stronger stuff than she appeared to be.

"In the words of your adopted homeland, you're welcome," she said, hitting him with a pretty knockout smile of her own. "Leave the Shogun in the car park here when you're all done and mail the keys from the airport," she added. "There's a stamped addressed Jiffy bag in the glove box. I'll have one of the guys come up and collect it, but just be sure to let me know if it needs any special . . . cleaning of any description."

Sean grinned at her. "I'm sure I don't know what you mean," he said, the picture of injured innocence.

"Well, call me if you need backup," she said, keeping it brisk. "I can have some of my people up with you in about three hours, depending on the traffic, with thermal-imaging gear, night-vision equipment, the works. We've gone very high-tech these days. Just say the word."

I saw Sean's minuscule flinch as she said "my people," where once they had been his, but he smiled.

"Thanks, but no thanks," he said. "We thought we'd give this a whirl the old-fashioned way before we go for a full-scale assault from the roof."

" 'The old-fashioned way'?" Madeleine queried.

"Hm," I said. "I know it sounds radical, but we were going to try knocking on the front door. . . ."

EIGHT

"Take the next lane coming up on the right," I said. "The house is about a mile and a half further down, on the right."

The instructions were probably unnecessary. Sean had been to my parents' place on at least three occasions over the years, which meant he could have found it again blindfolded. He had that annoyingly uncanny sense of direction.

Now, I clutched for the center armrest as the Shogun swayed violently. "And can you please try and remember they still drive on the left over here? These roads are too narrow to go bowling down the middle at this speed."

"I haven't forgotten," Sean said mildly, not slackening his pace. "I'm just making best use of the visibility — hedging my bets."

"*Hedge* will be the operative word if you meet one of the locals towing a trailer with half a ton of horse in it," I snapped.

"Calm down, Charlie," Sean said, sounding irritatingly placid. "We need to decide how we're going to handle this. We don't know what — if anything — we're walking into."

"Simple," I said, aware of a tightness in my chest that made it difficult to breathe. "We knock on the front door and, if there's anyone I don't recognize in the house with my mother, we kick the shit out of them and go home. Next?"

He pursed his lips as he stuck the unwieldy 4×4 into a narrow, blind left-hander, his movements deceptively slow when things seemed to be happening around him so fast.

"In essence, I like it," he said lightly. "What it lacks in style it makes up for in dumb simplicity." His voice hardened. "What makes you think you'll get further than the threshold before they cut her throat?"

His choice of words was deliberate, I knew. It jolted me out of my focused little bubble of anger, made my hand stray automatically towards my own throat, to the fading scar that lay hidden beneath the high neck of my sweater.

I thought suddenly of Madeleine. "Feminine wiles," I said. I sat up straight in my seat and gave him my most brilliant vacuous smile. "Oh, Mummy, I'm *awfully* sorry to barge in on you like this, but I just *had* to bring my new boyfriend home to meet you." I clapped my hands together a couple of times, a proper spoiled little princess, then clasped them together under my chin and put my head on one side like a particularly stupid spaniel. "Isn't he just *super?*"

The utter disbelief on Sean's face would have been more comical if he'd kept his eyes on the road. As it was, he only managed to jerk the nearside wheels out of the gutter at the last moment.

"Oh my good God," he spluttered, hardly able to steer for laughing. "You do that terrifyingly well."

"Super," I said, and let the bimbo act drop. "You're going to have to do it, too. You can be something in the City that doesn't require a brain. You'll just have to pretend you don't have a chin, either."

"Investment banker?" Sean suggested, lips twitching. "No, I know — I'll be a political spin doctor."

"No," I said. "It needs to be something where they're *not* going to suspect you're capable of sticking a knife in their backs. Civil servant?"

He shook his head. "These days, all the

bad guys know that's doublespeak for MI5," he said. "Are we really going to let things go far enough for me to need a cover story?"

"Probably not, but you were the one who taught me the value of good prep. You'll need a different name, though. Sean makes you sound too tough."

"Blame my mother," he said carelessly. "She was very big on James Bond when I was born."

I twisted in my seat. "You were named after Sean Connery?" I said in wonder. "Really?"

He frowned, as though he'd just realized that was one piece of family history he probably shouldn't have shared. Then he nodded and gave a wry smile.

"My sister's called Ursula and my younger brother's Roger. You work it out," he said. *Ursula Andress and Roger Moore. Who would have thought it?* "We even had a dog called No — it was a bugger trying to teach it anything."

I laughed out loud and registered that we were nearly at the ivy-clad gateposts that marked the entrance to my parents' driveway and he'd humored the nerves out of me, made the last mile or so that much more bearable.

"So, pick a suitable upper-class-twit name

or I'll pick one for you," I said, ruthless nevertheless.

"How about —" that beatific smile — "Auric?"

"As in Goldfinger? Get real. Okay, you've had your chance, mate. . . ."

"Mummy darling!" I squeaked as soon as the front door opened to my knock. "I'm awfully sorry to arrive unannounced and all that, but I *had* to let you meet Dominic. Isn't he just divine?"

Sean had time to glare at me before he shouldered his way through the narrow opening, looking for all the world as if I was the one thrusting him eagerly inside. My mother, without a chance of mounting a viable defense, backed up into the tiled hallway, nothing but bewilderment on her smooth features.

She looked normal. Normal for my mother, that is. Hair set and face perfect, she was wearing a high-neck cream silk blouse with a fine-knit wool cardigan over it, probably cashmere, and, yes, pearls at her throat and ears. She'd finished off the ensemble with a tweed skirt and sensible shoes. Every inch the countrified English lady.

And not the slightest sign that she was being held here under duress.

For an expanded moment, we stood there, the three of us. It felt to me that I saw everything in that austere space in the blink of an eye. The gleaming black-and-white diagonal set of the tiles underfoot, the old church pew that doubled as a repository for car keys and unopened mail, with a line of scrubbed Wellington boots beneath, the polished dark wood staircase stretching to the upper floor.

And the two unidentified jackets on the pegs below the antique mirror.

I glanced up at it, saw the crack of the slightly open door to the drawing room reflected there, and instinctively held out my arms wide.

"Mummy, it's so lovely to see you," I said, my voice still loud and as guileless as I could make it. "Now, I know it's naughty of us to just pop up from London like this, but Nicky's just *so* impulsive." I threw Sean an adoring glance and he, to his credit, managed to smile indulgently at me rather than vomit.

For another second my mother stared at me with a kind of horrified expression, but that could have been wholly accounted for by my lunatic behavior. I waited a beat longer. If I was totally off base, all I'd done was make an ass of myself. But, if not . . .

Then, numbly, she shuffled forwards and allowed herself to be engulfed in a big daughterly hug, when the most physical contact she'd initiated in years was a chaste hello/good-bye kiss to her powdered cheek. She vibrated with tension in my arms. I put my mouth very close to the pearl stud in her ear and murmured, "Where are they?"

If that was possible, she stiffened, as though I'd suggested something indecent, and pulled back. Then her eyes swiveled, very deliberately — towards the staircase and back. Towards the drawing room and back.

"Darling," she said, her voice croaky. She cleared her throat. "Um, how wonderful to see you. What a nice surprise! I'm afraid I — I can't really offer you lunch or —"

"Oh, gosh, we couldn't possibly put you to all that trouble at such short notice," I interrupted gaily. "Besides, I promised darling Nicky I'd show him a real country pub." I gave a tinkling little laugh. "He's fully expecting a bunch of yokels with straw in their mouths and string round their trouser legs. I've told him he's more likely to rub shoulders with the same stockbrokers here that he does up in Town."

My mother stepped out of my embrace

and turned to Sean, who'd been waiting politely for us to finish our show of familial affection.

"Mrs. Foxcroft, it's such a pleasure," he said, in that kind of drawling, slightly bored upper-class voice you can't escape from in the trendy parts of Soho. "I've heard *so* much about you." He grasped my mother's arms and made a production of air-kissing her on both cheeks. I thought she was going to faint. "And now that I've met you, all I can say is that you must have had your daughter when you were *awfully* young."

My mother flushed and preened automatically, a knee-jerk response to the heavily ladled charm. Then she threw me an utterly confused look and stumbled back a pace.

"We just thought we'd stop off for a nice cup of tea, then we'll be on our way," I said deliberately, moving forward to take her arm. "And perhaps one of your scrummy cakes? I've been telling Nicky what a total angel you are in the kitchen." I glanced at Sean with a huge smile and added wickedly, "Mummy's buns are absolutely to die for."

Sean's expression froze momentarily as he fought for control over it, then relaxed into courteous attention. "Oh I'm sure they are," he murmured, and threw me a warning glance. *Don't push it. This is not a game. Trust me. I know.*

"Oh, er, well, please do come through," my mother said, any double entendres going straight over her head. She pushed open the door to the drawing room and led us inside.

I don't know quite what I'd been expecting, but the sight that greeted me wasn't it. The only occupant of that starchily formal room was a tall blond woman, who sat on the sofa with her legs gracefully arranged, her long shins slanted alongside each other, knees pressed demurely together.

She had apparently been flicking through the pages of the magazine that lay open on her lap — *The Field,* if the photo spread of gundogs was anything to go by. When we walked in she put the magazine aside and glanced up with nothing but polite inquiry on her strong-boned face.

I took one look at the way she emptied her hands and knew she was a player.

"Oh, gosh, Mummy, we didn't realize you had visitors," I cried, going all aflutter. "How *awfully* rude of us!" I bounded forwards, closing rapidly on the woman on the sofa. My intention was to overcrowd her but she unfolded her legs and got to her feet faster than I'd hoped.

"Awfully rude of us," I repeated, having to lift my gaze to look her in the eye as I pumped her hand with a purposefully limp grip. The short-sleeve dress she wore showed off lean, well-defined muscles, but, even close-up, her face bore no scar tissue to show she was a fighter, and no hint that she'd had surgical help to remove it.

Now, I pulled a little moue and treated this stranger to a conspiratorial smile. "I just couldn't wait to show off darling Nicky."

"Well, I can't say I blame you for that," the woman said, dropping my flaccid hand as soon as she was able to.

Her accent was American — educated midwestern, if I was any judge. As she spoke, she ran her glittering eyes over Sean in a slow predatory survey. He bore it with an arrogant indifference, as though this kind of female adoration happened all the time and was just another cross he had to bear. "Wherever did she find *you?*"

Sean's expression became ever more languid. "Polo," he said, and smiled at me as though the sun rose and fell in my eyes. "I have a small string."

"Really?" Blondie said, swallowing it and impressed, despite herself. "Well, you should talk to my . . . associate. He's the horse nut."

My mother had slunk silently into her

favorite armchair next to the original Adam-style fireplace during this brief exchange. Her gaze was not inside room and her hands were trembling. She'd been knitting — something she did only when she was upset — the beginnings of an Aran sweater, by the looks of it. The heavy-gauge wool and number-two needles and all the related paraphernalia were stuffed into an old brocade bag at the side of the chair. She picked it up now, stared at the partially completed garment, then put it down again without seeing a thing.

"Your associate?" I queried, moving to my mother's side. I put a reassuring hand on her shoulder but she didn't respond to my touch.

"Yes — Don," Blondie said, eyes narrowed slightly as she watched my mother's nerve start to fail. "He's just upstairs. I'll call him down."

"Why don't I make us all that cup of tea?" I suggested. "Nicky, could you —"

"No," the woman said. A command, delivered like one. I stopped and regarded her with wide, innocent eyes. "No tea," she said, sharper now.

"Coffee, then?" I said brightly.

"No goddamn drinks, okay?" she said. Her voice went surprisingly harsh when it was raised. "Don! Get your goddamn ass down here, right now!"

The mysterious Don must have already reached the hallway, because the door opened with barely a pause. A big man stepped into the room and I saw at once why he'd been sent to lurk upstairs while Blondie handled the social interaction.

He was huge, with a shaved head and a slightly Oriental slant to his eyes, and wearing a gray suit. After our earlier discussion on James Bond, the only thing that went through my head was: Oddjob. All he needed was a bowler hat with a steel brim. I guessed his only connection to horses was that he could probably lift one.

Sean had been standing with his back almost to the door when it opened. Without a flicker, he brought his right arm sweeping back, elbow bent, to smash it into Don's windpipe. His reaction was instinctive, deadly as a striking snake. He hardly even seemed to look to find his target.

The big man staggered back against the wall, hands to his throat, making urgent gurgling noises. Sean crouched and spun, using the momentum to load his full body-weight behind a punch to the man's groin. Don's gurgles momentarily rose in pitch and volume, then he went utterly silent and started to slither floorwards.

Blondie, meanwhile, overrode her natural startle reflex to leap for Sean. I ducked and hit her hard with my shoulder as she flew past me, deflecting her back onto the sofa. She bounced straight up again, eyes slitted, and instantly threw a vicious kick. Whatever that dress was made of, there was plenty of stretch to it.

She must have been used to sparring with male opponents. It was the only reason I could think of that she automatically aimed for testicles I clearly didn't own. I twisted slightly and took the brunt of it on my hip. Left hip. Bad idea. The pain sizzled down through my leg like hot fat.

I blocked it with adrenaline and anger, and charged her. If you're fighting someone with a short weapon, you stay out of range. But against a long weapon, you have to get in close. I reckoned those well-muscled legs counted as a pair of long weapons. She was quick, though, grabbing both my upper arms with viselike fingers, her breath hot in my face.

Her skill so far had told me she was trained but was not a fighter by nature. And she clearly didn't spar with anyone who was willing to mess up those elegant features. I snapped my head forwards to butt her full

137

in the middle of her long slim nose with my forehead, hearing the solid crunching tear of cartilage right before the scream.

Mother!

I reared back. My mother had shrunk into her chair, terrified into silence by the sudden eruption of violence around her. It was only when she saw the blood start to squirt that she'd let rip.

Blondie tried to boot me in the stomach but I was close enough to downgrade the blow into a shove. Even so, I cannoned back into the arm of my mother's chair. As I sprawled over it, the abandoned knitting loomed large in my field of vision. I grabbed for one of the needles and yanked it straight out of the web of wool that anchored it.

When Blondie tried to launch another venomous kick — towards my head this time — I stabbed the twelve-inch needle straight through the fleshy part of her right thigh with enough force to penetrate the muscle completely and tent — but not break — the skin on the other side.

She collapsed back onto the sofa, yelping in her distress. I glanced at Sean. He'd got Don on his knees with his face jammed hard up against the wall by the doorway. He had the big man's feet crossed at the ankles and fingers linked on top of his head. Sean's hand almost disappeared into the folds of flesh at the back of his captive's neck with the force he was using to keep him there.

He nodded to me. I nodded back.

"I'm guessing the polo was pushing it too far, huh?"

I managed a rusty half smile. Blondie was still rolling around on the sofa, trying to evade the pain. She certainly knew a lot of very innovative swearwords for someone so well-bred but, other than invective, she was out of fight. The shock of the unexpected blow to the face had more to do with it than the severity of either injury, in my opinion.

Her nervous system had certainly prioritized the broken nose over the hole through her leg. I'd managed to split the skin of the bridge as well as damage the underlying structure. Hardly surprising that my forehead felt like I'd a lump the size of a golf ball on it. Blondie needed her nose packed and set and probably glued back together as well, but it wasn't life-threatening. She could damn well wait.

Meanwhile, I wasn't going to leave her with a weapon, albeit an embedded one. I leaned down and, before she could protest, yanked the needle back out of her flesh with deliberate carelessness. That seemed to bring the leg wound back to prominence again. I felt the ache in my own thigh and was aloof to her pain.

I glanced over at my mother. She was quiet now, but with that dangerously calm demeanor that usually denotes a part of the brain is refusing to accept the input offered to it and has temporarily closed for repair.

Very slowly, she got to her feet, her movements jerky and stiff.

"Actually, I think a cup of tea might be a very good idea, Charlotte," she said, her voice rather reedy. "Don't you?"

"For heaven's sake, Mother —" I began, but Sean caught my eye and gave a tiny shake of his head. *Let her do it. Something normal. It's her way of coping.*

I took a breath. "Yes, please," I said meekly. "That would be lovely."

She headed for the kitchen, carefully stepping over Don's feet almost without seeming to register the nature of the obstruction. At the doorway she paused, turned back, and her eyes swept slowly over the alien tableau that had just been acted out in her drawing room, as if seeing it for the first time.

"I'll bring a tea towel and some ice for that nose," she murmured vaguely. "Try not to make too much of a mess on the sofa."

Her eyes focused on me, on the bloodied

knitting needle drooping from my left hand.

"I do wish you hadn't done that, Charlotte," she went on, a little pained note in her voice. "It was a rather complicated pattern and you've made me drop all my stitches."

NINE

"They arrived five days ago," my mother said. "Introduced themselves as colleagues of your father, from America. Said that he'd issued an open invitation to look us up whenever they were in England. I — I had no real reason to doubt them. From the things they said, they clearly knew Richard, and they seemed very pleasant . . . at first."

She took a deep breath that wavered on the way out, and sipped a mouthful of tea from a delicate Spode cup. It rattled slightly when she put it back onto its saucer and she frowned at it, as though the cup had shaken of its own volition.

"When did you realize they were . . . serious?" I asked.

We were at the long table in the kitchen, sitting across the corner from each other, so I was close but she didn't feel I was staring right at her, accusing her. Like this was some kind of interrogation.

Sean had found a roll of duct tape in the back of the Shogun. I'd helped him drag my mother's unwanted houseguests out to the garage and left him to deal with them. I didn't ask what he intended to do and, if I'm honest, I didn't much care. I was too busy trying not to concentrate on the throbbing in my left leg, or how easily I could assuage that ache with one of the painkillers I'd wanted ever since we'd got off the flight.

Instead, following Sean's silent prompting, I'd sat at the table and let my mother go through the ritual of making tea, spooning loose leaves into a warmed pot, adding water right on the boil, letting it brew, and then filtering it through a strainer into cups so translucently fragile that you had to pour the milk in first or they'd shatter. By the time she'd stopped fussing she seemed more settled, but it proved a transient state.

"More or less as soon as they'd finished their first cup of tea," she said in answer to the last question, looking fretful again. "I should never have let them into the house, but you just don't expect . . ."

"They're professionals," I said dryly. "I'm not surprised you didn't clock them."

She tried for a smile but couldn't summon the will required for it to stand up by itself. As soon as she let go, it fell over. "As a JP who's heard I forget how many cases of fake Gas Board inspectors conning their way into old ladies' houses and rifling their handbags, I feel very foolish to have been taken in by them," she admitted, "however briefly."

"I would say you've coped extremely well for a hostage," I said, taking a sip from my own cup. I don't know if it was the pot or the china, but it tasted perfect. Unless it's over ice and awash with slices of lemon, the Americans just can't do tea. A bag on a string dunked into a cup of lukewarm milky water. I'd given up drinking the stuff.

"I didn't want them to see how afraid I was, so I tried to ignore them as best I could," she said in a small, austere voice, gesturing to her hair and clothes. "Not let them get to me. Carry on as though nothing was happening. I suppose you find that rather silly."

"Not at all." I shook my head. "Most people would have totally fallen apart. Trust me — I've watched it happen."

She stared at me for a moment with a slightly puzzled expression on her face, and I realized with a sense of guilt that I couldn't remember the last time I'd offered her praise for anything.

But that one, I reminded myself, was very

much a two-way street.

I swallowed and asked with great care, "Did they . . . hurt you?"

She gave me a quick glance, but her gaze wouldn't latch with mine and went sliding off past my shoulder. "Not as such," she said, evasive. "But the chap — Don — made it painfully clear what he was prepared to do if I wasn't 'a good girl,' as he put it."

Her gaze skated round the kitchen walls and finally dropped into my cup, which was three-quarters empty. Relieved by the excuse, she jumped up and stretched for the teapot from beneath its cosy in the middle of the table. I tried not to let my impatience show while she did what she needed to in order to settle. And to come to a decision about how much of it she was willing to let out into the open.

"He seemed to have some particular perversions of a sexual nature that revolved around older women," she said at last, prim but all in a rush, sitting ramrod-straight on the hard-backed chair. "He spent some time expounding on the subject, about what he —" She broke off, pressed a shaky hand to her mouth as though just to speak of it made her physically sick. I started to reach for her, instinctively, but she waved me off.

And I could empathize with that completely. I knew exactly what it was to abhor the thought of being touched. By anyone. It didn't matter who.

"I'm sorry, Charlotte," she said, low, when she could speak again. "I'm so sorry."

"Don't be," I said, my voice rough with a prickling sense of rage that wasn't directed at her but had no other outlet. "What the hell have you got to be sorry about?"

"I never understood what it was really like for you, did I?" she murmured, and the sudden unwelcome swerve in the conversation made the hairs stand bolt upright all along my forearms.

Oh no. Don't go there. Not now. . . .

I had to look away from her at that point, focusing instead on an errant fleck of tea leaf that had escaped into my cup and was floating on the surface, because my mother had begun to cry.

Although, *cry* was the wrong word to describe it. *Cry* suggested a maelstrom of unbearable feeling but if I hadn't been watching her face I would never have known. She cried almost without emotion, without great sobs racking her body, without the telltale catch in her voice or the clog in her throat. Instead, as she stared into the past the tears fell unheeded from her eyes and dropped onto the surface of the table

146

below her, like offerings to a long-forgotten god.

And just when I was considering prayer myself, I heard the slam of the front door and footsteps on the tiles. A moment later, Sean appeared in the kitchen doorway.

He saw the pair of us like that and froze in mid-stride. It was only when I threw him a desperate *Don't leave me here alone* smile, that he came forwards. He was wiping his hands on one of the old rags that my father kept stored in a corner of the garage, although for what purpose I'd never discerned. My father's idea of do-it-yourself was *personally* telephoning for a tradesman.

My mother suddenly seemed to register both Sean's presence and the unaccustomed wetness of her eyes at the same moment. She turned her head away sharply and whipped out her handkerchief.

"Well," Sean said to me, tactfully ignoring her distress, "either that pair are better versed at not answering questions than I am at asking them, or they genuinely don't know anything."

He moved across to the sink, raising an eyebrow at me over the top of my mother's head as he went. I shook my head a little.

He ran the hot water and squeezed washing-up liquid onto his hands. The rag he'd put down on the draining board was, I saw, stained a distinctive dark red that would no doubt turn brown as it dried. I got up, took the sugar bowl off the table and tipped half the granulated contents into his hands as he scrubbed at them, so the sugar would act as an abrasive. He nodded and his eyes went to my mother again.

How is she?

I don't know.

I shrugged, but it was a truthful response.

"If we're going to turn them over to the local police, we have to do it soon," he said out loud. "We've already delayed almost longer than we can justify, not to mention interrogating them."

My mother's brittle poise had recovered, but at Sean's quiet comment it seemed to shatter afresh.

"Oh! Do we have to?" she said wanly. "Can't we just let them go? I mean, surely, now you're here . . ."

"Mother, what do you think will happen if we let them go?" I demanded. "We can't stay more than a day or so. Do you expect them to give us their word that they'll leave you alone in future?"

She swung a beseeching gaze towards Sean, but he proved no softer touch.

"I'm sorry," he said, face grave, "but we

really do need to get back to the States as soon as possible."

Her face began to crumble. She jerked her chin away from us and busied herself by fetching Sean a mug from the row hooked under the shelf on the Welsh dresser and pouring tea from the pot. Still no best china for him, I saw with a little spurt of anger.

We sat. Sean took the chair alongside me to give my mother space, and sedately drank his tea. As I watched his fingers curl through the handle of the mug, I realized that the delicacy of a Spode teacup would have discomfitted him. Perhaps that was why my mother hadn't offered that choice. Belatedly, and somewhat ashamedly, I gave her the benefit of the doubt. Even more so when she offered Sean a tentative but apparently genuine smile.

"Well, thank you — both of you — for coming so quickly," she said. Her eyes flicked back to me. "I wasn't sure, when you rang, if I'd said enough, but that dreadful woman was listening in and I couldn't say more —"

"You said enough," Sean assured her.

"Yes," she said faintly. We were all silent. Then she took a breath and said, "I know I should prosecute them, for what they did, but I . . . can't. Besides anything else, we

149

don't know what that might do to Richard's situation."

"Did they say anything to you at all — about why they were here?" I asked. "Or what this is all about?"

She shook her head, frowning. "Not really," she said. "I knew something was wrong, of course, but until you told me, I'd no idea it was . . . as bad as you say." She looked up suddenly, hope growing on her face. "But he can come home now, can't he? That would solve things."

"Not yet," I said, feeling mean for dashing her back down again. "I'm sorry. He was still in jail when we left."

"You said he'd been arrested in a b— brothel," she said bravely, wincing either at the sound or the very thought of the word. "What on earth was he doing there?"

I felt my mouth start to open while I scrambled to cobble together a believable lie, but my brain refused to do anything other than replay the memory tape of us barging into that room and finding my father well on the way to a compromising position with the naked, painfully young Asian girl. It was an image I didn't think I'd ever fully erase.

"He was most likely coerced," Sean said coolly, stepping in. "Charlie saw him picked up from his hotel and taken there, and he didn't exactly look willing. They were probably holding the threat of your safety over him." He glanced at me. "It would explain why they didn't need to stay with him to make sure he . . . played his part."

He'd been putting a little too much realism into that particular piece of acting for my taste, but I didn't voice the opinion.

"I see." She was silent for a moment. "But what I don't understand — about any of this — is why? Why pick on us to . . . *torment* in this way?"

"We were rather hoping," I said, "that you might be able to tell us that."

"I can't!" she said, voice climbing towards shrill. She stopped, took a breath, and continued in a lower register. "What I mean is, I have no idea why those . . . *people* turned up on my doorstep. Richard never mentioned anything before he left."

"Are you sure?" I said, adding quickly, "I'm not suggesting you're going senile, Mother. But with hindsight, has he seemed distracted, or worried about anything lately?"

"Well, he certainly hasn't been himself since he last returned from America," she admitted, sliding me a reproachful little look over the rim of her cup.

I don't remember much about the four days immediately following my near-fatal shooting, which was probably just as well. But when I was finally allowed to wake in that hospital in Maine, my father's un-friendly face was the first thing that greeted me. He'd made his displeasure at my situation pretty clear without, it seemed to me, managing to express much concern for my welfare. I'd taken what comfort I could from the fact that he was there at all but, afterward I'd wondered if he'd been lured across the Atlantic mainly by a professional interest in the intricacies of the surgery I'd undergone.

"What about this doctor friend of his they mentioned on the news?" Sean asked, cut-ting into my gloomy thoughts. "Jeremy Lee. They were dropping hints that your husband might have had something to do with his death."

"He most certainly did not," my mother said stoutly. The speed of her response had a knee-jerk quality to it, but the words were underwritten by a tremor of doubt. She rushed to cover it. "Richard believes life is absolutely sacrosanct. He's dedicated his career — his life — to its preservation," she said, more firmly now. And, just to prove she was feeling more like her old self, she added, "Something *you* might have difficulty understanding."

Sean was hard to read at the best of times, and now he gave no indication that he took offense at her remark. Whether he did or not was immaterial. I took offense enough for both of us.

Instead, he rose and nodded to her, expressionless. "I'd better go and check that our guests are still sitting uncomfortably. If you'll excuse me?" he said with excruciating politeness. "Thank you for the tea, Mrs. Foxcroft."

He walked out and, a few moments later, I heard the front door slam behind him.

My mother, as if only just realizing what she'd done, showed her distress in the flutter of a hand to her throat, the tremulous mouth and doe eyes.

I rose, too, unmoved by the tricks I'd seen her use too many times before. At least it was a sign she was almost back to normal.

Didn't take her long after a four-day ordeal, though, did it?

"Pack some things," I said, abrupt. "If we can't bring my father to you, we'll have to take you to him, and try to get to the bottom of this. Make sure you've got your passport."

I gathered Sean's and my empty crockery

and took them to the sink to rinse out. When I was done, I turned back to find my mother had risen but not approached, as if she wasn't sure of her reception if she got closer.

"Charlotte, I'm sorry," she said, sounding convincingly wretched. "I didn't mean —"

"No, you probably didn't," I said tiredly. "But just bear this in mind, Mother, before you're so quick to condemn Sean. If he wasn't the way he is — if we both weren't, come to that — you'd still be stuck here listening to Don's plans for a fun-filled evening by the fire."

TEN

"Okay, people, we're faced with a bit of a dilemma," I said cheerfully. "What do we do with you two?"

I glanced from a subdued Don to his sullen companion and smiled. They were both lying on their sides on the cold painted floor of the garage, well away from my father's dark green Jaguar XK8 and the dust cover that hid my laid-up FireBlade, tucked away behind it.

Sean had bound them efficiently, so their wrists and ankles were bent back behind them and taped together. I'd been tied like that during Resistance to Interrogation exercises during Selection and I knew it was bloody uncomfortable for anything longer than a few minutes at a time. I reckoned they'd probably been like that now for more than an hour.

Sean had also added a nasty refinement. Several bands of the reinforced tape went from their feet and looped up round their necks, so if they relaxed they ran the risk of asphyxiating themselves. Blondie seemed to be coping with this better than Don, who had clearly chosen muscle bulk over flexibility and was starting to suffer for it.

He hadn't been looking too good to start with. I don't know what methods Sean had employed in his attempts to get information out of the pair of them, but Don's skin had now taken on the color and texture of a melted candle.

Sean had also used Steri-Strips to put Blondie's nose back together, and had affixed a dressing to the wound in her leg using more duct tape around her thigh, but I daresay he hadn't been particularly gentle with any of it.

"You're obviously aware that we can't let you loose," I said. "Just as you know we're not going to turn you over to the police. So, what choices do we have?"

I crouched and made eye contact with Blondie. Of the two of them, she seemed to be the leader and I knew that if she folded Don would follow.

"From here, we're about forty-five minutes from a place called Saddleworth Moor," I said, still conversational. "Out in the Pennine hills. It's very . . . isolated." I let my voice harden. "During the 1960s, a couple called Ian Brady and Myra Hindley abducted a number of young children, raped and murdered them, then buried the bodies out on the moor. Some of those bodies," I continued placidly, "have never been found."

Sean's timing was perfect. He walked in at that moment, having just raided my mother's toolshed. In his right hand he held a garden spade. He let the steel blade drop to the concrete floor with a ringing clatter that made both of our prisoners flinch. His face wore a cold, featureless mask that offered no hint of mercy.

"We're all set," he said, leaning on the handle of the spade. "And we don't have much time."

I turned back, to see Blondie's fearful gaze jump from Sean to me. Don closed his eyes briefly, as though he might have been praying.

"The alternative," I said to them, "is that we take you up to a friend of mine, who will keep you incommunicado for a while — as long as it takes — and then release you unharmed. For that, we need some level of cooperation. It's up to you." I made a show of checking my watch. "You've got, oh, around three minutes to make up your minds."

I rose, nodding curtly to Sean, and we walked out. I noted that he made sure to grate the spade on the ground with each stride, just to drive the point home.

We halted just outside the garage door, leaving it open slightly so we could keep a surreptitious eye on them.

"What exactly did you do to Don?" I asked quietly.

Do you really want to know?

I shook my head as though he'd spoken out loud. "No, on second thoughts, don't answer that. Will they cooperate?"

He shrugged. "I would, given that kind of a choice — and so chillingly delivered." He tilted his head and regarded me with studious eyes, an almost mocking smile on his lips. "You play the psycho very well, Charlie."

"Thank you — I think," I said. "I learned from a master."

At that moment, my mother came out of the front door and hurried across the gravel towards us. She saw the spade in Sean's hands and her face blenched white.

"Oh, you *haven't* . . . ?"

"No, we haven't," I said, moving forwards to meet her and registering the way Sean

158

casually shifted to block her view into the garage. "We've given them some options, that's all, and they're talking them over."

"Oh," she repeated, more blankly this time. "Well, er, I'm just packing some things, but I'm not sure what to take. How cold is it in New York at the moment? And how long am I likely to be away? I have a lot of responsibilities that can't just be dropped at the last minute, you know," she added in a peevish tone that lasted until she asked, suddenly more forlorn, "And . . . what do I tell people?"

"Tell them your husband's been taken ill," I said, starting to run out of patience. "He's a doctor, for heaven's sake. Hospitals are full of sick people. Tell them he caught something. Or tell them he got knocked down by a bus crossing the road and broke his ankle."

"But that's simply not true."

Give me strength! "Okay. How about you tell them he broke it falling down the stairs during a police raid on a Brooklyn brothel? That closer to the truth for you?"

She gave me a hurt look and scurried back into the house without reply. I turned and found Sean watching me, expressionless.

"What?" I said, but he only shook his head and pushed the garage door open again.

As they heard our footsteps approaching, both Blondie and Don squirmed round to try and see us coming, as though that would somehow make a difference.

"Okay," Sean said to them, his voice even and pleasant, but that of a stone-cold killer nevertheless. "Decision time. What's it to be?"

They chose internment over interment. Of course they did. We folded the Shogun's rear seats flat and slid them in like coffins into a hearse, on a sheet of folded heavy-duty plastic from the greenhouse. They lay flat on their backs, side by side. We secured their hands and feet with more duct tape so they posed no risk to us, and covered them with a picnic blanket my mother insisted on providing. She thought comfort — we thought concealment.

I made a phone call and got the promise of help I needed. Then Sean and I drove them north. About an hour and a half up the M6 motorway, over the high-level bridge at Thelwall, and into Lancashire. Back to my old stamping ground.

Aware of our audience, we didn't talk much on the drive up. At one point Blondie's muffled voice demanded we stop so she could use the rest room. Classic hostage technique — get your captors to do you small favors. I wasn't buying.

"It's not much further," I told her. "You'll have to wait."

"And what if I can't wait?"

"That's up to you — only you might want to bear in mind that this isn't our vehicle, so we don't really care what happens to it," I said blandly. "Whereas you might not have a change of underwear for a while."

She fell silent for the remainder of the journey.

Sean left the motorway at the north Lancaster exit, drove up the Lune Valley and then struck out along the winding back roads towards Wray. Eventually, at my direction, he turned off the main road and the Shogun clambered easily up a potholed farm track. At the top was a scruffy yard with an old stone barn at one side and a couple of dead pickup trucks fighting a losing battle with the weeds in front.

We passed through a set of stone gateposts, one of which was cracked clean in half, and drew to a halt. A moment later, the barn door opened and a big man with shaggy hair and a scarred face stepped out and glared at us, even though he'd known full well we were coming. At his heels was a mammoth rottweiler bitch. The dog appeared to be glaring, too.

I opened the door and climbed out. As soon as he recognized us for certain, the man broke into a grin that revealed several gold teeth.

"Charlie!" he said. "How are ya, girl?"

"Good, thanks, Gleet," I said, shaking the oil-ingrained hand he offered. "You remember Sean?"

"Course I do, mate," Gleet said, a certain amount of respect in his voice. He clicked his fingers dismissively to the dog who, with one last, longing look in our direction, turned and disappeared back into the barn. Gleet jerked his head towards the Shogun. "You got these two bodies you want storing, then?"

"Yeah," Sean said, opening up the rear door. "Don't take any chances with either of them."

"No worries. Got a space cleared out at the back of one of the old pig sheds. They'll be safe as houses back there and they'll not get out across the field past that lot with their fingers intact, I can tell you." He gave an almost delicate shudder. "Vicious little buggers, pigs."

Gleet might live on a farm, but the day-to-day running was handled by his morose sister. He spent his time building beautiful custom motorcycles out in the barn, which was how I'd first come into contact with him.

His sister appeared now, a stocky masculine woman, silent and scowling, in a baggy flower-print dress over Wellington boots, and a knitted hat with a frayed hole in the crown.

Between us, we hauled our cargo out of the Shogun and untied their feet so they could walk. Don thought about making some kind of a play at that point, but his restricted circulation wasn't up to it. Gleet's sister manhandled him across the yard and through a galvanized metal field gate with all the careless skill of a woman who's spent the last forty years dealing with bolshy cattle.

The free-range pigs were a new addition since my last visit to Gleet's place, and they hadn't done much for the landscape. Pigs like to dig, and the ground we staggered across was ankle-deep in muddy ruts, like the Somme after particularly heavy bombardment.

The pigs looked happy, though — and big, too. And intelligent in a sly, cunning kind of way, as if they knew full well they had the upper hand out here and they couldn't wait for you to miss a step so they could prove it. They stopped wallowing and tunneling long enough to watch our halting progress across the field, past their corrugated iron arks to a dilapidated wooden shed.

Close up, the shed was a lot more solid than it had first appeared, with a shiny new padlock on the door. Inside, it stank of its last occupants, to the extent it made your eyes water. Blondie's face showed her disgust.

"This isn't over," she said, her voice flat and buzzing slightly from the busted nose. "This isn't anywhere *close* to being over."

"Any time you feel up to a rematch," I said, meeting her gaze, "you let me know."

Her lips twisted into a grimace that might have doubled as a smile. "You have no idea, do you," she said, "who you're dealing with?"

"Perhaps you'd care to enlighten us?" Sean said. He gestured to the pigs, who'd edged nearer like they were hoping to pick up gossip. "Might make all the difference to the company you keep."

"I'll take my chances," Blondie said, closing down. "I think they're probably better than yours."

Gleet's sister gave her a shove backwards and bolted the door to their temporary cell behind the pair of them. It was only then I let the bravado fade from my face.

"Don't worry, they'll be fine," Gleet said. "May and me'll look after them."

I realized with some surprise that I'd never known his sister's name before. I turned to her and, aware of the listening ears, asked casually, "Are you still handy with that crossbow of yours?"

"Don't need to be no more," May said darkly, with the faintest glimmer of a twinkle in her dull gray eyes. "Them daft buggers at t'local council gave me my shotgun license back."

Eleven

We spent the night down in Cheshire. A phone call on the way back had Madeleine arranging seats for the three of us on the first available return flight to New York, but it didn't leave until the following morning so there was nothing we could do except sit tight overnight. I called ahead to warn my mother of the schedule. The conversation was brief and when I rang off she was fretting about canceling the milk and the newspaper delivery at such short notice.

For the rest of the journey, we speculated about Blondie's and Don's purpose, employer, and identity — mostly fruitlessly.

The only thing that was obvious was that they were both Americans. Accents aside, their clothing was all U.S. chain-store brands. No need to cut out the labels, because hundreds of thousands of each item were sold every year.

Sean and I had been through their belongings meticulously, but they were real pros and they'd carried nothing incriminating. No passports, no ID, no personal mementos or convenient books of matches, no credit cards. Just a stack of cash in a plastic envelope from an airport exchange bureau, and a pay-as-you-go mobile phone with the call register purged.

They'd arrived by taxi, my mother had told us, but in Blondie's handbag we'd found a ticket for parking at Manchester airport, dated the day of their arrival, and a set of car keys. The keys were for a Citroën, so they obviously didn't belong to Blondie's own vehicle in the States, where Citroëns weren't imported. That meant they were from a rental, which they'd picked up and almost immediately abandoned in one of the sprawling car parks. They'd carefully removed the key fob identifying which company it was hired from.

"I suppose that's where they'll have stashed their personal stuff," I said. "Hire a car as soon as you land, leave everything you don't want found on you inside, then dump it in long-term parking and pick it all up again when you leave."

"It's good operating procedure," Sean said. "These days, the authorities are too nervous to let you leave luggage at the airport."

They'd stuck to protocol over communication, too. My mother had never heard them make any outgoing calls, and they had always been very careful to take incoming ones well outside her earshot. Apart from Don's increasingly creepy behavior, they hadn't given any sign that things weren't going according to whatever plan they'd devised.

"Interesting that they had no weapons on them," I said, "but I suppose if they flew in they couldn't exactly bring anything with them."

"Mm, still, they're not difficult to pick up over here — particularly so close to Manchester. Perhaps it's fortunate they didn't think of that," he said with a wry smile. "But they must have known they didn't need them. There were two of them against an untrained woman in her fifties, and they had the additional threat of doing something nasty to her husband if she didn't play ball. They knew she wasn't going to try anything."

"But . . . she did," I said, a little blankly as the realization hit. "She warned us."

"Yes, she did," Sean agreed. He threw me a little sideways look. "There's more to your mother than meets the eye."

"Well, let's face it," I said, unwilling to be impressed, "there could hardly be less."

He smiled openly at that, reaching into his jacket pocket without taking his eyes off the road and pulling out his mobile phone.

"Here," he said, handing it over. "Before I started asking those two any difficult questions, I took a couple of mug shots of each of them. They're not very good — I'm no David Bailey, and they weren't exactly willing subjects — but if you e-mail them across to Parker, he might be able to ID them."

"You're right," I said critically when I'd scrolled through the menus and found the shots. I peered closer at the small view screen. "This one of Blondie's so bad she ought to be using it on her passport."

He glanced across. "I don't think she trusted me to capture her best side, so she would keep shutting her eyes."

After some fiddling, I managed to send the photos on, then called Parker to check they'd come through. I heard the rattle of computer keys in the background.

"No . . . nothing yet," he said. "How's your mom — she okay?"

"She is now," I said.

"Ah. Trouble?"

"No more than we were expecting."

"*That* bad?" Parker said grimly. "Ah, hang on . . . yes, the pictures have just landed. Let me just check that they open okay. . . . Jesus! Is this woman actually dead?'

"No, she's faking it."

"I guess she's faking the blood all over her face, too, huh?"

"Ah, no, that was me," I said, and he laughed at the cheeriness of my tone.

"Okay, leave it with me. I'll e-mail these to a guy I know who works with the Feds. He should be able to run them through a database or two and at least tell us if they've got any history."

"The guy — Blondie called him Don — seemed to have some fairly distinctive behavior quirks," I said, and summarized my mother's halting admission. "That might help nail him down."

Parker's voice hardened. "Damn right he oughta be nailed down," he said. "She must have been terrified."

She'd certainly had a taste of the grim realities of life, I reflected, where previously her only brush with the dark side had been somewhat vicarious.

"Yeah, well, she bounces back pretty quickly."

"Oh," Parker said, sounding a little nonplussed but, at the same time, cynical. "So that's where you get it from."

It was dark by the time we got back to the house. My mother had cooked us an evening meal that was as elaborate as it was exquisite. She served it, accompanied by best china, starched linen and hallmarked silver cutlery, with all due pomp and ceremony in the formal dark red dining room. I imagined she'd done the same thing every night for her captors, a pointlessly stiff-upper-lip example of not letting standards slip, no matter what the circumstances. If she'd been any good at carpentry she'd have built them a river bridge in the jungle, too.

I was starkly reminded of the last time Sean had eaten a meal in that stuffy room, during the one and only time I'd brought him home to meet my parents on an illicit weekend pass from camp. I'd been filled with the vain hope that they'd be impressed by his quiet self-containment. Instead, they'd been horrified by his obvious working-class origins and gone out of their way to expose him, in their opinion, as little more than a vulgar, uncouth yob. Although he'd hidden it rather better, he'd been just as intimidated by their upper-middle-class snobbery.

In truth, I never should have been involved

with him in the first place. Not then. Not only was he a sergeant when I was a lowly private, but he was one of my instructors as well. As far as the army was concerned, the relationship was taboo on every level, and undoubtedly doomed from the start.

Now, I watched him in the flickering light from the twin candelabra, as he lifted a long-stem glass to sip the excellent wine he'd chosen from my father's cellar to go with the main course. There was still an unmistakable lethality to him that anyone with half a brain couldn't fail to recognize, but it was sleeker, slicker, more heavily disguised.

He could have been a corporate raider, a ruthless entrepreneur, even a prowling tiger on the Stock Exchange floor, rather than the obvious enforcer he'd always seemed in the past. My mother certainly responded better to his present gloss, but I wasn't sure how much of that was due to some kind of residual gratitude. And, if it wasn't, a part of me bitterly resented her belated approval now, when neither she nor my father had bothered to look beyond Sean's rough-diamond exterior before.

After we'd locked down for the night, we quizzed her again about my father's recent behavior, but it was heavy going.

"I simply can't believe he could possibly be involved in anything illegal or immoral," she declared resolutely, and wouldn't budge from that standpoint, despite firsthand reports to the contrary. "I'm sure when I've spoken to him, everything will be all right."

Eventually, I gave up and announced my intention of turning in, and that provoked more prudish maneuvering on my mother's part. Anyone would have thought I was in my early teens rather than my late twenties.

She made a big song and dance out of showing Sean to the room she'd made up for him specially, as though that was going to persuade him to stay put for the duration of the night.

He just favored her with a bland smile and assured her he would sleep very soundly there. And, as she was fussing over pointing out clean towels in the neighboring bathroom, he passed by me close enough to murmur in my ear, "Won't we?"

"If you were a gentleman *you'd* be the one doing all the creeping from bed to bed," I whispered back, scalp prickling at the thought of trying to get away with that kind of thing under my parents' somewhat puritanical roof.

"Yeah, but I'm assuming your childhood bedroom doesn't have the luxury of a double bed." He smiled, wolfish. "Besides, I'm not sure I could stand the thought of being stared at by a shelf full of raggedy old stuffed animals and dolls."

"Good point, although I was never a big fan of dolls." I waited a beat. "Had an Action Man and a Meccano set, though."

He rolled his eyes. "Now why doesn't that surprise me?"

My mother came out of the bathroom in time to catch us grinning at each other. She was too polite to glare at us with outright suspicion, but it was lurking fairly close to the surface nevertheless.

I woke early and disorientated. Over the last few months I'd successfully managed to work my body clock round onto U.S. time. A day back in England seemed to have skewed all that careful programming.

My mother went for thick curtains, lined like there was likely to be another blackout, but I could see the first strains of dawn leaching in around the edges and the birds were already in full song. There was a wren somewhere close by — I'd recognize that strident little voice anywhere. But no traffic, no sirens. Weird.

Stretching with care, feeling the twang of sleep-shortened muscles, I turned my head to see Sean's alongside mine and felt the familiar giant leap of emotion that simply being with him always provoked.

He lay quiet and still. The nightmares that had so often plagued him seemed to have diminished in both quantity and quality since we'd moved to New York, but maybe that was just my rosy-tinted perception.

For a few moments I took advantage of the lightening gloom to indulge myself and simply watch him. He lay on his back with his head turned slightly towards me, lips parted, those severe features relaxed and almost boyish. Viewed with a dispassionate eye, I acknowledged the cold beauty in the lines of his face and wondered what it was about him that inspired me to such devotion.

Back when we'd first met, when we'd both been in the army, an immediate, incendiary attraction had flared between us. I'd fought against it with a desperation born of the knowledge that any involvement with him could leave me badly burned. I'd known then that Sean was way out of my league.

In some ways, he still was.

I resisted the urge to smooth a stray lock of hair back from his forehead, aware that even the lightest touch would wake him when he deserved to sleep a little longer.

Neither of us had got much rest during the night, that was for sure.

Shortly after one in the morning, feeling more nervous than on any covert operation, I'd crept soft-footed along the darkened corridor, stepping over the floorboards whose age-old creaks and groans had formed the sound track of my early life. I didn't knock, just gripped the old brass handle firmly to stop it rattling, opened the door a crack and slipped into his room, with my heart already hitting the rev limiter in my chest and my temperature rising as the blood flushed my skin.

The bedside lamp had still been on. In its subdued glow, I could see Sean lying on his side with the covers pulled up only to his waist and his naked back towards me. I'd stood for a moment and watched the regular rise and fall of his rib cage, uncertain whether to approach him. Creeping up in the middle of the night on a man with Sean's reflexes and bitter-won experience was not likely to be good for anyone's health.

Just for a moment the doubts resurfaced and I was tempted to retreat. Then Sean had lifted his head slightly and said quietly over his shoulder, "The longer you stand there, the colder your feet are getting."

You don't know how close you are with that one, Sean. . . .

I crossed the room in half a dozen strides, lifted the heavy satin eiderdown and slipped in alongside him. And, shortly after that, any doubts I might have had about the exercise were comprehensively blown away.

And now, as I tried to slide out stealthily from under the rumpled covers less than six hours later, his eyes blinked open. I took their hazy focus as an enormous compliment. It meant that Sean felt safe enough with me to let his guard down completely. At least some of the time.

"Hi," I said, hearing the catch in my voice.

He smiled, utterly transforming his face, stealing away the brutality that lurked beneath the surface.

"Hi yourself," he murmured. He blinked again and his eyes sharpened as he correctly interpreted my intentions. "Leaving so soon?"

"I have to," I said. I propped myself on one elbow and gave in to temptation, touching my fingers to that rogue lock of hair. He caught my hand and turned his head to press a lazy kiss into my palm. The nerves fizzed as far up as my elbow.

"Stay," he said, his voice muffled against my skin.

I stiffened, tried to pull back and found he wouldn't release me, relaxed my arm rather than fight him.

"I can't, Sean," I said, my voice twisted into a groan by regret and desire in equal measure as his tongue gave way to his teeth, nipping at the crease of my lifeline. "I want to — you know that — but my mother's highly likely to bring you an early-morning cup of tea at any moment, just to check up on us."

He did let go then, and part of me wished he hadn't.

"And what's she going to do if she finds you here?" he said, and I didn't like the cool delivery. "Scream? Faint? Throw things?"

"All three, probably," I said, careful to keep it light. "Come on — she's my mother. I wouldn't feel comfortable being caught by her in bed with —"

"Me?"

"With *anyone*," I said, firmer now. "It wouldn't matter if you really were something in the City with a string of polo ponies. I still wouldn't feel right about it."

"Sure about that, are you?"

"Yes!" I hissed. "She knows we're living together in New York and she accepts that — inasmuch as she actually accepts anything she doesn't like or approve of. In real-

ity, that means she sticks her head in the sand and pretends it doesn't exist. I may not be a child any longer, but this is my parents' house. When I'm here, I have to abide by their rules and —"

His hand snaked across my hip, cutting off my voice in one laser-guided caress that blanked my mind and filmed my eyes. I arched back onto the pillows, gasping. Sean always did fight dirty.

"We're both consenting adults, Charlie. I think we proved that last night, don't you?" He leaned in close enough to whisper tauntingly against my throat. "So, what was that — lip service? I never would have taken you for a hypocrite."

With a monstrous effort of will, I jerked out from beneath that clever mouth and those devastating fingers and tipped myself over the edge of the bed. My mother didn't believe in heating the bedrooms and it was cool enough outside the covers to make me shiver instantly.

Sean watched in brooding silence as I quickly snatched up my discarded robe and shoved my arms into the sleeves. I darted for the door, hugging the fabric around my body as if for comfort. When I looked back, his expression did nothing to warm me. I felt my chin come up.

"You should know as well as I do, Sean," I said, "that half the point of breaking the rules is *not* getting caught doing it."

"That depends on whether you think more of the people making the rules than you do of the rules themselves," he shot back darkly. He sighed, let his voice gentle. "After all they've said and done, that pair, are you still *so* desperate to win their approval?"

"They're my parents." I swallowed. "It's a natural reaction, don't you think?"

"It's a pointless quest." He shook his head, a quick jerk of frustration. "They're never going to respect or understand you." *Not like I do.* Coaxing now. "Give up on it, Charlie — on *them.*"

I tried to ignore the lure of his words. I opened the door, checked that the corridor was quiet and empty outside, turned back and gave him one last, helpless shrug.

"I'm sorry," I said. "I can't."

TWELVE

Because Madeleine had arranged our tickets back to New York, the three of us sat up towards the sharp end of a British Airways Boeing 767. She'd managed to pull some strings to get us a good last-minute deal in Club. Besides the obvious comfort and convenience factors, it made sense from a defensive point of view.

The check-in line for BA Club World was short and enabled us to fast-track through Security, minimizing our exposure time in public areas. We didn't know if Blondie and Don were working independently in the UK, or if they had assistance from someone who might be keeping a watching brief. As it was, we cut things fine enough so that by the time we'd been through the usual rigmarole of metal detectors and pat-down searches, we went more or less straight to the departure gate.

My mother was subdued on the flight. She

had adopted a mournfully tragic air at being dragged away from her home under these circumstances and she kept it up throughout the journey, graciously weary in allowing the cabin crew to dance attendance on her.

We got into JFK around lunchtime. Sean rang Parker as soon as the plane pulled up to the jet bridge. The call was short and to the point.

"He wants us in the office right away," Sean said. "He's sending McGregor to pick us up."

I nodded but didn't get the chance to do much more than that. The aircraft door finally clunked open at that point and the press of people began pushing towards freedom.

Sean had been cool with me since I'd left his bed that morning, carefully placing himself across the aisle to leave me alongside my mother, where the layout in Club meant our seats faced each other. I'd tried to persuade myself he was just being professional, that the alternative was to sit with her himself or leave her somewhat out on a limb. But the fact I knew there was more to it than that created a low-level anxiety I couldn't seem to dispel.

By the time we walked out through the

main doors of the terminal into the weakening autumn sunshine, there was a huge dark blue Lincoln Navigator idling by the curb, with limo-black tint on the rear windows. If Parker's employees shared one common denominator, it was their efficiency.

Behind the wheel was a young black Canadian called Joseph McGregor. He'd joined Parker's outfit fresh from two tours in Iraq. I'd worked with him before and he was an excellent driver — he reckoned New York at its worst was a walk in the park compared to the streets of Basra under fire.

He stayed behind the wheel and kept the engine running while we loaded our bags. Even my mother's voluminous hard-shell suitcase looked a little lost in the SUV's cavernous rear load space.

She allowed us to hustle her into the plush leather upholstery of the backseat without seeming to notice the speed of our departure. I climbed in alongside her, leaving Sean up front, and McGregor gunned the V-8 and sped away.

"So, what's the panic, Joe?" Sean asked.

"Better ask the boss," McGregor said, uncharacteristically evasive.

Sean merely shrugged.

McGregor took the Queens–Midtown Tunnel under the East River and into

Manhattan. Once we emerged, my mother spent the journey with her neck cranked to take in the towering buildings. I could identify with that, at least. Much as I tried not to let it show, I was still frequently overawed by the sheer scale of New York City, and Manhattan was tightly packed yet sprawling at the same time. As we approached midtown, the affluence of the area seemed more apparent.

"Where are we going?" my mother asked at last, starting to look flustered. She waved a hand towards her outfit — a stuffy tweed skirt and pale pink twin-set with the cardigan draped around her shoulders. "I mean, I don't know if I'm suitably dressed."

"Just the office." Sean's face gave away nothing of his opinion about such a trivial worry. "You'll be fine."

My mother was still fretful. "Perhaps I ought to have changed," she said.

She looked carelessly smart in a well-bred, English kind of way. I debated on telling her that in New York, black was the new black, but decided against it. Informing my mother she was in danger of making a fashion faux pas would be enough to send her into a tailspin, and I reckoned we were going to have more than enough on our plate coping with her today.

"You'll be fine," I repeated, aiming for re-assurance rather than exasperation. I'm not sure I quite pulled it off, but she let the subject go.

Instead she said, in a rather small voice, "When do you think I might be able to . . . see Richard?"

If it was me, I thought savagely, *and it was Sean who was in trouble, I would never have stopped asking that question from the moment we got off the plane. It would have been my first — my only — concern. Why wasn't it yours?*

"That depends," I said curtly, "on whether he's out on bail."

She looked hurt. Sean half-turned in his seat and I saw McGregor's head tilt slightly to the rearview mirror, so that I was re-garded by three reproachful pairs of eyes instead of one.

Despite the traffic, the journey didn't take long. Parker's offices were in a newly reno-vated building with an imposing entrance onto the street and a uniformed doorman. McGregor treated my mother with defer-ence, calling her "ma'am" as he led her across the lobby. If he'd been wearing a cap, he would have tipped it.

I turned my head away so I could avoid the speculation that formed in her eyes as she now regarded me. As if maybe her daughter wasn't associating with quite the thugs and peasants she'd always feared.

We took one of the express elevators, which whisked us up to the agency offices, and stepped out into the discreet opulence of the reception area. I saw my mother register the newly installed Armstrong Meyer nameplate behind the desk and resented the quickening of her interest.

Bill Rendelson toned down his habitual hostility in front of outsiders. He led us straight through to Parker's office without his usual snide comments, pulling the door closed behind us. Inside, sitting drinking coffee, we found Parker Armstrong — and my father.

Both men rose when we entered. My father was still in the same suit he'd been wearing when I'd last seen him, but the shirt was clearly freshly laundered and he looked clean-shaven, showered, even rested, damn him. Only the discolored patch across his cheekbone gave away that he'd been through any kind of rough treatment. And that, I knew, was due to me.

I was suddenly very much aware of having just got off a seven-and-a-half-hour flight after very little sleep for the last three nights.

He went straight to my mother and, just

for a second, I thought I might actually be about to witness genuine emotion between them. Then, when they were just a couple of paces apart, he seemed abruptly to remember the circumstances that had brought them here, and faltered, settling for a brief kiss on the cheek that was herculean in its restraint.

"Oh *Richard,*" my mother said, her voice wobbling as her face dissolved, as if she'd only just been holding it all together until now. "I've been so very frightened."

"I'm so sorry, my dear," he said, sounding somehow rusty. "It's all over now."

A gross exaggeration, in my view, but I didn't like to point that out.

"They came into the house, Richard," my mother went on, as if he hadn't spoken. She dug in her handbag for a handkerchief and dabbed at her eyes. "Into our *home,* and threatened me." Tears broke her voice. "They said such a— awful things would happen."

"I know." With a sigh, he finally folded her uncomfortably into his arms and they stood there for a while in that stiff embrace.

Then, over my mother's bent head, his gaze shifted past me to Sean. "Thank you . . . for going to my wife's aid," he said in a quietly frozen tone, like he could hardly bring himself to express gratitude to Sean. Still, he couldn't bring himself to express it at all to me.

Sean nodded. "You can repay us with a little honesty," he said coolly.

My father tensed, as though his first response was denial, closely followed by the realization that he had very little choice. Gently, he put my mother away from him, guided her to a chair and handed her off into it with the kind of practiced delicacy I imagined him using on a critical patient's dazed and grief-stricken next of kin. When he spoke, it was over his shoulder and with quiet dignity.

"I'd like a moment alone with my wife first, if you don't mind."

We'd all of us been through the military machine at one time or another, enough to respond instinctively to the innate command in his voice. My father ran his operating theaters with an iron hand tougher than any general's and he was used to being obeyed utterly.

"Of course," Parker said. "Just let Bill know when you're ready."

We filed out. As I closed the door behind me I saw my father take the chair next to my mother's, close but not touching, and begin to speak in a low voice. Whatever he had to say, I considered, it had better be good.

Parker led us into the same conference room where we'd had our last confrontation, and took the same seat at the head of the table. I hoped we weren't in for a rematch.

"Damn, he's good," he said with a rueful smile, blowing out a breath. "I don't think I've ever been elbowed out of my own office before."

"How long has he been here?" I asked. "I mean — I'm surprised they let him out of jail."

"Well, they didn't so much let him out as our legal team wrestled him loose," Parker said. "The amount they charged for it, I was right about our lawyer putting his kids through college. I just didn't realize he'd be able to fly them there in his own Lear 55."

"Quit stalling," Sean said, parting his jacket and taking a chair. "You were being very cryptic on the phone. What's happened?"

"We're taking serious heat," Parker said bluntly. He ran a frustrated hand through his prematurely grayed hair. "Somebody's been digging and they've been digging hard and deep. The Simone Kerse thing, for starters."

"But that was nothing to do with you," I said, then caught the look on his face and instantly regretted my unguarded choice of words. One of Parker's men had been killed on that job and I knew that wasn't something he took lightly, by any means.

"I'm sorry," I said quickly. "What I meant was, Simone wasn't your responsibility — she was ours. Mine, to be exact. And I was the one who lost her."

"You didn't lose her, Charlie," Sean said. "Under the circumstances —"

"Nobody listens to circumstances," I cut in, self-recrimination making my voice harsher than it should have been. "The hard facts are that I was the one tasked to protect her and she died on my watch. After that, nobody cares about the how and the why."

It was my own argument, but it hurt that he recognized the truth of it enough to fall silent.

"I realize it wasn't your fault, Charlie," Parker said. "But you know as well as I do how easily the newspapers put their own spin on things. And that's not the only thing they've come up with."

I recalled the report he'd practically thrown across this very table at me only two days previously, and knew whatever they'd found now it had to be worse.

Parker flicked his eyes at Sean, then back to me and said, "Look, I don't believe half of what they've printed, but —"

"Tell me," I said through suddenly stiff lips.

He sighed heavily. "I don't know where they've gotten half this stuff, but they seem to think you've had run-ins with the cops not just here, but in the UK and Ireland, and with the security services in Germany. They're claiming that you've killed at least half a dozen people, making out you're some kind of crazy . . ."

He looked at my face and his voice trailed off.

"If you believe that about Charlie," Sean said coolly, staring Parker straight in the eye, "then you should never have taken either of us on in the first place."

Parker shrugged. "What *I* believe is immaterial," he said, but he was rattled. "It's other people's perceptions that are the problem here."

"Why?" Sean demanded, letting the word crack out. "If she was a guy, everyone would be queuing up to buy her a beer and listen to the war stories. But because she's a woman, the fact that she's good at her job and has proved it in the field is considered somehow indecent." He tilted his head as though he had the other man on a microscope slide. "I thought you were more enlightened, Parker."

"Tell that to our clients, Sean," Parker snapped back. "We lost another contract this morning. They're leaving like rats off a sinking ship!" He held up a hand when Sean would have countered, pinched at the bridge of his nose for a few long moments, trying to relieve the tension. "I'm sorry," he said at last.

"Don't be," I said roughly, trying not to make my despair obvious. "You brought us in as an asset not a liability, and I've brought this trouble down on you."

He waved away my latest apology and seemed to make an effort to focus. "What we need —"

There was a sudden knock on the door and Bill Rendelson stuck his head round without waiting for an invitation, his expression sour.

"You got calls stacking up, boss," he said shortly. His eyes slid to Sean and me and, if anything, his face grew even more thunderous. "And they're ready for you to go back in."

"Cards on the table time," Sean said, and his coolly indifferent tone was a challenge all by itself. "I assume you don't have a significant drinking problem?" The wording was a nicely irritant touch, implying as it did that the older man did indeed have an issue with alcohol and the only subject under discussion was the severity.

My father didn't so much glare at Sean as subject him to a withering scrutiny most people would have shriveled under. Probably me included.

"Of course I don't."

He and my mother had seated themselves in two of the client chairs, side by side, forming a united front. Parker had taken his customary seat behind the desk and I wondered if he was trying to reassert his authority by such a move. I hovered in between, leaning on a corner of the desk as though ready to play for either side, depending how things were going.

"In view of your somewhat public confession, there's no 'of course' about it," Sean said with a deadly smile. He sat down in one of the client chairs opposite my parents and crossed his legs, apparently totally at ease, before adding quietly, "So, are you going to tell us what the real story is here? What really happened to this patient of yours who died in Boston?"

For a moment my father didn't speak,

then he gave an audible sigh, as though gathering his inner resources. "Jeremy Lee had severe spinal osteoporosis," he said at last.

"Osteoporosis?" Parker queried as we exchanged blank looks. "That's the kind of thing little old ladies get, isn't it? Makes them fall down and break their hips."

My father gave a pained nod at this somewhat simplistic view. "In essence, yes," he allowed. "But it affects in excess of two hundred million people worldwide — twenty percent of whom are men. That's more than forty million, and the problem is growing."

"What causes it?" I asked. "And what caused it in this case?"

"It's a popular misconception that it's down to calcium deficiency, but that's not the whole story. We have an aging population, more sedentary lifestyles." My father shrugged. "But in half the cases of osteoporosis in men, the cause is unknown," he said. "Although smoking can affect bone cells, and drinking inhibits the body's absorption of calcium, Jeremy did neither."

"If you don't mind me saying so, Mr. Foxcroft," Parker said, "we have a lot of home-grown medical talent over here. Why were you called in?"

My father favored him with an austere smile. "To begin with, Jeremy was misdiagnosed and had lost a certain amount of faith in his colleagues," he said. "By the time he contacted me — or rather, his wife did — he was very ill. Miranda was hopeful that there might be a surgical option that would offer him some relief, and I think it's fair to say I have a recognized level of expertise in that area."

At this point it seemed to occur to him that the events of the last few days might have sullied that spotless reputation somewhat. A shadow, no more than a flicker, passed across his face. My mother, sitting next to him, snuck her fingers through his and squeezed. For a moment he squeezed back, then disengaged his hand. He never once looked at her directly.

"Miranda called me and asked for my help," he added simply. "So I went."

It must be nice, I thought with fierce jealousy, *to have the kind of friendship with my father that motivates such an instant response.*

"And was there anything you could do?" Sean asked.

My father shook his head. "I did some tests to see if there was the possibility of installing titanium cages to support Jeremy's vertebrae, but it was too late for that. His bones were like chalk. By the time I got there he was in a wheelchair, his spine had almost totally collapsed and he was in constant pain." That shadow again, darker this time. "It was . . . difficult to see him like that."

I felt the transfer of his anger. "And what was being done for him?"

"Not much beyond palliative care," he said, dismissive. "They'd tried him on synthetic bone-stimulating hormones in an attempt to increase his bone density, but without success. According to his notes, over the past few months his condition had deteriorated at a rate I would normally have expected to take years. I ruled out anything environmental, went back several generations to eliminate the hereditary angle. It seemed to me that the hospital was making little attempt to find out the root cause of his illness."

"Surely," Sean said, frowning, "if he was getting older —"

"Jeremy was in his early forties," my father cut in. "I met him when he was a young student over in London. Hardly an old man, would you say?"

"So, what happened?"

"I discovered that the hospital was involved in clinical trials for a new treatment for osteoporosis developed by the pharmaceutical giant, Storax. It's not yet licensed, but they've had some remarkable successes so far. I contacted them to see if it might be possible to use it in this case."

"I didn't think you were such a risk taker, Richard," Sean said.

"Sean," my mother said in quiet censure. "A man's life was at stake."

My father acknowledged her intervention with a faint nod. "Miranda voiced her doubts but, by that stage I felt there was very little to lose and I convinced her we should give it a try. I felt we had few options left open to us."

"And what did Jeremy Lee feel about this?"

"Jeremy had picked up an infection and lapsed into a coma," he said, no emotion in his voice. "Storax were reluctant to extend their trial at this stage, but in the end I . . . persuaded them." He gave another small smile. "They sent two of their people up to Boston to administer the treatment. And that's when we discovered that Jeremy had already received it."

"Hold on," Parker said. "You mean he'd already been given this Storax treatment and was still getting worse?"

197

"That's how it appeared. My suspicion was that the hospital had been using him as an unwitting guinea pig." He took a moment that might have been to calm himself, and his expression afterwards was almost rueful. "I'm afraid I may have made my dissatisfaction with this state of affairs somewhat clear."

I suppressed a smile. My father in full righteous flow would be a sight to behold.

"Can you prove any of this?" Sean asked, and although his tone was absolutely neutral, my father bristled anyway.

"Sadly, no," he said sharply. "The Storax people were doing more tests to confirm it when I was asked to leave — politely, of course — by the hospital administrators."

"And you agreed?"

He shrugged. "I had no choice. My position there was afforded as a courtesy, not a right. Before I left, I made it clear to the hospital that I was intending to take the matter further. Unfortunately, I never got the chance."

"What happened?"

"Jeremy died that night. Miranda got the call around midnight and I drove her to the hospital, but it was already too late."

Again, he paused, took a breath — the only outward sign of his distress. He was talking about the death of a friend and he might have been discussing having missed a bus.

"What actually killed him in the end?" Parker asked quietly.

"In my opinion, a hundred milligrams of intravenous morphine," my father said.

"Are you sure?"

"As I can be — and before you ask, no, I can't prove that, either," he said, glancing at Sean. "Not without access to his notes. Maybe not even then."

"But you were sure enough at one point to make a public accusation to that effect," Sean said, quirking one eyebrow. "Wasn't that somewhat . . . foolish if you didn't have any proof?"

My father's chin came up. "Yes, as it turned out," he said calmly. "The following morning I received a telephone call informing me of my so-called drink problem and telling me what would happen to Elizabeth if I didn't participate in my own downfall." His eyes flickered closed for a moment. "They were rather graphic and very detailed," he added with grim restraint.

"Oh, Richard," my mother said softly, her eyes on his face.

"We have to take this to the police," Parker said, reaching for the phone on his desk.

"If we —"

"No."

There it was again, that quiet command. It was enough to bring Parker up short. His hand stilled and he regarded my father in steady silence for a few moments before he asked in a level tone, "Why not?"

My father didn't reply immediately. He leaned forwards in his seat, clasping his hands and seeming absorbed by the way his fingers linked together. Eventually he looked up, his gaze taking in the three of us, ranged against him.

"You must think I inhabit a very rarefied little world," he said, his voice reflective and almost a little remote. "And I suppose that in some ways, I do. I am not accustomed to being manhandled, to having my family threatened, and I find I . . . don't care for it."

"They won't do it again," I said, fast and low. "Trust me. They won't get the chance."

"No, they won't," my father said with a brittle smile. "But not because you'll be there to take on all comers, Charlotte, I assure you." He straightened the crease in his suit trousers and brushed away a piece of lint from the fine cloth before he looked up again. "When I was a medical student I had a bit of a reputation as a poker player," he said. "I always knew when to bluff and when to fold a bad hand."

"And you feel this is a bad hand," Sean said. "So you're going to fold, is that it?" He couldn't quite keep the sneer out of his voice, but my father didn't rise to it.

"I don't know who was behind my coercion and Elizabeth's unfortunate experience, but I can only assume they have some connection to the hospital," my father said. "They had a major civil action brought against them last year for medical negligence, which they lost — somewhat disastrously — and they can't afford another. It would appear they're prepared to go to extreme lengths to ensure it doesn't happen again."

Sean ducked his head in acknowledgment of the point. "That's a fair description," he said. "But what about your supposed friend, Jeremy Lee? What about his widow? You're just going to walk away and leave things as they are?"

My father's face whitened. "The longer I stay, the worse I'm making the situation for Miranda," he said. "I've been totally discredited as any kind of expert witness. Trying to redress things now will only make them worse still. My best course of action is to go home as soon as possible, so we can try to put this whole thing behind us."

My father rose, automatically buttoning the jacket of that immaculately tailored suit, and helped my mother out of her chair. She clung to his arm. He turned to face us.

"Thank you — all of you — for your assistance," he said, not quite meeting my eye. His gaze just seemed to scutter across me from Sean to Parker and back again. "But there is nothing more you can do here."

THIRTEEN

Until the arrangements could be made for them to go home to the UK, my father booked a room for himself and my mother at the Grand Hyatt, which was somewhat more in keeping with his tastes and made me realize I should have questioned who'd chosen his previous hotel.

There were a lot of things I should have questioned.

My father refused Parker's offer of the use of McGregor and the Navigator while they were in New York. Instead, much to my mother's obvious disappointment, he insisted that they would catch a cab on the street, and Sean and I went down with them to the lobby. It was a good opportunity to have one last go at getting my father to make a stand, but he'd fallen back on frosty formality.

My mother did her best to fill the awkward silence with nervous, inconsequential chatter that put nobody at ease. I wasn't the only one who was glad when we reached ground level.

Sean nodded to the doorman, who whisked outside to summon a cab, something he seemed to achieve almost instantly.

"You should have told me you were in trouble," I said, making one last effort at getting through, aware even as I spoke of the stiffness in my voice that would prevent me from doing so. "Whatever you may think of me, this is what I do."

My father looked down his nose at me. "I'm well aware of your capabilities, Charlotte," he said curtly. "That is precisely why I didn't."

We saw the yellow Crown Victoria pull up smartly outside, and moved towards the doors. My mother seemed to have some spring back in her step, as though now she was reunited with her husband, all was right with the world again. With a sense of panic, I felt my parents slipping away from me. Unwilling to let it end like this, I walked with them, out into the pale slanted sunshine.

Sean had carried my mother's heavy suitcase as far down as the lobby without apparent effort, setting it down while he tipped the doorman. My father picked it up, clearly surprised by the unexpected weight, and began lugging it across the sidewalk to the waiting cab while my mother paused in the doorway to rifle through her handbag for her sunglasses.

I had started to follow him when I heard an engine, away to our left, even above the normal background sounds of traffic. American engines are generally big and torquey. They don't need to rev in order to provide power unless you want a lot of it, and you want it now. This was being thrashed and I turned instinctively towards the noise.

I was just in time to see another taxicab mount the curb about ten meters away, trailing sparks as it graunched over the concrete, front suspension taking the hit. It came barreling along the sidewalk towards us.

Like the one idling by the curb, the second cab was a yellow Crown Victoria. The big car leapt towards us, seeming wide enough to totally fill the space between the building and the street, engine roaring. The front wing grazed off the front façade, striking yet more sparks like it was breathing fire, and it kept on coming.

My father froze in its path, still clutching the handle of the suitcase. Adrenaline fired into my system like a shot of nitrous. I took three or four rapid, boosted strides and hit him shoulder against shoulder, the force of my momentum enough to send him pitching clear of the cab's flight path.

Spinning halfway towards the threat, I saw nothing but the black plastic of the front grille and a vast sea of yellow steel that made up the car's bonnet. I even had time to notice the taxi medallion riveted to the center.

In that weird, slowed-down way things have, I recognized that I didn't have time to run, and nowhere to run to. My only thought was to minimize the hit.

Years of falling off horses as a kid taught me not to try and break a fall with my limbs outstretched. Later, years of martial arts training of one form or another taught me how to use them to slow my descent much more scientifically.

So I jumped, straight up, tucking my knees in like I was dive-bombing into a swimming pool. I didn't have nearly enough height to clear the Crown Vic's front grille, which clipped my left leg halfway down my calf as the car shot underneath me, causing me to tumble violently. As I somersaulted across the expanse of yellow bonnet, I slapped my hand and forearm down hard onto the steel to lessen the impact, but hit the windscreen hip and elbow first with enough force to break the laminated glass anyway.

I had visions of continuing to roll right up over the roof, at which point the huge slant-sided advertising hoarding that ran full length along it would probably have broken my back. Then the driver of the rogue cab slammed on his brakes.

The Crown Vic lurched, slithering, to a stop, jolting as it hit something that I could only pray wasn't my father's body. The sudden deceleration was enough to spit me straight off the front edge of the bonnet and send me thumping back down onto the ground, knocking the wind out of me. The last time I'd been hit by a moving vehicle while on foot, I recalled whimsically, at least I'd had the forethought to be wearing bike leathers.

Rid of his inconvenient hood ornament, the cabdriver punched the accelerator before I'd even hit the deck. I flinched, trying to roll out of the way of the fat front tire that was now heading straight for my chest, and knowing I didn't stand a hope in hell of doing so. All I could smell was hot oil and burned rubber and rust.

Game over.

Just when I knew he couldn't possibly

miss me, the cab jolted to a stop again, engine revving high enough to send all the hairs up on the back of my neck. I realized, to my amazement, that my mother's heavy-duty suitcase was rammed between the opposite front wheel and a mammoth concrete tree planter at the edge of the curb. I started scrabbling backwards on my bruised backside, arms flailing. The cab's rear wheels spun up more smoke as the driver forced it on. The planter trembled. The suitcase began to buckle and twist.

The shell of the case gave up its last breath and collapsed completely. As it did so I felt a hand grab my shoulder and another hook under my armpit to wrench me up and out of the way. I was peripherally aware of a yellow blur flashing past as I flew through the air, before I slammed up against a solid male body, robbing me of what little air I'd managed to draw back into my lungs.

Dazed, I looked up, met Sean's near-black eyes only a few inches from my own. The sheer fury in them shocked me back into life. I wrenched myself out of his grasp and staggered back a pace.

I turned. For a moment everything was imprinted on my brain in minute detail and total silence.

The doorman was standing in the middle

of the sidewalk, staring after the disappearing cab with an expression of outraged disbelief on his face. The driver of the cab he'd summoned had leapt out and was gesticulating wildly. I could see his mouth moving, but could hear no sound coming out. My mother was crouched in the shelter of the doorway where Sean must have practically thrown her to keep her out of harm's way. She was clutching her handbag to her chest like it was her sole means of protection, knuckles white around the straps.

But my father was the one who worried me. All I could see of him, sticking out from between the planter and the cab waiting by the curb, were his legs from the knee downwards, good dark gray socks and highly polished black lace-up shoes. For a moment, I felt a dreadful cold leap of fear, then his feet twitched and he sat up abruptly, brushing the dirt from his suit jacket. He looked annoyed rather than hurt, and pale as dust.

The world kicked back into gear. I heard our cabdriver's raucous shouts in what sounded like Ukrainian, the squeal of brakes and the blowing of horns all the way up the next two blocks as the cab that had tried to hit us swerved through traffic. I could only hope the crazed windscreen was making it harder for him.

Sean brushed past me to bend over my father and his eyes were everywhere.

"Can you move?" he demanded.

My father glanced up at him with irritation. "Of course I can."

Sean yanked him to his feet without another word and hauled him back inside the building, covering his back all the way. I did the same with my mother, depositing her onto one of the low sofas on the other side of the entrance lobby, well back from the doors. She threw herself at my father and held on tight, sobbing.

The reception staff were fluttering with shock, telling each other in loud voices what it was they thought they'd seen. A moment later the doorman dragged the sorry-looking remains of my mother's suitcase into the lobby and jerked his head at the Ukrainian cabbie.

"The driver says he thinks the other cab was stolen," the doorman told Sean. "Says one of their guys got 'jacked in Murray Hill 'bout an hour ago. The word was out to the other drivers to keep an eye out for his ride."

"Looks like they found it," Sean said.

The doorman nodded, eyes flicking over my shocked parents and the ruined case.

"You want I should call the cops, Mr. Meyer, or is this a . . . private matter?"

"I think this was too public for that. You'd better call them.'

"Got it." He paused. "What about a medic?"

I turned fast at that, scanning my father. He'd moved awkwardly when Sean had rushed him inside, but he'd seemed basically okay — no obvious injuries, no blood, and I didn't think he'd hit his head or lost consciousness when he fell.

"No, he seems fine," I said, turning back to find the doorman staring at me like I'd totally lost it.

"Er, I meant for you, ma'am."

I followed his gaze and looked down, realizing for the first time that I was the one with blood on my hands. I turned them over to find I'd scraped the palm of one and cut the other. I'd put a hole in the knee of my trousers as well. The blood didn't show up much against the dark brown fabric, but I could see grit stuck to the wetness around the torn edges. I swore under my breath.

My jacket was ripped, too, one sleeve almost hanging by a thread where Sean had grabbed at it. When I went to step forwards I realized my left leg was already stiffening up, and by the feel of it I was going to have a bruise the size of Wales from hip to ankle.

I glanced at my father again. He was staring at me over the top of my mother's weeping head with an expression on his face that I couldn't quite decipher, and didn't have the patience to try.

"You may think it's all over," I said bitterly, jerking my head in the direction the cab had taken, "but nobody seems to have told the opposition."

Parker's office had its own private bathroom and that's where I stripped off. The designers had lined the place with mirrors, so I practically had a three-sixty view of my injuries, such as they were. One scraped knee and elbow, two scraped hands, and a sizable grazed bruise that started in a remarkably neat line halfway up my left calf and was spreading rapidly. Nothing that wouldn't heal up or scab over in a few days.

All in all, I reckoned I'd got away pretty lightly.

I fumbled with the mixer tap to sluice the dirt out of my hands, and had just wadded up tissue paper to wipe the worst of the grit out of my knee when there was a knock at the door.

I expected Sean, but it was my father who stood in the gap.

For a moment we stared at each other. I saw him survey me with a professional gaze and I was suddenly very aware of standing there in just my underwear with all my scars, ancient and modern, on show for him to judge me by. I resisted the urge to reach for one of the large towels hanging by the shower, and faced him with as much pride as I could muster. Not much, under the circumstances.

"Was there something you wanted?" I asked, icy.

"I brought you this." He lifted his right hand and I noticed for the first time there was a first-aid kit in it. His voice was cool for the intended victim of a hit-and-run. "And I thought you might appreciate my professional expertise, if nothing else."

I'd been through enough emergency medical training, military and civilian, to deal with such minor injuries myself, but I shrugged and turned back to the sink, wringing out another piece of paper towel and shaking the excess water out of it. "Feel free," I said.

In the mirror, I saw him approach and put the case down on the marble surface. I'd half-filled the sink with lukewarm water, which was now a grubby pink color and had disgusting mushy clumps of tissue floating in it. For a moment he stood there, watching my efforts, then he reached into his jacket to pull out his gold-framed glasses.

"Sit down, Charlotte," he said with quiet authority, and snapped open the first-aid kit.

For once, I didn't put up a fight. Pointless to cobble something together myself when there was an expert on tap. I sank onto the closed lid of the toilet and let him empty the sink in order to wash his hands.

"I'm assuming you didn't hit your head?" he said when he was done, tipping my chin up to watch the way my pupils reacted to the strong overhead spots.

"I'm not concussed and there's nothing broken," I said, twisting my face out of his grasp. "Trust me, I know what broken bones feel like."

"Yes," he murmured. "So you do."

"Where's Sean?" I asked, trying not to sound too hopeful.

"He and Mr. Armstrong are giving statements," my father said shortly. "The police want your side of it, naturally, but Meyer's stalling them until you feel up to it."

I pulled a wry face. Sean was very good at keeping the unwanted at bay. "Are they really willing to wait that long?"

He picked a handful of sterile wipes out

of the kit, tore them open and began cleaning my left palm.

"The man driving the cab," he said, almost conversational as he worked. "I think I recognized him."

I looked up sharply from what he was doing to my hand but his face, bent close to mine, was a picture of closed concentration.

"Who was he?"

"I don't know his name, of course," my father said. "But I believe he may have been the one who drove me across the river to Brooklyn. I hadn't seen him before that. It was always the other chap who called or visited — the one with the short-back-and-sides."

Buzz-cut.

He straightened, ripped open another packet. This one contained a pair of tweezers, which he used to pinch a sliver of glass out of my flesh. Probably from the front screen — I'd certainly hit it hard enough.

"I see," I said. "So, they've tried to discredit you and blackmail you, and, now that's failed, they're just settling for a spot of good old-fashioned murder. Nice people you're mixing with."

He dug the tweezers in again and I flinched, letting my breath out on a hiss. Just when I thought he'd done it simply for badness, he emerged with a second chunk of glass, which he dropped into the stainless-steel waste bin. It was big enough to bounce when it hit the bottom.

"You do realize that he was there, don't you?" he said suddenly. "In the hotel, the morning you came to see me and brought me that bottle of rather expensive whisky." He smoothed his thumbs over my palm, searching for any residual splinters. There weren't any.

"Buzz-cut?" I said, and even as I asked I remembered the tightly closed door to the bedroom in my father's shabby little suite. No wonder Buzz-cut had looked at me twice when I'd pulled up outside the hotel the next morning.

My father glanced up at me for a moment, frowning before he got the reference. "Hm" was all he said.

He put my left hand down and picked up the right. I'd sliced into the heel of my thumb, small but deep, and the cut was dirty but the damage was generally less widespread. In fact, my knee was shouting loudest. I ignored it.

"Is that why you told me I was a cripple?" I asked without rancor.

He cleansed the cut and applied the self-adhesive closure strips. His hands were cool, dry and confident.

"I was under the strictest instructions — I'm quite sure you don't need me to go into details. It was impressed upon me that I was not to counter any attempts made to discredit me. Nor," he added grimly, "was I to elicit any help or assistance from anyone. Any offers were to be firmly . . . rebuffed, or the consequences would be severe. They were most definite about that."

Rebuffed. Well, I suppose you achieved that one. . . .

"So you chose brutality to get your message across."

My father finished a fast cleanup of my elbow, which had come off best in the injury stakes, and put the tweezers down roughly, almost slamming them. He touched a finger to his discolored cheekbone. "It seemed a method you would best understand," he said, almost haughty. But underneath that veneer of pride I caught just a glimpse of genuine sorrow. I recalled my own bitter, angry words, hurled without thought to the wounds they would inflict, only aware of the desire to cause him as much pain as he had caused me.

And I had, I realized, by so readily believing the things I'd heard about him were true. Just as I'd been left stripped and wasted by his lack of belief in me, all that time ago.

"Besides," he went on, remorseless, "I knew if I wasn't hard enough on you, you would be too stubborn to give up." He allowed a glint of bleak humor to break through as he bent to examine my knee. "As it was, I think I was convincing, don't you?"

I forced my mind to concentrate on what he was saying, rather than on what he was doing. The grit seemed to have gone a long way into my knee, and the patella itself felt strangely disconnected. All that work to rid myself of my limp, and now I'd gone and got myself another. And in that distracted moment, I finally understood.

"You weren't simply rebuffing me," I murmured as the thought coalesced.

"You're going to need to take some painkillers for a few days, Charlotte," he said. "Please don't be stubborn about it."

"I've got some . . . something in my bag I can take," I said, dismissive, suddenly wary of telling him what. My left leg had settled into a sullen throb along most of its length, burning brightest around my knee. "You weren't just rebuffing me, were you?" I repeated. "You were trying to make me seem too weak to be a threat to them. You were trying to protect me."

He paused, frowning slightly again. Then he was tearing open more wipes, leaving the packets scattered across the marble surface next to the sink. He was used, I recognized, to having a team to clear up after him.

"Yes," he said at last, cautiously. "Yes, I suppose I was."

"Why?"

His eyes flicked to mine in silent censure. "In case it escaped your notice, Charlotte, I'm your father." He sprayed me with a coat of sealant dressing and straightened, nodding to signify he was done. "It's what fathers do."

And I realized then that, despite my earlier jealousy, whenever I'd called on him in the past, he'd come. He might not have agreed with my actions. In some cases he might not even have fully supported them, but he'd come nevertheless.

I stood, trying not to stagger as I put weight through my left leg, testing the knee to make sure it wasn't going to fold on me.

"You know you can't leave this here, don't you?" I said. "Not now."

My father looked up from scrubbing his hands, met my eyes in the mirror for a moment. Then he was back to his brisk rubbing.

"I was prepared to," he said remotely, "but

219

clearly *they* are not." His face pinched and I wondered, briefly, what might happen if my father ever relaxed that ruthless self-control for long enough to well and truly lose his temper.

"So, are you going to tell the police the whole story?"

He had been drying his hands, and that halted him for a few long moments while he gave it due consideration. "What good will it do?" he said, sounding weary. "Do you honestly think they'll give due credence to anything I have to say?"

I opened my mouth to respond but got no further. There was another knock on the door and Sean put his head round without waiting for an invitation. His eyes slid darkly from me to my father, who turned away, throwing the last paper towel into the waste bin and straightening his shirt cuffs.

"You okay?" Sean asked.

"I'll live," I said.

He advanced and folded my new clothing onto the counter next to the sink — a spare suit and shirt, still in their dry-cleaning bags. It was a rule of Parker's that everyone kept a decent change of clothes at the office, just in case of emergencies. In his early days he had once had the misfortune, he'd told us, to have to face a widow when he was still spattered with her late husband's blood. He'd taken considerable precautions not to be put in the same situation again.

"Are you ready for the police? They want your side of it."

"Do they think I might have been jaywalking?"

He smiled and, just for a moment I saw the relief and the anguish swimming deep in his eyes, then it was gone.

"Getting hit by a car hasn't knocked any sense into you, I see," he said dryly. "I'll tell them you'll be another fifteen, shall I?"

I nodded, and he went out. I turned to find my father watching me with an expression that might have qualified as distaste. He removed his glasses and folded them into their slim case, which he tucked back into the inside pocket of his jacket.

"What?"

He shook his head and I shrugged, stripping away the plastic bag to remove the shirt from its hanger.

"What do you intend to say to the police?"

"What would you like me to tell them?"

He made a gesture of frustration. "Don't play games, Charlotte," he said, clipped. "It doesn't become you."

I raised my eyebrows. "Who's playing games?" I said mildly, buttoning the shirt.

By the time I'd eased my way into the trousers, he still hadn't answered.

"Your reputation's been blown, your home invaded, your family's secrets smeared across the newspapers. And now some-body's just tried to kill you," I said then, keeping all the emotion out of my voice.

I lifted my jacket. Underneath it was my SIG P228 in a Kramer inside-the-waistband sheepskin clip. Sean must have been into the office gun safe. My father watched me go through my habitual checks and slide the holstered weapon into position just behind my right hip. There was absolute disapproval in his every line.

"If you'd trusted me and Sean enough to come to us when they first started threaten-ing you, we could have dealt with it there and then and avoided it coming to this." I pulled on my boots and straightened, stifling a groan the movement caused. I shrugged into my jacket, smoothing the cloth to make sure it covered the outline of the SIG. "Whether you like it or not, I'm bloody good at what I do. We could have taken out Buzz-cut and his friend before they got you anywhere near Bushwick."

"Oh, I've no doubt you could have 'taken out' my aggressors, as you so coyly put it," my father echoed bitterly. "Perhaps that was what I was afraid of most."

FOURTEEN

One way and another, we were tied up with the police for most of the day. After the uniforms came the plainclothes men. World-weary and sardonic New York cops, they'd seen everything and heard more. And they made it quite clear that the story my father was now telling was more far-fetched than most.

They were obviously aware of Richard Foxcroft's name — anyone who had read a newspaper or seen a news report in the last week couldn't fail to be. I got the distinct impression that the only reason they didn't outright laugh in our faces was because Parker Armstrong's name carried weight, despite recent events. The hatchet job that had been done on my father's reputation, however, was a resounding success.

They'd investigate, the cops told us, but what was probably no more than an accidental hit-and-run wasn't high on the priority list. If we could bring them some-thing more — like the faintest shred of evidence to support our fanciful claims of attempted murder — they might be more inclined to devote some man-hours to the case.

While they were interviewing him and my mother, I brought Parker and Sean up to speed on the conversation with my father while he'd been patching me up. When I'd finished, both of them looked thoughtful and no less worried than they had before.

"We need to put a lid on this quickly," Parker reiterated, although I was heartened by his continued use of the word *we*. He glanced from one of us to the other. "If he's finally agreed to make a stand, we can do something. Let me make some calls."

He stood, decisive, and regarded us gravely. "Meanwhile, you're going to have to keep those two out of trouble. They've already come after them once. They'll try again."

I got to my feet, too. I'd taken the op-portunity to swallow a couple of painkillers and they'd done a decent job at floating the edge off things. Rising was considerably easier as a result. "Thank you," I said. "And I know you don't like to hear it, but I'll say it again — I'm sorry for all of this."

"Jeez, I know that, Charlie." He offered me a tired smile and, a rarity, put his arm around my shoulder in a more fatherly gesture than I'd ever had from my own. "Don't worry, we'll see it through. And anyhow, you can't be held responsible for your parents."

"Tell me about it," I muttered. "Can't live with 'em. Can't kill 'em and bury 'em in the garden."

After the police had rolled up their crime-scene tape and departed, we gave my parents a choice. Either Sean and I would put them up in the spare room at the apartment, or we'd put a guard on them at the hotel and stick with them whenever they were outside it. After the briefest of consultations, they went for the latter option, which was both a relief and a snub as far as I was concerned.

I noticed Parker go a little pale when I bluntly offered this ultimatum. His whole ethos for executive protection was to keep clients as safe as possible without cramping their style. Some saw it as risky, but it certainly seemed to work for him. Time and again, I'd come across agencies who'd been fired for letting their operatives crowd the principal and vetoing what the client considered normal activities. I liked Parker's attitude. It went a long way towards explaining why, family money aside, he was doing well enough to run a substantial office in New York and a weekend place in the Hamptons.

Nevertheless, this was not a normal situation, nor the kind of clients he was used to dealing with. I knew that if we didn't lay some ground rules right from the start, in an emergency things were going to go pear-shaped at somewhere approaching the speed of sound.

I was coward enough to let Sean tell it to them straight. I didn't think they liked me any better, but at least I felt my father was likely to hold whatever Sean said in rather higher esteem.

"You are not under house arrest and we will not restrict your movements unless our experience and our judgment of the situation tell us it's vital that we do so," Sean said, disregarding the cynical twitch of my father's mouth. "But, these people, whoever they are, are serious. If you take risks with *your* safety, just remember that you take even bigger risks with *our* safety. As today should have shown you, we will always attempt to put ourselves between you and the threat. That's what we do." He let his eyes slide over me briefly, making a point of it. "Is that clear?"

"We understand," my father said stiffly.

"Good," Sean said, and although he kept his face and voice and body entirely neutral, I could tell how much he was enjoying this. "In that case, there are a couple of things you'll need to remember in case of attack. If we shout 'Get down!' at any point, all we want you to do is bend double and keep your head low, but stay on your feet and be ready to move unless we actively push you to the ground. Don't try and stick your head up to see what's happening. Don't try and look round to see where the other one is. You're going to have to trust us to have you both covered, yes?"

He paused and, after a second's hesitation, they both nodded.

"One last thing," Sean said, and now he did allow his voice to go soft and deadly. "This is not a democracy. We will do whatever we have to in order to preserve your lives and keep you safe. What we will *not* do is stand there in the middle of a firefight and discuss alternatives as you see them, or justify our actions. If we tell you to do something, just do it. Afterwards, we can talk about it all you like."

"So," my father said, matching his tone to

Sean's almost perfectly, "what happens when, in the cold light of day, you find you *can't* justify your actions?"

There was a long silence while they stared each other down. Here were two men who had both handled death, from one direction or another, and never flinched under the weight of that responsibility.

"I don't know, Richard. It's never come up," Sean said deliberately. He checked his watch, a wholly dismissive gesture, and started to turn away. "But if it ever does, I'll be sure to let you know. . . ."

Sean, Parker, and I formed a three-man detail to get them out of the building and into the Navigator that Joe McGregor had waiting by the curb. This time, we took no chances, but whoever had been behind the wheel of the rogue cab did not spring out at us for a second attempt.

Nothing happened on the journey to their hotel, where McGregor took station. He had nothing to report when Sean and I arrived to relieve him in the morning, and nothing untoward happened the following day, either. Unless you counted the excruciating politeness with which Sean and my father treated each other. It screeched at my nerves like a tone-deaf child with their first violin.

We spent the day shopping for a replacement suitcase for my mother, and new clothes to fill it. She picked out another hard-shell case just like the last one. Where previously I might have tried to talk her into something lighter, now I voiced no such objections. Structural suitcases, I decided, were my friend.

Parker, meanwhile, was working furiously behind the scenes and providing us with regular updates on progress — or lack of it.

He'd sent to his various contacts Sean's rudimentary photos of the couple we'd found baby-sitting my mother back in England. Apart from the fact that everyone seemed to think Blondie's pic had been taken post mortem, nobody initially offered any clues as to their background.

Then Parker got a possible hit on Don, last name Kaminski. It turned out he was an ex-marine with a disciplinary record, who'd been spat out by the military machine two years previously and disappeared into the private contractors' market. In other words, he was either a bodyguard or a mercenary.

Parker had uncovered the firm Don apparently worked for. Unfortunately, due to delusions of grandeur on their part, they seemed to think they were equal to — and therefore direct rivals of — Parker's outfit. The result was that they refused to tell him anything about what their guy might or might not have been up to.

They wouldn't even confirm Don was outside the mainland U.S., which I felt was a bit pointless, given the circumstances. But, Parker did at least manage to pick up a useful little snippet from an unguarded comment. From that, he deduced that Don Kaminski's employers were growing increasingly alarmed by the fact they'd lost contact with their man. I thought of May and her shotgun, and the aggressive porcine guards around his temporary prison, and decided that it was probably going to be awhile yet before he got in touch.

It took longer to get any information on the woman I knew only as Blondie, although I admit that the state of her face probably didn't make her any easier to identify.

We were just coming out of Macy's department store when Parker called on Sean's mobile. Sean let the answering machine pick up and didn't make any attempt to respond to the call until we were back in our vehicle and on the move again. I returned Parker's call while Sean dealt with the lunchtime traffic.

"Are you all together and close by?" Parker demanded.

"Yes," I said, being cagey over the phone. "About ten minutes, give or take traffic. Trouble?"

"Nothing desperate," Parker said. *Yes, it could be trouble.* "Just get back to the office as soon as it's convenient, would you?" *And yes, it's urgent.* And he ended the call before I could satisfy my curiosity any better than that.

By dint of only a small number of minor moving-vehicle violations, Sean made it back to base inside my ten-minute estimate. We rode the elevator in silence and Bill Rendelson intercepted us before we'd taken more than three steps out into the lobby.

"The boss wants to see you two alone first," he said quietly to me, not giving away any clues. He turned to my parents. "If you'd come with me, sir, ma'am?" I saw a flicker of impatience cross my father's face, but he allowed the pair of them to be ushered into one of the conference rooms. Bill promised to be back soon with refreshments, then shut the door on them smartly and hurried across towards Parker's office, jerking his head much less deferentially that we should follow.

Inside, Parker Armstrong was sitting in his usual position behind the desk. Opposite him, in one of the client chairs, sat a nondescript little man in a badly cut gray suit. He looked like a second-rate salesman or a clerical drone who has trudged the same furrow for so long he's worn a groove deep enough to bury himself.

The man looked up quickly as Sean and I entered. He had a mournful, rumpled face, with baggy eyes that were slightly bloodshot, but they didn't miss a trick. I knew before the door had closed behind us that he'd pinpointed the fact we were carrying, and we weren't exactly being obvious about it.

A pro, then. But what kind?

"This is Mr. Collingwood," Parker said as both men rose for the introductions. "He's with —"

"Er, let's just say I'm with one of the *lesser-known* agencies of the U.S. government and leave it at that, shall we?" the man said, glancing at Parker almost with mild reproof. He offered us both a perfunctory handshake, letting go almost before he'd gripped.

Parker stared back, unintimidated. "I like to keep my people fully informed," he said.

Collingwood ducked his head, smiling apologetically. "I'd be a whole lot happier, at this stage, if we kept this whole thing as *low-key* as possible, Mr. Armstrong. I'm sure you can understand our . . . concerns."

I was getting better at placing regional American accents. Not quite Deep South enough to be Alabama or Georgia. Maybe one of the Carolinas.

Parker nodded reluctantly and waved us to sit down. Sean and I took the chairs on either side of him, positions of support and solidarity that weren't lost on the government man. Those heavy-lidded eyes gleamed a little as they regarded us.

Despite his observant gaze, Collingwood struck me as an official rather than an agent — the kind who'd once been in the field, but was now firmly anchored behind a desk. His suit had the bagged knees to prove it. He had a briefcase lying closed on the low table near his right hand and a buff-coloured folder, also closed, in front of him, which he fiddled with while he waited for us to settle, fussily lining it up with the edge of the table.

His hands were misshapen across the backs, I noticed, like he'd spent his youth bare-knuckle fighting or suffered from premature arthritis. Perhaps that explained the lackluster handshake.

"Why don't you bring everybody up to speed," Parker suggested.

The little man ducked his head again and

smiled at us. His hair was very thick, its glossy blackness at odds with his lived-in face. It couldn't have looked more like a wig unless it actually had a chin strap.

"This business came to our attention because Mr. Armstrong was attempting to identify, ah . . . *this* woman," he said, opening the folder just far enough to peer inside and lifting out a blowup print, which he spun the right way up and slid across the table towards us.

"Yes," Sean said, barely glancing at the picture. He didn't need to. It was the one he'd taken of Blondie lying on the floor in my parents' garage with her eyes closed. The blood from her obviously broken nose formed a mustachelike stain on her upper lip.

Collingwood sat back and rested his elbows on the arms of the chair, steepling his fingers and tapping the ends together so his nails clicked.

"What can you tell me about this photograph?" he said carefully. "First off, where did you, ah, *obtain* it?"

He looked from one of us to the other. We stared right back, giving him nothing. Collingwood cleared his throat, trying to hide his desperation behind a nervous laugh. "I mean to say, we know *when* it was taken.

That's the beauty of digital these days — there's a time code embedded in the image. But we don't know *where*. Or under what, ah, circumstances."

"Perhaps it might help if we knew why you need to know this," Sean said, pleasant but noncommittal. "Who is she?"

Collingwood's gaze swung across him, then he gave a weary sigh, raising his hands a little.

"Okay. Her name is Vonda Blaylock," he said, eyes still on the photo, lying untouched on the tabletop. "And she's one of ours." He looked up, his face ever more sorrowful. "Or, leastways, she was. . . ."

Oh shit.

I glanced back at the photo, as if knowing Blondie's real name and status as a government agent might change my memory of her in some way. No, I decided, it didn't. She and her heavy-duty sidekick had still conned their way into my mother's house, threatened her, frightened her, and been prepared to do untold damage to whoever came to her aid. I relaxed, shrugging off the guilt that had been nudging at my shoulder. All things considered, she'd got off lightly.

Vonda. Not a name I'd come across before. It suited her, sort of, although she'd always be Vondie to me.

"When you say she's one of yours, does that mean she was on an assignment of some kind?" Sean asked, picking his words to be as neutral as possible.

Collingwood winced, as if he'd been hoping for something more reassuring than that. Or at least something different. There was a light sheen of sweat coating his forehead. "Not exactly," he said. "She's been on leave for the last couple of weeks. Look, can you at least tell me if she's still alive or —"

"She was when that picture was taken," I said, taking pity on his patent distress.

"Well, thank the good Lord for that," he said, slumping back in his chair, hands dangling. "That shot came down the wire and we thought . . . *I* thought . . ." He stopped, shook his head and added, almost to himself, "Whatever she's gotten herself into, she didn't deserve —"

"Just what *has* she gotten herself into, Mr. Collingwood?" Parker asked, still in that dangerously quiet tone.

"Hm?" Collingwood looked up, distracted, and Parker had to repeat his question. "Well, I can't go into details — you understand — but we suspect that Miss Blaylock has been doing a little, ah, *freelancing,* put it that way. Either on the company dime, or on her own. I had a conversation with her about it, gave her the opportunity to come clean." He looked at the photo again. "She didn't take it — just put in for vacation time. An internal inquiry was scheduled for when she got back at the start of this week, but she never showed, and all our attempts to locate her have failed — until that arrived." He jerked his head to the photo. "What *happened* to her?"

I did.

Rejecting brutal honesty, I said, "She took part in a scheme to blackmail my father, Richard Foxcroft, by kidnapping my mother." I was watching his face while I spoke to see if any of this was news to him. If it wasn't, he gave a pretty convincing display of bewildered consternation. "In England," I added, as though that made it so much worse.

"Are you sure about this?" He looked blankly around us, as if we were all going to crack up and admit that we were joking. "I mean, ah, how *reliable* is your intel?"

"Very," I said. "By the time we arrived to, ah, *remedy* the situation," I went on, matching my style of delivery to his, "your Miss Blaylock was pretty well dug in and prepared to repel boarders. How else do you think she ended up with her nose splattered all over her face?"

Collingwood wiped a thoughtful hand across his chin and I heard the slight rasp of his fingers against the stubble. The guy had a few tufts of body hair protruding from the ends of his shirt cuffs and just below his Adam's apple, too. He must have had to shave twice a day just to stop people calling out Animal Control.

"So *you* took the picture," he said.

"I did," Sean said. He shrugged, untainted by guilt of any kind. "We wanted to know who she was and who she was working for, and she wasn't keen to tell us."

"So all you did was *ask,* huh?" Collingwood demanded with outright suspicion. "No rough stuff?"

"I may have raised my voice towards her," Sean said blandly, carefully sidestepping what he'd done to her companion instead. "But the fight was over by then. And I'm hardly a torturer."

No, he wasn't, I reflected, but he was a damned good interrogator. Cold, ruthless and utterly relentless. I'd been on the receiving end during my Special Forces training and, even though a part of me had always clung to the shrinking reality that it was all just a game, his innate menace and his aptitude for arrowing in on fear and weakness had terrified everyone who'd had to endure it.

"We reasoned that identifying her would be by far the best way to neutralize whatever threat she presented," Sean continued, sounding perfectly reasonable.

"And afterward?"

Sean met his gaze straight and level. "We left Ms. Blaylock relatively unharmed." He always was a better liar than me, too.

"But you're telling us you had no idea of where she was going, or what she was doing?" Parker asked at that point, deflecting whatever doubts Collingwood might have been about to express. "Do your people normally inform you if they're traveling overseas, for instance? Are they flagged at Immigration?"

"No — o," Collingwood said slowly, sounding like he was drawing the word out to give himself time to think. "They're not *obliged* to tell us. It was only after she disappeared that we ran checks and found she'd bought a plane ticket to the UK."

So, he'd known Vondie had left the country long before I'd told him about my mother, I realized. And knowing *we* knew meant the rules of the game shifted slightly, that now he had nothing to lose by giving us a little more. Collingwood reached for the buff folder again and leafed through it, still careful not to let us get a look at the contents.

"Here you go — she flies into Manchester, England, just over a week ago. After that, we lose her. She just drops right off the grid. According to the Brits, she hasn't used any of her credit cards or even switched on her cell phone since she landed. She missed her return flight, didn't turn up at work when she was due. I don't mind telling you that we're *seriously* concerned for her safety."

"Was she traveling alone?" I asked, trying to keep any inflection out of my voice.

Collingwood ducked his head again, then made a little side-to-side movement, which I took to mean yes/no/maybe.

"She booked and paid for the flight herself, but we pulled the manifest," he said cautiously, opening his case for that piece of paperwork and handing it over. I took it without comment, leafed through the pages. It came as no surprise to find Don Kaminski on there as well, but I let my eyes drop past his name without a waver, sedately read all the way to the end and put the sheaf down onto the table.

When I looked up I found Collingwood had been watching me closely. But if the disappointed twitch in the side of his face was anything to go by, I hadn't shown him what he'd been hoping to see.

Where his left hand hung over the arm of the chair his fingers performed an unconscious little dance, rubbing the pad of his thumb across his fingertips, back and forth like he was checking the viscosity of oil, or asking for a bribe. I wondered if he was even aware he was doing it.

"Okay, people — cards on the table time," he said at last, tiredly. "We believe Agent Blaylock has been working with a guy called Don Kaminski, but I'm sure this information comes as no surprise to any of you — seeing as how you initially sent around a mug shot of Kaminski at the same time as that picture." He nodded to the blowup of Vondie and allowed himself a wry smile. "I'm assuming from the fact that you stopped asking about him, that means you ID'd him pretty fast. Am I right?"

Parker inclined his head a fraction, a faint encouraging smile on his lips. It was the first movement he'd made since he sat down again. On either side of him, Sean and I were doing our best impersonations of the sphinx at Giza.

Collingwood gave a snort of frustration at our lack of a more emphatic response.

"Look, I know the business you're in is pretty tight-knit, cliquey, so if you identified Kaminski and the outfit he works for, you'll already know about his current contract and you'll understand our, ah, *interest?*"

If Kaminski was working for the Boston hospital, I couldn't for the life of me work out how someone like Collingwood might be involved, but I had a feeling if we played this right, we might just be about to find out.

I tried not to hold my breath, tried to force my muscles not to tense. Parker, with heroic restraint, merely gave a polite, almost bored nod, as though this was all information we were well aware of and he wished Collingwood would cut to the chase.

"So, what exactly *is* your interest, Mr. Collingwood?" he said, his face deceptively placid.

Judging by his weary expression, Collingwood took Parker's question as awkwardness rather than ignorance. He gave a gusty sigh. "Storax Pharmaceutical, of course."

Storax.

The name couldn't have hit me any harder if it had been plastered all over the front of the taxi that had tried to run me down.

Storax. The company that manufactured the drug Jeremy Lee had been taking before he died — with or without his knowledge. The company that had obligingly sent two of their people up to Boston allegedly to assist in his treatment. Where had *they* been, I wondered, when the good doctor had been administered his fatal overdose?

My father had been convinced that it was the hospital who'd been covering up some kind of clinical error, but now Collingwood had shed a whole new light on the situation. The question was, what should we do about it?

"And why exactly is one of the *lesser-known government agencies* interested in Storax?" It was Sean who asked the question, which was just as well — I wasn't capable of speech. I was amazed that Sean could sound so calm in the face of the information Collingwood had just dropped, apparently unwittingly, into our laps.

Collingwood's eyes narrowed, as if he realized he'd said more than he should, and I could see his mind backtracking, trying to work out what advantage we might gain from it. After a moment he seemed to come to the conclusion that he had nothing to lose by saying more.

"Storax Pharmaceutical contracts with the U.S. government to produce certain, ah, vaccines. Anything more than that is classified information," Collingwood said, ducking his head again like a boxer expecting to dodge blows. "But let me just say that we keep an eye on their other activities. A very *close* eye. Storax is just about to be granted worldwide licenses for this new bone drug of theirs, based largely on the success of clinical trials to date. If there's a problem and they're covering it up, we need to know and we need to know fast."

"If Storax holds government contracts, surely you have some authority to go in and do some kind of audit," I said.

He gave a sad little shake of his head at my naïveté. "Storax is a *global* corporation," he said. "A multibillion-dollar enterprise. Heck, they probably have more people on the payroll just to *lobby* for them in Washington than our agency has on its entire payroll, period. We can't fight that unless we have an ironclad case. They'll shut us down in a heartbeat. And that brings me to your father, Miss Fox. Where is he, by the way?"

"Somewhere safe," Parker said, jumping in before I had the chance to answer, even if I'd had the inclination to do so. "What is it you want with him?"

"If Storax is falsifying any of its research, I'm sure you can appreciate the implications for the national security of this country, Mr. Armstrong," Collingwood said heavily. "If Richard Foxcroft has any evidence to support his claims that Dr. Lee was given that overdose as some kind of cover-up, we need to talk to him."

"Why should we trust you?" I said flatly. "If Storax *are* behind what's been going on, they've fought dirty so far and it's damn near ruined him. Don't you think he's had enough?"

"We need to know what he knows," Collingwood said, stubborn. "I don't suppose I need to remind you how, ah, *difficult* we could make life for your father if he doesn't cooperate?"

Parker pushed his chair back and rose, the movement sudden but smooth and controlled all at the same time. He leaned forwards slightly and planted both his fists very deliberately onto the desktop, letting his shoulders hunch so that Collingwood was left in no doubt about the width of them, normally so well disguised by careful tailoring.

"Do I need to remind *you* that one of *your* agents is guilty of kidnapping?" he asked, his voice gentle enough to make me shiver. "That she and Kaminski threatened to torture and rape a defenseless old lady?

How would that look on tomorrow's front page?"

"Almost as bad as the old lady's highly respectable husband getting caught in a bordello with a teenage hooker," Collingwood shot back. He gave another gusty sigh. "Look, this is getting us nowhere. I just want to recover my agent and find out what her involvement is with Storax, and what they're hiding. Foxcroft can help."

He returned Parker's glare with a cool stare of his own before shifting its focus to me. The upper corners of his eyelids folded down until they almost touched his lashes, making his gaze seem deceptively sleepy. "You want a way to get your father out of the mess he's in, and no doubt *he* wants to get to the bottom of this other guy's death up in Boston. Am I right?"

Slowly, reluctantly, I nodded.

Collingwood smiled at me. "See? Same goal."

"This is all very romantic," Sean said, his voice dry, "but how do you intend to consummate this marriage of convenience?"

Collingwood frowned briefly at the flippancy. "We trade," he said. "First off, you, ah, *assist* me in recovering my rogue agent."

"Always assuming that we have any ideas in that direction," Sean agreed placidly.

"And in return?"

Collingwood shrugged. "I listen to Fox-croft's side of the story, drop the word in the right ears to make sure all that, ah, *trouble* he got himself into over in Brooklyn goes away," he said, "and in return he gives me his professional take on the death of this guy Lee, and any possible connections he can make between that and Storax."

We fell silent. It was an answer. In fact, from where I was sitting, it was the only answer — or the start of it, at least. Collingwood's fingers were twitching again as he regarded us.

"Well?" he demanded. "Do we have a deal?"

"I think that's up to the good doctor, don't you?" Parker murmured. He glanced at me, eyebrow slightly raised. I nodded slightly and he leaned forwards, pressing the intercom button on his phone. Bill Rendelson's voice barked from the speaker in acknowledgment.

"Bill, ask Mr. and Mrs. Foxcroft to step into my office, would you?"

Parker let go of the intercom button and sat up to face Collingwood's obvious consternation that one of his objectives, at least, had been within such easy reach. "Why don't you ask him yourself?"

FIFTEEN

My father listened with absolute concentration to the proposal the government man put forward, as though he had any number of choices in the matter. When Collingwood was done outlining what he had in mind, my father's face was grave despite the fact that he was being offered deliverance, or something pretty close.

It was my mother who spoke first.

"What are the risks?" she asked, glancing around the group of us. "These dreadful people have already threatened us and only a few days ago someone tried to kill my husband — and my daughter, too," she added, a touch belatedly for my taste. "Will agreeing to help you make them stop? Or will it only make them try harder?"

Collingwood pursed his lips, but I saw that gleam was back in his sad-looking eyes again. He'd clearly dismissed my mother from his calculations almost as soon as they'd been introduced. She was the dictionary definition of *genteel,* if far from the defenseless old lady Parker had described. I sometimes found it easy to forget that under that blue-rinsed exterior lay a formidable, albeit largely dormant, brain.

"Ma'am, we'll do our best to ensure your safety. We need your husband's testimony if we're going to make anything of this. Besides," he added with a reassuring smile, gesturing around Parker's office, "these people are the best in the business. My recommendation would be for you to put yourself entirely in their hands."

"In that case, are you also going to foot the bill for their services?" she said pleasantly.

Collingwood looked momentarily taken aback. "I will certainly put that to my superiors, ma'am," he said, noncommittal.

She nodded and smiled, seeming placated. Collingwood waited a moment, as if to make sure she wasn't going to come back with anything else, then began gathering up his papers. He picked up the flight manifest I'd looked at, and in doing so uncovered the blowup of Vondie Blaylock that had been hidden underneath it. The photograph suddenly seemed to lie starkly exposed in the center of the table and was all the more shocking because of it.

I heard a simultaneous sharp intake of breath from both my mother and father.

Then my father stretched out and picked up the photo and there was the slightest hesitation in the reach, as though he didn't really want to look but couldn't help himself. He took his time studying the image and, when he was done, he glanced across at Sean with taut disdain curling his lip.

"Your handiwork, I presume," he said coldly.

"No, actually," I said. "Mine."

For a second he allowed his bitterness to have free rein before he ruthlessly clamped down on it. But there was something in his face when he looked at me that hadn't been there before. Or perhaps it was the other way around. Perhaps now when he looked at his only child, the product of both his genes and his nurturing, there was something missing.

I turned away and caught Collingwood watching our frosty exchange with apparent amusement lurking in those mournful eyes. They were a dark brown color, I noticed. That, together with the drooping lids, gave him the appearance of an elderly bloodhound. But one who had suddenly picked up a hot new scent, and was hunting.

"So," Collingwood said, dropping his hands onto his thighs as though preparing to get to his feet, "no doubt you'll need to discuss this —"

"I don't believe so," my father said, interrupting him. Just when I thought his arrogance had reached new levels, he did cast his eyes sideways at his wife, for all the world like her opinion mattered. She nodded, and the slightest flicker of a smile crossed my father's thin lips. He turned back to Collingwood. "I'm prepared to help you all I can."

Collingwood continued to rise, but only to lean across the table and offer my father a solemn handshake. "Glad to hear it, sir," he said, shaking my mother's hand also, almost as an afterthought, and subsiding again. He shifted his attention to Parker, waving a hand towards Vondie's picture, which he'd left — deliberately, I'm sure — on the table. "So, Mr. Armstrong, can you help me to, ah, *locate* my agent so I can bring her in?"

My mother gave a start of surprise. "Oh, but surely that's —"

"The woman who held you hostage — yes," I cut in to stop her blurting out that she'd watched Sean and me take both her unwanted houseguests prisoner and that they were still being held at our behest. Regrettably perhaps, the only quick way I could think of to shut her up was to remind her. "The woman who allowed her partner to threaten to rape you."

She paled, then a dark, mottled flush bloomed across her cheeks. Peripherally, I saw my father's head snap round, but I held on to my mother's distraught gaze until I saw the understanding creep into it and strip from her tongue whatever words she'd been about to voice.

When I let go, I expected to find my father glaring at me for raking it up. Instead, he had picked the photograph up again and was studying it afresh. It occurred to me that it was probably the first time he'd got a look at one of his wife's captors. I don't know how much she'd told him about her ordeal, but it must have been enough.

Parker, who'd missed nothing of my father's brooding double take, got easily to his feet and came round the desk to shake the government man's hand. "Would you give us some time to make a few calls, Mr. Collingwood?" he asked politely.

"No problem," Collingwood said. "I'm grateful for any assistance you can offer."

Parker favored him with a bland smile. "We'll see what we can do."

Sean and I followed Parker out into the reception area, closing the office door behind us.

"Okay," Parker said quietly. "Get on the phone to whoever's holding those two and cut them loose." I nodded and started to reach for my mobile. I had carefully erased the number for Gleet's farm from the phone's memory, but I had it stored in my own instead.

"Oh, and tell your guy to make sure he gives them back a cell phone or access to a landline, okay?"

I paused in mid-dial. "Okay."

He smiled. "Good," he said, then half-opened the door and added, louder, "Bill, would you show Mr. Collingwood into one of the conference rooms while we make some inquiries on his behalf?"

"Yeah, boss," Bill said, emerging from behind the reception desk. As he passed Parker, he gave him a slight nod. Obviously, there was something going on here and I didn't fully appreciate the finer details. But before I could ask, Gleet's number in the UK began to ring out and I didn't have time to wonder about it. I crossed quickly to an empty office where I wouldn't be overheard.

"Good thing, too," was all Gleet had to say when I passed on Parker's instructions.

"They was starting to stink in there. Even the pigs was complaining."

"Just watch yourselves when you let them go," I warned. "The woman's got a nasty kick to her, and I wouldn't trust the guy anywhere near your sister."

I heard Gleet snort even at the other end of a transatlantic phone line. "He'll be a brave one if he tries anything on with May. She sleeps with that fuckin' shotgun alongside her under the covers," he muttered. "Don't you worry, Charlie. I'll stick the pair of 'em in the back of the van and drive 'em round in circles for a while before I let 'em go. I'll make sure I dump 'em far enough away that they wouldn't find the place again in a month of Sundays."

"Great. Don't forget to let them have a phone, though."

"They had one with 'em, didn't they?" he said. "I'll make sure it's charged up when they get it back. No worries."

"Thank you," I said, heartfelt. "I owe you a big one for this, Gleet."

"Nah, I 'aven't forgotten Dublin," he said, and his voice had entirely lost its joky edge to turn stone sober. "I think this just about makes us even."

We let Collingwood stew for half an hour

while we sat in Parker's office, drinking his excellent coffee as he chatted with my parents. Parker was erudite enough to bring my father out of his simmering silence and coax conversation out of my mother. All things to all men — or all women, come to that. By the end of it, I could see my parents drawing unfavorable comparisons with Sean, but by then I didn't care.

Sean preferred not to take part in this conversation, sidelining himself. Perhaps he'd tried to talk with my parents too many times in the past, under too many sets of circumstances, and had tired of having the effort thrown back in his face. He wasn't used to failure. It wasn't a state of affairs he had to deal with very often.

After I'd finished my phone call with Gleet and joined them, I'd tried to catch Sean's eye with a question mark in my expression.

What the hell's Parker up to?

Sean had just given me a faint knowing smile.

Patience, Charlie. He knows what he's doing.

I shrugged, feeling outside the joke. And that feeling only increased when, some thirty-five minutes later, Bill Rendelson brought Collingwood back through. All Parker did was thank the government man courteously for his time and tell him we'd be in touch.

I expected Collingwood to show some signs of annoyance at what must have seemed a pointless delay at the very least, but instead he just ducked his head in that strange nervous little gesture of good-bye, and limply shook hands again all round.

"I'm sure we'll meet again soon, sir," he said to my father, in a hurry to leave now. "As soon as we've recovered our rogue agent, I'll talk to the cops in Bushwick and see if we can get some of this mess straightened out."

"Thank you," my father said with understated dignity, as though Collingwood was offering to grant him some minor favor rather than possibly salvaging his entire career. Maybe he just took exception to the veiled threat — no Vondie, no clean slate.

After Collingwood had gone it was my mother, again, who cut to the heart of the matter.

"It all rather sounds like our salvation," she said, her voice tragic, "but how do we know we can trust him?"

"At this stage, we don't," I said. She looked confused, but for a moment the only analogy that came to mind involved urinating in tents.

It was Sean who glanced across and said, "Remember the old quote about keeping your friends close but your enemies closer."

My mother frowned, enlightened but not reassured. "That sounds like something out of Machiavelli — *The Prince*?"

"Possibly," Sean said with a twitch of his lips. "But I was thinking more of Michael Corleone — *The Godfather Part II.*"

"Oh," she said blankly. "And how do we know who is a friend and who is an enemy?"

Parker merely smiled at her and a moment later, as if on cue, Bill knocked and entered, brandishing a computer memory stick in his remaining hand, like it was an Olympic torch.

"I've edited out the twenty-five minutes of tuneless humming and him clearing his throat," Bill said, "and homed right in on the heart of it."

Parker took the storage device from him with a nod of thanks. "Mr. Collingwood did make life a little too easy for my suspicious mind," he said, "so I asked Charlie to make sure Blaylock and Kaminski had a way to make a phone call as soon as they were released, and I arranged for Collingwood to be somewhere we could monitor his incoming calls."

Suddenly, all that sophisticated audio equipment in the conference room where Collingwood had been waiting took on a whole new meaning.

"You bugged him," I said with admiration. "Clever."

"I will neither confirm nor deny that allegation." Parker curved me a smile, more in the eyes than the mouth, but when he spoke his tone was serious and somber. "And I certainly have no intention of doing so outside this room."

While he was speaking, he'd plugged the stick into a USB port on the slimline laptop computer that sat open on his desk, and hit the relevant keys.

Parker's laptop had a tiny high-tech-looking pair of external speakers connected to it but, even so, when the audio file started to play we crowded more closely around the desk to listen.

The first thing we heard was the warbling note of a cell phone ringing, some heavy sighing as it was fumbled for in some hard-to-reach pocket, then Collingwood's voice.

"Yeah?" he said by way of universal greeting, sounding almost bored. Then his voice sharpened and there was a slight clatter in the background, as though he'd been leaning back on a chair and had let it jolt forwards flat onto its feet with the shock of the unexpected caller.

"Vonda! My Lord, where are you? Are you all right?"

The microphone was good but not that good. We could hear some squawking in the background, but not enough to begin to decipher actual words at the other end of Collingwood's line. It was just audio scribble.

"Hey, hey, just wait a goddamn minute!" He cut right across the top of whatever she was saying. "I don't know what the hell you got yourself mixed up in, kiddo, and I don't *want* to know. . . . No, *you* just listen to *me*. You come on in and we'll work this whole thing out. You stay out there, off the grid, and I can't help you."

He sounded sad rather than angry. Tired, as though this was a ritual he'd been through many times before, a procedure he had to go through, but he knew it never ended well.

Vondie launched back in at this point — strident, if the cast of what she was saying was anything to go by. Collingwood barely let her get into her stride.

"Believe me when I tell you, you're in a world of trouble right now, kiddo, but it'll be worse if you run." His voice turned almost pleading. "Look, I know you're hurting. That busted nose needs to be fixed if you're gonna stay looking beautiful, huh?"

Parker reached out and paused the playback, looking round the assembled faces. "Immediate thoughts?" he asked crisply.

"Well, he doesn't sound like he knew what she was up to," Sean ventured. "Unless he was aware you were recording him, of course, and he was playing to his audience? If it'd been me, I'd have assumed you were monitoring."

Parker shrugged. "It cost a lot of money to have surveillance gear installed in that room," he said, offering me a wry smile. "We know he didn't sweep it, so unless he's had cleaners in that we don't know about, I doubt he would have spotted anything."

"He sounds almost . . . *fond* of that woman," my mother said, a dent forming between her eyebrows, as if she couldn't understand why anyone could possibly want to show affection for one of her erstwhile tormentors.

"Protégée," I said shortly. "He trained her, that would be my guess. If she's cocked-up and he can't fix it, or if he can't bring her to heel — and quickly — it's going to reflect as badly on him as it does on her," I added, echoing Sean's remarks the day of my abortive fitness test. "*If* he's on the level."

"I think you're right," Parker said. He glanced at my father but only received a brief shake of the head in response. My father had never been one to speak just to hear the sound of his own voice unless he had something of value to say. Parker nudged the mouse and Collingwood's voice re-emerged.

"Come on in, kiddo," he repeated. "Whatever you got yourself into, you can still make it right. . . . Hey, hey, I know. I just want to help you, kiddo. I stand by my people." Coaxing now. "Just come on in. Come home — please?"

There was a long pause but this time we couldn't hear anything of Vondie's voice. Either Collingwood had shifted his position, or she was no longer screeching at him. Or she was giving his words long, silent consideration.

Eventually, Collingwood said, "Okay, but call me and let me know which flight. Promise? I'll meet you. . . . Yeah, I'll bring you in myself. . . . It'll all work out, you'll see. . . . Yeah, take care of yourself, kiddo. Bye."

We heard a muted bleep as he ended the call, then a long slow exhalation and a single quietly muttered but entirely heartfelt word, just before the recording ended: *"Shit."*

"Yeah," Parker murmured, clicking it off with a thoughtful air. "I'd say that just about sums it up, wouldn't you?"

"Pretty much," Sean replied. "The question is, Do you trust him more, or less, after hearing it?"

It had been a general question, but he cocked an eyebrow at my father as he spoke, making it direct and personal.

My father gave an elegant shrug. "I'm not entirely sure that I have much of a choice in the matter," he said, indifferent. "But I've always found that actions speak far louder than words. If he's to be trusted, I would rather suggest that we'll know soon enough by what he does."

"But, Richard, surely if this man *isn't* to be trusted, that means they'll make another attempt on you, doesn't it?" my mother demanded, her voice taking on distinct overtones of Vondie's shrill note.

My father gave a grim smile. "In that case, my dear," he said with utter calm, "we'll find out just how good Charlotte is at her job."

Sixteen

We heard nothing from Collingwood for several days, during which time my father's frustration grew. Parker used the lull to mount a major low-key public-relations campaign within the industry and managed to stem the flow of clients who had suddenly decided to seek the services of other firms.

One or two even came back, slightly sheepish. But there were more who stayed away for no better reason than to save face. Parker seemed to be practically living at the office. Despite his denials that he didn't hold me — or my family — in any way personally responsible for his current woes, I knew there were others who didn't feel the same way. Bill Rendelson, for one, could hardly bring himself to speak to me.

Sean and I stuck with my parents, on a rotating shift pattern with a couple of Parker's other guys, 24/7. By Sunday morning, when we'd heard nothing and seen nothing, all of us were going a little stir-crazy stuck in the hotel, however luxurious.

In particular, my mother's nerves were strung so tight we could probably have got a recognizable tune out of her. I suppose it was inevitable that it was she, eventually, who demanded we get out and take in some of the sights.

"I haven't been to New York with your father since before you were born, Charlotte," she protested when I expressed my doubts about the wisdom of going walk-about. "We went to Greenwich Village, I remember. It was just like something out of a Woody Allen film. And I would very much like to do it again." It was a royal command rather than a request.

My father, who'd spent much of this voluntary incarceration reading obscure medical textbooks of one type or another, glanced up from his page and frowned over the top of his glasses.

"Are you sure that's wise, Elizabeth?" He used such a mild dry tone that I knew he didn't really need to ask.

My mother's chin came out, mulish — was that where I got it from? "Frankly," she said with some asperity, "I need some air."

He paused a moment as if considering the

validity of this argument, then inclined his head. "In that case," he said gravely, "of course we'll go." He turned his gaze to Sean, who was sitting at the room's desk, typing onto one of the office laptops. He had taken off his jacket and his tie, but not the paddle-rig holster for the Glock 21, which he'd carried since we'd returned to the States. Somehow, he didn't look quite dressed without it.

"I trust you have no objections?" my father said in a steely voice, daring Sean to raise any.

Sean didn't reply instantly. When he did, it was without looking up from the screen.

"If you're sensible — no."

"Of course." My father rose almost gracefully, tucking his glasses into an inside pocket as he smiled at my mother. "Shall we go?"

McGregor was back on call that day and he obligingly drove us south on Fifth until we hit the huge ornamental white stone archway that makes a grand entrance to Washington Square Park.

As we stopped at the light, my mother leaned across to stare out of the window. "Oh Richard," she said, her voice husky, "do you remember?"

I twisted in my seat in time to see him

give her a strangely indulgent smile.

"Yes," he said softly, "I do." And, louder: "We'd like to walk from here, if you don't mind."

McGregor checked with Sean, who was sitting alongside him. Sean did a fast sweep and nodded reluctantly. "Okay, Joe," he said. "Set us down outside the park and keep close by."

McGregor pulled over to let us out. We crossed the road and passed under the ornate archway to enter the park proper, heading towards the circular central fountain. It was warm enough to make being out in the open air pleasant, and plenty of people were taking advantage.

As if by some unspoken agreement, Sean and I reached into our respective pockets for sunglasses and slipped them on at the same time, making it easier to move our eyes but not our heads, keeping track. I kept my coat unbuttoned and my left hand wrapped round my phone, with McGregor's number on speed dial just in case we needed a rapid extraction, and my Bluetooth headset in place.

The crowds gave us cover but also provided it against us. Sean and I closed in, casually, on either side of my parents. He was slightly behind my father, to his left. I was a pace in front of my mother, on her right.

Between us, my parents strolled along, arm in arm, apparently oblivious to such measures. They wandered through the park, murmuring to each other, pointing out landmarks they recalled, or admiring the skills of the jugglers and the busking musicians, the studied concentration of the chess players, and the skateboarders' laid-back cool.

While my mother and father stayed on the move it wasn't so bad, but when they became entranced by the slick patter and slicker hands of an elderly magician down near the southwest corner and stopped to watch, I was pricklingly aware of our vulnerability. The park was bordered by trees, but Washington Square itself had plenty of buildings high enough to have a perfect view — and unobstructed trajectory — into the place.

I turned my back on my parents and quartered north and east without needing to look to know that Sean was covering west and south on the other side of them. Watching the buildings for the light and dark of closed or open windows. Watching people's hands and eyes for movement that didn't fit pattern. Looking for the people who didn't fit in, the ones who were trying not to be seen.

I saw her because she wasn't moving at all. And in the bustle of the park on a Sunday morning, that alone made her stand out — just as she'd intended it to.

Vondie Blaylock.

I would have known that cool blond figure anywhere, even without the flesh-colored dressing across her broken nose and the intense hatred that was coming off her in waves.

She was wearing a long black coat that hung heavy enough to be leather or suede and was big enough to be concealing just about anything underneath it. She was a hundred meters away, on the low flat steps leading into the fountain. There was a light breeze from the northwest, enough to distort the fall of spray and partially obscure my view of her.

What the hell are you doing here? And what the hell is Collingwood doing, letting you out?

I stepped across so I was directly between Vondie and my parents. My right hand had shifted automatically, just a fraction, my fingers brushing against the front edge of my open jacket, ready to push back the material and reach for the SIG lying hidden beneath it, but her hands gave no answering twitch. I raked the area surrounding her, looking for the additional threat, the backup, but she seemed to be alone.

I let my eyes do a fast flick behind me. Enough to check my parents hadn't moved out from under my surveillance, that they were still watching the magician pick the pockets of an audience volunteer and laughing at the man's bewildered expression as all his possessions were solemnly returned to him, one after another.

"Sean," I murmured.

"Hm-mm. Got her. And I don't like it any more than you do." A pause, weighing up our options. "Let's get out of here."

My thumb had been hovering over one key on my phone and, almost before he'd spoken, I'd already pressed it. McGregor picked up before it had time to ring a second time. Quietly, I gave him concise exit instructions for the west side of the park, and Sean and I began surreptitiously to pincer in on my parents. I had every intention of practically taking my mother off her feet, if necessary, to get her out of there in one piece.

And then, as if she could read our intent, Vondie gave us a mocking, jaunty little salute, and turned away. We froze, watching her stride under the arch, her back directly towards us like a provocation. She moved with only the slightest limp on her right leg and I experienced a momentary pang of regret that I hadn't made sure it was more pronounced.

She reached the curb just as a black Lincoln Town Car pulled up alongside her, and climbed in without a pause. She didn't look back. We watched the Lincoln until it reached the next corner and disappeared from view.

I felt my shoulders drop and widen as the tension oozed away. I turned and found Sean staring narrow-eyed after the Lincoln.

"They're playing games with us," I said.

He nodded. "I agree. 'Look how easy I can get to you, anytime I want.'"

"Yeah," I said tightly. "I thought Collingwood was supposed to be putting a muzzle on that bitch."

"Maybe he has," he said flatly. "Just imagine what she might have done if he hadn't."

I glanced at my parents, expecting they would still be caught up in the show, only to find my mother also staring after the black Lincoln. Her body was rigid and I knew it wasn't just the car, which would have meant nothing to her. She must have seen Vondie and recognized her. So, maybe that taunting wave wasn't just for me. My father's eyes were on his wife, concerned but questioning, as though he didn't know what had caused her sudden reaction.

I moved in, touched my mother's arm and found she was vibrating through her coat.

"Are you all right?" I asked.

She finally tore her gaze away from the other side of the park and swept it over me. I was astonished to see, not fear, but anger lighting up her features.

"Yes," she said at last, calmly, and added through gritted teeth, "I utterly refuse to allow *that woman* to frighten me any longer."

"That's . . . good," I said slowly. "But she scares the hell out of me, so we're leaving." I caught my father's eye. "Unless you feel we're overreacting?"

"No." He shook his head, clearly more shaken than he was prepared to admit, and cast a jaundiced eye over the magician. I could see that whereas before his act had seemed fresh and funny, now it had taken on a rather tawdry air. The sun had gone in unexpectedly and left the day bathed in cloud and shadow that was reflected in my father's face. "I think I've seen more than enough."

Parker managed to reach Collingwood at

home, or wherever the crumpled little man went at the weekends. Collingwood called me direct on my mobile a short while later.

"I'm very sorry," he said, sounding genuinely mortified. "Agent Blaylock is temporarily suspended until the internal investigation is complete and, believe me, I made it, ah, *totally* clear to her that she's in a *world* of trouble."

"Not clear enough, obviously."

I heard his sigh. "She's hurting right now," he said, aiming for reproach. "She's gonna need surgery on that nose. You really messed her up."

"I did no more than she was undoubtedly prepared to do to me," I said mildly. "Sort her out, Collingwood, or I'll do it for you."

"Hey, let's not let things get out of hand, huh?" he said, sounding worried now. "I think it might be a good idea if you took your folks away for a few days, though, get them out of harm's way."

"They won't be dictated to," I said. "Fortunately, they've already decided to get out of New York for a while. Use that time to talk some sense into your agent, will you?" I didn't tell him Parker was arranging tickets as we spoke.

"I will," he promised. "Meanwhile, you be sure to let me have your travel plans — so I can stay in touch."

"I don't think so," I said, shaking my head even though I knew he couldn't see it. "Parker can always get hold of us if he needs to."

"But —"

"No," I said. "That's going to have to be enough. You told my parents to put themselves in my hands, Collingwood. If you trust me enough for that, leave me to do my job. So far you've done nothing. Not even pick up the tab for our services."

"I'm sorry," he said, apparently chastened. "I guess it looks that way, but bureaucracy moves slowly. You have my word that I'm working on it. And of course I don't want to compromise the security of your parents in any way. Do what you think is best."

"Don't worry," I said. "I intend to."

SEVENTEEN

I hadn't been to Boston since an assignment the previous winter when my principal had died and, technically, so had I. For a brief period at least. On the whole, I wasn't sure if that made me feel any better about the way things had turned out.

And I certainly wasn't sure that it put the city on my list of top ten places to revisit. But, Boston was where Jeremy Lee had lived and worked and died, and that's where my father was determined to go.

"This chap Collingwood doesn't seem to be getting anywhere, despite his earnest promises," he said, dismissive. "And I can't sit around doing nothing. One may as well just be covered in honey and pegged out for the ants."

"I agree," I said. "So, what do you hope to find in Boston?"

"I need to talk to Jeremy's wife, Miranda, and go over his medical records again, in detail," he said. "And I hardly think, under the circumstances, the hospital authorities will courier them down for my inspection."

He gave me a slightly tired smile, looking almost human for a change. "I still find it hard to believe that a company as large and well thought of as Storax Pharmaceutical would stoop to this kind of behavior because one patient out of a considerable number suffered side effects. Yes, Jeremy's reaction was severe, but medicine is never an exact science and one must expect the occasional unexpected result."

It was hard, listening to him, to remember that he'd counted the dead man as his friend.

"Nevertheless," I said, "licensing the drug when they know this might happen makes no sense, surely?"

"No, it doesn't." He frowned, removing his reading glasses to pinch at the bridge of his nose. "I'm missing something," he admitted, almost to himself, "and I can't work out for the life of me what it is."

"It'll come to you," I said. "But what makes you think the hospital will let you see the records, even if you go up there in person?"

He cleared his throat. "Ah, well," he said, looking as uncomfortable as I'd seen him, although there was the faintest glimmer of amusement in the back of those usually humorless eyes, "I wasn't exactly planning on asking their permission. . . ."

The four of us flew into Logan on a mid-morning flight out of La Guardia, making the usual knuckle-whitening approach over the dark gray waters of Boston Harbor.

Sean and I had declared and checked our guns, locked in their polymer cases, with ammo separate. All strictly aboveboard and legal. Until we reached Massachusetts, that is, which has no reciprocity regarding concealed-carry licenses with New York. Most of Parker's operatives solved this problem by going through the rigmarole of getting additional licenses for nonreciprocal states, but Sean and I were still plowing our way through that particular forest of paperwork.

If we were caught, we'd be in just as much trouble as we would have been getting ourselves arrested with a pair of unlicensed handguns in a police raid on a brothel in Brooklyn. But I'd thought of the threat I'd read in Vondie Blaylock's stance that day in Washington Square Park, and made my decision without a qualm.

We picked up a rental car at one of the

off-airport lots. Sean had chosen another capacious Navigator SUV, despite the abysmal fuel economy, on the grounds that sometimes it was good to have the advantage of bulk over speed.

We drove sedately through the Ted Williams Tunnel and into the city itself, glowing with autumn browns and golds. More sedate than New York, less brash, Boston nevertheless showed the petticoats of its history like a prim old lady secretly proud of a wild and somewhat rowdy past.

Bypassing glitzier accommodation, we settled for a more low-key chain hotel in the Back Bay area. The rooms were dull and as much in need of refurbishment as the shabby New York place where I'd first confronted my father after that damning news report. It seemed half a lifetime ago. Since then, I'd been mildly kicked about by Vondie and much less mildly kicked about by the pointed end of a yellow cab. Thank God for Vicodin.

I knew I was leaning heavily on the painkillers to see me through this rough patch, and I was rationing my intake as much as I could stand. But I'd learned a long time ago that there's nothing heroic about being in pain. Nor does it allow you to function at anything like full speed, mentally or physically. When recovery time wasn't an option, chemical respite would have to do.

We used the bellboy service to haul our luggage up to the eighth floor, leaving our hands free. Sean and I had taken an adjoining room to my parents, with a dividing door that we unlocked but left closed while we freshened up after the flight.

It hadn't occurred to me, until my father knocked and entered, that this arrangement might cause a problem for his old-fashioned sensibilities. But as soon as he walked in I saw him pause, eyes skimming disapprovingly over the huge king-size double bed that filled the floor space in the small room. There wasn't even a pullout couch so we could make any pretense about it.

At that moment Sean came out of the bathroom, drying his hands, looking very much at home. And the fact that we intended to share a bed together, in the room right next to theirs, was suddenly very loud and very obvious. I felt seventeen again. It was all I could do not to squirm.

"Can I help you, Richard?" Sean asked pleasantly, moving past him close enough to make the older man step back.

My father tore his eyes away from the bed and our partially unpacked bags, which were sitting cosily side by side on the counterpane. Without thinking, I reached out and grabbed the handles of mine and swung it onto the foldout luggage rack in the alcove next to the bathroom, then tunneled through the contents to find my toiletries.

"We wondered about dinner," my father said stiffly. "Elizabeth and I are quite happy to eat here in the hotel, if you do not wish to go out again."

Even with my back to him, I could feel that Sean had followed my movements. I knew damn well he read me like an open book and, by the way he flicked the towel sharply over the back of a chair, that I'd have to answer for my cowardice later.

"I wouldn't recommend staying in," Sean said, nothing in his voice. "The rooms are okay, but the last time I ate here I went down with food poisoning and I've no desire to go through that again — even with such an eminent medicine man on hand."

"Very well," my father said, inclining his head despite the danger of cracking his neck because he was holding it so rigid. "We'll knock when we're ready." And with that he went out, closing the door oh so quietly behind him.

I shut my eyes. Sean's voice, when it came, was viciously soft and close enough to make me jump, though I hadn't heard him move round from the other side of the bed.

"You're an adult. When are you going to stop apologizing to them, Charlie, for the way you live your life?"

I opened my eyes again, turned and found him crowding in on me so I had to tilt my head back to meet his. Briefly — just briefly — I thought about lying, but there wasn't any point.

"Respect for the attitudes of an older generation hardly counts as an apology," I tried instead.

"No excuse," he dismissed. "Times change. Attitudes change. They should be the ones to adapt, not you."

It took me a moment to find some spine and, when I did, it brought my chin up in defiance. "You're the one who used to take Madeleine home with you and pretend intimacy, just to stop your mother match-making."

His head went back in surprise and his anger dissipated just a little under the force of wry amusement.

"You're right," he allowed, his voice still cool, "but I did it to stop my mother worrying about me working too hard and not having a life. Not because I was ashamed of anything."

"I am not ashamed of you, Sean."

"Really?" He stepped back, and it was like he'd stepped back in time as well as space, to the arrogant, unsettling superior he'd been during my short and inglorious military career. Someone to whom my success or failure had appeared to be of minor interest because he had nothing invested in the outcome. "So, prove it."

I didn't, of course.

We went out and found a fabulous seafood place down near the water but I was so jittery that I couldn't remember exactly what I had to eat or drink.

I told myself it was because I was on duty. And not just any duty, but guarding principals I cared about too deeply for it ever to be purely professional. Sean, on the other hand, was the model of the perfect executive protection officer — polite, remote, focused.

But, unusually for him, he made no attempt to blend with us on a social level. He'd disconnected himself from the family group, deliberately emphasizing his status as an outsider. Rather than a party of two related couples, it appeared more like we had inexplicably invited a servant along for the evening and were perhaps now regretting such a display of largesse. And I knew I was trying too hard to pour oil on troubled waters, otherwise I would have berated my parents for their supercilious demeanor. It was a long and uncomfortable evening.

After we got back to the hotel and settled my parents in for the night, I expected Sean to bring things to a head, but he didn't. He'd never been a sulker and this new attitude scared me.

When he came out of the bathroom, he stripped with impersonal efficiency, and climbed into his side of the bed. It was big enough for the gap between us, when I slunk in silently on my side, to seem wider and more frozen than one person could hope to cross — even with dogsleds and an affinity for polar bears.

EIGHTEEN

The following morning we risked breakfast in the hotel restaurant and then headed for the suburb of Norwood, where we would find Jeremy Lee's widow. Norwood was southwest of Boston, just outside the I-95 ring road that cupped the city to Massachusetts Bay, skirting round the growing sprawl on its landward, western side.

The mammoth construction job that had been disrupting Boston the last time I'd been there didn't seem to have changed or progressed overmuch. We sat in traffic, inevitably, which my parents bore with stoical patience and which Sean maneuvered his way through with expressionless skill. He'd hardly spoken to me all morning, a state of affairs that my father observed minutely, as if monitoring a patient for the manifestation of fatal symptoms.

We hadn't picked up any signs of surveillance since we'd landed in Boston, but went through a series of routine countermeasures even so. They all came up empty. By the time we hit the main freeway, we knew we were clear. Sean kept our speed up, making good time, but the journey still seemed to take forever.

It was a little after ten when we pulled up outside a pretty two-story house in a quiet street of others, all painted beautifully contrasting pastel shades with white trim around the windows, like the residents had been to a color-coordination meeting before they all went out and bought paint in the spring.

Miranda Lee was not what I was expecting. The name sounded tall, refined and elegant, but the person who opened the screen door onto the covered porch was short and rather chunky, dressed in black leggings and a baggy football sweater, with her long wiry dark hair tangled around her face. But there was no debating the delight with which she greeted my parents.

"Richard! Elizabeth!" she cried, flinging herself onto each of them in bone-crushing hugs while Sean and I stood a little apart and watched the street, the neighboring houses, the wooded area behind. "Oh, I just can't tell you how glad I am to see you both. I'm *so* sorry for all of this," she added, sounding genuinely distraught. "But what am I thinking? Come in, come in . . . all of you."

As she said this last bit she cocked her head towards Sean and me, scanning us with shrewd dark eyes as we walked into the house.

"This is my daughter, Charlotte," my father said without any particular pride. "And . . . Sean Meyer, who is helping to ensure our safety."

As introductions went it was a cop-out, as he well knew, but Sean kept his expression bland as he shook hands with the widow. He refused a seat and instead stayed at one side of the room where the windows gave him two separate views of the street.

The ground floor was spacious and open, with a large kitchen off the living room, and a dining room separated by fold-back double doors. It was decorated in a haphazard style with splashes of vibrant color that should have jarred but somehow didn't. The house was rammed with cheerfully disjointed clutter, easygoing and largely unpretentious.

I declined our hostess's offer of herbal tea, which she went into the neighboring kitchen with my mother to make, and chose to stand alongside Sean, just far enough apart to keep the doorway to the kitchen in my field of view. It was not a gesture that went unnoticed by either man present.

When I glanced over, I found Sean and my father had locked gazes like two rutting stags battling for supremacy. I shifted uncomfortably under the weight of knowledge that I was the dubious prize they were fighting over.

It was juvenile and pointless and would not, I thought bitterly, help any of us to do what we had to.

Miranda came back through, balancing a tray containing cups and a china teapot and set it down on the low table in the living room.

"There now," she said brightly, plonking herself down on the comfortably faded sofa and patting the cushion alongside her. "Come and sit, Elizabeth, and I'll pour."

"Miranda, we need to talk," my father said gravely. "About Jeremy."

For a moment it was as if she hadn't heard. Then something of the light dimmed out of her, sending her shoulders drooping. I looked at the top of her bowed head and realized that the pale line of her part revealed gray roots. When she looked up and her face had lost its animation, the lines framing her eyes and mouth seemed deeper cut and much more apparent.

"I know," she said quietly, hands restless in her lap. "I've been following the news — I haven't been able to avoid it." She looked up suddenly, her gaze flitting nervously before finally coming to rest on my father. "So . . . *did* you give Jeremy morphine, Richard?"

My father's head tilted. "No," he said, his voice utterly calm and laced with regret rather than anger. "Actually, I was going to ask you the same question."

"No. No, I didn't," she said. She sat up straighter, looked him firmly in the eye. "I wish I had, but I was selfish enough to treasure every moment I had with him, right to the end. And yes, when it was all over, I admit I was relieved, for both of us." Her voice wavered, taking her lower lip with it. She took a moment to steady both. My mother put a comforting hand on her arm. "I wish I'd been brave enough to put an end to his suffering, but I wasn't."

My father closed his eyes briefly in acknowledgment and I saw a fraction of the tension go out of him.

"Somebody was," he said, with no more than a trace of irony, "and now they seem determined to cover up that act of mercy."

"But surely the hospital's to blame," she

said, anger leveling the wobbles out of her voice. "A mistake —"

"Miranda," my father said gently. "There are no circumstances under which one would give a patient such an amount of morphine."

Not if you wanted them to live.

She took in a sharp breath, as if he'd spoken the words out loud, a soft gasp.

"He was in tremendous pain. I thought, maybe . . . but you're right, of course."

"The thing is, darling," my mother said carefully, "that someone's trying to make it look as though Richard's lying about this whole thing. The hospital are denying poor Jeremy was given the morphine at all and the drug company, Storax, seem to be doing everything they can to . . . silence us." She ducked her head, waited until Miranda met her gaze. Something the other woman seemed suddenly reluctant to do. "So you see, if there's anything you aren't telling us — anything at all — we do rather need to know."

Miranda didn't answer right away, mutely pouring the tea as though grateful for something to do with her hands. She filled and passed cups to my parents, her brows knitted.

"Your husband is dead," Sean said quietly.

It was the first time he'd spoken since we'd entered the house, and Miranda's head turned almost blindly towards him. "There's nothing you can do for him now except tell the truth."

She sat for a moment longer, a small huddled figure, then got restlessly to her feet. With an impatient frown my father opened his mouth to speak but my mother shook her head and, to my surprise, he buttoned his lip.

Miranda went to the bookcase near the fireplace and picked up a framed photograph that had been lying facedown. She stared at it a moment and ran a hand lovingly across the glass, then caught herself in the self-indulgent gesture and hurried over to thrust the frame into Sean's hands.

"That was taken four years ago," she said, not breaking stride, crossing to a bureau against the far wall and digging through one of the drawers, throwing sentences back over her shoulder. "Virgin Islands. Our wedding anniversary. Three weeks. It was glorious."

I edged over to Sean and glanced at the framed photo. In the foreground was a tanned man wearing close-fit swimming trunks, leaning out from the rail of a small yacht. From the angle of the horizon, the yacht was heeled over close into the wind, sails snapped bar-taut.

The man was standing on the side rail, supported by a safety wire, with his feet spread wide to highlight well-defined calves and muscular thighs. His back was braced, giving the impression of strength and agility. Wrapped in his left hand, like the reins of a Roman chariot, were the cleated-off lines for one of the sails, a brightly colored spinnaker.

Behind him, at the tiller, you could just see a woman. She was wearing sunglasses and a shade over her forehead, and she was slimmer and undoubtedly happier, but the brilliant smile could only have been Miranda's. Both of them were waving to whoever held the camera, their movements synchronized.

I looked up. Miranda was back in front of us, waiting. She pushed a second picture into my hands. An unframed snapshot, curling at the edges, one corner bent over as though it had been shoved away out of sight rather than proudly displayed.

The second photo had been taken in this very room, I realized, the décor turned stark and gaudy by the harshness of the flash that had been used to illuminate the shot.

It was of an old man, sitting slumped

awkwardly in the chair my father currently occupied. He was smiling determinedly for the camera, an orange party hat slanted on his head. But his face was gaunt, the graying skin tight across his protruding bones. Like it hurt him almost beyond endurance to produce such a show of happiness, but he would have died rather than admit it.

Pain was written loud and clear in every line of his body, from his twisted spine to his clawlike hands, the unnatural tilt of his neck. His feet were encased in ill-fitting Velcro booties and part of a Zimmer walking frame was just visible at one side of the shot.

There was something about the line of his mouth, the shape of his teeth, his ears, that was familiar, but it took a moment to put it together.

"This is Jeremy?" I said, not quite positive enough for it to be a statement.

"They both are," she said sadly. "That was taken in April this year — on his forty-third birthday."

I flipped back and forth between the pictures. His Korean heritage showed, I noted, in the fold of his eyelids, the shape of his nose. Even through the wastage, he retained a residual attractiveness.

Sean silently handed me the framed photo and I gave them both back to her. She put them down on the table, near the tea tray, careful to leave the one taken on the yacht uppermost.

"I'm very sorry for your loss," I said. Not just his death, but the manner of it.

She glanced at me, dully, and gave a mechanical nod. A standard meaningless acknowledgment of a standard meaningless line of condolence. But what else did we have to offer?

"When did he start to get sick?" Sean asked into the uncomfortable silence.

Miranda cleared her throat. "A year ago, in the spring," she said, her voice very calm. "He always went mountain biking in the White Mountains with some of his buddies from the hospital every year, soon as the snow cleared. They'd been gone a couple of days when I got a phone call. He had a fall, they told me. A bad one. I expected . . ." Her voice trailed off into a helpless shrug. "I don't know what I expected, but when I got to the hospital, the doctors there said it looked like he'd been dropped off a building. His spine had practically exploded. It didn't make sense."

She broke off, gulped in air to steady herself before she could go on. "We went from specialist to specialist but nobody seemed to have a clue. Over the months that followed the accident, the breaks wouldn't heal. Jeremy lost more than three inches in height and his back began to curve from the constant fracturing of his ribs and vertebrae." Her eyes traveled almost resentfully over the width of Sean's shoulders, his obvious strength, and swapped to me. "My wonderful, athletic husband was crumbling to dust right in front of me." She drew in a shaky breath. "Eventually, they diagnosed spinal osteoporosis, but by then it was almost too late to do anything about it." She flicked a quick glance across at my father. "That's when I called you."

My father put down his teacup. "Almost," he said, "but not quite."

"What do you mean?" Miranda tried to hedge, but the flush that stole up her neck told another story.

"When I first suggested trying Jeremy on the new Storax treatment, you were opposed to the idea, at a time when one would have assumed that you'd pursue any avenue open to you. I had to convince you to give your permission as his next of kin. At the time, I thought it was because the treatment was still in the experimental stage, but you knew it was pointless, didn't you, Miranda?" he said slowly. "You knew he'd already tried it and that it hadn't worked."

"I — yes," she muttered. "He knew the pharmaceutical company were screening their test patients very carefully and he was afraid he wouldn't be selected, so . . . no, he didn't tell them he had tried it already." She met his level gaze and flushed again, but then her chin came up in a kind of defiant appeal that he understand the motives for her duplicity. "He was desperate."

"It would seem there was a very good reason Jeremy wouldn't have been selected," my father said, ignoring her mute plea. "I believe Storax knew that with certain patients there would be catastrophic side effects, a rapid acceleration of the progress of the disease. And I believe they're doing everything in their power to cover that up."

"But that's terrible," Miranda said, frowning, shaking her head. "I can't believe it."

"After Jeremy died," my mother put in, her voice calm and a little remote, "Storax sent some people over to England to . . . threaten me, if Richard didn't admit to things — awful things — designed to ruin his reputation."

Miranda groped for the back of the nearest chair, stumbled round and sank into it as her knees buckled.

"But they've been so kind," she said, face blank. "I've had e-mails from someone in their legal department, offering me advice. They've been so helpful, I —"

"Who from in their legal department?" Sean demanded. "And what kind of advice?"

Miranda's head turned blindly in his direction, but I knew she didn't see him. "From someone named Terry O'Loughlin," she said. "We've never spoken — just e-mails — advising me to sue."

I glanced at Sean. "Why would Storax advise Miranda to file a claim if they knew about the side effects?" I said. "I can't believe this is an isolated case, so surely they're setting themselves up to lose millions in similar suits?"

"Not if the case against them collapses because Miranda's expert witness has suddenly lost all his credibility," Sean said pointedly. "Because he's a drunken lecher, for example."

My father folded a little in his chair, unconsciously reminding me of the picture of a sunken Jeremy Lee at his last birthday party.

"The people Storax sent must have known that as soon as it was confirmed Jeremy had already taken the drug, I'd start asking questions," he murmured, running a hand across his forehead. "He was dying anyway, but they couldn't afford to wait . . . and so they finished him."

"And then sent Blaylock and Kaminski over to the UK to baby-sit Elizabeth," Sean agreed. "They moved fast to cover this up."

My father allowed himself a brief dismissive glare. "Jeremy's records should speak for themselves," he said stiffly. "I need to see them."

Sean shook his head at this display of naïveté. "Don't you think that the first thing Storax would have done after getting you thrown out of the hospital and tying you in knots with that reporter, was to walk off with his records, or alter what they didn't want known? Without them, you can't prove a thing."

"Jeremy kept his own records," Miranda said suddenly. She looked up and her eyes had cleared, focused. "A journal of his illness. How it progressed, symptoms, treatments. Everything he tried and the effect it had. It's in the den. Would that help?"

"A journal?" my father said, sounding vaguely offended that secrets had been kept from him. As if the keeping of private notes alongside his own somehow signified a lack of trust. "Yes, yes it would. If you're sure you don't mind our reading it now?"

"Of course not. There's nothing really

private in there." Miranda jumped up and hurried towards the door. "I'll get it."

"If we have Jeremy's own account, that might save us a lot of time and trouble," my father said when she'd gone, giving us a tight, tired smile. "I wonder why he felt the need to keep it?"

"If he knew he was either taking or being given something that wasn't aboveboard, he might have wanted his own record. Just as long as it can be relied upon."

"Jeremy was not only a doctor of some repute," my mother said, as though that fact alone put him beyond question, "but he was also meticulous as a person."

Sean's eyebrow lifted. "Even when he was in constant pain and pumped full of morphine?"

"It's very reliable." Miranda's voice from the doorway was distinctly chilly. "Considering I was the one filling it in for him during his last weeks. Everything they gave him, every time he cried out with the pain, I wrote it down in that damned book."

"Sorry," Sean said, not looking particularly contrite even so. "It's part of my job to play devil's advocate."

She nodded. "He stopped taking the Storax treatment as soon as he realized it wasn't helping, but he never thought for a moment it might actually have been making him worse. He made me swear not to tell you, Richard," she added, throwing my father another anxious look. "He knew he was dying and he was afraid if it came out that he'd dosed himself, our medical insurance might be void. He was trying to protect me. . . ."

It was only then that we noticed her hands were empty.

"Miranda," my father said, rising, "I can assure you that I will not allow confidential medical information about Jeremy fall into anyone's hands but my own. You needn't worry about —"

"It's not that," she said, looking baffled and not a little afraid. "After his death I put the journal away — I could hardly bear to look at it. It was just a reminder —" She broke off, shook her head as if to clear it. "I put the journal in the top right-hand drawer of his desk, same place as always. But when I went to get it just now, well, it was gone. . . ."

NINETEEN

"Collingwood's pissed," Parker said.

"Tell him to take more water with it," I said recklessly. Even at the other end of a bad mobile phone line, in a moving vehicle, I heard his sigh. Parker was a pretty cosmopolitan guy and he got British humor better than most, but there were days when he simply didn't find it funny. Plainly, today was one of them.

"Okay — Collingwood's pissed *off,*" he amended heavily. "That any clearer?"

"Crystal," I said, letting my voice drawl. "What's he got to be so pissed off about?"

"By the sounds of it, he expected you to keep your father closer to New York, so he'd be available to answer questions about Storax."

"Well, he's the one who left us dangling for days," I said, allowing my irritation to flare. "And he's the one who told us to get out of town for a while."

"Yeah," Parker said dryly, "but I think he hoped you'd go to Long Island, someplace like that. Not Boston."

"And *I* hoped that when he said he'd keep that blond bitch on a tight leash, he meant it," I said, as quietly as I could. Even so, I caught an offended clearing of throats from the rear seat. Across to my left, Sean took his eyes off the road for long enough to flash me an amused smile. It was the most animation he'd shown all day.

"Hey — you can't always control your people as much as you'd like," Parker said pointedly. "Don't push it, Charlie. *He's* doing *you* a favor."

"It was supposed to be a two-way street," I said. "But so far, the traffic's been traveling only in one direction. What's he been doing all this time?"

Another sigh, longer this time. "Government departments move slowly — you should know that."

"Yeah, well, this guy makes a glacier look positively speedy."

We were on I-95 again, heading north. It was a little after 1:30 in the afternoon. We'd spent the last couple of hours searching Miranda Lee's house for the missing journal of her husband's last days — without success. Suspicious that this wasn't merely a case of absentmindedness, Sean and I went over the place thoroughly and it was Sean, naturally, who found the slight scratches around the face of the lock on the back door, showing that it had been recently finessed.

Miranda had been coping fine until the realization really sank in that someone had invaded her home and had picked through her most private belongings. At that point, she spent some time in the downstairs loo, clutching the toilet bowl with both hands while she heaved. My mother stayed with her, gently pulling Miranda's hair back out of the way and wringing out damp cloths to wipe the clammy sweat from her face.

Meanwhile, my father collared Sean and me in the living room. "She needs protection," he said, his face almost as pale as Miranda's. Across the other side of the hallway we heard the muffled sound of renewed retching. "What would have happened if she'd been here when they broke in? It isn't safe for her to be left alone."

"She should go and stay with friends or a relative," Sean said. "There's only two of us, covering the two of you, twenty-four/seven. We can't be everywhere at once."

"So, call in more people," my father said, his arrogance surfacing again.

Sean just stared. "And who's going to pay for that?" he demanded in that quiet deadly tone of his. "Charlie and I have stuck with you like bloody glue since this happened, which is costing Parker thousands of dollars in lost revenue. Not to mention the damage your exploits have already done to the business."

"I might have known it would be the money you cared about," my father sneered.

"I don't care about it and wouldn't have accepted anything, had you offered it," Sean said coldly. "But that's just the point. Not once — *not once* — have you offered to pay the going rate for our services."

"But . . . Charlotte's family," my father said, sounding scandalized.

"Yeah," Sean said, his face cold, "but — as you've always made *so* abundantly clear, Richard — I'm not."

The end result of Sean's parting shot was that my father grudgingly announced he would personally pay Parker's fees for someone to come and stay with Miranda. It was the lady herself who turned him down flat.

"I have a friend over in Vermont I haven't seen since college," she said. "She just had a baby and I've been promising I'll go visit with her for a few days — a week maybe.

Help her out with the older boys, let her get some rest." She gave a watery smile. "Give me something else to think about, too."

"We'll get to the bottom of this," my father said gravely, in the same tone of voice I imagined him assuring a patient they'd diagnose some mystery illness. "I promise."

Miranda had no idea who'd taken her late husband's journal, but, whoever they were, they'd been pretty subtle about it. Despite my father's concerns over her safety, so far there had been no overt threats made towards her. And she had no idea when the robbery might have taken place. She hadn't noticed anything amiss and claimed it had been weeks since she'd last looked in the desk drawer where it had been kept. She'd looked sad when she'd said it. Too many painful memories there, I guessed.

We'd left her organizing her trip and were headed back up towards Boston when Parker called to inform us of Collingwood's displeasure.

Now I asked, "And how did he know we *aren't* on Long Island, anyway?"

This time, I heard the smile in Parker's voice at my naïveté. "He's with the government, Charlie," he said. "They have access to just about anything that's logged-on to a computer — credit cards, cell phones, flight manifests, car-rental companies, hotel registers. You name it."

"Shit," I muttered, earning me another clearly audible intake of breath from the rear.

"That's one way of putting it," Parker said dryly. "One last thing," he added. "Collingwood knows that you're carrying — must have pulled the flight details and picked up that you checked firearms — and he knows you don't have the permits for Massachusetts. He's hinted that he could have you both picked up just for that. If things get hairy up there, they're going to go bad pretty fast. Just remember. And watch your backs, both of you."

"We will," I said gravely. "Thanks, Parker."

"You're welcome," he said, matching his tone to mine. "Keep in touch."

As soon as I'd hit the button to end the call, Sean said brusquely, "It's obviously not good news. So, what gives?"

Briefly, concisely, I told him Parker's latest information about Collingwood, aware as I spoke of the solid weight of the SIG at my waist. Already, I'd feel lost without it, especially in light of this morning's discovery.

"So, what do we do now?" I said when I

was done, twisting in my seat so I could take in my parents' anxious faces. "I'm open to suggestions."

"We go to the hospital," my father said slowly. He glanced up, mouth thinning as the decision firmed. "We go and look at Jeremy's records at the source, so to speak."

"Don't you think," Sean put in, "that whoever took the journal from Miranda's house will also have covered that angle? And be expecting us?"

"Probably," my father said, frowning, "but they may well have assumed that the records were secure where they were, and best left alone."

"Interesting you should use the word *secure* there," Sean said, flicking his eyes to my father in the rearview mirror. "How difficult is it going to be to gain access to them?"

My father gave a tight little smile. "Well," he murmured, "let's go and find out, shall we?"

But first he leaned forwards in his seat and directed Sean through the suburbs to one of the numerous small shopping malls, and then to a particular store that seemed to sell brightly colored pajamas, if its window display was anything to go by. It was only when we got inside that I discovered the place sold surgical scrubs.

"If one wants to blend in with a forest," my father murmured, "it's best to dress like a tree, don't you think?"

The question that formed in my head — how my father knew the place was even here — was answered as soon as we walked through the door. The elderly man behind the counter greeted him by name like an old friend, and asked how the bone work was going. He greeted the next customer with the same easy geniality.

We moved deeper into the store and Sean nudged my father's arm as soon as we were out of earshot. "Is this the only surgical-garb shop in the area?"

"Of course not," my father said, nonplussed by the question. "But this is the place Jeremy recommended. He used to use it all the time, and they should have everything we need here."

Sean suppressed an annoyed sigh. "Yeah, including an owner with photographic recall," he said, "who will no doubt remember us six months after we've gone — and be able to describe us very nicely to the police. Did it not occur to you that picking somewhere you're *not* known might have been a better idea?"

"I'm not planning on engaging in any

activity that would interest the police," my father shot back in a savage whisper, trying to hide the pink stain that had risen from his shirt collar. He had, after all, engaged in plenty so far. "Besides, all we're going to do is look at some records, not burn the place to the ground."

"Well, just supposing things get a little more *involved* than that?" Sean said.

My father looked him up and down with insulting calculation. "Well, I'm sure I can rely on you to start a fire, if need be."

He stalked along the shelves and quickly outfitted the pair of us in dull hospital garb. It was not, I concluded quickly, designed to flatter. My father was annoyed that Sean wouldn't carry his selections to the cash register for him.

"If you want to shop, carry it yourself," Sean said flatly.

There was a very good tactical reason for Sean needing to keep his hands free, but by not explaining it, he just came across as rude and argumentative. I scowled at him behind my father's back. Sean gave me a bland stare in return.

I had to give my father a swift nudge in the ribs when he would have dragged out his platinum AmEx to pay for the gear. We were already leaving a trail that a bloodhound with a heavy cold could have followed through a nest of skunks. There was no point, I reasoned, as I avoided eye contact with the security camera on the way out, in making things worse.

TWENTY

The hospital where Jeremy Lee had been both a doctor and a patient was set a long way back from the road on a huge sprawling piece of land south of Boston itself.

I still had trouble getting my head round how wasteful America was with its land. Unless you were in the heart of a big city, nobody seemed to bother about redeveloping brownfield sites. They just boarded up the old building and went and broke ground somewhere fresh. Even the smallest business had a car park the size of Sweden.

It seemed to take forever to reach the hospital entrance. We drove in through carefully landscaped grounds that looked more like a golf club than a medical facility, with fiercely posted speed limits. I hoped the ambulances had a faster approach road, or their emergency patients were likely to expire between the main road and the front door.

We'd already detoured via a roadside rest stop for Sean and I to change into our disguises. My father had decided to bluff it out in the role he played best — arrogant surgeon. He would walk my mother in through the front entrance and we'd meet up inside. Entirely from memory, he gave us precise directions to the elevators and the stairwell.

"They're highly unlikely to have removed Jeremy's records from the system yet," he said. "All I need is an empty office with a computer terminal." His eyes flicked over the pair of us. "You won't be able to take your guns."

Sean's silence spoke louder than any verbal disagreement would have done but eventually he sighed and shoved the Glock, still in its holster, into the Navigator's glove box. I added my SIG and, when I glanced at him, caught my father's satisfied little smile, like he'd just won a point of principle rather than necessity.

I knew Sean was as unhappy about this as he was about relying on my father's intel, but he bore it without comment. He'd always been able to listen to orders and evaluate them in a detached manner, even when they were given by officers he despised.

The plan we loosely devised was that Sean and I would go in via the underground ambulance entrance in the guise of nicotine junkies. To this end, Sean had even picked up a discarded cigarette packet and straightened it out, to add a layer of verisimilitude. The empty packet sat on top of the dash and the strange pervasive smell of unburned tobacco leached into the atmosphere inside the Navigator.

"What about me?" my mother asked. She had no surgical wear. "I can play some useful part, surely? If you recall, darling, I was awfully good at amateur dramatics when I was younger."

"You were." My father smiled at her fondly if somewhat patronizingly, I thought, and patted her hand. "In that case, we'll hold you in reserve as our secret weapon."

She sat up a little straighter and smiled back, hearing only praise.

"Look, can we go and get this over with before I go old and gray?" I said, a little tartly, earning a reproachful look from both of them. When was I going to outgrow *that*?

We parked up as far away from the security cameras as we could manage and parted company, walking quickly. As my father had predicted, nobody paid us the slightest attention as we ambled inside the building, discussing a nonexistent cop show we were supposed to have watched on TV the night before.

The unflattering skullcap was uncomfortable to someone whose only regular headgear was a bike helmet. I tugged the cap down over my forehead, rubbing the skin carefully as I did so. The lump from when I'd head-butted Vondie in my mother's drawing room seemed to be taking a long time to disappear. I wondered how her nose was feeling.

The four of us rendezvoused in the ER, where we were swallowed up in the usual bustle. My mother was sitting in the waiting area, close to the stairs, leafing through a magazine. My father, I noticed, had already managed to purloin a white coat and a stethoscope from somewhere, together with what looked suspiciously like an official ID card on a lanyard around his neck. No doubt he knew the layout of the place well enough to know where such things were kept, and the overwhelming self-confidence to simply help himself. I'd no idea his criminal tendencies were so well developed.

"Why couldn't *we* just do that?" I grouched quietly, gesturing to my shapeless garb.

Sean's brow quirked. He was also wearing

the delightful little skullcap, but on him it looked good. That wasn't a stretch. On him, just about anything looked good.

"Because there would be too many chiefs and not enough Indians," my father said.

"These days," Sean said, "I think you'll find that's *Native Americans.*"

"If you've *quite* finished," my father muttered, "perhaps we could concentrate on the matter at hand? There are a couple of security people loitering near the lift and I'd rather not push my luck *too* far, if I can help it." He gave a small, almost embarrassed smile. "They may have been briefed to keep an eye out for me."

"So, we need a diversion," Sean said, eyes narrowed. He turned to me and opened his mouth but my father held up his hand.

"Leave this to me." He strode away, looking very much at home in this environment.

Along one side of the emergency room was a row of three glass-walled rooms where patients could be treated more fully. There were Venetian blinds for when more privacy was required. Like watching a movie with the sound turned off, we saw my father enter the middle room where an unattended patient appeared to be either unconscious or asleep, wired up to various monitors. After a quick flick through the chart, he moved alongside the bed and did something that we hardly caught, before leaving quickly. For a few moments nothing happened. Then an alarm began to sound and the nearest medical staff rushed past him to deal with it.

My father calmly walked back to us.

"Shall we go?" he suggested quietly, not breaking stride as he reached us and swept past, heading for the stairs. "It won't take them more than a few moments to work out what I've done."

"What the hell *did* you do?" I demanded in a whisper. "Kill him?"

"Hardly." He shot me a pained little glance as we sidestepped the security personnel whose eyes, naturally enough, were on the drama in front of them and not on us. "I merely loosened his blood-oxygen sensor. Even a *very* junior intern," he added with a slightly scathing note in his voice, "would know enough to check that before attempting to resuscitate him."

"Oh well," I said under my breath as we took the stairs two at a time and the clamor dropped away behind us, "*that's* all right, then."

He led us without hesitation to the elevator, then up another two floors and through a maze of corridors, finally halting outside an unmarked door that looked no different from any of the others. He tried the handle. It wouldn't turn. My father's face took on a piqued look, as if the locked door was a personal affront.

"This one, I think you *can* leave to me," Sean murmured, producing a pick set from his pocket and moving my father aside. The lock was clearly intended to keep out casual trespassers rather than those with more serious intent, and it yielded to Sean's nimble fingers in less than a minute.

He straightened and pushed the door open, meeting my father's sharp gaze with a bland expression on his face. I could see that my father really wanted to snipe at Sean further for his obviously illegal abilities, but even he recognized it would be hypocritical to do so under the circumstances.

Inside, the room turned out to be a cramped office, its floor space three-quarters occupied by two chairs and a desk, which was empty apart from a double filing tray, a telephone, and a blank computer terminal. All the usual office detritus of books, photographs and paperwork was missing, leaving shadows in the dust and faded patches on the walls.

My father crossed to the desk and sat behind it, hitting the power button on the computer as he reached for his glasses.

"How did you know this would be empty?" I asked.

His eyes flicked over me briefly. "This was Jeremy's office," he said shortly, and turned his attention back to the screen. "His was a particular specialty. Recruiting his replacement will take some time."

"Are you sure you can access his records from here?" Sean asked.

"I'll answer that in just a moment," my father said, attacking the keyboard once the computer had booted itself up. I tried not to hang over his shoulder as he tapped his name and password into the required boxes.

The computer thought for a moment, then came up with the message: ACCESS DENIED.

"Damn," I muttered. "What now?"

"Hm, they have been thorough, haven't they?" my father murmured, not sounding at all surprised. "But not *that* thorough, I think."

This time, he typed *Jeremy Lee* into the name field, and a seven-character password. I caught only the first couple of letters — *M* and *I* — but I could guess the rest. His wife's name. I remembered the photograph Miranda had showed us of the pair of them on the yacht, happy, carefree, and my throat constricted.

My father hit ENTER. The computer clicked and whirred again, thought about being awkward while we held our collective breath, and then gave up its secrets.

It didn't take more than a few seconds for my father to navigate his way to the appropriate section of the Electronic Medical Record system and key in the name of his dead colleague. Within moments, Jeremy Lee's official patient records were on screen for us to see.

My father leaned closer, scanning the information with the mental dexterity of a natural speed reader. His face darkened as he read on in silence, his only movement to stab the key to page down. We didn't interrupt him until he was done.

"Fabrication," he snapped, almost throwing himself back in the chair. "Maybe they've been more thorough than I first thought."

"What does it say?"

"That Jeremy suffered multiple fractures of his thoracic vertebrae in his fall, causing hemiplegia — lower-body paralysis — which led to a urinary tract infection, in turn leading to septicemia, which killed him."

"And is that feasible?"

"As a course of events? Perfectly," my

father said, even more clipped than usual. "Hemiplegia often causes such problems, in that the patient can't adequately empty his bladder. Having a lot of urine in the bladder at all times is a situation ripe for a UTI." He nodded toward the screen. "They note that he had an indwelling Foley catheter to keep his bladder empty, which is a common enough route for infection. All very logical," he said bitterly. "All very made up."

"So, no mention of osteoporosis?" Sean said. "Spinal or otherwise?"

My father gave a snort. "Oh yes, as a minor side issue. But as a major factor of his condition? No." He scrolled back up through the document. "Nor is the Storax treatment mentioned anywhere in his records, despite the fact that the technicians Storax sent clearly identified its presence. They state he was on heavy-duty antibiotics for the infection, and OxyContin for the pain. Nothing else."

"What about cause of death?" I asked.

"Well, I'd hardly expect them to admit in black and white that it was the hundred milligrams of morphine injected into his IV line that did the job." He unhooked his glasses and almost threw them onto the desktop, hard enough for them to clatter against the surface, and stared after them as though he was going to be able to divine some kind of answer in the grain.

Eventually, he looked up, hollow-eyed. "We're at a dead end. Jeremy's already been cremated and they've covered their tracks to the point where it would be just my word against theirs. And they've ensured that my word would not carry very much weight at the moment."

Sean glanced at his watch. "We need to get out of here," he said. "That little stunt you pulled downstairs is likely to have them looking for a practical joker."

My father reached towards the keyboard again, but Sean leaned across him and switched on the printer. "Print it all out and we'll take it with us," he said. "Mrs. Lee will be able to testify how much of it is false."

For a moment, my father looked scandalized at the thought of actually stealing a patient's records. Then I saw the realization hit that the originals had been stolen well before he'd been anywhere near them.

A watched printer, like a watched kettle, takes forever to boil. This one looked modern but might as well have been a monk with a quill pen dipped in ink for all the time it took to go through its start-up routine and begin spitting out the pages.

Just as the last one settled into the catch tray, the phone on the desk began to ring.

My father glanced up. "They're on the ball," he said tightly. "They must have the file flagged on the EMR and they're checking up on who's accessing it."

Sean snatched the papers out of the printer. "Okay, we're out of here," he said to my father. "You may as well leave the computer on — they already know we've been in there." He jerked his head to me. "I'll take him out the way we came in. You get your mother and meet us, okay?"

I nodded and opened the door a crack as if expecting to see security men rushing to detain us. The corridor outside was deserted.

I slipped through the gap and made for the nearest staircase, taking it at a run and jumping the last few steps onto each half landing as I went, heedless of the residual bruises from my taxi encounter. After the first couple of flights my left leg started complaining bitterly at this treatment, but I ignored it.

I reached the ER and spotted my mother sitting in the waiting area, pretending to leaf through a magazine. She looked tense and awkward, but so did everyone else there. They all looked up when I hurried into view.

"Ma'am, would you come with me, please?" I said in my best generic East Coast drawl.

I didn't have to feign the urgency in my voice, nor she the way her face paled at my words, but nobody watching saw anything amiss. Some even threw her sympathetic glances as she jumped to her feet and followed me out.

"What it is?" she said as soon as we were out of earshot. "Where's Richard?"

"He's fine," I said. "We got what we came for, but they know we're here."

I was aware of a tension in my chest that had nothing to do with running down a flight of stairs. We'd pushed our luck coming here to begin with, and were pushing it even further with every minute we stayed. If anything, the disguises made it worse, like being caught out of uniform behind enemy lines. As if it made the difference between being treated as a legit prisoner of war, or being shot outright as a spy.

Not that I was expecting hospital security to gun us down if they got hold of us, but when we turned what should have been almost the final corner to our escape route, I found it was a close run thing.

The two security guards we'd slipped past earlier had cornered Sean and my father by a bank of elevators. They looked up sharply when I appeared.

"What the hell is going on?" I demanded, East Coast again.

There was a pause, then one of the guards said, "Nothing that need concern you, ma'am."

My brain clicked over. Clearly, they'd been looking for my father alone. Sean, I surmised, had been caught up in this purely by association. Any threat I might present was quickly weighed and dismissed.

"Of course it does," I said, pushing a note of weary belligerence into my voice. I advanced, careful in my positioning, forcing the guard who'd spoken to turn away from Sean slightly to keep me in full view, just in case we couldn't talk our way out of this. Out of the corner of my eye I saw Sean shift his balance. Almost imperceptible, but enough.

I stabbed a finger towards my father. "This man's a doctor — a damned good one. I need his expertise for a consult. Right now."

"We got orders to hold him," the guard said, but I saw the crease in his brow as the indecision and the worry crept in. He glanced at his partner for support, received only a halfhearted, puzzled shrug in return.

I sighed and deliberately lowered my voice. "Look, whatever the problem is, can't it wait? I got a kid about to go into the OR whose legs are in a million pieces. You want to explain to his mother why he's gonna spend the rest of his life in a goddamn wheelchair?"

I waved an arm vaguely behind me and felt rather than saw my mother step in closer. The guard who'd been doing all the talking let his eyes flick over her. Then he frowned again, his expression hardening.

My eyes met Sean's. *He's not going to buy it.*

I know. Be ready.

The guard opened his mouth, got as far as, "Look, Doc, I got my —"

"Oh, Doctor!" my mother cried suddenly. "Is this the surgeon? Is this the one who can save my poor Darcy's legs?"

Darcy? Where the hell did that *come from?*

I turned. My mother had come to a faltering stop, a picture of anxiety, twisting her hands together in front of her breast like a tragic Shakespearean actress. All she needed was a handkerchief to dab at her eyes, but I thought that might have been overplaying the role a little, even for her.

"Ah, Mrs. Bennet," I said, as the *Pride and Prejudice* reference finally sank in. Besides, wasn't Mrs. Bennet supposed to be a scatterbrain? "There may be some kind of problem, I'm afraid. These *gentlemen,*" I said ominously, indicating the security guards as I moved to comfort her, "want to detain Mr. Foxcroft and —"

"Oh, but you can't!" my mother cried, her voice rising, jagged. Her eyes swiveled wildly from one to the other. They couldn't hold her gaze, shuffling awkwardly. They fetched and held and ejected people. They didn't get into conversation with them. Not for minimum wage across a twelve-hour shift. And clearly not enough to be thrown by my mother's obvious English accent, either.

"Look, lady —" the guard tried again.

"Tell them, Dr. Wickham!" my mother said, wheeling to face Sean, her face imploring. *My God, were those actual tears?* "Tell them he's my only hope!"

And with that she gave a kind of a wail and collapsed into the arms of the guard who'd been doing the talking.

"Aw, lady, for Chrissake . . ." He tried to paw her away, like she was contagious, keeping his head back and his chin tucked in. Finally, he managed to get a grip on my mother's upper arms and hoisted her away. "Go on, get him out of here," he said to me in desperation. "But if anyone asks, you ain't seen us and we ain't seen you! Okay?"

"Okay," I agreed gravely. "Don't worry, you won't see us."

The four of us disappeared along the corridor as fast as we could manage, round a corner and out through the first exit we came to that didn't claim to be alarmed.

"My God, Elizabeth," my father muttered, and his voice might have been shaky and breathless purely because we were all but running across the car park towards the Navigator, but that wouldn't account for the note of wonder I heard there, too. "My God . . ."

Sean hit the remote and the locks popped. We piled in and he had the engine cranked and the vehicle already rolling before the last door was slammed shut behind us.

My mother fastened her seat belt and smoothed her skirt, frowning a little at a crease in the material. Then she looked up and smiled and, just for a moment, there was a distinct twinkle in her eye — a frisson of pleasure, excitement, even pure thrill.

"That was nicely played — well done," Sean said, but his praise was guarded. "You took quite a risk, though. If they'd tagged even one genuine member of staff, we'd all have been sunk."

I glanced at him, surprised by the downbeat tone. "Come on, Sean," I said. "It was inspired and, anyway, it worked! Isn't that what counts?" I smiled at him, but he didn't return it. "Anyway, what alternatives did we have?"

He didn't answer right away, concentrating on his driving. He was making a series of random turns, fast enough to put distance between us and the hospital, unobtrusive enough not to get us pulled over.

I frowned. Sean was cautious, yes, but he'd never been mean when it came to giving due credit, and he admired inventiveness. At that moment he glanced sideways and the brooding darkness of his gaze almost made me flinch.

What the hell . . .

My father leaned forwards in his seat. "What's the matter, Sean?" he said in a clipped, almost taunting tone. "Did Elizabeth's actions disappoint you in some way?"

"*Disappoint* me?" Sean echoed, his expression blanking as his voice grew lethally soft. "Of course not. Just how would they do that?"

I fired my father a warning look but his eyes were locked onto the narrow slot of the rearview mirror, which was all he could see of Sean's set face, and he didn't catch the gesture. Or, if he did, he chose to ignore it.

"You were about to start a fight," my father said on a note of disdain. "It seems to be your first instinctive response to any difficult situation. Then Charlotte and Elizabeth managed to talk our way out — rather successfully, I thought. Does that fact wound your ego in some way?"

I was torn between pleasure at the unexpected praise, and anger at his attack on Sean.

"It never hurts to plan for the worst," was all Sean said. "And I think you'll find that Charlie was just as prepared to take direct action."

"Hm," my father said. He let his eyes slide over me, and there was something vaguely dissatisfied in that brief appraisal. "How much of that is due to your influence, I wonder."

"Some," Sean said. "But have you considered how much of it is down to you?"

"Oh, cut it out — both of you," I snapped. "Stop talking about me like I'm not damn well here. Or at least have the decency to wait until I really *am* not here before you dissect my character."

"I think you'll find what we're doing is vivisection," Sean said, showing his teeth in a tight little smile totally devoid of humor. "For it to be dissection, I believe you'd have to be dead."

"Well then," I said coldly, thinking back to February, to a few long seconds in a frozen forest in the snow when my heart had briefly given up the fight. "In that case you missed your chance, both of you."

TWENTY-ONE

Despite Sean's evasive driving techniques — or perhaps because of them — there were no signs of anyone following us after we left the hospital. Eventually, we headed back towards the Back Bay area, stopping at a little Japanese noodle bar, little more than a storefront café, for an early meal.

My father and Sean kept up their quietly confrontational stance throughout, leaving me and my mother to play peacemaker. My mother was, understandably, still invigorated by her performance at the hospital. I had to keep trying to muffle her enthusiastic recall.

It was fortunate that we were the only customers in at that hour, and the blank-faced girl who took our order didn't seem able to process more than the basics in English. Still, I didn't like the idea of anyone being close enough to eavesdrop on our conversation.

Stopping my mother chattering on about every thought process she'd gone through, however, proved easier said than done. In the end I had to distract her with talk of distant family holidays and old school friends I'd long since lost touch with, but who, for some strange reason, still seemed to be in regular contact with my mother.

And even that turned out to be a bit of a double-edged sword as far as topics went. Every single damn one of them, it seemed, had married well and produced hordes of startlingly precocious and beautiful children for their grandparents to dote on.

Eventually, her excitement dimmed enough even for her to recognize the static silence that clung between Sean and my father. The pauses grew longer, then joined up into one long pause, unpunctuated by speech altogether. By that time I was thankful for the respite.

When we'd finished our last pot of green tea, my mother pushed her chair back and announced she needed the ladies' room. When I rose to join her, she gave me a blank look, then nodded gravely as she realized why.

The waitress didn't understand that question, either, but she caught the general gist and jerked her head towards a doorway near the rear of the restaurant. The little girls' room turned out to have two cubicles with a tiny sink wedged to the side of them. There was barely room to turn on the tap and, when you'd managed that, you struggled to get both hands in the bowl at once.

To my surprise, perhaps, my mother didn't seem perturbed by her surroundings. Neither did she seem desperate to use the facilities, but instead fussed around washing her hands and tidying her hair in the mirror on the wall next to the sink. I got the distinct impression she was stalling.

Eventually, she glanced up and met my eyes in the reflection.

"I do wish you wouldn't keep sniping at each other, Charlotte," she said, attempting to soften the slightly pained note with a hesitant smile. "Nothing good will come of provoking him."

"Me?" I said, feeling an annoyed twitch run sharply across my shoulders. "I'm not provoking anyone."

Her sigh brought me back. "You're provoking each other."

"I see. And are you planning on also having this conversation with him about not winding *me* up?"

She frowned. "I wouldn't dream of it,"

she said in a slightly affronted tone, bending to peer at the little strip of paper towel that was sticking out of the bottom of the dispenser on the wall. "I just think you should be careful not to push him too far, that's all." She tugged ineffectually at the towel, but it wouldn't budge.

It was my turn to sigh. I took a step forwards and pumped the handle on the side of the dispenser, twice. It rolled out two sheets, which I tore off and dumped in her hands.

Can lie us out of trouble, but can't dry her hands unaided. Full of surprises, my mother.

"I'm not the one who's doing the pushing," I said then, aware that I was scowling. "But if he shoves me, he can only expect me to shove back."

"Two pigheaded people . . ." She shook her head. "He only does it because he cares. I didn't realize just how much, but he does," she said, with an almost wistful look on her face as she dropped the scrunched-up towels into the waste bin and took a last look at her appearance. "Strange."

"I know he's a cold-blooded bastard, but why is that so strange?" I said, cut to the bone. "Isn't a man supposed to care about his daughter?"

She turned with an oddly puzzled look on

her face, which cleared as she made the connection. "Oh my goodness," she said, her voice chiding. "You think I mean Richard."

My own face went totally blank. "Don't you?"

"Oh no," she said. She gave a breathless little laugh as she reached for the door. "I was talking about Sean. . . ."

When we got back to the table, I could tell from the stony expressions on both men's faces that they hadn't been chatting about the cricket scores while we'd been gone. As soon as he saw me, Sean got to his feet and, though his movements were as smooth and coordinated as they always were, there was a darkness simmering beneath the surface.

I thought of my mother's warning, and something bright and cold slithered down my spine in response.

"The bill's taken care of," Sean said, scanning my face and clearly not liking what he saw there. "Let's go."

We didn't talk at all on the way back to the hotel, when we left the Navigator in the adjacent parking garage and walked to the elevators, nor from the elevators to our two adjoining rooms, but the silence was deafening. I found myself almost wishing for trouble. Something — *anything* — to give me a reason to lash out, relieve the tension that was mushrooming inside my skull and prickling my fingertips.

We said an abrupt good night and saw my parents locked down for the night. And when Sean very quietly shut our own door behind us and flicked on the bedside light, the room suddenly seemed very small and very close. We must have accidentally altered the setting on the air con before we went out, too. There was no other explanation for why it seemed hot enough in there to have the sweat break out across my palms and send it crawling along my hairline.

"We should talk about the plan for tomorrow," I said, desperately scrabbling for casual as I shrugged out of my jacket and slipped it onto a hanger. "For a start, what do we say to Collingwood about —"

Sean's hands on my shoulders made me jerk in reflexive surprise, going for an instant block before I could countermand the action. He evaded without thinking, spun me round so my back hit the door frame to the bathroom, hard enough to jolt. He'd stripped off his own jacket, I noted dumbly, draped it carelessly across the bed. His face was so tightly controlled he was white with the pressure of it.

"Your father suddenly seemed to remember something of his obligations over dinner," he said, and his voice was deceptively light. "While you and your mother were out of the way, he took the opportunity to give me the full parental speech."

"The parental speech?" My heart rate picked up. Not in pace, just in ferocity, so I could feel each vibrating beat like a punch behind my rib cage. "I didn't think we were gone that long."

"He was concise — you might almost say pithy — and I got the gist."

"So . . . what did he say?"

Sean feathered his grip, letting his hands fall away from my shoulders as though he couldn't trust himself to leave them there any longer. Bereft of his touch, I shivered.

"He told me not to hurt you any more than he seems to think I have done already," he said with the careful blankness I'd once heard him use to give an operational briefing on the aftermath of a massacre, disconnecting himself. "He knows I'm pushing you to finally sever ties with the nest and, perhaps, you're not ready to take that step."

"I see," I said, matching my tone to his, detached and impersonal. "If that's the case, why push me to take it?"

"Apparently, it's mainly because I'm a selfish bastard — I'm paraphrasing here, you understand," he said.

He took a pace backwards and leaned his shoulder on the wall opposite, folding his arms so his fingers were tucked under his armpits. He tilted his head back, staring past me at a point of nowhere as if he had to put effort into remembering words I knew would be acid-etched into his brain.

"He told me you'd already been through more than most people ever have to face in a lifetime. That you'd been broken in every way that mattered — mentally, physically, emotionally. And, in his opinion, the blame for most of it can be laid squarely at my door."

"That's rich," I said, rough with a dangerous cocktail of emotions, "coming from him."

Sean shrugged. "But, the trouble is, he's probably right," he said, and the casual acceptance in his own voice sent a greasy fear sliding through my gut. "So, first thing tomorrow I'll call Parker and get him to send up Joe McGregor to take over from me. He'll help you keep them safe until this bloody mess can be sorted out."

I'd always thought that phrase about your heart sinking was purely metaphorical, but I felt the sudden lurching contraction in my chest. I wanted to say a hundred things, but when I opened my mouth all I actually managed was, "What about you?"

"I'll go back to New York, see if I can help Parker untangle things at that end." He sounded matter-of-fact, as though he had nothing to gain or lose by the action.

For a moment I couldn't react, couldn't break the paralysis his announcement caused. When he could bear my shocked gaze no longer, Sean lifted himself abruptly away from the wall and moved further into the room, almost restless as he pulled off his tie.

I found my voice, used it to say, "I don't want McGregor," and hated the plaintive note.

"Why?" Sean turned back, impatient now, hands on his hips. He carried the Glock high on the right side of his belt, with a slight forward cant. "He's young but he's good, and his experience is solid."

"But he's not you," I said, small and subdued. "I want you."

He let his head snick down and left, biting off whatever retort was forming on his lips, closed his eyes and took a breath.

"You don't know what you want, Charlie," he said wearily. He glanced up and the defeat in his eyes terrified me. "I thought, last summer when we were in Ireland, that

338

you knew, that you'd made up your mind. But it only takes a few days in the delightful company of your parents before your resolve all goes to shit."

He sucked in a breath, let it out slowly as though willing the fragile hold on his temper to last just a little longer. "I'm tired," he said, flat. "Tired of not being sure how you feel about me. Tired of being shunted out of sight when it suits you, like some dirty little secret — okay to fuck in private, but God forbid you should ever have to acknowledge that fact in public."

"That's not fair," I said, grinding out the words over my distress. "You know damn well we *can't* make a show of being a couple, not in the job we do. Even Parker doesn't quite trust us not to let it get in the way!"

He shrugged, like it wasn't worth arguing about anymore, and started to turn away, unfastening the cuffs of his shirt.

Fury blazed. I shoved away from the wall and reached him in two fast strides, grabbing his arm, flipping him to face me.

If I'd been expecting to catch him off form, off balance, I should have known better. Sean twisted out of my grip with the kind of fluid, practiced ease that had always made him so deadly at hand-to-hand. He sidestepped, graceful as a fencer, and sent me sprawling onto the bed like he was brushing away an unwanted fly. Now I wasn't even worth the trouble of fighting properly.

He'd been carelessly gentle but, even so, I had acquired a lot of new bruises lately and the thump as I landed reminded me of every one of them. I elbowed up and stared at him, my vision starting to shimmer.

"Is that all I am to you, Sean?" I demanded, using anger to drive the shake out of my voice. "A quick fuck?"

He went very still and stared down at me, the only movement in his face a muscle jumping at the side of his jawline.

Nothing good will come of provoking him, my mother had warned.

Maybe if that cautionary note had been sounded by anyone else but her, I might have paid more attention. As it was I cast aside all sanity and threw another stupid, reckless challenge his way. "Only, I've been *fucked* before, and I didn't think what we had together was quite in that category."

For a moment he didn't react. Then, with an almost feral growl deep in his throat, Sean pivoted and swept the ornate lamp off the desk behind him with a single backhanded blow. It yanked the plug out of the socket and spun the glass base against the bathroom wall, shattering it into fragments. The explosion of violence was stark and shocking.

Appalled, I threw myself sideways off the bed, dropped onto my feet on the far side of it, scrambling to meet his eyes. They were burning, ferocious, in the face of a stranger. The fear caused a massive spike like an electrical short. I'd always sensed the beast in Sean ran very close to the surface but he'd never fully uncaged it before. Never with me. Until now.

He advanced, head down, utterly focused, kicking aside a chair. I backed up, my heart thundering against my breastbone, the blood roaring in my ears as the adrenaline rampaged shrieking through my system.

He reached me, reached for me, ramming me backwards until the wall brought us up short. I told myself I could have stopped him, could have evaded him, but I wanted — no, I *needed* — to know how far he would take this. How far he would hurt me.

Because then I'd have my final answer.

His fingers clamped around my wrists, jerking my arms up and out, pinning me against the wall. He crowded me with his body, forcing an awareness of the height and the breadth and the weight of him.

The memories triggered by that deliberate

341

act ripped through me, caving my chest until I could barely breathe. He leaned his face close to mine and watched with a cold hard gaze as every scrap of color bleached out of my face and I struggled to hide the sudden bloom of panic in my eyes.

"Sean!" The words were torn from me, weak and watered. *"Please . . ."*

I'd pleaded that night, too — begged and pleaded. For all the good it had done me then.

Donalson, Hackett, Morton and Clay.

"I'm not them, Charlie," he said, almost a whisper that I struggled to hear above the rasp of air in my clogged throat. "I've never been them — except inside your head. And every time you flinch away from me — yes, just like you're doing now — you're blaming me for what they did to you."

"I *don't* blame you." Was that pathetic little voice really mine?

"Yes, you do," he said, certain as stone. His eyes flicked down to my mouth and back up again. Eyes so dark they were almost black, with the tiniest flecks of gunmetal and gold around the pupil. "Just as your bloody parents blame me, for not teaching you better, for not protecting you."

"Sean, you weren't even there!" I protested, still reedy but stronger than before.

"You didn't know —"

"*I* blame me," he said, and the quiet admission undid me. He let go of my wrists and stepped back, a flicker of self-loathing in his face as he saw the reddened marks his grip had left on my skin.

Just then, there was a tentative rapping at the dividing door. My father's voice from the other side: "Charlotte? We heard a noise. It sounded like . . . Is everything all right in there?"

Sean raised his eyebrow in my direction.

Well, are you going to lie to them again? Pretend there's nothing wrong?

"Everything's fine," I said, a pain in my belly like a twisted knife as I watched the light fade out of Sean's eyes. "We knocked over a lamp. It's fine."

There was a long, dubious pause. "All right," my father said heavily. "If you're sure."

"Yes," I said, almost normal. "I am."

Sean started to turn away from me, closing down. I knew I was losing him and I couldn't have been any more scared if he'd been dying.

I levered off the wall and went for him again. This time, when he tried another almost dismissive throw, I countered, stepped in close, got my hip under his and

343

used his own demonstrated advantage in size against him.

The room was too small for fighting. Sean landed hard and awkwardly, halfway onto the bed, and jackknifed straight back onto his feet again, light as a cat, but there was a glitter in his eyes now. I told myself that anything was better than the dull-eyed beaten stare he'd had before.

"You knew what you were taking on with me, Sean," I told him harshly. "If you wanted somebody perfect, you should have taken Madeleine home for real, while you had the chance."

"I never wanted Madeleine," he said, quietly vehement. "I only ever wanted you, from the very first moment I laid eyes on you. Wanted you so badly it was like a bloody sickness. I've never changed my mind about that. But sometimes I think you have."

The words were spoken with such soft certainty that I felt something break inside. It must have been something connected to my eyes, because they began to flood with tears.

"You know how I feel about you, damn it," I said, keeping my chin up and my gaze on his even though my sight had blurred away. He tilted his head to one side and regarded me as though he could see right through to my soul. He probably could. I'd laid it bare for him. "I love you. That's never changed for me, either."

"Hasn't it?" He held his arms out, in challenge as much as invitation. "Then prove it."

I moved into him without hesitation, reached up and fisted my hands in his hair and pulled his mouth down to mine. Despite that, the kiss started out slow, smooth, tender. I had no intention of letting it stay that way.

Something ignited, as it always did when I was with Sean. Sometimes I thought that fire was never entirely extinguished, like a pilot flame waiting for the explosive rush of fuel to become a full-fledged ferocious burn. All consuming, unstoppable.

In moments, I had his shirt peeled open and was fumbling with his belt. He yanked the holstered Glock out from his waistband and dumped it behind him onto the bed. He'd already done the same with my SIG, had parted my shirt from my trousers and jerked it upwards to dance his fingers across the heated gap of skin between the two.

I don't remember him unclipping my bra, but suddenly my breast was in his hand, his mouth. I let my head fall back, gasping, as any logical sections of brain fell over and refused to reboot.

Eyes blind now, I was barely aware of his hands lifting me onto the desk. My trousers and the rest of my underwear had gone somewhere along the way and those diabolically knowing fingers teased and tormented until it was all I could do not to implore him for release.

My shirt was off my shoulders, bunched and tangled around my elbows, riveting my arms behind me. I fought the terror of being restrained, battled it down, opened my eyes as Sean leaned in close, bit my lower lip oh so gently.

"Trust me," he murmured and I knew he'd seen both the fear and my attempts to resist it. "I'll never hurt you, Charlie. . . ."

"I know."

He smiled at me, an utterly beautiful, heart-stopping smile, and began to trail slow burning kisses along the length of my neck, almost reverently across the scar that circled the base of it, and down the bow-tight, quivering arch of my body.

His breath accentuated the sweat dewing my skin, created an acute sensitivity that made me flail helpless under his touch. The thrumming moan in my throat was guttural, barely human. The need was prowling through me, starting to rage as he kept me teetering on the knife edge of utter ruin. My hands thrashed weakly and the telephone followed the lamp onto the floor, crashing off the edge of the desk.

Glazed with desperation, I lifted a weighted head on the end of a feeble neck and found him watching me through slitted lids. And then I understood what he was waiting for. I'd spent the last few days kicking him squarely in the ego and now he wanted total surrender by way of recompense. More than acceptance, only a kind of mindless subjugation would do.

I gave it to him.

His hands and mouth demanded more. I was panting, crying, clawing towards a peak I couldn't quite reach.

"Sean! For God's sake . . ."

"What?" he demanded, and the grip he was having to exert on himself made his voice sound coldly furious. "What do you want?"

"You!" I nearly shouted it, throat raw. "I want you!"

"Careful, Charlie." He spoke in my ear, whisper rough, almost mocking. "These walls are terribly thin, you know, and we don't want your parents to know what we're about, now do we?"

I fought my arms free, tearing my shirt into tatters in the process, and grabbed him with vicious fingers.

"I don't give a shit about my parents," I managed through gritted teeth. "Just do it. Right now. And don't you dare hold anything back or I swear I'll kill you where you stand."

He was too far gone to laugh, but I just had time to see the triumph, the pure male exultation blaze into his eyes. Then he was inside me in one long driving thrust. I hadn't touched him but he'd done enough for both of us. A wild cry leapt from my throat as my body closed greedily around him, and that was all it took. The twisted mass of frustrated tension that had been building up inside me burst loose, bellowing with wrath and glory as every sense overloaded.

"Hold on to me!" Sean demanded, hoarse. "For the love of Christ, hold on to me. . . ."

Still his hands gripped my hips, almost cruel, heedless of bruises old and new, balancing me at the edge of the desk and making it slam into the wall with every wild plunge of his body into mine. He'd tortured himself as well as me, making both of us wait. But by the time he let go with an almost primal roar, I followed him over again.

And disintegrated, like an overrevved race engine, pushed too hard to the finish. I was dying and certain of it. No way could my heart hit that hard, that unevenly, without one or other of us going into full cardiac arrest.

And then I realized the pounding was a fist on the dividing door.

"Charlotte! Are you all right?" My father's voice again, sounding shaken to the core. "Open this door! What the *devil* is going on in there?"

Sean's face was buried in my shoulder, arms wrapped tight around my body, muscles trembling violently. We both were. I let my head fall back against the wall behind me, closed my eyes and felt his lips brush against the side of my neck.

"Haven't you ever heard two people making love before?" I called back, croaky. "Go away and leave us alone. . . ."

Twenty-Two

I faced my father's staunch disapproval over breakfast the next morning.

He'd called horribly early — a little before six — and announced, almost defiant, that he intended to go down for breakfast and assumed one of us would feel obliged to accompany him.

Sean was still spark out, lying in a face-down sprawl diagonally across the massive bed. It was odd he hadn't woken at the phone, but considering the energy he'd expended during the night, I reckoned he deserved to sleep a little longer. So did I, come to that.

"I'm just going to jump in the shower," I said quietly. "Give me ten minutes — all right?"

My father agreed, reluctant, seemed about to say more but changed his mind.

"Very well," he said instead, clipped, and left me to it.

True to my word, I was out of the shower, dried, dressed and armed inside nine minutes. Sean stirred as I came back in, rolled towards me. His face was shuttered.

"All right?"

"Yes," I said, feeling suddenly awkward as the memories resurfaced. "His lordship demands breakfast, so I'll go down with him."

He nodded. "And, no doubt, an explanation about last night."

My face flooded and I paused with one hand on the door handle. "Well," I said, "he might have to whistle for that."

My father answered his own door sharply to my knock, already dressed in another of his immaculate, conservative suits. He gave me a narrow-eyed stare as though looking for something he could complain about. Not finding anything immediate seemed to annoy him all the more. He was positively glowering in the elevator, and the waiter who intercepted us at the hotel restaurant entrance almost stepped back in the face of such an obvious black mood, stuttering through his seasoned greeting.

I waited until we were both seated. My father took out his reading glasses and studied the breakfast items on offer with fierce concentration. He closed the menu with a distinct snap when the waiter returned to pour iced water.

"Eggs Benedict and a pot of Earl Grey tea," my father told him, brusque, peering over the top of his frames. "And please be sure to *boil* the water for the tea."

"Yes sir," the waiter said, flustered. "And, er, are you ready to order, ma'am?"

"I'll have a half Florida grapefruit, a bowl of Raisin Bran with two percent milk, wheat toast — dry — and a decaf," I said. "And a glass of juice. Do you have cranberry?"

"Yes ma'am."

"Great. Make it a large." For some reason, I seemed to have worked up an appetite.

The waiter almost grabbed our menus, took a last look at my father's scowling face as though debating the wisdom of some further question, then fled.

"You've picked up the language, I see," my father said when we were alone once more.

"Funny that," I said equably. "What with us and the Yanks both speaking English."

He made an impatient gesture with his left hand. "You've picked up the inflection," he amended. "You still sound English, but you ask questions like an American. And what on earth is two percent milk?"

I shrugged, tugging the linen napkin out

of its starched origami folds and draping it across my lap. "After the first few weeks you fall into the phrasing, otherwise you repeat yourself a lot. It seemed easier to adapt to survive — at least so I didn't go hungry in restaurants." I smiled. "And two percent milk is semi-skimmed."

"Adapt and survive," he murmured. "Yes, I suppose that's what you do best."

I would have queried that, but the waiter had hurried back again, with a pot bearing an orange tag for decaffeinated coffee, and my glass of juice.

"Your tea will be right out, sir," he said to my father, beating a hasty retreat before an opinion could be expressed.

I took a sip of my coffee, which was unusually rich and dark and smooth, and propped my elbows on the table while I held the cup under my nose, just for the smell of it.

And all the time my eyes were circling round the restaurant, checking out the other diners, the reinforced glass panels in the service doors that gave me a view into the harshly lit kitchen, the exits, and the positioning of the staff. It was all becoming second nature now and knowing that was so made the colors brighter, the sounds sharper. I lived in that explosive sliver between the *what if* and the *when.*

"You better just come right out and say it," I said mildly. "Whatever's on your mind, I mean. Right now, there's an elephant in the room that everyone's avoiding mention of, and I don't really fancy it sticking its trunk into my breakfast cereal."

My father's face ticked before he could stop it. He took a moment to control the surge of his temper, straightening his knife and fork until they were exactly aligned with his place mat. His hands were absolutely steady but then, in his profession they had to be.

"I used to find your flippancy at the most inappropriate moments somewhat difficult to take, Charlotte," he said. "But I find it particularly distasteful after last night."

"Ah yes — last night," I murmured, keeping my voice lazily amused even though I felt my fingers tense around the coffee cup. I compelled them to unclamp and set the cup down in its saucer without a clatter. "O-kay, let's get this over with."

The waiter was back again, sliding a rack of toast and a teapot onto the table before running away. My father winced a little when he saw the string for the teabag dangling out from under the lid, but he heroically restrained himself from complaint.

"I'm not entirely sure what's worse," he said then, conversational. "The fact that he obviously hurt you, or the fact that you evidently enjoyed it."

"Sean didn't hurt me," I said in a similar matter-of-fact tone, snagging a slice of toast and a little pot of strawberry preserve from the middle of the table.

My father linked his fingers together and regarded me over the top of them. "You have fresh bruises on your wrists that weren't there yesterday," he said, a dispassionate diagnosis. "Which means not only that you were held down with considerable force, but also that you resisted."

What do I say to that? That Sean was angry? That he didn't mean it? That I'd witnessed all too clearly the wave of disgust that had crossed his face when he'd seen what he'd done? So, which was the greater evil to admit to my father — deliberate cruelty or careless brutality?

And because I couldn't think of anything to say that wouldn't make it worse, I didn't say anything. Instead, I shrugged and took a bite of my toast, but my throat had closed dangerously and I had to chase it down with a mouthful of juice.

"Has he ever . . . hit you?"

"Yes," I said, leaving just enough of a pause to push him for a reaction. There wasn't one. "We spar together. Of course he has."

A sigh. "Don't be obtuse, Charlotte," he said, and the clip was back with a vengeance. "You know exactly what I mean."

"No, he's never beaten me up, if that's what you're getting at." I allowed myself a small smile as I took another swig. "I'm hardly in danger of becoming a battered wife."

That got a response. Instant, more of a flinch than anything else.

I put down my glass, smile fading. "My God," I said softly. "Is *that* what you're afraid of? That we might get married and then it would be official — he'd be your son-in-law and you'd *have* to accept him? Is that it?"

"Of course not," my father evaded sharply. "Do you find it quite so difficult to believe that I — we — might be concerned for your welfare?" And, when my skepticism was clearly demonstrated by my lack of answer, he glanced away and added carefully, "People who have been through the kind of trauma that you experienced, often have a certain amount of difficulty forming normal relationships afterwards." He looked up abruptly, met my eyes. "They self-harm. They look for sexual partners who will hurt them. They need the pain in some way, like worrying at a nagging tooth. I find it . . . pitiful."

"Is that what you think I'm doing?" I asked, limiting my physical response to a raised eyebrow when what I really wanted to do was reach for his throat. "Trying to alleviate some kind of karmic toothache?"

The waiter returned, this time bearing a large oval tray at shoulder height, which he put down on a foldout trestle and began to decant plates onto our table with all the flourish of a casino croupier dealing cards. My father waited until the man had scurried away again before he spoke.

"It defies logic that someone who's been gang-raped would take any kind of pleasure in being forced," he said, quietly frozen, "unless they have severe psychological problems. Problems for which we attempted to get you some professional help over a year ago. Yet you stopped going to Dr. Yates after only a few sessions."

"I don't have a problem forming a 'normal relationship' — whatever you might deem that to be," I said, outwardly calm as I poured milk onto my cereal, hating the way my skin heated at his words. "It's the fact that I've formed one with someone you despise that really pisses you off."

My dip into coarseness was deliberate but he let it slide this time, and that in itself was interesting.

"We don't despise him," my father said, and I noted he could rarely bring himself to use Sean's name. I realized, also, that by using "we," he was off-loading part of the blame for his attitude towards Sean onto my mother. *How convenient.*

"Well, you make a pretty good show of it, unless he's useful for" — I paused, miming exaggerated thought process — "oh, I don't know — *keeping you alive,* maybe?"

"It sounded like a war was breaking out in there," he muttered then, his voice low, near to shaken. "It sounded like he was killing you, Charlotte. What the devil were we supposed to think?"

I put my spoon down with great care.

"How about anything but the worst all the time?" I said, fixing him with a stare that was as laconic as I could make it. "He's a good man, with standards and a sense of honor, if you could only see it. And we love each other."

I paused, hoping for some kind of acknowledgment of a valid point. Not surpris-

ingly, I didn't get one. "You were young once and in love, surely? Did you never have that desperate, all-out, break-the-furniture-and-to-hell-with-the-consequences kind of sex?" I demanded. "If not, then I rather think *I* pity *you*."

I expected a cutting retort. To my utter amazement, not to mention my embarrassment, something flickered through his face and he blushed. My father actually blushed. He opened his mouth to deny it, of course, but I held up a peremptory hand.

"No!" I said quickly. "Don't tell me! On second thoughts, I withdraw the question because, to be quite honest, I really do *not* want to know. . . ."

We finished breakfast largely in uncomfortable silence, with me desperately trying to dislodge the unwanted mental image of my parents engaged in rough sex. The metaphorical elephant was back, but for some reason now the picture in my head had it wearing a PVC corset and fishnet stockings, and carrying a saucy lash.

My father signed both meals to his room, and we rode the elevator up again without speaking, reaching his door first. He swiped the key card through the lock and pushed the door open almost without a pause. I followed him in, both of us coming to an abrupt halt just inside the doorway at the sight which greeted us.

My mother was sitting on the small sofa near the window, washed and dressed. Sitting alongside her, almost knee-to-knee, was Sean. He was wearing yesterday's suit with a fresh shirt and his usual tie, his hair still damp from the shower. Both of them were laughing and they looked up sharply at our unexpected entrance. Briefly, I saw the flash of guilt from my mother, that she'd been caught fraternizing with the enemy.

I shot a quick sideways glance at my father's face and saw something cold and dark and tightly furious blaze there before he slammed the shutters down.

Sean met his gaze in cool challenge, as if daring him to make a big thing of this. For a moment they dueled silently, then my father turned away with the excuse of asking my mother if she wanted breakfast. His voice was politely neutral, but his shoulders told a different story.

"Thank you, no," she said. "We've just had a cup of tea and that will be quite sufficient, I think."

Sean pointedly continued his stare, then rose with casual grace and strolled towards us.

"I think perhaps we should go back and see Miranda Lee this morning," he said. "See if she knows about the alterations that have been made to her husband's records. If she saw them beforehand, she's another witness. If we leave soon, we should miss the morning rush."

My father nodded stiffly, moving aside to let him pass. I stood my ground and, as Sean drew level, I reached out and grabbed his sleeve.

He stopped, flicking his eyes down to my hand and then up to my face. His expression was wary, almost uncertain.

I stepped in to him, let go of his jacket to reach up, curving my hand to his clean-shaven cheek and pressing my lips very softly against his. For a moment, sheer surprise kept him immobile before he responded. A gentle chaste kiss that nevertheless served as an instant inflammable reminder of how the night had progressed.

I kept my eyes open, watched his flutter closed and open again slowly as I pulled back a little. There was confusion in them, yes, but a kind of joy, too. His pupils were huge.

"Good morning," I murmured, husky and a little defiant, acutely aware of our audience.

He reached up, brushed a stray lock of hair back from my forehead with an infinitely gentle finger, as if needing to demonstrate he could touch me and not leave a mark.

"Yes," he said, and he was smiling. "It is now."

By the time we'd packed, loaded up the Navigator and checked out, it was a respectable-enough hour to call ahead and warn Miranda Lee that we were coming back, just in case she'd made plans.

I called her from my phone as Sean swung the Navigator through sunny Boston streets. It was warm enough not to wear a jacket unless you had something you wanted to conceal underneath it. Both Sean and I wore jackets.

My father had been terse since my little display of open affection towards Sean in their hotel room, but I felt liberated and reckless. Even though there was a part of me that was desperate to know what the hell Sean and my mother had been discussing so earnestly while we'd been gone.

Now, I recognized, was not the time to ask.

Miranda took awhile to answer her phone,

and sounded distracted when she finally did so.

"It's Charlie Fox," I said. "Um, Richard and Elizabeth's daughter," I added when she didn't immediately respond.

"Oh yes, of course! I'm sorry, Charlie. I'm a little out of it right now, but I'm glad you've called," she said and gave a nervous laugh. "In fact, if you hadn't, I'd probably have tried to call you."

"Why?" I said, and it was the tone as much as the question that had Sean's attention snap in my direction. "What's happened?"

"You know how I mentioned about Terry O'Loughlin — in Storax's legal department? Well, I had another e-mail just in — but it's kind of weird."

"*Weird* how?" I said. Now, my father was leaning in close from the rear seat.

"Well, it's really brief — a warning. Just tells me to be careful and not to trust anyone." Another short laugh. Definitely nerves. "I mean, after yesterday — discovering the house was broken into and everything, it's freaked me out, you know?"

"I'm not surprised," I said. "It sounds like Storax are playing mind games with you. Trying to scare you."

"Yeah, well, it's working." She let out a

shaky breath. "But what should I do?"

"Have you made any plans to go to your friend's place — Vermont, wasn't it?"

"I'm already packed," she admitted. "I checked into a motel last night and only came back to the house this morning to get a few things. I was going to leave again right after lunch."

I checked my watch, calculated the journey time. "Hang on till we get there, can you? We're just getting onto the interstate. Unless we hit traffic, we should be with you inside an hour."

"Okay, yes," she said, in a rush. "I didn't want to ask, but . . . thank you."

I ended the call and relayed the gist of it to the others. "It sounds like Storax have got her rattled," I finished. "Which is probably the point of the exercise."

"Yeah," Sean said, pulling out to overtake a line of Kenworth trucks, "and at the risk of scaring her even more, what do we tell her about what we found — or more to the point, what we *didn't* find — at the hospital?"

My father took a moment to reply, but whether this was because he was considering his answer, or trying to bring himself to have a normal conversation with Sean, I wasn't sure.

Eventually, he said, "We still don't really

know what Storax hope to achieve by all this."

"They're covering their backs, surely?" I said, twisting so I could carry on a conversation with him in the rear seat more easily. He was sitting directly behind me, which made it more difficult. "They have to know there's a chance that some of the patients being treated will suffer the same kind of side effects that Jeremy Lee did. And if they didn't know that before his death, then they sure as hell did afterwards. It makes no sense that they haven't completely withdrawn it and stopped the trials. By continuing, aren't they opening themselves up to another thalidomide fiasco?"

"Withdrawing it could potentially cost them a great deal of money," my father said. "And might allow a competitor to steal a march on them. Better for Storax if they can work on the problems quickly, without anyone finding out about them."

"But if the rate Miranda said her husband deteriorated is anything to go by, surely the side effects would have shown up pretty quickly?" I pointed out.

My father shrugged. "Not necessarily. Jeremy was of Korean descent. Korea has one of the lowest instances of osteoporosis in the world. Of course, there's considerable research to suggest this is largely due to environmental factors rather than genetics, but it's an interesting point."

"None of it's enough to go to all this trouble over, though, is it?" Sean demanded. "Overdosing Lee, falsifying his records, setting up an elaborate operation to ruin your career? Never mind what they were prepared to do to your wife." He tilted his head slightly to smile reassuringly at my mother in the rearview mirror — a gesture that had my father's frown deepening into a scowl.

"How much does Storax stand to make out of this — if it goes ahead?" I asked, as much to distract him as anything else.

"Osteoporosis is becoming a major problem," my father said, mentally shaking himself like a dog coming out of water. "When you take the worldwide licensing, a treatment as successful as Storax's *seemed* to be, would be worth hundreds of millions, if not billions, in annual revenue."

"Even so," I said. "I feel we're missing something. There's got to be more to it than that."

"I agree," Sean said. "One thing that's been bothering me is how Storax managed to get their hands on someone like Vonda Blaylock at such short notice. Kaminski was already contracted to them for security —

that much we know — but Blaylock is a government agent. How did they recruit her? And why?"

"Perhaps they knew that something like Jeremy Lee's death would happen, sooner or later," I said. "And, it never does any harm to have a backup plan."

For once, the gods of congestion smiled on us. We made better than average time and left the main freeway at the exit we'd taken only the day before, following what I would classify as a fast A road that began to twist and turn. Then off again onto a minor road that sliced, curving, through a thickly wooded area.

There was very little other traffic now. Sean drove with easy precision, to the point where I could leave him to it and stay sitting mostly sideways to chat face-to-face with my parents.

So, I wasn't in the best position to brace myself when Sean jumped on the brakes hard enough for the antilock system to activate. There was a whump, and the Navigator lurched sideways abruptly, wallowing, the quiet hum of its tires on the asphalt transformed into a harsh metallic grinding.

"What the — ?" I began.

"Stinger," Sean managed, fighting to control the abruptly unwieldy vehicle.

"A *missile?*" my father demanded, more outrage than alarm. "Someone just fired a Stinger missile at us?"

"Wrong Stinger. Spikes on a chain across the road," I said shortly. "We just lost all four tires."

The SIG was out in my hand, but I didn't remember drawing it. I was twisting constantly in my seat, scanning the road all around us, searching for the ambush that could only be moments away. "Will it drive?"

"I'm doing my best," Sean said. "But if it comes to a chase, it may well be quicker to walk."

A flash of movement to the driver's side caught my eye. The front end of a bloodred Ford pickup truck, big as a fire engine, shiny bull bars reinforcing the grille like a battering ram. It was heading straight for us out of a narrow side road that disappeared up into the trees. The truck covered the ground rapidly, with a roar of its massive V-8 engine that I heard even over the racket made by the Navigator's stripped and battered wheels.

"Incoming!" I shouted.

Sean let go of the steering wheel and got

his hands out of the way. Good job, too, or the vicious kick when the pickup hit us would have broken both his thumbs. Both doors and the B-pillar buckled, the side-impact air bags exploded and the windows shattered, raining down glass onto both Sean and my mother, who was sitting directly behind him.

The force of the crash whipped the Navigator into a graunching broadside across the road and onto the grass. The bare rims of the alloy wheels dug in and nearly flipped us, thrashing the cabin around like we were being shaken in the jaws of a monster. I clung to the door grip, peripherally aware of my mother's terrified screaming in the backseat.

"Down!" I yelled at Sean. He instantly threw himself sideways, flat across the center console. I reached over the top of him with the SIG and put three rounds into the front screen of the pickup where I judged the driver's head would be, the empty brass pinging off the inside of the Navigator's dash. "Clear!"

"Out — now!" Sean said, rearing up to launch himself over to my side of the vehicle.

As soon as we'd come to a stop I'd punched my seat belt release and piled out backwards, keeping the SIG up to cover Sean as I checked our escape route.

Sean wrenched open the rear door and bodily dragged my father out. He landed heavily on his knees on the grass, dazed, shaking his head as if to clear the ringing from the cumulative concussion of explosive air-bag charges and gunshots. The shock of close-proximity live firing in a confined space took some getting used to, and he hadn't had anything like the practice.

"Take him!" I reholstered the SIG and went back in for my mother.

Sean left me without hesitation, scooping up my father and thrusting him towards the tree line with one hand wrapped in the collar of the older man's jacket. The Glock was out in Sean's right hand and he kept the muzzle up all the way, moving at a sideways crab so he could cover my father's back and still be ready for the occupants of the pickup to make their move.

I jumped into the backseat and found my mother in full-flight panic. Her seat belt had jammed and she was clawing at it uselessly, eyes wild with fear as I slid across the seat towards her. I flipped out the largest blade on my Swiss Army knife and hacked through the webbing of the belt itself, ignoring the locked buckle.

As soon as she was free, my mother nearly trampled me in her desperation to escape. If I hadn't grabbed her, she would have scrambled right over the top of me and hit the ground running.

A man had jumped out of the driver's door of the pickup — unscathed, I noted with irritation — and was heading round the front of the Navigator to cut us off. I almost slung my mother back into her seat and drew the SIG, bringing it up so my target's head would appear in my gun sights as soon as he came into view.

He did so, moving in a fast professional crouch, holding a semiautomatic handgun in a double-handed grip, up and level in front of him. As soon as he had sight of us, he pulled the trigger. He was hasty and the shot went wide, hitting the headrest of the rear seat just to my right and kicking out a flurry of foam and stuffing.

"No!" my mother screamed and I realized in the fraction before I returned fire that her cry was as much to me as it was to our attacker. Ignoring her, I snapped off two rounds at the blur of moving target.

One shot went wide but I put the second through his upper thigh. He gave a yelp of pain and scuttled for cover, dragging his injured leg. Well, I had a certain amount of sympathy there.

I glanced towards the tree line but couldn't immediately see my father and Sean, which meant they were safe in concealment. *And if they've any sense,* I thought fiercely, *that's where they'll stay.*

Then, behind us, another vehicle hove into view, a dark blue nondescript Chevy. It arrived at speed, the driver showing no astonished twitch at finding an apparent pileup half-blocking the road in front of him, which meant he was expecting this — or something like it.

The odds of successful evasion had just got longer.

"Out — *now!*" I said roughly to my mother before the approaching car had come to a full sliding stop. "We need to move! And keep your bloody head down."

She looked confused, as though the new arrival might have brought assistance rather than further danger, but at least she didn't argue.

As we jumped out of the backseat of the Navigator, I fired off another shot in the direction of the pickup driver just to keep *his* head down, and dragged my mother into a run for the trees.

As I did so, I heard shouts from the occupants of the Chevy. I spun, fisting my left hand into my mother's coat and ducking my shoulder to haul her halfway onto my back, covering her body with my own as I brought the SIG up in my right hand.

I fired before my arm was at full stretch, aiming intuitively. Two figures had emerged from the Chevy, and some part of my brain registered a man and a woman. Their body language told me instantly that they were armed for immediate use rather than merely for threat. I chose the man as my primary target based purely on experience, knowing that he would likely pose the greater risk to our safety.

I sighted directly at the center of his body mass and squeezed the trigger twice in quick succession.

Running, weighted, my aim wouldn't have won me any marksman badges, but it got the job done. Both rounds took him high in the shoulder, jerking him back and to the right. I just had time to see the mist of blood spray out, then he was falling.

Still lurching sideways, protecting my principal, I swung my arm towards the woman. She had moved into a shooter's stance, legs spread, arms locked in front. If she'd any training at all she was in the far better position for a decent shot.

And, with shock, at that moment I recognized her — if not the face then certainly the white tape across her fattened nose.

Vondie.

So, not only training but also a damn good motive for wanting me dead. Looked like Collingwood still hadn't managed to put a muzzle on his rogue agent — not enough to stop her from trying to take a big bite out of me, at any rate.

Suddenly, the car window alongside Vondie shattered as two fast shots from the trees put it through. She spun but clearly couldn't spot Sean's position. Outflanked, she jumped for the safety of her vehicle, abandoning the kill. The Chevy's engine was still running, and she had the gearlever rammed into drive before the door was even shut, leaving her fallen colleague writhing alone on the ground in her wake.

Vondie swerved round the wreckage and, just when I thought she was completely faithless, the brake lights blazed as she anchored on and leaned over to throw the passenger door wide open. The man I'd lamed came hopping out from behind the Navigator and dived inside. Vondie stamped on the accelerator and the Chevy took off with enough anger to leave two long black streaks of burned rubber scarring the asphalt, and the bitter smell of gun smoke, blood and gasoline behind her.

Twenty-Three

Sean came out of the trees with soft-footed caution, staring after the disappearing Chevy, eyes narrowed and the Glock still clasped loosely in his hands. He glanced at me and nodded, just once. I nodded back. That was enough.

My father ducked round him and began hurrying to the man who was jerking and twitching in the middle of the road, the blood pool widening around him by the moment.

"Wait," Sean snapped.

We shouldered past my father and approached the fallen man, staying wide to present two difficult oblique targets. I knew he'd been carrying and I hadn't seen him drop a weapon. Sean edged in, not letting the Glock's point of aim waver, and kicked away a big Colt semiautomatic. He leaned down then and checked the man roughly for a backup piece, not mindful of his injuries while he was doing it.

"Look who it is."

I moved closer, saw beyond the blood and the contortion of the pain, and realized my victim was Vondie's partner in crime, Don Kaminski. Hardly a surprise to find them hand in hand, when I thought about it. I wondered how he felt about Vondie abandoning him when he went down.

My father brushed Sean aside then, almost with contempt, and crouched next to the injured man, who was panting with the effort it took not to cry out. Blood pulsed from one of the wounds in his shoulder in oxygen-rich scarlet spurts. *Artery.* He had a few minutes, maybe less.

My father ripped at the clothing around the wound. "Press there — hard," he said to me. "We have to slow the bleeding."

Reluctantly, I holstered the SIG, put the heel of my hand over the hole in Kaminski's shoulder and leaned my weight into it, hearing the squelch. The acute pain that action caused sent his muscles into spasm, arching his back off the ground as his body went rigid. I had a pretty good idea that it would, because I'd once had something very similar done to me.

Kaminski's pain threshold must have been considerably higher than mine, though. His only verbal reaction was a grunt when he should have been screaming. But I saw the almost feral panic in his eyes and knew it was fear as much as anything that kept him silent as he twisted beneath my hands.

"We don't have time for this," Sean said, eyes scanning the road in both directions. "We need to get out of here."

My father threw him a vicious glance.

"We can't simply leave him. He'll die."

"We didn't start this and we don't have time to finish it," Sean said, equally brutal. "He knew the risks."

Under his breath, my father muttered something that sounded very much like an instruction for Sean to go to hell.

My mother gave a short laugh that was way too high-pitched to signify amusement.

"Oh for heaven's sake, you're as stubborn as each other!" she said crossly. "Let him do what he can, Sean. If anyone comes it will look like what it is — a doctor treating someone at the scene of an accident."

"I'm more worried about his friends coming back with reinforcements, rather than keeping up appearances," Sean said. He stared down at the injured man with entirely dispassionate eyes. "All right," he said, letting out a fast breath. "Charlie, stay with him." He turned to my mother and added, almost politely, "Elizabeth, if you wouldn't mind helping me get our gear, let's see if their truck will still drive, shall we?"

"Do what you have to," my father said, dismissive, unfolding his glasses from his inside pocket and sliding them on.

I leaned harder into Kaminski's shoulder but seemed to be having very little effect on the rush of blood. My hands were awash with it. I glanced up at my father and saw by his face that he knew my efforts were futile. If Kaminski's frantic struggles were anything to go by, he must have known it, too.

"You must calm down if you want me to help you," my father told him, quietening the man by the sheer authority in his voice. Or perhaps the lessening of Kaminski's movements was simply due to the fact that he was bleeding out as fast as his accelerated heartbeat could accomplish the task.

Nevertheless, knowing that death is stalking your shoulder doesn't make you entirely see sense. Kaminski clearly didn't like the option of letting a man he'd just been sent to kill get close to him. His rib cage heaved, shuddering with the sheer effort he was expending to drag in each sodden breath.

"You know this man's a top-flight surgeon, and you also know that without his help you'll be dead in minutes," I told him. "Now, just let him save your miserable little life."

"You know him?" my father said.

"Yes," I said coldly, meeting Kaminski's eyes, seeing the pain and the dread in them and feeling nothing. "He's the one who — if you'd refused to cooperate in New York — was planning to take such delight in raping your wife."

For a moment my father's hands stilled and I thought perhaps he might simply abandon his efforts and walk away. Maybe I wanted him to.

Then he glanced at me and seemed to shake himself. "I need a sharp knife and some form of clamp," he said. "Anything will do, but quickly!"

One-handed, I dug my Swiss Army knife out of my pocket again and flicked out the smaller, cleaner, of the two blades, thrusting the knife towards him handle first. He took it like a typical surgeon, without either eye contact or thanks, and began to slice away the clothing around the wound site.

"Here." Sean was back just long enough to dump one of the vehicle's first-aid kits, a roll of duct tape and a tool roll down next to us. My father barely acknowledged him, just ripped the kit open and dug out sterile wipes, dressings and bandages. He searched through the rest of the contents quickly, but there was nothing intended to deal with anything this severe.

Kaminski, I recalled, had once been in the military. I bet he wished he still had his standard-issue ampoules of morphine with him now.

My father ignored the ties holding the tool roll together, cutting it open instead, his fingers slick with blood. With a grunt of satisfaction, he slipped a pair of pliers out of the roll, ready, and turned back to his patient.

"Hold him," he warned. "This is going to hurt."

Kaminski must have outweighed me by nearly two to one, but he'd been shot twice and bled for long enough to weaken him sufficiently that I had the upper hand. I knelt on his chest, letting go of the wound, which surged afresh like floodwater.

Swiftly, surely, my father stabbed the knife into the dense pectoral muscle at the top of Kaminski's chest and sliced up towards his collarbone, his face ticking with irritation as the man screamed and bucked under us.

My father used one of the unpacked dressings to clear the welter of blood enough to see what he was doing, then stuffed what seemed to be his entire hand into the incision he'd just made.

I don't count myself as squeamish, but that made me look away. I had to remind myself that this was, after all, what my father did for a living. The inner workings of the human body held no mysteries for him. It was just a machine that went wrong, and he was a highly trained and highly paid mechanic. I glanced at his face and found him calm, frowning slightly in utter concentration as he worked by feel alone.

"Ah," he said at last. "Got it. Hand me the pliers."

I grabbed the pliers. They'd been sitting in the tool roll for some time, by the look of them, and were covered in a film of oil and dirt.

"Shouldn't we clean them first?" I asked as I slapped them into his outstretched palm, reaching for a sterile wipe from the first-aid kit.

"The man's bleeding to death," my father snapped. "I think infection is the last of his worries at the moment, Charlotte, don't you?"

Slowly, carefully, he withdrew his hand from the gaping hole in Kaminski's shoulder, a thin piece of rubbery tubing gripped tight between his forefinger and thumb.

My God, I thought. *That's an artery.*

Delicately, he wrapped the tube in a piece of dressing and clamped the pliers onto it before looking round. I grabbed an elastic band that had been holding one of the bandages together and handed it over. "Use this."

He took it with a nod this time, stretching the band around the handles of the pliers to hold them shut. Then he sat back on his heels, head tilted slightly, his lips pursed slightly in disapproval.

"Not exactly the neatest bit of surgery I've ever carried out," he said, wiping his forehead with the sleeve of his jacket, "but under the circumstances it will do the job."

He leaned over Kaminski, eyes skimming the blanched features until he was sure the man had him in focus.

"If you dislodge or attempt to remove the temporary clamp I've placed on your artery, you will undoubtedly bleed to death," he told him, voice cold and entirely matter-of-fact. "Do you understand me?"

Fear was not the only thing holding Kaminski immobile. Eventually, he gave a slow blink, which we took to signify assent.

"Good." My father glanced at me. "Dressing, if you please." I ripped off the cellophane wrappings and slapped the wadded gauze and cotton wool into his outstretched palm, too. He packed them over the wound, but ignored the bandage I offered in favor of duct tape, which he applied liberally across Kaminski's chest, holding the pliers as well as the dressings firmly in place.

He was just adding the last strip when Sean approached.

"The truck's drivable, no problem," he said as he drew near. "Hitting us hardly even put a dent in the chrome. If you've quite finished playing Dr. Kildare, *now* we need to leave, okay?"

"We should take him with us — get him to a hospital at the very least," my father argued.

Sean hid his exasperation behind a formally blank face, but it edged out around his words, even so. "He'll slow us down, decrease our chances of evasion," he said. "And I should hardly need to remind you that he and his lady friend have just tried to kill the lot of us."

For a moment my father didn't speak, but his face turned grave. Then he nodded, brusque. "Very well," he said. He rose, dusting off his knees. "If you get medical assistance soon, your chances of survival are fair. You may even retain the use of your arm," he told Kaminski in a disinterested tone, turned on his heel and walked away.

I bent to retrieve my Swiss Army knife, carefully wiping the blood from the blade onto Kaminski's jacket. Between us, Sean and I managed to drag him to the side of the road, where at least he wasn't going to get run down by passing traffic. Not that there'd been any since the Chevy's exit. Vondie and crew had chosen their ambush site well.

Kaminski was very weak now, passing in and out of consciousness, too far gone even to cry out when he was moved. I couldn't find it in me to pity him.

Sean crouched and looked into the man's eyes and made sure he was just aware enough of us to register.

"This is the second time we haven't killed you when we had the chance," Sean murmured, almost regretful as he got to his feet. "Make it the last."

The Ford turned out to be an F-350 on a Pennsylvania plate. It was a double cab, which meant there was more than enough room inside for the four of us and our luggage. And, apart from the trio of bullet holes in the front windscreen, it was relatively undamaged.

Sean drove us away from the scene, making as much speed as he could without attracting too much attention, pushing the big pickup hard. I'd retrieved boxes of ammo from our bags before we set off and now I occupied my hands topping off both magazines while I had the chance. Sean's Glock had only two rounds gone. My SIG was light by eight.

At one point Sean reached over and gave my hand a quick hard squeeze. I squeezed back and that was it. For several miles, nobody spoke.

When I glanced over my shoulder to check on my parents, I found them holding each other close in the backseat. But, to my surprise, it seemed to be my mother who had her arms wrapped around my father, when I would have expected him to be the one to be offering the most comfort. She met my eyes over the top of his bent head and gave me a faint smile. After a second, I smiled back.

"So, where now?" I asked Sean. "Miranda Lee's?"

Sean shook his head. "They must have been there, or they're intercepting her calls," he said. "We didn't decide we were going back there until this morning, and she's the only person we told. Either way, she's compromised."

"So, has Vondie gone rogue again, or is Collingwood pulling her strings?"

He shook his head. "If Collingwood's behind this, we're so far up the creek they've never even *seen* a paddle," he said. "I think we'd better assume the worst. Turn off your phone, just in case they're tracking us through the system. We'll find somewhere with a landline and call Parker."

"If Collingwood's bent," I said, fishing my mobile out and holding down the power button until the screen went blank, "he's going to have Parker under surveillance, too, surely?"

"Of course." He flashed me a grim smile. "We'll just have to make sure we're suitably cryptic, won't we?"

Cleaning up was a priority if we were to remain at large. We stopped at a little roadside fuel station that seemed to have branched out into garden furniture and windmills as well as the usual supplies. The rest room was round the back of the building and we had to get a key from the cashier before we could use it.

We sent my mother in, seeing as she had come out of the encounter relatively un-scathed and had the least amount of blood on her. She returned with a rusty key on one end of a piece of weighted chain, just in case any of us took a fancy to it.

There was only one — unisex — rest room, which my mother took one look at and declined to use, regardless of need. It was lined largely with scuffed stainless-steel panels held together with antitamper fastenings. The cracked sink was minus a plug, but at least there was soap in the dispenser and the water was hot.

My father's nose wrinkled, but he rolled up his sleeves and got on with it. He'd even fetched a nail brush from his overnight bag. I wadded paper towels into the bottom of the sink and kept one hand on the top of the push-down tap to fill the bowl with water.

He washed his hands with technique born of long practice, thoroughly cleaning each area of skin, including the backs and round the base of his thumbs. It was so obviously methodical that you knew he would be able to get them spotless even in the dark.

I leaned on the cracked tiles under the long slot of a window and watched him scrub at the blood I'd caused to flow. I saw again the way Vondie and Don Kaminski had got out of the Chevy, the guns in their hands, the clear intent. It was as if I needed the reassurance that it had been a necessary shot, a good clean kill. Kaminski might yet not die but, if he did, I supposed I could live with the consequences.

The adrenaline had left my hands unsteady, and increased the ache in my thigh until it was a fierce burn that I longed to alleviate with Vicodin. I was thankful we'd had a chance to grab our luggage before we'd fled the scene and I was mentally sorting through my bag, trying to remember exactly where I'd left my painkillers, in order to make their retrieval when we went back outside as unobtrusive as possible.

"Does it make you feel differently about him?" my father asked suddenly.

I'd been thinking about Kaminski and my brain immediately turned back in that direction. I blinked. "Does what make me feel differently about whom?"

My father sighed, as though I was being deliberately difficult. "Sean," he said, all but curling his lip at being forced to say the name. "The fact that he ran, back there, and left you and your mother to be slaughtered."

I stared at him. He met my eyes for a moment as he emptied out the dirty water and filled the bowl again to repeat the process.

"What do you mean, 'he ran'? Of course he did — I told him to," I said, a little blankly. "You should be bloody glad that he ran! If he hadn't, it might have been *you* who was shot."

"He left you both to die, Charlotte," my father said. "Are you so blinded by the man that you can't accept the unequivocal facts of the situation?"

"I'm not blind to Sean's faults," I said. "But I'm damned if I'm going to let you call him a coward when he's not." I elbowed off the wall, stalked towards him. "We told you the ground rules back in New York. Did you think we didn't mean any of it? What you think you saw back there, that wasn't what happened, and until you have a better understanding of what we do, I'd thank you to keep your half-baked bloody opinions to yourself, okay?" I threw him a contemptuous glance. "I'll wait outside."

I turned and went for the door, suddenly needing to get out of the same room before I did something both of us would regret. *Damn the man to hell!*

"Charlotte —"

I turned back, fully prepared to give him both barrels, but he'd stopped his scrubbing and was standing there, head down and shoulders bowed, gripping the edge of the sink with both hands, as if holding on for dear life.

Then I saw his head come up with that

arrogant tilt I knew so well, and the moment of apparent vulnerability passed like it had never been.

"You're right. I don't understand," he said, stony. "I saw a man who professes to love you turn his back and run in the middle of a gun battle, leaving you in danger. So . . . explain it to me. What exactly did I fail to see?"

I let go of the door handle and took a breath. When I let it out my voice was calmer. "We were under attack. One principal outside the vehicle, one trapped inside," I said in a clipped tone that, ironically, must have made me sound very much my father's daughter. I cast my eyes up and down him.

"You must outweigh my mother by — what, forty or fifty pounds? Sean outweighs me by sixty. Purely from a logistical point of view, it made no sense whatsoever for me to try and get you to cover, and leave my mother to Sean. If you'd been injured, I *would* have carried you, make no mistake, but I knew he could do it so much more easily. And that would make him more efficient. Better at his job."

"But —"

"But what?" I demanded, not letting him cut me off. "All I had to worry about was getting my mother out. I didn't have to worry about you, because I knew Sean would keep you safe — would *die* to protect you, if he had to. I knew exactly how he was going to react because he's always the absolute professional and that makes him utterly dependable when the chips are down."

I stalked forwards, got right in his face and took mean satisfaction in the way he flinched back. "If he'd come back for me, there was a chance he might have just got in my way, cluttered my backgrounds when I was taking a shot. As it was, I knew Sean had my back, but not at the expense of yours."

I paused, took a breath that went in fine but came out less steady than I would have liked. "If things had been reversed, if it had been you stuck in that car, and we'd got my mother out, I would have taken her and run, just the same," I went on. "And, if I had, would you now be accusing *me* of cowardice?"

"No," he said, low. "Of course not."

"Well, halle-bloody-lujah," I threw back at him. "Are *you* really so blinded against Sean you can't see anything good in him?"

My father paused, brow creased in concentration. "I'm never going to be able to think of it as normal behavior," he said at last, slowly, "that he's prepared to kill or die for a stranger."

I hate to break this to you, Daddy dear, but so am I.

I sighed, a long expulsion of air that did nothing to allay my frustration. "Well, try not to think about it, then," I said tiredly. "Why don't you just settle for being fucking grateful instead?"

TWENTY-FOUR

When we'd cleaned up, I called Parker's office in New York from the little payphone outside the gas station. The line was faint and I had to stick one finger into my ear whenever there was traffic so I could hear the other end of the conversation.

To begin with, Bill Rendelson was very reluctant to put me through, but that was par for the course with Bill. And as soon as Parker himself came on the line, I knew we were in trouble.

"Charlie!" he said, a little too brightly. "Where are you?"

I took a moment to answer, raising an eyebrow at Sean, who was standing alongside me, listening in as best he could. He gave a brief shake of his head.

"Somewhere safe — for the moment," I said cautiously. "Listen, we found out the hospital severely modified Dr. Lee's medical records. There's no mention of Storax or the treatment he was on. They're saying the fall killed him — indirectly, of course. My father reckons it's all bullshit."

"Great," Parker said mechanically, and my trace of uncertainty solidified. "I'm sure Collingwood will check it out. Charlie, we need you to come in — you and Sean and your parents. Can you do that?"

"No — sorry," I said without regret. "Not until we find out whose side everybody's on. At the moment, there are too many loose ends flapping around. Not least of which are our old friends Vondie Blaylock and Don Kaminski."

Parker sighed loud enough for us both to hear. "What about them?" he asked, but there was a little more steel and snap to his voice.

"She just threw a great party in the middle of the road and invited us to dance," I said, keeping my own tone laconic, casual. "We declined. I imagine the car-rental people are going to be all over you sometime soon about what's left of the Navigator we hired, though — seeing as it was secured on the company credit card."

"Totaled, huh?"

"Totally," I agreed cheerfully. "And I'm afraid I had to get serious with our old friend Don Kaminski, but he *was* pointing a gun at my mother at the time. My father treated him at the scene, and he informs me he might even make it. Vondie, incidentally, bravely ran away and left him to die."

"Dammit, Charlie, you can't go around killing people."

"I can when they're having a bloody good go at killing us first," I shot back. "Of course, we realize that by the time Vondie puts in any kind of official report, we'll be the villains of the piece, but whether she's believed or not rather depends on whether she's working *with* Collingwood, or in spite of him." I let that one sink for a moment, then asked softly, "Which is it, Parker?"

"Why don't you ask him yourself," Parker said calmly, "seeing as he's right here?"

The phone went quiet for a moment. I jammed the receiver hard against my ear and heard increasingly frantic muttering going on at the other end, like Parker was holding the phone out to someone, trying to persuade them to take hold of it, and they weren't keen on the idea.

Eventually, I heard a slight rattle, the uncomfortable clearing of a throat.

"Mr. Collingwood," I said. "How is Vondie after her failed ambush? And the guy with the limp?"

"Vond*a*," Collingwood corrected auto

matically. "And how would I know that?"

"Because she's either got some rich uncle who's funding her in a little private enterprise, or she's using Uncle Sam's money instead," I said. "One way or another, she's not working alone in all this."

Collingwood said nothing. I suppose, looking at things from his point of view, there wasn't much he could say. I imagined they were recording this phone call, and on tape was the last place he'd choose to say something that might come back to haunt him under oath.

"There is another alternative, of course," I said. "And that's the possibility that you are totally incompetent."

He was cool enough to swallow the insult and not allow much more than a touch of irritation to creep through into his tone. "And just how, exactly, do you work that one out?"

"You told us there was an internal inquiry scheduled for Vondie as soon as she got back from leave," I said.

"That's correct."

"So how come she's just managed to turn up in sunny Massachusetts, armed, with a backup crew, when you're supposed to be reining her in?" I asked mildly. "Either that's down to the fact you're crap at your job,

Mr. Collingwood, or she's merely following orders — *your* orders."

There was an even longer pause this time and Sean began to make "Wind it up" motions, tapping the face of his Breitling. I nodded to him.

"I take your silence to mean you're having difficulty defending your position, Mr. Collingwood," I said. "Or difficulty tracing this call. One or the other."

"Give it up, Charlie," Collingwood shot back. "Like I said before, I can make things damn near impossible for you out there. And now you've injured two men — shot them with an illegally carried gun. You a poker player?"

"No," I said, "I'm not."

"Shame," he said. " 'Cause I was just gonna come out with a clever analogy about you bluffing with an empty hand. You got nothing but trouble coming your way if you don't turn yourselves in now. You have zip to bargain with."

"Not happening," I said. "Just one last thing, though, Collingwood."

"And what's that?"

"How did you know how many people I'd shot and injured, unless you've talked to your agent in the last half an hour?"

And when he didn't answer, I hung up.

with a sharp snick.

Sean raised an eyebrow in my direction. "So Collingwood's crooked."

"As a dog's hind leg, by the looks of things," I said, rubbing a tired hand round the back of my neck.

"And we're in the shit again?"

"Up to our ankles at the very least."

He gave me a half smile, one just vivid enough to sap a little of the weariness. "That's only a real problem," he said as we headed for the truck, "if you're standing on your head."

"Great," I muttered. "I'll remember that if I'm ever inclined towards gymnastics."

Sean gave a low groan. "Oh please," he said. "Don't get my hopes up."

I backhanded him in the stomach, just hard enough to sting the unbraced muscle, and dodged out of reach before he could retaliate, though he was grinning. Then I looked up and found my father watching us. He didn't say anything, just turned and climbed into the back of the pickup with grim disapproval plastered all over him.

Sean sobered instantly, everywhere but his eyes. There had been a distinct bounce in his step, I realized, ever since I'd kissed him in my parents' room that morning. A secret bubbling happiness that even a firefight and our current predicament couldn't dispel. If only we didn't have Collingwood's spooks and a global corporation on our backs, everything in the garden would have been rosy.

As we climbed into the truck, Sean glanced over his shoulder. "We need to find somewhere out of public view while we work out our options," he said. "And we need to do it quickly. It won't take them long to start looking for this vehicle."

He'd already disabled the tracker he'd found attached to the underside of the chassis, but that didn't mean Collingwood hadn't put out the pickup's registration to try and run us to earth the good old-fashioned way.

"And if we're going to run far, or for long, we need some cash," I said, pulling a fold of dollar bills out of my pocket. "I'm down to my last few bucks and, if Collingwood's put a block on our credit cards, we're going to have to try a bank or an ATM."

Sean nodded. "We'll do it sooner rather than later," he said. "They may well have already traced the phone we've just used, in which case we won't be giving them much else that's new if we use a bank close by."

A police car rushed past the gas station, sirens blazing as it went. I craned forwards in my seat to watch it go, mainly to make sure it didn't do a sudden U-turn and come back after us instead but, for now, our luck held.

Sean had just put the truck in gear and was preparing to move off when my father said, abruptly, "What about Miranda?"

Sean didn't quite sigh out loud, but inside his head it must have been another matter. "What about her?" he said, expressionless. "Either Collingwood's got people all over her, in which case she helped — willingly or unwillingly — to set us up, or they've got her phone tapped. Either way, the most sensible thing for us to do is stay as far away from her as we can."

For a moment I thought my father was going to argue, then he closed his eyes briefly and said with stiff-necked calm, "I told her we would get to the bottom of this, but I never dreamt that would put her in any danger. I gave her my word." He took in a breath, as if he needed to work his way up to this. "It's not something I do lightly and I would rather not break it, if I can avoid it."

Sean was silent for a moment. Glancing back, I saw my mother sneak her hand into my father's, give it a reassuring squeeze.

"Darling," she said, anxious to the point

of timidity. "If Sean thinks it's not safe —"

"We'll go," Sean said abruptly. "We'll swing by the house, but if we think it looks dodgy, we're not going in. All right?"

My father bridled at the steely tone, but he had the sense not to make an issue out of it when he was ahead. He nodded. "Thank you."

"And if we pass any banks on the way there, we stop," I said. When my father's face darkened, I added quickly, "Five minutes isn't going to make any difference, one way or another." And I hoped that it was true.

We washed out on both counts. A slow drive-by of Miranda Lee's house revealed no car in the driveway and no signs of habitation. We risked a phone call, but it rang out without reply.

And when I tried cards from three different accounts in the first hole-in-the-wall ATM we came across, the cash machine gave what I imagined was a mechanical gulping noise as it ate each one and passed on the indifferent advice that I should seek financial guidance at my earliest opportunity.

"So, we need cash and we need shelter," I said when we were back out on the road again. A state trooper passed us. I watched warily until he was out of sight. "A safe house. Somewhere to hole up."

"If Collingwood's put the squeeze on Parker, anything on the company's books will be compromised," Sean said. He glanced at my father in the rearview mirror. "If you have any wealthy ex-patients around here who owe you big favors, now would be a very good time to call them in."

"What about your ex-clients?" my father batted back at him. "Wouldn't any of them be grateful enough to assist?"

Sean pulled a face. "Our clients are Parker's clients," he said. "And if they're in Parker's system, Collingwood will have accessed their details by now."

"So, what do you suggest?" my father asked, a little of the old bite back in his voice. "That we keep driving round until we simply run out of petrol?"

"We can't run for long," Sean said, ignoring the tone, if not the question. "Not in this vehicle. And unless we nick one, we can't get another."

"We need Parker," I said. "Or unhindered access to him, at least."

Sean flashed me a tired smile. "Collingwood's got him sewn up tight," he said. "Clients, colleagues, friends — ours and

Parker's. Collingwood will have them all under surveillance."

"Ah," I said as a sudden thought struck me. "But what about someone who *isn't* a friend?"

His eyes flicked sideways. "You've thought of someone."

"I might have," I said, and told him who I had in mind.

Sean laughed, a short bark of sound, and cocked a cynical brow in my direction. "You really think you can talk him into helping us?"

"It's worth a try."

Still smiling, he shook his head. "Never let anyone tell you that you haven't got balls, Charlie."

"Well," I said, "you should know. . . ."

TWENTY-FIVE

We found a big shopping mall with four main department stores at its center and a rake of smaller shops scattered in between. The best thing was that one of the big stores had underground parking as well as the sprawling acres of asphalt up top. Sean drove the pickup into a corner of the second level underground and we left it there, nose to the wall. It left the plate on view, but we reckoned the bullet holes in the front windscreen would attract much more attention. And if the cops came checking plates on every red Ford F-350 they could find, we were likely screwed anyway.

The phone call was not one I was looking forward to making, but there was nobody else I could nominate. Determined to get it over with as fast as possible, I left Sean and my parents in the truck and took the nearest elevator up into the mall itself, pausing only to check the location of the payphones.

They turned out to be in the bustling Food Court, a recessed area at the far end of the mall. Restaurants lined three sides of a central square filled with tables and chairs like a school canteen. It seemed odd to find ladies in power suits, their feet surrounded by high-class carrier bags, lunching together in such a setting.

The mingling smells of fast food — stir-fry Chinese as well as the usual pizza, burgers, pretzels, and frosted doughnuts — hit my stomach hard and, though it quavered a little, I found I was actually hungry. It seemed a long time since breakfast, despite the fact that my watch told me lunch wasn't yet strictly overdue.

Nevertheless, my stride faltered. Whoever said an army marches on its stomach knew their human nature. And, besides, who knew when we'd get the chance to eat again? I fingered the diminished fold of dollar bills in my pocket.

Let's see what happens in the next ten minutes before we go blowing the funds, shall we?

The phones were halfway down the painted block corridor that led to the rest rooms, so there was a constant stream of people passing by, but nobody lingered as if to catch me making my illicit call, and there were no obvious surveillance teams at work. I shook myself for this creeping paranoia. Did Collingwood really have the manpower — not to mention the clout — to cover every payphone in the area, at this notice, just in case?

Get a grip, Fox!

I reached the phones and dialed the number quickly, before I had a chance to back out. The phone seemed to ring out for a long time before anyone picked up but, when they did, it was the guy I'd been hoping for.

I listened while he went through his ritual greeting, welcoming the caller to the facility and identifying himself by name.

"Hi, Nick," I said, trying for casual and not quite bringing it off. "You know who this is. Please — don't hang up."

I had no idea if Collingwood might be using some kind of recognition software to monitor phone calls made to anywhere connected to Parker or to me and Sean. If so, that would naturally include the gym a few blocks away from the office, where I'd so recently had my dramatic run-in with my personal trainer. Was it enough of a link that Parker's company had a group membership there? *One way to find out.*

I'd rarely had cause to speak to Nick on

the phone and I wasn't sure if he'd recognize my voice without a name attached to it. His sharply indrawn breath told me that he did.

"I got nothing to say to *you,* lady," he said, aggressive and sulky both at the same time. In the background I could hear the clank of fixed-weight machines being worked through innumerable sets of reps, the beat of music from the aerobics studio next door. "You nearly got me fired!"

"Then just listen," I said. "This is serious, Nick. We need your help."

"Huh!" The dismissive sound came out explosively loud in my ear. It clearly turned some heads at his end, too, because he suddenly lowered his voice to a savage whisper. "Why should I lift a goddamn finger to help you, Charlie? You damn near broke my freakin' *arm,* lady!" And, less angry, more plaintive: "Made me look like a fool."

I shut my eyes a moment. Acting in anger never worked out well for me. I should have learned that by now.

Two thickset men in jeans and work shirts were approaching along the narrow corridor, walking slightly spread out, not speaking, their gaze seemingly directed right at me. I shifted my weight slightly, just in case, but they kept on moving past, disappearing into the men's room doorway.

"I'm sorry, Nick," I said carefully, brain racing ahead. What did I know about Nick? What had Parker said about him? *Vain. Ambitious. A wanna-be.* I was suddenly aware of how hard I'd been gripping the phone. I forced my hand to relax a little. "But this is a matter of life and death. We need a guy we can trust. A guy who's coolheaded and tough, and the first person we thought of was you. But, if you're still too sore because I hurt your pride, I understand. Shame, though. Parker would have been so grateful, but —"

"Hey, wait up," he said, fast and anxious now. "I didn't say I wouldn't do it. If Mr. Armstrong's in trouble, I'm your guy!"

"No, I'm sorry, Nick — this was a mistake," I said, glad he couldn't see me smiling. "Look, it could be dangerous. I would hate to —"

"Tell me!" He almost squawked it out, then dropped his voice again, conspiratorial. "I can do it, Charlie. Just give me the chance to prove it to Mr. Armstrong, okay?"

"Okay," I said, aiming for reluctant admiration. "I need you to call Parker at his office and get him down to the gym as soon as you can. How you do it is up to you, but you've got to be casual, so anybody listening in doesn't suspect you're acting as an agent for us."

I used the word *agent* deliberately, knowing it would go straight to his ego like a tequila slammer to an empty stomach. I fed more coins into the phone and waited.

"Sure, no problem," he said, excited as a kid. "Er, what do I tell him?"

I held back a sigh. "I don't know, Nick," I said, reining in my impatience. It was a reasonable question. "Tell him you need to go over the results of the last fitness assessment you did for him — but whatever you do, for God's sake don't mention me by name. Or Sean. We've got some very bad people after us."

Some very official people. But I didn't tell him that.

"Tell Parker you think he'd want to know if he was going to put operatives into the field who might get themselves into trouble because they weren't fit. How's that? I'm sure you'll think of a way to dress it up so it sounds just right." I checked my watch. "I'll call back every hour until you get him there."

"Should I take your number, then he can call you?" Nick asked.

"No, it's not safe."

He bridled at that. "I ain't afraid of a little trouble."

"I didn't think for a moment that you would be, Nick," I said, keeping my voice as straight as my face. *To be afraid, first you have to fully appreciate the dangers involved.* "But nobody can hold out under interrogation forever. The less you know, the safer everybody is — you included. Standard operating procedure."

"Okay, okay. I get that," he said, more subdued. There was a pause like he was writing something down. "Supposing Mr. Armstrong, he doesn't go for it?"

"He will," I said, projecting more confidence than I felt. I waited for a woman to wheel a puce-faced, wailing toddler in a buggy past me and out into the Food Court. "Parker's a smart guy."

And I hoped to hell that I was right.

TWENTY-SIX

We met up with Parker in a rest area on I-95, just south of Boston. It was six hours since my initial phone call to Nick. Five hours since Nick had managed to get a sneaky message through to Parker, and my boss had given his watchdogs the slip and hotfooted it down to the gym to be waiting by the phone when I called back. And four hours since I'd called again, by which time he'd arranged a substantial float and instructions for a rendezvous.

So, not only smart but bloody efficient, too.

We'd hung around at the mall for as long as we reckoned we could get away with it, then headed towards the meeting point, staying as far away from the populated areas as we could manage.

According to Parker, the story Vondie was putting out — via Collingwood, naturally — was that they'd attempted to flag us down on the road in order to escort us back to New York. At which point we'd opened fire on them in a vicious and unprovoked attack. I'm not sure quite how they explained the obvious signs of a Stinger hit and heavy side impact on the Navigator, but I'm sure the empty brass I'd left behind inside it didn't help our cause any. Nor did leaving gunshot wounds in two of her team.

New York to Boston, if Parker kept it legal and didn't get too badly snarled up in traffic, was a four-hour drive. We timed our own arrival at the rest area to be a couple of minutes after his ETA. The less time we had to hang around in the open in a bullet-ridden — and technically *stolen* — vehicle, the better.

I'd told Parker what we were driving and we'd parked up out of the way to wait. Eventually, we spotted him behind the wheel of a nondescript silver five-year-old Toyota Camry. He did a slow circuit of the car park, showing himself to us, before pulling up. Sean restarted the engine and maneuvered the pickup in alongside him.

Parker had dressed down in jeans and a Tommy Hilfiger stripe shirt, worn with the collar open so it looked natural to have the tails out. As he walked round the back of the car to join us, a Honda Integra on big chrome wheels pulled in about a hundred meters away. Part of me half-expected someone like the young Canadian, Joe McGregor, to be driving the second car. Instead, it was Nick who climbed out and gave us a sketchy, self-conscious wave.

Sean merely raised an eyebrow at Parker's unusual choice of traveling companion. Parker gave him a look that said clearly, *don't ask.*

My mother got out of the pickup with her arms out, ready to embrace her savior. Parker ignored her. He was wearing sunglasses, but I could tell that his eyes were everywhere.

"Get your gear into the trunk of the Camry," he said. "Do it now."

Chastened, my parents began transferring luggage. Despite the size of my mother's suitcase, it didn't take long. Sean's and my squashy bags fitted in round the others, tight but snug.

When we were loaded, Parker installed my parents in the rear seat, got back into the Camry again and sedately drove it over to join the Integra. Sean and I gave the pickup a quick once-over, wiped down the obvious touch points, locked it up and walked away from it, towards the Camry. We walked away quickly, I noticed, without looking back —

as though the Ford were going to start whining like an abandoned dog.

By the time we'd rejoined him, Parker was back out from behind the wheel and standing by the driver's window. He stood, I noticed, casually relaxed with his hip turned side on to the car, not obviously using it for cover but using it just the same. He handed over the keys, jerked his head towards the interior.

"There's five grand in cash in the glove compartment," he said. "A couple of boxes of ammo, and two clean pay-as-you-go cell phones. But don't use them unless you have to — that goes as much for the hollow-points as it does for the Motorolas."

"Parker, we're not exactly virgins at this," I said mildly.

He smiled just a little, shrugged. "Better to tell you and risk offense, than not tell you and risk blowing the whole thing to hell and back."

"Speaking of which — what's he doing here?" Sean asked quietly, nodding in the direction of Nick, who was hurrying to join us.

"He got me the car," Parker admitted. "Belongs to his sister. She's out of town for another month — Europe. Besides, the Camry's the most common car on the road.

You couldn't blend in better if you tried."

"My sister's a real motorhead," Nick said, enthusiastic. "It's got the V-six under the hood, in case you need to make a run for the border." He suddenly realized what he'd said and his face fell comically. "Uh, but I'd appreciate it if you didn't."

I didn't like to point out that running from someone with Collingwood's resources was one car chase destined to be over very quickly. Instead, I offered him my hand.

"Thanks, Nick," I said with a warmth I didn't have to fake. "Good job."

He grinned at me. Still a big adventure for him, I saw. *Wait till the first time you get blood on your hands — either literally or metaphorically. See how much of a game you think it is then.*

Last thing, Parker handed over a scrap of paper. "I've set up temporary e-mail addresses for both of us," he said. "This is yours, and the password. Might be easier sometimes to use that than to phone. Any intel I can dig out for you — on Storax or this O'Loughlin character you mentioned — I'll send."

"Parker, you're a wonder," I murmured, studying the random series of numbers and letters that made up the e-mail address. "At the moment, it's a toss-up whether I want to adopt you or have your children."

He lifted an eyebrow, smiled a little and gave me a firm handshake, the same for Sean. "I'd settle for you straightening this mess out and getting back to work," he said.

"One more favor," Sean said. "When Vondie's crew jumped us, we were on our way back to see Jeremy Lee's widow, Miranda. We haven't been able to raise her since. Can you look into it for us? Check she's okay?"

Parker nodded, climbed into the passenger seat of Nick's Integra. "I find out anything, I'll e-mail." He slammed the door and dropped the window. "Make sure you get receipts for what you spend," he warned. "The five grand's for expenses — it's not a bonus, okay?"

We watched them pull out of the parking area and get back onto the highway before we climbed into the Camry, my parents still in the rear seat and Sean behind the wheel. It was clean and remarkably free from clutter inside. Nick's sister had a vanilla-scented air freshener hanging in front of one of the vents on the dashboard. I unhooked it and dropped it into the ashtray, which was part full of spare change.

When I checked the glove box, I found the money Parker had promised, in bundles of mixed-denomination used bills, held together with an elastic band. A brand-new-looking road map of America was tucked down the side of my seat. It was nice to work for a man who thought of everything.

Sean started the motor. The V-6 sounded polite rather than powerful. Parker must have filled up not long before he met us because the needle on the fuel gauge canted well to the right. Sean adjusted the driving position and glanced over his shoulder.

"So," he said. "Now we have clean transport, the question is, where do we go — apart from anywhere the hell away from here?"

"Houston," my father said, surprising me with the immediacy of his response. "It's where Storax have their U.S. headquarters and, as they seem to be at the center of this, it's where I should imagine we'll find some answers."

"Do you have any idea of how far it is to Texas?" Sean asked. "Or how long it will take us to get there?"

"No," my father said, unashamed. "Do you?"

"Roughly two thousand miles," Sean said without a blink. "That works out to the best part of two days' solid driving — if we don't want the luxury of stopping to sleep."

My father gave him his most arrogant surgeon's stare. "We'd *best* make a start, then, don't you think?"

We drove southwest, out of Massachusetts, down through Connecticut and slipped across the corner of New York state bypassing the city itself. A few hours later we were passing Scranton, Pennsylvania. The Camry wasn't exactly the rocket ship Nick had boasted, but it had cruise and air con and allowed us to make competent, inconspicuous progress.

We rolled on, mile after mile of undulating freeway, rocked by mammoth trucks that gained on us with relentless ease in the gathering dark, like supertankers crossing the English Channel.

Just after midnight, we hit Harrisburg and crossed the Susquehanna River. As oncoming headlights raked the interior, I glanced back and found my parents soundly asleep. My father had taken off his jacket and was using it as a blanket for my mother, who had curled up over the center armrest, her lips slightly parted as she slept, face pillowed on her hands like a praying child. My father had draped his arm across her shoulders, his head lolling sideways against the door glass. He was going to wake up with a hell of a stiff neck.

"They okay?" Sean asked, keeping his voice low.

"Out of it. How about you?"

In the dim glow from the instrument panel I saw him smile, little more than a twitch at the corner of his mouth.

"I'm okay," he said. He'd discarded his jacket and rolled back the cuffs of his shirt, revealing the lines of muscle definition in his forearms.

He drove without apparent effort, shoulders relaxed. I'd once driven through the night with Sean from Stuttgart to Berlin and back, at hair-raising speeds of over a hundred and sixty miles an hour for most of the journey. Going a steady sixty-five on an arrow-straight freeway should have been child's play by comparison, but there was so little stimulation that the hardest part was staying awake.

"Not getting tired?" I persisted. "Let me know as soon as you are and I'll take over for a while, let you get some shut-eye."

"I'm fine," he said. He glanced across at me. "You maybe ought to grab some sleep yourself, though, so you can spell me later."

"Yeah, I know," I said, lifting a wry shoulder. "Still too wired, I suppose."

"Well, you could always talk to me, Charlie. Keep me awake that way."

Something in the silky way he said it had my heart rate accelerating. "What about?"

He must have heard the way it slightly changed my voice, because he laughed softly. "Not that," he said dryly. "Although, if you *really* want to talk dirty to me while your parents are dozing lightly in the back-seat then feel free, by all means."

"No, I don't," I said, aiming for stern but badly let down by the hitch in my breath. "And it was a reasonable question. It's only your dirty mind that puts any other slant on it."

"Guilty," he said cheerfully. A pause. "Actually, I wanted to talk about us. About last night."

My pulse had begun to slow, but at that it took off again like someone had fed in a squirt of nitrous oxide. I felt the liquid burn under my skin, firing a primitive flight response that translated into such a fierce blush I was glad of the surrounding dark-ness.

"Wow," I said, surprisingly sedate. "I thought it was supposed to be the woman who always initiated conversations like that."

"Don't hedge, Charlie," he said, and though his voice was mild, I heard the underlying serrated edge to it. "I promised I wouldn't hurt you and . . . I did."

"No," I denied quickly. "It —"

"I hurt you," he repeated, more harshly. "And I'm sorry for it. More than you'll ever know." The last part was muttered under his breath, hardly audible.

"It doesn't matter," I said, and saw the frustrated twitch that crossed his features.

"Well, it damn well should," he said quietly. "In one breath I tell you that I'm not the same as the bastards who raped you, and then, in the next, I'm practically doing the same thing myself. I let my temper get away from me." His fingers flexed round the steering wheel and I had a flash recall of them braceleting my wrists with the same unforgiving grip. If his hollow tone was anything to go by, he remembered it, too. "It's not something I'm proud of."

"Do you honestly believe what you did — what *we* did — was rape?" I said, cracking the last word like a whip, even though I kept my voice down to a fierce whisper. "Nowhere near. It was wild, yes. A little rough, maybe. But if you think that qualifies, you're a bloody fool!"

"I disagree," he said icily.

I tried to let go of my anger. "Okay, have it your own way — yes, you raped me," I snapped, still keeping the volume as low as

I could manage, feeling the slightest tremble of the car as he controlled his reaction. "I didn't enjoy it for a second and I faked my orgasms — all of them. Happy now? Hair shirt uncomfortable enough for you?"

For a second Sean's face had frozen, then all the tension went out of him and he made a spluttering sound that might have been suppressed laughter, but could just as easily have been anguish.

"Oh my God, Charlie," he said at last, almost a groan, shaking his head. "I've always tried so hard not to remind you —"

"You don't," I said, cutting him short. "And do you think I don't know that, anyway? Do you honestly think I would stay with someone who deliberately set out to intimidate me? To hurt me?" I huffed out a breath. "You must have a pretty low opinion of my own sense of self-worth, Sean." A wisp of an earlier conversation drifted through my mind. "And you're not the only one," I muttered.

It took Sean all of a second to latch on to that. "Your father?"

"He made his feelings clear over breakfast," I said lightly. "Told me how pitiful he found me — that I must be a whack-job to have enjoyed any of it."

"Your father actually used the expression

'whack-job,' did he?" Sean murmured. "Don't you just hate it when he comes out with all that technical medical jargon?"

I shrugged, more an annoyed roll of my shoulders. "So I'm paraphrasing," I allowed. " 'Pitiful' is definitely one of his, though." I debated silently for a moment about how much of the rest to tell him, then said, "When I told him I wasn't likely to turn into a battered wife, he nearly had a heart attack."

"At the 'battered' part or the 'wife' part?"

"Either — or both. Take your pick."

A mile passed in silence. The periphery of the Camry's headlights picked out some unidentified large bird of prey lying as crumpled roadkill on the shoulder of the highway, the feathers of one stiffened wing ruffling slightly in the wash from the passing cars like it was waving for help.

"Does the prospect have any appeal for you?" Sean asked then. "Marriage?" There was nothing in his voice, no clue to which way he hoped I'd answer.

"I'm assuming that *wasn't* some kind of proposal," I said, with the same care I'd use to approach a suspect device. "I think, at the moment, I like things the way they are. What's that old saying? If it ain't broke, don't fix it. Besides, I'm not sure I'm good wife material — battered or otherwise." I only caught Sean's shoulders shift by some infinitesimal amount because I was looking, and looking hard. "Why?"

Sean pulled out to overtake a truck that seemed to be going only a few miles an hour slower than we were, despite hauling a double trailer-load of tree trunks behind it. The driver was tired enough to wander slightly into our lane as we drew alongside. Sean accelerated out from under him, then let the cruise control pick up again.

"Because it's not a question that's occurred to me before," he said. "And this is the kind of journey where no doubt we'll get to say all kinds of things that haven't occurred to us before." He took a breath, cocked his head as if considering. "I don't think I'm good husband material, either. And, if genetics are anything to go by, I'd make a lousy father," he added, his voice hardening just a touch.

"Well, like I said — if it ain't broke . . ."

"That's not to say it will never need fixing, at some point in the future," Sean said then, his voice calm, almost remote. "It's just, right now, I think this is probably all I have to give you . . . to give anyone. But, *if* — or *when*, but more likely *if* — I ever get to the stage where I feel inclined to propose, it would be to you, Charlie."

Inside my head I heard a soft hissing sound, like a lover's gasp or spray on summer lawns, followed by a smooth vortex of tightly spiraling, conflicted thoughts.

Too much.

Not enough.

As good as you're going to get.

"Thank you," I said quietly, listening to the rhythm of the tires over a section of mended road surface. And I found myself smiling. "My parents would utterly freak out."

"All the more reason for you to say yes, then — *if* or *when* it ever happens." I saw the answering flash of his teeth. And, as if I'd asked the question out loud, he added, "And no, you'd never be battered if you were my wife. Not by me, at any rate."

I reached across and brushed my fingers along his cheekbone, where the hollow dipped it into shadow. The skin was tightly stretched. He was concentrating on the road ahead and almost flinched under my touch.

"I'm not made of glass, Sean," I said, keeping my voice deceptively gentle. "Four of them couldn't break me. You won't come close. And I meant what I said last night."

"Which part?"

"The part where I told you if you dared

hold anything back, I'd kill you where you stood."

He let a laugh form, even if it was a shaky one. "Ah, *that* part," he murmured, and his voice turned wry. "I think you almost did."

I grinned at him, mostly in relief. A feeling that lasted right up until a disembodied voice spoke up from the backseat.

"I'd like to stop for a short break when it's next convenient," my father said, sounding cool and collected and not at all like a man who's only just woken from an uncomfortable nap. "No rush," he added. "Please — do finish your conversation first. . . ."

TWENTY-SEVEN

We drove through the night, Sean and I, heading steadily southwest, one town blurring into the next on the endless road. We passed signs for familiar English place names in unfamiliar locations, all jumbled together until it was like something out of a long bizarre dream.

Dawn broke as we crossed the border from Virginia into Tennessee, the sun rising ragged over the Appalachians. It sparkled on the dew in roadside pastures, stretching the outlines of the trees and the dozing horses. We chased our own shadow for a hundred miles before it fell away and was trampled beneath the Camry's wheels. The daylight, which started out so softly tentative, sharpened to a vicious edge by noon.

By 3:30 P.M., allowing for the hour we'd gained going from Eastern to Central time, we were approaching Memphis, Tennessee. We stopped at a roadside diner that had been cryogenically frozen sometime in the mid-fifties. An antique jukebox played a series of old maudlin country numbers, to which the wait staff sang along with more enthusiasm than technical accuracy. Raucous, but welcoming.

Our waitress must have been sixty-five, with skin the color of bourbon and the legs of a woman half her age, which she showed off beneath a skirt that was barely longer than her apron. She also had an accent thick enough to slice as she called my father "sugar" and bumped him with her hip as she declared how much she just loved the way he done talk.

I half-expected my father to tighten up like a clam's armpit at her impertinence. To my surprise he seemed happy to chat to the woman, whose name was Glory, even going so far as to compliment her on the caterwauling she'd been subjecting us to.

"I *knew* you folk must be believers," she said, beaming at us. "You on this road, headin' west, and you gotta be goin' to Graceland." She finished scribbling on her pad, already heading for the kitchen, which we could see into behind the long counter, calling back over her shoulder, "You see the King, sugar, you be sure to done tell him Glory never lost the faith, now. We know he ain't dead. It's all some gov'ment con-spiracy. Yes sir."

"Of course," my father said gravely. "I'd be delighted to pass on your message."

" 'Delighted,' huh?" She laughed and shook her head as she slapped in our order. "You sure talk pretty, sugar."

My father waited until she was out of earshot, then looked at the rest of us, totally puzzled. "The king of where?" he said.

Once we'd stopped, it was hard to get going again. We drove for another couple of hours before Sean finally caved and agreed that we needed to rest up until morning. By that time, we were just approaching Little Rock and night had fallen hard on Arkansas. The city looked very bright as it loomed on the horizon, initially beautiful against the utter black. It was only when we got nearer that the glitter seemed to take on a slightly tarnished quality.

We picked out a small nondescript chain hotel near the airport. It was close to the interstate and promised Jacuzzi rooms, free HBO movies, and a business center.

We left the Camry under the impressive portico at the front entrance while we gave the woman on the desk a sob story about having our passports and wallets stolen. We assuaged her immediate suspicions by producing a large enough cash deposit to counterbalance any qualms that we were about to trash the place and skip out. I think our air of bone-deep weariness mixed with English respectability won her over.

She gave us adjoining rooms, told us what time the complimentary breakfast would be laid out in the lobby, and had already wished us a pleasant stay before it occurred to her that might be difficult.

As we trudged back out to fetch our luggage I was aware of being so tired my vision was vibrating with the effort of keeping my eyes focused. I noted the movements of the people in the lobby almost on autopilot. If someone had pulled an Uzi out from under his coat I would have seen it, but I was probably too far gone to comprehend what it meant.

More than twenty-four hours sitting in a car without sports seats made me feel like someone had been kicking me repeatedly in the base of my spine. I was praying that, sometime sooner rather than later, the nerves into my left thigh would overload and shut down.

Walking out of the hotel, I could feel the gathered heat releasing from the ground up into the darkness. The night air was hot, and humid enough to drink, sticking my shirt to my back almost instantly. Sean popped the boot and he and my father grabbed the bags while my mother wheeled out a luggage trolley from the lobby.

It was only as Sean swung my bag up with the others that I remembered I hadn't re-zipped it fully after our last stop. I stretched out a hand, but I was too tired and too slow. The little brown plastic bottle of Vicodin I'd stuffed just inside the top of the bag went spinning onto the ground and rolled to a stop by my father's foot.

He picked it up before I could stop him, recognized the type of the bottle and scanned the label automatically. He was halfway through handing it back when he stopped, frowning, and looked up at me.

"These are yours, I assume, Charlotte?" he said. He held the pill bottle top and bottom with a disdainful finger and thumb and shook it gently, gauging the level of the contents by the resultant rattle.

"Yes," I said, reaching for the bottle, but he whisked it out of reach. Fatigue is not a good sedative for temper. Mine lurched into life, leaving blotches of vivid color splashed behind my eyes. I held my hand out. "Do you mind?"

"That my daughter's on Vicodin? Certainly," he said. He shook the bottle again and peered at the date on the label. "And, it would seem, consuming them at a rate of knots. How long have you been taking these?"

I glanced to Sean for support, but he had that closed-up look to his face. He didn't need to speak for me to see his mind working it out.

"On and off," I said bluntly, "since I was shot."

"I see. Naturally, you are aware that Vicodin is addictive if taken long term."

"Of course I am," I said, aiming for haughtiness but not making it much past defensive instead. "I don't use them regularly — just when I need to. When my leg's bad." *Like now. Give me the damn bottle!*

"Were you taking them the day you passed your physical?" Sean asked suddenly, and the unexpected coolness of the question took me by surprise. Our closeness in the car, our solidarity, suddenly evaporated in the face of his veiled accusation.

"I —"

"Oh for heaven's sake, both of you, leave the poor girl alone!" my mother said. "Don't you think she's got enough on her plate without you both jumping on her over this?"

"I'm sorry if you feel that the danger of our daughter turning into a drug addict is something we should just ignore, Elizabeth," my father said.

My mother laughed. It was a bone-tired laugh, with a touch of hysteria skimming just under the surface. "Of course we shouldn't ignore it, but I hardly think this is the time or the place to make it into an issue, either," she said stoutly. "How many times have you told me people make bad decisions when they're in pain? Surely you agree that's the last thing any of us want at the moment — least of all Charlotte?"

"Vicodin is a mix of acetaminophen and hydrocodone," my father bit out. "Hydrocodone is a narcotic pain reliever and acetaminophen increases its efficiency. Among the many possible side effects are impaired reactions and reduced mental alertness. In other words, it can severely affect the decision-making process. One has to be careful about letting a patient drive, or operate machinery. But you're quite happy for Charlotte to be running around with *that*," he said, gesturing dismissively in the direction of my hidden SIG, "and very little compunction about using it, when she's on this type of medication?"

My father must have been tired, too. It

was the first time I think I've ever heard him sound so testy with her, but my mother was undaunted. She drew herself up straight as a duchess and treated him to a lofty stare.

"And have Charlotte's actions so far shown her to be anything but entirely rational?" she asked with brittle dignity. She allowed herself a shaky smile. "Terrifyingly so," she added, and her voice softened. "Whether we like it or not, Richard, our lives are in Sean's and Charlotte's hands and I, for one, am prepared to trust her judgment implicitly."

My father gave a single muffled tut, the only outward sign of his annoyance. He glanced at Sean, as if for support. I didn't expect for a moment that he'd get it.

"Why didn't you tell me you were still taking painkillers, Charlie?" Sean said quietly.

My brain was working too sluggishly to do more than gape at him for a moment. "Don't start, Sean," I snapped. "Nothing I'm taking has stopped me from doing my job. You said so yourself."

"Yes, but are you doing it in spite of the Vicodin?" he said. "Or because of it?"

My mother stepped between us and put an arm around my shoulders. "Be sensible and leave it for now, Sean," she said gently. "We're all tired enough to say things we'll regret in the morning. Come along, Charlotte," she murmured steering me towards the hotel entrance. "I think for once we can forget equality of the sexes and leave the men to bring in the luggage, hm?"

I shrugged her arm away. "I can still do my job," I said, dogged, stepping away from her and struggling not to stagger.

"Of course you can, darling," she said, "but at what cost?"

As we walked through the automatic doors into the lobby, I glanced back and saw Sean and my father, still by the open boot of the car, watching us. They were standing shoulder-to-shoulder, I noticed, unconsciously presenting a united front. Ironic that the first time they were in any kind of accord, it was to team up against me.

We slept like the dead, all of us. Ten straight hours. When I woke, I reached out a hand and found Sean's side of the bed already empty but still warm from his body heat. When I lifted my head I heard the sound of running water in the shower, and I rolled over slightly to check the time on the digital clock by the bed. It was 6:08 A.M.

And as I moved, I noticed something else on the bedside table that hadn't been there when I'd crawled into bed the night before

— my bottle of Vicodin. For a moment the fear ran through me that perhaps Sean had junked the contents, to prove some kind of a point. I reached out and picked it up. The plastic bottle had some weight and I couldn't help the sense of relief that went with that discovery.

"If you need them, take them," Sean said from the bathroom doorway. I hadn't noticed the water shutting off. The light was a little behind him, so his face was in shadow. He had one bath towel wrapped loosely round his hips and was wiping his neck with another.

I felt something hard and frozen tighten at the center of me. "For the moment," I said baldly, "yes, I think I do."

"I know," he said, moving so he was in the light. His eyes were very dark and very cold. "But when we get back to New York, you are going to come off them. And if you need help to do that, we'll get it for you."

My chin came up and I met his gaze steadily. "I'm not hooked, Sean," I said. "I won't need any help."

He regarded me for an elongated moment, then nodded just once.

"Okay" was all he said.

The business center was deserted when we

went down to the lobby, so Sean was able to log on to the e-mail account Parker had given us without fear of anyone looking over our shoulder. There were two e-mails in the Inbox from the nondescript address Parker had set up for himself. Not worried about downloading viruses, Sean opened the first one.

Parker had clearly spent some time digging into Storax — background and financials. The number of zeros on the end of their annual profit figures had my eyes crossing.

"French parent company," Sean muttered, scanning the highlights. "Subsidiaries in Germany, Switzerland and the Far East, as well as the U.S. government contracts for bird flu and anthrax vaccines. Fingers in lots of pies."

"Well, Collingwood told us they had clout," I said, "and he had no reason to lie about that."

"Habit?" Sean suggested. He kept scrolling down. "Ah, here we are — Terry O'Loughlin. Bit sketchy, but I don't suppose Parker wanted to raise any flags."

The information Parker had uncovered simply said that Terry O'Loughlin had been listed as an employee of Storax Pharmaceutical for the past five years, and was registered as living alone at an address in an affluent suburb of Houston.

"Looks like they pay their legal people pretty well," Sean murmured. O'Loughlin drives a two-year-old Porsche 911 GT3." To make identifying our subject easier, Parker had included the registration number of the car and the color — Guards red.

"If we're going to try approaching this guy, we might be better confronting him at home," I said. "We stand a better chance than trying to force our way into Storax's headquarters, at any rate. My breaking and entering skills are somewhat limited."

"Yeah," Sean said with the ghost of a smile. "One day, when we've got time, I'll show you how to do the job properly."

"It's a date." I gave a wry smile of my own. "And they say romance is dead."

He grinned at me then, if briefly, and I felt some of the tension go out of my shoulders, but when he opened the second e-mail from Parker, suddenly neither of us was smiling anymore.

Miranda Lee's body had been discovered by local law-enforcement officers the previous evening. They'd called at her home in response to an anxious request from the friend in Vermont, who'd been expecting her that afternoon and had grown concerned when she didn't show.

According to the reports Parker had accessed, Miranda had swallowed a large quantity of sleeping pills, washed down with an even larger quantity of vodka. She'd left a terse little note blaming loneliness and the involvement of one of Jeremy's oldest friends in the events surrounding her husband's death for her decision.

"Bastards," I said slowly, clenched with an impotent rage. "They suicided her."

"Looks that way."

"Bloody hell." I stood for a moment, then let my breath out. "What do we tell my parents?"

Sean erased the e-mails, dumped the cache and logged off. "The truth," he said. "As much as they can stand of it."

"It makes me keener than ever to talk to O'Loughlin," I said bitterly. "Did he know what they were planning — is that why the cryptic warning? And, if so, why not tell her straight?"

"I'll make a point of asking that when we meet him," he said, getting to his feet. "But we must still be nearly six hundred miles from Houston. I suggest we make a start as soon as your parents are awake. We can grab breakfast on the way."

"So, how do we approach this guy?" I

wondered aloud as we walked to the elevators and punched the call button. "Phone? E-mail?"

"I think we might be better just turning up unannounced. Less chance of him setting us up if he doesn't know we're coming. We'll get a more honest reaction face-to-face."

"Okay, as long as you're not planning that we go sneaking in there in the middle of the night," I said.

Sean raised his eyebrows. "We've done plenty of sneaking, in our time," he pointed out mildly.

"Yeah, but this is Texas, Sean," I pointed out. The elevator doors opened and we stepped in. "This is the state where you practically have to explain to the licensing authority if your vehicle *doesn't* have a gun rack. No way do I want to go sneaking into somebody's house in the middle of the night when they're likely to be armed and trigger-happy."

"Come on, Charlie. He's a lawyer."

"So?" I muttered. "That just means he knows how to shoot you and get away with it."

By 7:30 A.M. we'd raided the hotel breakfast buffet and hit the road. We left Little Rock and drove to Texarkana, which straddles the border between Arkansas and Texas. It was purely my imagination, but I could have sworn the sky seemed bigger here.

We dropped off I-30 at Texarkana and took the smaller roads, a mix of dual and single carriageways that meant progress was slower than before. The alternative was a long detour to stick to the interstate, going via Dallas.

We'd broken the news about Miranda to my parents as soon as we were on the road.

"Oh, Richard," my mother had murmured with a choked-off sob.

My father's face had taken longer to react. "We should never have left her on her own," he said, remote.

I braced myself for condemnation for not providing her with protection, even though she'd rejected our offer of help, but he lapsed into silent brooding after that, refusing to be drawn into conversation.

East Texas was more thickly wooded than I'd been expecting. We drove past lakes and forests, through small towns with curiously old-fashioned signs outside the local businesses, like they hadn't been updated for the past forty years. Getting into the urban sprawl of Houston was a shock after the seemingly slower pace. The journey had taken forever and now, suddenly, we were here.

Traffic was starting to build, but we were all anxious to take a look at our enemy. Storax had their base of operations on a twenty-three-acre site in an area called Pearland, just outside Beltway 8. The site was on a high-tech industrial park, and surrounded by a good deal of chain-link fencing.

Even on a cursory drive-by, we saw patrols with dogs and CCTV that had been positioned by someone who knew what they were doing, backed up by more sophisticated and much less obvious security.

The grounds were not as attractively landscaped as those surrounding the hospital in Boston, but they were much more carefully thought out from a defensive point of view. The building itself was mirror glass and pale gray concrete, giving nothing away. Apart from the name in letters a meter high along the front wall, it could have housed anything. It wasn't even easy to identify the main entrance.

"We'd need an army to break into this place," Sean muttered, eyes still on the image of the pharmaceutical giant in the rear-view mirror as we drove away.

"Well, Sergeant, considering we are all the troops you have," I said, glancing across at him, "let's just hope we don't *need* to break in."

The light was starting to drop and when it went, it went fast, the blue end of the spectrum fading to leave a soft lingering red and orange cast. In under half an hour it seemed to go from squint-inducing sunlight to dark enough for the Camry's headlights to make a difference. Night didn't so much fall in Texas, it plummeted.

We headed back towards Houston Hobby airport, where there were any number of hotels and motels to choose from, picked one almost at random. My parents weren't keen on being left there, but the lure of a real bed quickly overpowered their protests. Sean and I grabbed a couple of hours' rest ourselves to let the rush hour die. Then we had a hot shower and a change of clothes, used the business center to print out route maps, and headed out again.

"You do realize," Sean said quietly, as we pulled back out onto the freeway, "that they should have caught us by now, don't you?"

"Yes, I've been wondering about that," I said. "If Collingwood sounded the alarm after Vondie's ambush failed to net us, we never should have made it out of Massachusetts."

"Mm, so does that make us good?" he

asked. "Or just lucky?"

I flashed him a tired smile. "Can't we be both?"

TWENTY-EIGHT

Terry O'Loughlin lived in a large house that showed both modern and Spanish influences, in the quiet, well-to-do suburb of West University Place. It was an area of wide leafy streets, triple-car garages and lawn sprinklers, just inside the 610 Loop, an inner ring road that circled the skyscraper heart of Houston.

We drove past slowly, while I made a bit of a show of holding up the map and pointing at signposts, just in case the neighbors were nosy. I had a sudden abrupt sense of déjà vu — of cruising past Miranda Lee's house and of what had been lurking inside. The O'Loughlin house, too, was quiet and dark.

"Look's like there's nobody home yet," Sean murmured. I heard the slightest catch in his voice and knew he, also, was thinking of Miranda.

"Hey, he has a Porsche lifestyle to support," I pointed out. "That probably means long hours — even for a corporate lawyer."

Sean considered this, nodding his acceptance. "Plus, he lives alone, so there's nobody to rush home to."

"So, do we broach him on the doorstep, or let him get inside?" I asked.

Sean shook his head. "Neither, I think," he said. "A GT3 is a hundred thousand dollars' worth of motorcar over here. There's no way you'd leave it on the driveway." He nodded at the attached garage. "There'll be an electric opener on the garage door. He may never need to get out of the car outside the house. And once he's inside there's no guarantee he'll open up to us. Particularly if he's feeling jumpy after what's happened."

"So . . . are you suggesting we break in and wait for him to turn up?"

"That would be my choice," Sean agreed.

"What about the alarm system? A house like that is bound to have one."

He gave me an offended look. "Do I look like an amateur?" he said. "Besides, most people get lazy about setting the alarm. Particularly," he added, leaning forwards and pointing towards a gray shadow that had suddenly appeared in one of the front windows, "when they have house cats."

The gray shape solidified into a large

447

white cat, who'd jumped onto the window-sill and sat up to wash its own chest with an exaggerated nodding motion, one forepaw dangling.

We left the Camry parked on the main road, near a church, which we hoped would excuse its presence, and walked back to the house. The place was still in darkness when we arrived and Sean quickly led the way past the garage towards the rear. We walked confidently, like we had every right to be there.

The back door had a solid bottom half, complete with cat flap, and a series of small panes of glass at the top. Sean slipped his pocketknife out and, while I kept a nervous watch, sliced through the putty holding the nearest piece of glass to the lock. In moments, he was reaching inside.

Despite his confidence over the lack of alarm, I still held my breath while he turned the key left on the inside like he was removing the fuse from a booby-trapped device. The lock disengaged smoothly and the door clicked open without any fuss. I listened for the shrill beeping that usually means you've got thirty seconds to enter your disarm code, but there was nothing.

We stepped through into a small tiled hallway — over the doormat, just in case —

and Sean threw me a quick, if rather smug, smile which I pretended not to see. I'd taken the SIG off my hip as soon as we'd got inside. Sean's Glock was already in his hand, though I hadn't even seen him reach for it. The handling of a gun came so naturally to Sean that it just seemed a part of him.

The hallway had a utility room off, with a locked door that presumably led to the garage. We moved on, into a large modern kitchen in glossy white, its surfaces wiped down and clear of clutter. There was an automatic water bowl on the floor. The only noise came from the constant trickle that flowed into it, the shunt of the refrigerator, and the distant hum of an air-conditioning unit.

As we stood there, letting the silences of the house settle around us, we heard a thump. The white cat we'd seen washing itself in the front window came stalking arrogantly into the kitchen and sat down in the center of the tiled floor to fix us with an accusing stare. I swear its unblinking eyes shifted from us to the huge double doors of the fridge and back again, pointedly.

"Feeding time, huh?" Sean murmured. "No chance, pal. Go and catch something."

As if understanding perfectly, the cat's tail

lashed twice. It got up abruptly and trotted out again, giving a last annoyed flick just as it disappeared through the doorway.

Enough illumination from the street filtered in through the front of the house to light our path. We followed the cat out of the kitchen, past an open-plan dining room with a glass-topped table supported on what appeared to be two blocks of marble. Huge ornate lamps were placed at either end. The table had only one place mat set on it.

Past the dining room was the living room with its big front window, which was where we'd seen the cat from the street. Just as we drew level with the doorway, the lights in the living room clicked on, nearly giving the pair of us a heart attack.

I hit the wall, bringing the SIG up instantly to cover the vestibule. Light from the living room spilled starkly into it, showing it to be empty apart from another cat, a tabby with a startlingly white bib and paws, sitting on a side table near the huge front door. The cat regarded me with disdain.

On the other side of the doorway, Sean had swung the Glock round to cover the living room. I glanced across at him.

"Clear," he said tightly. "Lights must be on a timer."

"Oh yeah, one of those scare-the-burglarsto-death timers."

"We're not burgling."

"Mm," I said. "Try telling that to the local cops if we get caught."

"Well," Sean said, "I wasn't planning on it. . . ."

Aware we could be seen easily from the street through the uncurtained windows, I peered quickly into the living room without entering. Thick rugs, white leather corner sofa, big-screen TV in an open cabinet with what looked to me like top-end hi-fi. To one side of the TV were half a dozen bottles of various spirits. Most of them were full, or very nearly.

In front of the sofa, three or four different remotes were scattered across the glass-topped coffee table, which was a scaled-down version of the one in the dining room. On the shelf underneath were a couple of magazines about American football and what looked like a travel brochure for Tanzania.

"Real bachelor pad," I said quietly.

Sean raised his eyebrows and jerked his head upwards. We climbed the open-tread stairs out of the vestibule carefully, to avoid the creaks. The landing was also open-plan, with a gallery that looked down over a balcony into the living area. Everywhere was

451

white. Another cat — dark gray this time — streaked past us on the landing and bolted for the stairs, a long sly blur in the gloom.

How many damn cats does this guy have?

Before we had a chance to go nosing into the upstairs rooms, we heard the sound of a powerful engine revving slightly as it changed gear for the turn into the driveway. The motor dropped back to a throaty idle, but the sound grew louder and more echoing, which could only mean the garage door was rising.

"Utility room?" I said. We needed to grab O'Loughlin as soon as he came into the house, without giving him chance to run, counterattack, or call for help. The ute was the most sheltered spot, unseen from the street. And just about roomy enough to take him down physically, if it came to that.

Sean nodded. He was already moving for the stairs, stealth discarded in favor of speed. As we reached the utility room, we saw a thin stream of light coming in from under the door leading to the garage. There was the clank of a motorized mechanism moving slowly through its operation, and then the sounds of the street were muffled again.

Sean and I braced ourselves on either side of the door. I slotted the SIG back into its holster, making sure my jacket slid free over the butt, just in case. Sean watched me and lifted a brow.

We need him to trust us, don't we?

Yeah, but not that much.

The Glock stayed firmly in his hand.

The Porsche's engine had already shut off and we heard the plip of a car alarm being set. O'Loughlin might leave his house alarm deactivated, but he wasn't *too* careless with his toys, then.

Footsteps. A key fumbling into the lock, rattling the handle a little. The door opened, bringing a rush of warmer air with it into the coolness of the house interior.

Even as the figure stepped into range between me and Sean, I registered something was off. O'Loughlin was shorter than I was expecting, slightly built, shoulder-length hair, curves, soft voice.

"Hey, guys — mama's home!"

Terry O'Loughlin's a woman. This stupidly obvious fact hit me at just about the same time that something warned Terry she had more than cats in her house. The briefcase and papers she'd been carrying spilled from her suddenly nerveless hands, hit the floor and scattered. The woman's automatic flight reflex had her wheeling back for the door to the garage, for the safety of her car, but

Sean had already moved behind her and shouldered it shut.

The noise the door made as it slammed seemed to jolt her out of stasis. Realizing she couldn't go back, she gave a strangled cry and tried to bolt for the kitchen instead.

I grabbed her arms as she scrambled to get past me. She couldn't break my grip but she fought anyway, panic lending her strength. It was a short-term loan and the payments were steep. She struggled on for a few moments, exhausting herself in the process, then went limp. I relaxed my hold on her just a little, enough so we could talk to her.

"That's better," Sean said soothingly. The Glock was out of sight. "We're not here to hurt you, Terry. We just want to —"

"The hell you're not!" Terry said fiercely, surging forwards to lash out with her right foot, aiming for his groin.

Sean had the fastest reactions of anyone I've ever known. He managed to twist slightly and took the bulk of the blow on his hip, but it was still enough to make him stagger back, doubled over.

I yanked Terry round and shoved her up against the wall by the garage door, and I admit I wasn't too gentle about it. She cursed the pair of us with colorful defiance.

"Sean!" I said, over my shoulder. "Are you all right?"

For a moment there was no reply. Then he said in a thickened voice, "Yeah, give me a minute. Christ Jesus, she's got a kick like a bloody mule."

Terry gave a slightly hysterical laugh and I shook her roughly.

"For God's sake, Terry, we didn't come for this!" I snapped. "Don't make me finish what *you've* started."

There must have been something in my voice that got through, because she stopped struggling and went quiet under my hands apart from a slight tremble, almost a vibration. It could have been anger, or fear, or a mix of the two.

I realized I'd been holding on to her hard enough for the pain to stop her breath, and I relaxed my grip on her arms a little. The release made her gulp in air like a surfacing swimmer.

"I'm going to let go of you now and step back," I said. "But you make any sudden moves, Terry, and I swear I'll put you on the deck and you'll stay there. Do you understand me?"

She swallowed and nodded, as much as she was able to with her face against the wall.

I let go and moved back quickly enough to put me out of range, skimming a quick glance across at Sean as I did so. He was propped against the door frame to the kitchen, bent forwards with one hand braced on his thigh.

Terry straightened and turned carefully, a little jerky, like she wasn't sure she wanted to get a good look at us, although I certainly wanted to get a good look at her. She stood taut as wire, still with that slight quiver, as though her brain was trying to override her body's natural instinct to run and was having to fight to do so. There were two of us, we'd invaded her home and, in her eyes at least, had attacked her, but she was holding. I felt a sneaking admiration for her guts, if nothing else.

"What do you want?" she asked in a small voice.

"We're here because of Miranda Lee," I said. "You sent her an e-mail a couple of days ago, warning her to be careful, but you were too late. She's dead."

"I know. I just heard today," Terry said, and there was no disguising the wobble in her voice. "What do you want with me?"

"It wasn't suicide," I said bluntly. "We think she was killed and we think you might know why."

456

She stiffened. "Killed? But —" She broke off, bit her lip. "That makes no sense. She OD'ed."

"But you must have thought Miranda was in danger, or why send her a warning?" I said.

She swallowed, took a moment to smooth down the jacket of her suit. I was no expert, but it looked like a very expensive suit. Dark cloth that draped well and hadn't creased even after a long day at the office and a minor fracas with intruders. Good cut and it . . . suited her.

"How —" she began, and stopped. Started again, her eyebrow coolly raised this time. "How do you know I sent her anything?"

"Because she told me — a few hours before she was killed," I said. "Were you just trying to scare her? Because, if so, it worked."

Terry flushed. "Of course I wasn't." She flicked her gaze towards Sean, who was watching her with a brooding stare. Her head came up and she met my eyes steadily. "I'd heard she was relying on a guy — some Brit doctor she'd called in — to be an expert witness. But reports were coming in that he was unreliable. It was my opinion that using him would ruin the chances of her lawsuit being successful. . . ."

Her voice trailed away and her gaze sharpened on me. "You're his daughter, aren't you?' she said, almost accusing, like I'd tried to trick her. "I read about you. They said you'd —"

"Stick to the point, Terry," I cut in.

She swallowed. "I didn't know Mrs. Lee — at all, really. We never met. Never even spoke on the phone. Just e-mails. But I . . . liked her. I felt sorry for her."

"You're a lawyer," Sean said flatly.

Sensing insult, a hint of color lit her cheeks. "So?"

"I thought corporate lawyers had their emotions surgically removed during training."

She pulled a face that contained a rueful anger. "Not all of us," she said. Now it wasn't under strain, her voice had a gentle Texas drawl with a wisp of smoke going on underneath it. If she'd been less smart she would have been called pretty, but there was an intense intelligence clear behind her eyes that dared you to demean what she'd made of herself by reducing her worth to such terms.

Into this silent standoff, the white cat that had confronted us in the kitchen appeared, twining through her legs and looking up at her face imploringly. When she glanced down, the cat made an openmouthed mute plea, whiskers quivering with the effort it put into making no noise whatsoever.

Terry stared down at it for a moment, unseeingly. Then she bent and swept the animal up into her arms, heedless of stray hairs. The cat squirmed until it had both front paws draped over her shoulder and began to purr loudly. She kissed the top of its head, which made it drop a gear and purr even harder.

"I need to feed my guys," she said roughly, hefting the cat. "You going to stop me from doing that?"

Sean merely straightened and invited her towards the kitchen with the inclined head and regal bow of a maître d'. Terry, aware of being mocked, glared at him and marched past with her head high and her spine very straight. I saw her glance at the back door, just once, as we passed, but she didn't try to run. I think she probably realized that she'd taken Sean by surprise once and that wasn't going to happen again.

As soon as she switched on the kitchen lights and dropped the white cat onto the floor, another three of its furry friends appeared, muttering at Terry and bickering among themselves.

"So," Sean prompted, "you felt sorry for

Miranda and you decided to help her. Why?"

"Her husband was dying," Terry said, but she was hedging. "Isn't that reason enough?"

"You work for a drug company," Sean said. "The chances are that, even with the best will in the world, lots of your customers are either dying themselves, or they have friends or relatives who are. What was special about her?"

Terry was spooning some foul-smelling, gelatinous, vaguely meaty product out of a can into two double bowls.

"Because it shouldn't have happened," she said at last, banging the last of the cat food off the spoon more fiercely than she needed to. "He should never have died."

"So why did he?"

She lifted the bowls off the counter and turned to face us, pausing a moment. The feline tangle around her ankles became a frantic melee at the delay. The fourth cat, a black-and-white, stood up on its hind feet and dug its claws into Terry's leg at the knee by way of retribution, pulling a thread in her trousers. She shook the cat loose absently, without annoyance, and put the bowls down. Four heads dived in.

"I could be fired for discussing any of this

460

with you," she said at last, almost with a sigh. "I signed a confidentiality agreement."

"You could be killed if you don't," Sean said bluntly. "Storax don't seem to like loose ends."

"Jeremy Lee died because he medicated himself with a drug for osteoporosis, produced by my company — the company I work for," she amended. "The technical side of it is not my area, but from what I understand, the treatment's still being tested on a very carefully controlled group of patients. Dr. Lee fell outside that group and he suffered certain . . . side effects."

"You make it sound like headache and nausea," Sean said, acidic. "His bones crumbled away to nothing and he died in agony. Yeah, I'll say he suffered 'certain side effects.' What was different about him?"

She flicked her eyes between the two of us. "Basically, he wasn't Caucasian," she said. "Dr. Lee was a second-generation American, but his grandparents were Korean."

I felt my eyebrows arch. "Storax developed a drug that will work only on white people?" I said, not bothering to hide my disgust. "I'm not surprised they've been going to all this trouble to cover it up."

Terry flushed. "It wasn't intentional!" she

said through clenched teeth. "It's a genetic thing — I don't understand all the technical details. But I do know that our research scientists are working round the clock to come up with a solution. In the meantime, it's not something we want to shout about."

"Yes, but it's something your company will do almost anything to deny," I said. "No wonder they didn't want a top orthopedic surgeon sticking his nose in."

"Top surgeon, huh?" Terry threw back at me with a toss of her head. "From what I hear, he's a drunk who can't keep his hands off underage girls."

"So they didn't tell you about the dirty tricks campaign they've been running against my father?" I said, keeping my voice mild even though I could feel the rage building like a low-level background hum. "They didn't tell you about the threats they made to my mother — what they'd do to her — if he didn't cooperate?"

Terry glared back at me, but wisely held her tongue. She had more self-control than I did.

"So, you knew that Jeremy Lee's premature death was as a direct result of the Storax treatment," Sean said, stepping in, "but still Storax didn't suspend the drug or wait to put it out until the scientists had come up with the answer?"

She had the grace to look a little ashamed. "There are millions of dollars at stake," she muttered. "*Hundreds* of millions. Osteoporosis is a major problem and it's only going to get worse. The drug works brilliantly —"

"Yeah, on *some* patients. But it kills others," I put in. She wouldn't meet my eyes.

"Do you think I don't know that?" she said quietly. "Why do you think I got in touch with Mrs. Lee? I told her she should sue — that the company could afford it. I couldn't bring myself to tell her outright what had happened, but I dropped hints that she should look closely at what was happening to his bones. I don't know if she followed that advice or not."

"She did — she got in touch with my father," I said stonily. "He answered a cry for help from an old friend and, because he might have been getting close to the truth, your people administered a fatal dose of morphine to Jeremy, doctored his hospital records, and pushed all the blame firmly onto my father — whose reputation they then started to systematically trash."

"That can't possibly be true," Terry said, but there was a shaken note to her voice that hadn't been there before. "The people I work for are not murderers!"

She turned away, hands to her face, brow creased.

"Miranda Lee didn't kill herself," I said softly, certain of it. "They fed her with pills and booze and stood over her until she was unconscious, so she couldn't make any attempt to save herself."

"You don't know that," Terry said, her voice a shocked whisper. "She missed her husband. She was lonely, depressed. I could tell that from her e-mails —"

"We went to see her the day before she died," Sean said, cutting her off. "She wasn't suicidal then."

Terry had no response for that. Sean regarded her with a calm stare. "If you've got such a social conscience, Terry, why are you working for an organization that only cares about the bottom line, and to hell with who gets hurt, or dies, in the process?"

She pulled a face. "You make them sound like they're selling to junkies on street corners," she said. "The products Storax manufacture save countless lives."

"And that counterbalances the odd 'mistake' like Jeremy Lee?" he said, his cynicism uppermost. "Enough that you sleep at night?"

"Yes, I sleep at night," Terry said firmly, meeting his gaze. "Do you?"

464

"So, Terry O'Loughlin has agreed to help you," Parker said, his voice scratchy over the long-distance mobile phone line. Even so, the skeptical note in his voice came over loud and clear. "What makes you think you can trust her?"

"Basically," I said quietly, "because we don't have a choice." I was standing on the open-plan landing overlooking Terry O'Loughlin's living room, keeping an eye on her as she sat on the huge leather sofa below me. She had her feet curled up underneath her, watching a football game with the fixed concentration of someone who's not taking in what's happening on the screen. I couldn't really blame her for that.

It was nearly 7:00 P.M. Central, which made it an hour later in New York — well outside office hours. Parker had still answered his mobile phone almost on the first ring.

"All we have at the moment is my father's word against the Boston hospital on what was in Jeremy Lee's original medical records," I went on. "We need proof of what the Storax treatment does to people of his ethnicity — and the fact that they knew that and didn't put out any general warnings, or withdraw the treatment. And for that we have to get inside Storax ourselves. We can't rely on outsiders — or insiders, for that matter. We need firsthand knowledge."

"And she's agreed to take you in," Parker said flatly. "Just like that."

I sighed and passed a weary hand across my eyes. "The place is a fortress, Parker," I said. "Short of aerial bombardment and a small army, how else are we going to get in there?"

His silence spoke louder than his words. Eventually, he said, "I'd be happier if you'd wait and let me tackle it from this end. I'm working my way up the chain of command and the FBI are trying to locate Collingwood and Vonda Blaylock. The more they look into what Collingwood's been up to, the more they find."

"But they haven't arrested them?"

"Not yet," Parker said, adding quickly,

"but they will, Charlie. You can take that to the bank. And when they do, they can't help but follow the trail right back to Storax. This whole thing will be blown wide open."

"Yeah, by which time Storax will have shredded any evidence that they had a hand in Jeremy Lee's death — or Miranda's supposed suicide — or that they knew about the side effects of the treatment. My father will never clear his name."

"But you'll be able to come out of hiding."

"It's not enough," I said. "Not nearly enough."

Down in the living room, the TV announcers went into a frenzy as something exciting happened in the game, which promptly broke for ads. The black-and-white cat jumped up onto the sofa and tried to climb onto Terry's lap. She stroked its head absently.

"Where are you now?" Parker asked in my ear.

"Still at the house," I said, being careful not to use Terry's name to alert her. The last thing I wanted was Terry taking undue interest in who I was talking to, or what I was saying. As long as she didn't try to make any calls herself while she thought I wasn't looking. "Sean's gone to retrieve my parents from the hotel and bring them back here."

"Is that wise?"

"Probably not," I said, "but we don't particularly want to leave her to her own devices, and it's easier to keep an eye on everybody if we're all together."

"Yeah, it's a tough one," Parker said. "Just trust me when I say I'm doing everything I can to work it out at this end."

"I know," I said. "But if you can't come up with anything by tomorrow night, it looks like we're going in."

"Why the big hurry?"

"Well, for one thing, it's a weekend, so half the staff won't be there," I said. "And, for another, I don't know how much longer my father's going to hold together. This is putting a hell of a strain on him — more than we realized." *More than* I *realized, that's for sure.*

Parker was quiet again and I didn't hurry him. We'd drawn the curtains, but they were more for decoration than effect, made of thin material, so I saw the lights sweep across the front window. I heard the sound of an engine pulling into the driveway, the Camry's motor sounding a lot more mundane than Terry's Porsche. The garage door clanked upwards again.

"Who's going in?" Parker asked.

"I will — with my father," I said, mentally crossing my fingers and hoping I could talk Sean into staying on the outside.

"At risk of repeating myself, is that wise?" Parker said mildly. "Taking your father with you, I mean."

"I don't have much of a choice," I said. "We need complex medical information and I wouldn't have a clue what I'm supposed to be looking for. I don't like the idea either, but this is a one-hit deal. We only have one chance to get it right and we have to move soon."

"Okay," Parker said at last, the reluctance sounding like a bad taste in his mouth. "But keep me informed, Charlie — I mean it. Every step of the way. I don't know how much cavalry I can rustle up if you get yourselves into trouble, but I'll do what I can."

By the time I'd finished the call and reached the bottom of the stairs, Sean had brought my parents into the house from the garage and was conducting awkward introductions with Terry O'Loughlin. She'd pushed the cat aside and jumped to her feet as soon as she heard the handle turn on the connecting door between the house and the garage, and waited awkwardly until the three of them walked in.

My father barely seemed able to bring himself to acknowledge Terry, but my mother smiled at her with every appearance of sincerity.

"I so glad we've met because I wanted to thank you," she said, "for all the support you gave Miranda after Jeremy died. You didn't have to do that, I know, but she was *so* grateful."

Terry looked flustered, but my mother gave her hand a gentle pat and moved on into the living room, looking round. Her eyes were bright with curiosity. "What an interesting space," she said, although I heard the reservation in her voice. "Shall I make us a nice cup of tea?"

Sean glanced hopefully at her. "I'm sure we could all do with some food."

"Of course," my mother said. "If you've no objections?" she added politely to Terry, who was regarding her with confusion. "I'd hate to interfere. I know I don't like anyone else in my kitchen. You must be terribly unsettled to have strangers in your house like this."

She made us sound like distance relatives who'd unexpectedly dropped by, rather than fugitives from justice who'd ambushed Terry and were almost — but not quite — holding her at gunpoint.

"Sure," Terry said, suddenly aware that my mother was still pinning her with an inquiring stare. "Why not? Knock yourself out."

My mother beamed at her and bustled out to the kitchen. We could hear her opening the fridge and the cupboards to take a quick inventory, talking to the cats while she did so. The black-and-white one stayed on the sofa near Terry, but the others had decided to see if they could con a second meal out of this new arrival.

"I could do with a drink," my father said, with an intensity that rang all kinds of alarm bells. He moved over to the bottles Terry kept by the TV set. I glanced at Sean, found him watching my father with narrowed eyes.

"Why don't you wait until you've had something to eat, Richard?" he said, his voice so calm and reasonable it sent shivers down my spine. "Elizabeth's a wonderful cook. You wouldn't want to spoil your appetite."

"I'm quite aware of my wife's abilities," my father snapped, slipping on his glasses to inspect the label on a bottle of Scotch. He clearly found it to his satisfaction. "But I think you'll find that a good single malt would never spoil one's appetite."

For a moment Sean didn't move. He and

my father locked gazes, and somewhere in the back of my mind I swear I heard the crack of bone and muscle as they silently struggled for supremacy. Terry's eyes darted between the two of them. I felt the sudden mortification that can only be brought on by the embarrassing behavior of a close relative in front of strangers.

Sean let the challenge drop with a shrug, like it was no big deal, his expression carefully neutral. My father eyed him uncertainly for a second, then his gaze shifted to Terry. "Would you mind, Ms. O'Loughlin?"

She made a kind of "whatever" gesture, which he took to mean assent. He saw me still staring, though, and waved the bottle in my direction. "Will you join me, Charlotte?" he asked. Then, before I could answer, added with a definite taunt, "Ah, no. Best not to mix alcohol with what you're taking, hm?"

I hid the flinch under a flare of anger. Sean stepped between us.

"Back off, Richard," he said pleasantly. "This isn't the time or the place to give your daughter a hard time."

My father opened his mouth to respond, took one look at Sean's face and, uncharacteristically for him, shut it again. He settled for sweeping out in his best superior consultant's manner, taking the whisky with him — presumably in search of a glass. So, he hadn't quite lowered his standards far enough to swig straight out of the bottle.

I turned back and found Terry watching me, her face thoughtful.

My mother appeared in the kitchen doorway. She was drying her hands on a tea towel, her movements slowing as she registered the level of tension.

"You don't keep much in stock do you, dear?" she said, smiling nervously at Terry. "I'm going to need a few things."

"I eat out a lot, but I could run down to the store," Terry offered quickly. "There's a Randalls about two blocks east of here."

Sean threw her a swift glance that said *Oh, please,* and turned back to my mother. "It's okay," he said, reaching for the car keys again with a resigned sigh. "Give me a list."

My mother cooked mountains of lasagne and insisted we eat at the dining table with due ceremony. My father was halfway down his third shot of whisky by the time we sat down, and he was starting to show the effects. His speech was straight and his mind seemed as sharp as ever, but he was edgy and restless, his hands fidgeting with the cutlery, like he couldn't keep them still. It scared me more than I liked to admit.

I could have done with a drink myself, but I'd stuck to water and promised myself one Vicodin later, just to ease the dull background ache in my leg. Over the past few days I hadn't been able to exercise it at all, and spending hour after hour sitting in a car had a cumulative effect. The pain was grinding me down, I realized, dulling my responses when I couldn't afford for them to be anything but scalpel-sharp. I was doing my best to hide it from Sean, but I knew I wasn't succeeding, even if he had yet to confront me with it. And if my father had been on form he would have seen it, too.

"So," Sean said when we'd cleared our plates with a single-minded speed that was probably both gratifying and insulting to my mother's culinary abilities, "what's the plan for tomorrow, Terry? How do we get in?"

Terry sat with her forearms resting on the glass tabletop. She frowned. "I think the best idea is going to be the same way I go in every day," she said. "Through the front entrance."

"It has dash and cunning, with a healthy dose of stupidity," I said to Sean. "I like it."

"Ballsy, certainly," he said, turning back to Terry. "What about security?"

"Just the usual," she said with a shrug. "There are a couple of uniformed guys in the lobby area, another half dozen somewhere close by. I've only seen them called out for real once — we had trouble with some animal rights protesters a year or so back. I'm no expert, but our guys seem to know their job. You know, they move fast, take no prisoners."

I hoped that was just a phrase, rather than an accurate description.

"So, what's the setup at the front entrance. Do you have a swipe card?"

Terry nodded. "Outside the main door. You go through two sets of glass sliding doors into the lobby, then through the metal detectors into the rest of the building."

"Metal detectors?" I said. I glanced at Sean. *No guns.*

Damn.

"Isn't there a back way in or something?" The last thing I wanted to do was go into the dragon's den unarmed. "We might as well write 'Eat Me' across our foreheads and cover ourselves in barbecue sauce."

Terry allowed herself a small smile, but shook her head firmly. "The whole security system was overhauled at the start of this year," she said. "They brought in consultants and tested it pretty thoroughly. The only way you stand a chance of getting in is walking right in through the front door and having somebody they trust vouching for you."

The mention of the word *trust* brought a cloud to her face, as if the scope of her betrayal was really coming home to her.

My mother was sitting next to her at the table. She reached across and put her hand over Terry's, gave it a squeeze.

"You're doing the right thing, dear," she said. "You must know that. These people you work for, they're prepared to let patients die for the sake of profit, and then pass the blame on to someone else."

"It's not like —" Terry began, then broke off, bit her lip. "I'm sorry," she said. "You're right, of course. It's *exactly* like that." She sat back and gave us all a tired smile. "Would you excuse me, please? I hate to be a bad hostess, but it's been kind of a stressful day. I'm gonna call it a night."

Sean and my father both got to their feet as she did. She gave them another wan little smile and headed for the stairs.

"What about her phone?" I asked quietly once Terry was out of earshot.

"I removed the landline phones from every room except the living room, and I have Terry's mobile right here," Sean said, lifting a small gloss-black cell phone out of his pocket.

"She gave it up without a fight?" I said. "You surprise me."

"Did you have to remind me about that?" Sean winced a little. "I wasn't prepared to go another round with that lady."

My father, meanwhile, seemed to be paying little attention to our conversation but was focusing on his whisky glass, which was now all but empty. He tilted it and stared regretfully into the bottom, then pushed his chair back purposefully.

"I think you've had enough, Richard," Sean said, and this time he allowed the fangs to show through the veneer of civility that habitually cloaked him. It even made my father pause, but only for a second. With a careless shrug, he reached for the bottle of single malt.

"In your opinion, perhaps," he said.

"No, Richard, in my opinion too," my mother said with quietly commanding dignity. She looked across the table straight into his eyes and suddenly her face seemed much less soft than I could ever remember it. "Tomorrow's going to be a trial, but with any luck this will all be over soon," she said, her voice soothing. "We can go home — back to our normal life." She let that one sink in for a moment, then added gently, "Why don't you go to bed, darling? Get some rest. I'll be up shortly."

He seemed to waver, then nodded, his face grave. There was a very slight sway to him, I noticed. The food had not quite managed to absorb the amount of spirits he'd put away over the last couple of hours. He was not a drinker by nature and his system wasn't hardened. It was starting to land punches.

"It seems I'm outnumbered," he said stiffly. "In that case, I'll say good night." And, with an almost firm tread, he walked out of the room.

We watched him go. Sean glanced at my mother. "Thank you," he said.

She made a little self-deprecatory movement of her shoulders. "I didn't do it for you," she said simply. "I did it for Richard. And for myself, if I'm honest."

She looked down at her hands, at the plain gold band on her left hand. "And I'm going to do something else for Richard tomorrow — and I know you'll argue, Charlotte, but my mind is quite made up about this."

I saw it coming, felt the jolt of that realization like a fist to the stomach, knocking the breath out of me. "No," I said. "No, you can't —"

"Elizabeth —" Sean began at the same time, his voice a low growl.

"Yes, I can," she said calmly. "He needs me. You've seen that — both of you. He's been strong for me for most of our married life. Now it's my turn to be strong for him." She got neatly to her feet, her face almost serene now her mind was made up. "When you go into Storax tomorrow, I'm going with you. And I'm afraid," she added with a firm but apologetic smile, "that nothing either of you can say will stop me."

THIRTY

At precisely 8:15 P.M. the following evening, we drove through the main gate into Storax Pharmaceutical.

I was with Terry in the Porsche. The Camry containing my parents followed more sedately behind, with Sean at the wheel.

Terry greeted the guy on the gate with an easy rueful smile that made me wonder about her acting abilities. She behaved as though coming into work on a weekend evening was normal, rather than the exceptional circumstance of trying to smuggle four people into the building who might very well topple the company. It was only if you saw how tightly her hands were gripping the steering wheel that you would have realized anything was wrong.

Fortunately, it was a Saturday night and there was some kind of ball game playing from the radio in the gatehouse. The guard waved us on after only a cursory inspection.

Terry had driven the GT3 with verve and skill on the way there, zipping through the light traffic without appearing to take risks, or hold anyone up. She was immaculately dressed, too, every inch the successful corporate lawyer, in another suit that looked as if it cost about the same as the car. By contrast, I felt very shabby. No change there, then.

We'd spent a restless night from Friday into Saturday morning. Sean and I had taken turns to keep a watch, dozing on the sofa between times. The cats ambushed us at regular intervals, as though they'd been instructed to make sure we got little rest. I tried shutting them in the kitchen, but they just yowled until we let them out again.

We spent most of Saturday cooped up inside, waiting, each preparing in the way we knew best. With some reluctance, Terry had gone about her usual Saturday domestic chores. My father stayed largely in his room and I didn't feel inclined to disturb him. Sean went out to the garage to strip and clean our guns, one at a time. We wouldn't be taking them in, but it was a soldier's ritual for him, I recognized, soothing as a mantra or a rosary.

My mother, on the other hand, chatted

brightly with Terry over laundry and lent a hand with the ironing, commenting cheerfully that it was only what she'd be doing if she were at home.

I knew full well that my mother had a morosely efficient cleaning lady who came in twice a week and could iron with military precision, but I didn't spoil the illusion. My mother caught my eye with a faint smile and I realized she was quite intentionally mounting a charm offensive. As if that would make it harder for Terry to betray us, if she liked us.

Now, Terry wheeled the Porsche into a space that had O'LOUGHLIN on a little white marker board at the head of it, like a grave. Sean pulled into a designated visitor's slot further down. Terry switched off the engine and sat for a few moments, not moving, staring straight ahead at the huge building that loomed in front of us.

"As my mother said, Terry," I told her quietly, "you're doing the right thing."

"Am I?" She turned her head, regarded me bleakly. "So, why do I get the feeling that nothing good will come of this, either way?"

"We just need you to get us through the door," I said, sidestepping the question. "After that, you can walk away. Claim we duped you — threatened you, blackmailed you. Whatever you like. But don't back out on us now."

"I won't," she said, eyes flicking back to the building again. She let out a shaky breath. "I'm just not used to all this cloak-and-dagger stuff, you know?"

Sean appeared by my door, opened it for me. "All right?" he said.

I nodded. Last thing, before I got out, I slid the SIG, complete with its holster, out of my waistband and tucked it into the glove box, trying to ignore the deep sense of foreboding to be leaving it behind.

We climbed out and walked sedately towards the front entrance, the five of us. I saw my mother move close alongside my father, but she didn't take his hand, even though I knew she wanted to. Terry had warned us there were security cameras on the outside of the building that would be monitoring our every move.

We'd talked over a cover story that afternoon. If questioned, Terry was going to claim we were legal people, working on something to do with the licensing of the new treatment in Europe. Important enough to warrant a weekend meeting. We were all wearing suits. Even my mother had dug in her voluminous suitcase and brought out something businesslike for the occasion. And between us we had a smattering of enough European languages to be reasonably convincing, unless anyone really gave us the third degree.

The front entrance was well lit, spotlighting our approach. Terry led the way, swiping her ID card through a scanner outside the first set of glass doors, which slid open in front of us. I followed her through. My father's manners had him stepping back automatically to allow my mother to go ahead of him.

It was pure chance, then, that the three of us women entered the lobby first and, as we did so, I saw a figure emerge from one of the office doorways on the far side of the metal detectors. A blond woman, tall, slim. Familiar.

Vondie.

"Out, out, out!" I shouted, grabbing my mother as I started to wheel for the doorway. Sean didn't hesitate. He piled into my father like a rugby tackle, forcing him back through the outer doorway when he'd barely stepped inside the building. Alarms started to shriek all around us.

Terry froze. I reached for her arm but she darted out of my grip, and I wasted maybe half a second going for her again. By which time it was too late. The doors had slammed shut and red lights glared above them. I caught sight of Sean's face, bone white with fury, safe on the far side of two sets of anti-ballistic glass. Then he was gone, hauling my stunned father with him by the collar of his coat.

By the time I turned back, there were six Storax security men forming a semicircle around us. Big guys, not intimidated at all at the prospect of taking on a trio of un-armed women. Three had extending batons, two had TASER stun guns, and one was bare-fisted, carrying PlastiCuff restraints. Just for a moment, my own rage had me coldly calculating the odds.

Not good, I recognized. *Not good at all.*

Alongside me, I registered a tight little gasp. My mother. Slowly, reluctantly, the madness faded and I brought my hands up to shoulder height, empty. I'd nothing to fill them with but anger, in any case.

"Very, ah, sensible, ma'am," said a man's voice. "No reason for this to get *nastier* than it has to." I let my head turn slightly and saw the small, rumpled figure of Collingwood step into view from an office marked SECURITY. He'd been watching us all the way in. Which meant he knew we were coming. . . .

"What did they offer you, Terry?" I asked, bitter. I turned, only to find that the lawyer was standing, openmouthed and apparently frozen. For a moment her shock seemed so genuine I thought I might be mistaken, that she hadn't calmly and coolly set us up to walk into a trap. Her eyes flicked from Vondie's triumphant features, to Collingwood, and back again.

Vondie advanced, pushing past the Storax security men until she was standing right in front of Terry.

"What's the matter, O'Loughlin?" she taunted. "Seen a ghost?"

Terry took a step back, threw me a look of horrified realization and whirled towards Collingwood, gesturing to Vondie as she did so.

"You told me she was dead!" Terry said, face white as her voice cracked harsh. "You told me they'd killed a federal agent in the course of her duties and I'd be doing my country a service if I helped you bring them in. You showed me a goddamn photograph, for God's sake! What was it — a fake?"

"Not a *fake,* exactly. I'm sure Charlie here will testify that photograph was the genuine article," Collingwood said in that diffident manner of his. He exchanged a quick smile with Vondie. "Agent Blaylock wasn't dead, is all."

"You lied to me," Terry said quietly, her body so tight, she was shaking. I glanced at her, but she wouldn't — couldn't — meet my eyes.

"I was somewhat, ah, *economical* with the truth, certainly," Collingwood allowed, spreading his hands a little. "But when national security's at stake, ma'am, I believe the end justifies the means." I couldn't fault the zeal in his tone. It sounded for all the world like he believed every word of it.

"What 'means' are those, Collingwood?" I asked. "The ones that had Vondie and good old Don Kaminski threatening to rape my mother if my father didn't take part in his own downfall? That's *justified,* is it?"

That got Terry's attention. Her gaze shot past me to my mother's set face. I took a quick look myself and found my mother had clamped her jaw shut to stop it trembling. A dark flush stained her cheekbones, but her back was rigidly straight and her chin was up with as much pride as she could muster.

"Or the ones that had you forcing Miranda Lee to overdose so she couldn't reveal what had really happened to her husband?" I said, cold and clear. "How do you square it as a national security issue that this company knew what would happen to someone of Jeremy Lee's ethnic background if he took the Storax treatment, and yet they issued no warnings? What was he to you — some kind of lab rat?"

"You sure have formed some *interesting* conclusions about all this," Collingwood said, his fingers performing their habitual dance. "But I think we can continue this somewhere a little more, ah, private, don't you?"

The door to the security office opened again and two more men in plain suits came out. Their faces were vaguely familiar. One was big, with a buzz-cut hairstyle that had me instantly placing him — the guy who'd put my father into the Lincoln Town Car outside the hotel in New York and taken him to the brothel.

The other didn't ring quite so many bells, apart from the fact he was limping. That clinched it. The driver of the pickup truck we'd commandeered after the abortive ambush in Massachusetts. Both eyed me with something amounting to a dark glee.

Collingwood jerked his head and the Storax security men closed in on us. Or rather, on me and my mother, almost elbowing Terry aside. She stumbled blindly out of their way, clearly shattered.

The guard who reached for me was no more than twenty-five, dark-skinned, holding the PlastiCuffs so tight that the bones of his fist showed through. It was nerves that made him rough as he yanked my hands down behind me and zipped the restraints around my wrists. He moved across to pull my mother's unresisting arms behind her.

"Do you have to do that?" I murmured, letting the pain slide out through the cracks, letting him see it. "How would you feel if it was your mother?"

The young man hesitated, his Adam's apple bounced like a basketball in play. He shrugged, embarrassed to the roots of his hair.

"I'm sorry," he muttered. Around him, a couple of the others shifted their feet uncomfortably.

"Do these people know there's no 'national security' involved?" I demanded more loudly, eyes swinging to meet Collingwood's. "That you're working on your own, off the books? That, at this very moment, your superiors are as interested to find you — and in what you've been doing — as we were?"

Collingwood hesitated fractionally, his eyes meeting Vondie's as if to check she was going to stand firm. I don't know what passed between them in that instant, but it must have been enough. He let a smile curve his thin mouth.

"Nice try, Charlie," he said, and if his voice didn't have quite the same confidence to it that it had before, I was the only one who seemed to notice. "You sure do know how to, ah, think on your feet. I admire that," he said with a bit of a chuckle, which he allowed to fade before going on in his most serious voice. "Thank you, guys. We'll take it from here." He nodded to the two men who'd just joined him. "The U.S. government sure appreciates your co-operation in the capture and containment of this dangerous suspect."

"And her aged mother," I tossed over my shoulder, acidic, as Buzz-cut grabbed my arm. "Don't forget that heroic part, boys."

"Charlotte," my mother managed to protest, but I wasn't sure if it was the provocation or the reference to her advancing years she most objected to.

Another uniformed security man came out of the office behind Collingwood and whispered in his ear. Collingwood's face twitched and I knew, in that moment, that they hadn't got Sean and my father.

"Too fast for your rent-a-mob, were they?"

I said mildly. "Shame."

"Let me go after them," Vondie said, breathless with the want of it. She reached under her short jacket and pulled a Glock 9mm out of a belt rig. "They won't get far, I guarantee it."

"There won't be any need for that," Collingwood said grimly, eyeing the pair of us. "If there's one thing I've learned about your father, Charlie, it's that he's an honorable man. I think if we offer him and Meyer the chance to trade themselves for you both, they'll deal."

"In that case," I said icy, "you don't know Sean half as well as you think. The only way you'll get him in here is if you offer your own head." I waited a beat. "Detached, preferably."

"You're in no position to be clever," Vondie said, moving in on me with a sneer.

"You never were," I said. "And you can't go out looking for Sean and my father with all guns blazing, can you? We wondered why we weren't picked up on the way down here. But you're hiding from your own people just as —"

Vondie flipped the gun into her left hand and hit me in the stomach with her clenched right fist. I saw it coming just far enough out to brace, but she put some weight and

491

venom behind it.

I staggered back, heard Terry shout, "For God's sake, you can't do this!" but I was concentrating more on staying on my feet at all costs. The pain was a tight crunch in my gut that radiated out in sharp, nauseating waves. I forced myself not to let it show on my face as I straightened.

"I thought so," I said, as calmly as I could manage. "You punch like a girl."

Vondie bared her teeth at me, might have gone for a second shot, but Terry stepped between us. She took my arms, steadied me, her eyes on my face. "Charlie, I'm sorry," she said quickly. "You have to believe me. They approached me days ago, showed me pictures of Agent Blaylock and told me you'd killed her. That if you tried to contact me, I should play along and lead you here. It all sounded so damned plausible. I didn't have a choice!"

"No choice?" I laughed, and it wasn't a happy sound. "I would have thought when Storax are signing the checks, they'd have a say in how their hired help behaves, wouldn't you, Terry?"

Her shoulders dropped. "You think they're working for us?" she said, and I would have scoffed at the question, but I saw the sudden stillness, the awful realization as it hit her.

"Aren't they?"

"No," she said quietly. "We're working for them."

THIRTY-ONE

They separated us. It was the first thing they did.

Collingwood had me and my mother hustled out of the lobby and taken through into the security area. They had a holding cell back there, presumably used as a secure place to stash intruders until the local law enforcement arrived. Vondie opened the door and shoved my mother inside, twisting a painful lock onto her wrist when the older woman attempted to resist.

My anger flared afresh. I stepped forwards instinctively, but Vondie let go of my mother with a shove and yanked the barred door shut, separating us.

"Sorry," Vondie said, smiling. "No family rooms in this hotel."

The outer door behind us burst open and Terry elbowed her way through. She was struggling against the two security men who were trying, somewhat halfheartedly, to detain her.

"Collingwood, you can't do this!" she snapped. "You've violated their legal rights. Even if you had any kind of a case against these people, it will never get to a courtroom if you deny them their right to legal counsel. I'll stand —"

"You have a sister in San Francisco, don't you, Terry?" Collingwood interrupted, his voice gentle.

Terry stopped, baffled. "Yes," she said, frowning. "What —"

"How would you like her hounded by the IRS? How would you like your cousin's work visa to the UK revoked and her deported in leg irons? How would you like your parents in Concord accused of harboring terrorists and thrown in jail?"

Collingwood jabbed a finger to emphasize each point, jolting her with every new threat, pushing her back. And when she was reeling, he paused, smiled at her almost kindly, let his voice turn coaxing. "You want to do your duty, don't you, Terry?"

"Of course," she said. "But —"

"Well, you've done it. Now let us do ours."

For a long few seconds, Terry wavered, gaze skittering between us. She bit her lip, wouldn't quite meet my eyes. Then, at last, she nodded slowly. "I'm sorry, Charlie," she said, her voice low, and went out.

The two Storax guards had been standing, dumbfounded, listening to the threats Collingwood made against Terry's family. They clearly had no wish for their own relations to come under that kind of official scrutiny. All it took to send the pair of them scrambling for the exit was for Collingwood's gaze to swing in their direction. The door closed behind them with a grim finality.

"You choose your people well, Collingwood," I said, bitter, aware of a faintly shiny taste in the back of my mouth. I faced him. "But if you're not being paid by Storax to clear the way for the licensing of this new drug, what the hell *are* you up to?"

Collingwood didn't answer right away, just jerked his head again and Buzz-cut closed in on me, the pickup driver keeping his injured leg at a safe distance. I must have just nicked him, otherwise he'd be on crutches.

I braced myself, glancing across at my mother, who was pale as death behind the bars.

"I'm not going anywhere without her," I said.

Collingwood swung round, got right in my face.

"Come now, Charlie," he murmured. "Do you really want her to see what we're about to do to you?"

The soft words hit harder than Vondie's punch to the gut. Before I knew it, I'd allowed myself to be dragged out, down a short corridor, into another room. It was empty with painted block walls, a concrete floor, and concealed lighting panels in the ceiling. It might have been a storeroom or an empty office, but it felt like a cell, or worse.

It was a reasonably sized space, but with Collingwood and Vondie, and the two men, it felt oppressively overcrowded in there.

Vondie set about searching through my pockets and quickly found the switched-off mobile phone. I'd emptied out everything else before we'd left Terry's house. I thought of Sean's phone and hoped that he was using it to call Parker right now.

I don't know how much cavalry I can rustle up if you get yourselves into trouble, Parker had told me, *but I'll do what I can.*

The only thing I could do was give them both a little time.

Vondie showed the phone to Collingwood, who nodded back towards me.

"Let her turn it on, just in case."

"Do you really think we've rigged it?" I

asked. "Wow, you're more scared of us than we thought."

The pickup driver stepped up behind me and cut the PlastiCuffs. I flexed my hands a few times, then obligingly thumbed the phone into life. Vondie snatched it out of my hands and pressed a few keys, scowling.

"Nothing."

"It's called being a professional," I said sweetly. "You should try it some time."

"Where will Meyer have taken your father?" Collingwood asked, folding his arms and leaning against one wall.

I shrugged. "Who knows," I said. "He could go anywhere. I hear Phoenix is nice this time of year."

"How much have you told your boss?"

"Everything," I said without hesitation. "We've kept him fully briefed and he's making moves as we speak to have the pair of you hauled in for treason — if that's a recognized crime over here. Back home, you'd probably be sent to the Tower of London and beheaded with an ax for what you've done."

Collingwood's face showed emotion for the first time. "I'm doing my job," he said, darkening with the fervor of a true fanatic. "My superiors may not like my, ah, methods, but I love my country, and if we don't get the jump on this nation's enemies, you can be sure as hell they'll try and get the jump on us."

"Your superiors don't know what you're up to," I said. "Come to that, if you're not taking a backhander from Storax, why the hell are you trying to bury a drug that doesn't work?"

"But it does work," Collingwood said, levering himself off the wall abruptly and pacing, and there was a zealous gleam in his eyes now. "It targets a particular genetic code. Do you have any idea what could be done with that?"

I stared at him blankly. "You're talking about a bioweapon," I said. I laughed. "Jeremy Lee's family were originally from Korea. Is that what this is all about? You've gone to all this trouble for the possibility of developing a side effect into a weapon. What are you intending to do, Collingwood, stand on the battlefield and wait for your enemies' bones to crumble?"

Collingwood stared at me for a moment, then shook his head. "You don't understand the possibilities, just like the bureaucrats above me when I first got wind of this. The Storax people were trying to play down the whole thing, so they could get their license, but I saw what could be done with it, even if they didn't."

I didn't want to let him reel me in, but I couldn't help asking, "How?"

He gave the slightest of smiles, as though he'd known I wouldn't be able to resist his rhetoric.

"Any company that handles government contracts has to be checked out regularly," he said. "I have unlimited access to Storax's files and I like to be thorough."

"So you're a glorified filing clerk," I said.

His face tightened. "You're not an American, Charlie, and you don't understand the threats facing this country," he said. "But, right now, you're one of them." He glanced across at Vondie. "We need to contain this as fast as possible. Find out what she knows and who she's talked to — and where Meyer and Foxcroft are likely to be," he said. "Do it, but with no . . . *outward* damage. If we have to trade her, she needs to *look* to be in one piece, if nothing else."

"There won't be a mark on her," Vondie promised, almost a purr. "Don't you worry about that."

Collingwood nodded and walked out without a backward glance. The door closed behind him.

"Well, *hardly* a mark," Vondie amended. She eyed me, triumphant, savoring the moment. "Okay, boys," she said. "Strip her."

I fought them then, hard and dirty. Knowing what they were trying to do set off all kinds of echoes back down the line, reaching viciously into the past and slashing through reason and training to carve a strake of outright bloody fear.

Even through the white-hot smear of rage, I recognized the fact they had their hands tied. They'd been told not to do anything to me that was going to show, and I was giving it everything I had and a little more besides. So, even outnumbered, I was more than holding my own and I reckoned we were pretty much at stalemate.

And then, as Buzz-cut staggered back, doubled over and starting to retch as he clutched at his balls, Vondie finally stepped in with an exasperated bark of, "Oh, for fuck's sake . . ." and stunned me.

I didn't see her pull it. She reached under my thrashing arms and dug the double electrodes of the TASER directly into my rib cage just below my left breast, which was probably as close to my heart as she could get it.

There was an almost infinitesimal delay, then the stunner's electro-muscular disruption technology stampeded over my neural pathways with all the tact and delicacy of a boot camp drill sergeant. It didn't bother trying to modify the control signals from my brain to my muscles, it blasted them into the ether, screeching commands in their place that I was unable to ignore or defy.

I'd been trained against the older type of stun guns, to focus and to fight through the charge they delivered, but this was like nothing I'd experienced before. I gave it a damn good go, flailing, but my coordination was blown to shit. Fifty thousand volts through your chest will do that to you.

The pain had a jagged quality all its own, ripping out chunks of my nervous system and spinning them away like debris from an explosion, so that some parts of my mind seemed magnified a hundred times and others were just big blank holes of frenzied nothingness.

Next thing I knew I was on the floor, my body rigid. I was peripherally aware that my head was banging on the concrete and that was probably not a good thing, but I couldn't stop the twitching dance of my limbs. My hands had distorted into the twisted claws of an arthritis-ravaged geriatric. I couldn't see, couldn't breathe. It was the worst cramp I'd ever had in my life, the most violent fever, the meanest hangover, all rolled into one.

After that, I don't remember much. They handled me roughly, yanked at my clothes, stuck something sharp in my arm. I think I heard someone groaning out the word, "Bitch!" over and over.

Then the corners of the room folded in neatly over my head, and I went under.

The first things that struck me, when I came round, was the nagging ache in my shoulders and wrists, and the nasty tingling in my fingers. I'd been sleeping, but something was very wrong with the angle. My head was lolling forwards into space, overextending my neck muscles.

They had strung me up, I realized belatedly, with all my weight hanging from restraints round my wrists. Padded restraints, by the feel of it, so they didn't mark me. *How kind.*

I lifted my head, miscalculated how heavy it had suddenly become and had to right myself with a jerk that did nothing for the pain everywhere else. I wondered how long I'd been left like that. Not long, I reckoned, or I would have suffocated like a crucifixion victim.

"Back with us, huh?" said a woman's voice I couldn't immediately place. There was something familiar about the words, though.

I waded sluggishly through my memory, sifting. My father. That was it. He'd said the same thing when I came round in hospital after I was shot. Shot. My father. My mother. New York. Boston. Parker. Texas. Storax. Terry. *Vondie.*

Reality arrived like a subway train, bringing with it a wheezing rush of information. On reflection, I think I preferred things when they were more fuzzy.

I opened my eyes. Somebody had brought in an easy chair and Vondie was reclining elegantly on it in front of me. The chair had been carefully placed out of my reach, even if I'd had the energy to try. She was leafing through a file contained in a thick manila folder and swinging her crossed foot negligently.

She'd taken the time to primp while I'd been gone, I saw. Her platinum blond hair was immaculately pleated behind her head and her makeup was flawless. It helped to disguise the thick nose I'd given her, even if it failed to conceal the damage completely.

It didn't take long to work out why she'd gone to the trouble, and the realization sent a greasy slither of fear coiling through my belly. They'd stripped me naked before they'd dangled me from the ceiling. Never a state of affairs that's going to make you

504

compare well to another woman and feel good about yourself. Not when she's tall and slim and wearing a fistful of designer labels, at any rate. Quite a change from the chain-store brands she'd sported on the UK job.

I forced my stiffened legs to uncurl, biting back a groan as I straightened my feet out with slow, deliberate effort onto the cold floor beneath them, so I could take some weight off my arms.

They'd hung me just high enough so that, when I stood upright, the best I could do with my arms was bend my elbows a little, but they were still largely numb from the restricted blood flow. Eventually being cut down, I recognized ruefully, was going to hurt like a bastard.

"Did I miss anything exciting while I was asleep?" I said around a furred tongue.

Vondie smiled without looking up from her study, as though I wasn't worth any greater response. I waited in silence, muscles shivering, while she played her games, knowing I'd been through this before, or something very like it, and emerged more or less intact.

When I'd been undergoing my Special Forces training, they'd allowed the full-fledged boys to have first crack at interrogating us. It was a matter of pride that they broke us, as they'd been broken in their time, and though I'd held out longer than most, they got to me in the end. They got to everybody in the end.

Vondie finished reading her page and looked up with a smile.

"Your record's impressive, Charlie — in places," she said. "Shame you didn't make the grade for Special Forces, though. That must have stung — being one of the dropouts. The failures. Tell me, were you really raped, or were you just hoping you could screw your way to a pass? Should have started with the instructors. Oh, wait a minute —" She glanced back at the page briefly, raised her eyebrows in mock surprise. "You did."

"Why?" I asked, still breathless from the constriction in my chest. "Is that how you managed to make it?"

Her smile didn't waver, but something tightened around her eyes. "I passed out in the top five percent of my class," she said, and there was no mistaking the pride.

"Yeah," I drawled, aiming for languid as I rolled my head round a few times, trying to work out the giant kinks. "I've heard that can happen in a slack year."

Vondie let her breath out fast. She closed

the file, held it over the arm of her chair and let it go, very deliberately, so it hit the floor with a sharp smack. *Of no further interest.*

I blinked a few times. I don't know what they'd given me, but it was dispersing fast. I'd lost the muzzy feeling in my head and my vision was almost clear.

"Where's my mother?" I said. My mind revolted at the thought of them doing this to her, treating her like this. She didn't have the resources, the resolve, to cope. It would finish her.

Vondie got to her feet and came closer, the limp I'd given her in Cheshire almost imperceptible now. She was smiling broadly. "Well, well, I have to admit that normally it takes my interviewees a little longer to cry for their mommies," she said, making a big show of looking at her platinum wristwatch. "Congratulations, Charlie — I think that's a new record."

I stopped forcing my eyes to lock onto different distances around the bare room and focused totally on her instead.

"If you've hurt her, you know I *will* find you and I *will* kill you," I said with utter calm. I'd never meant a promise more, but I felt nothing. No emotion, no anger. Just certainty. Utter, cold, glittering, diamond-tipped certainty.

Vondie flinched before she could control it, saw that I'd registered her involuntary reaction, and damped down a scowl. Instead, she began to circle, lips pursed, eyes flicking up and down my body in slow, deliberate insult.

"I kind of thought you'd be in better shape — someone in your profession," she said in a beautifully disparaging tone.

I didn't respond. She disappeared out of my field of view and I forced myself not to move my head to try and follow her path. But I couldn't stop myself tensing up, like seeing the fin slice under the surface of the water and waiting for the first crushing bite from the depths.

When it came, her touch was almost a caress, and far more creepy because of that. I felt a cool finger very softly trace the ugly scar of the bullet wound in my right shoulder blade and forced myself not to twist out from under it.

"Got it in the back, huh?" Her voice was soft, too, and very close to my ear. "Running away, were you, Charlie?"

I let my head come up a fraction, just enough to reinforce the memory of the head butt that had smashed her nose. I heard her quick sidestep, the little gasp the sudden movement provoked, and knew I was walking a very dangerous line here.

She stalked back round to stare me in the eye — but not too close. "What a pity you took Don out like that," she said, her voice regretful. "They're still not sure if he'll lose the arm." She paused for another dismissive visual sweep. "He would have had such fun with you. . . ."

"Like to watch that kind of thing, do you?" I said, ice in my chest now, flooding my limbs with such cold I struggled not to tremble. "Is that how you get your kicks?"

She smiled, and it wasn't a pleasant smile. "You can indulge yourself in this little round of bravado all you like," she said. "But it's all going to be for nothing. News flash, honey, this is a pharmaceutical company. They got stuff here that will have you screaming for mercy and spilling your guts — in every sense of the word — in minutes."

She gestured to my left. I twisted my head and noticed, for the first time, that someone had wheeled in a little trolley, on which was a steel tray containing several sets of latex gloves and a number of hypodermic syringes. I had no idea what was in them, and even less desire to find out.

I felt my chin come up. "So, what's keeping you?"

She sat down again, smoothing her skirt as she did so. "We want you to suffer, not to die," she said casually. "We took a little blood while you were out and the lab boys have been running a full tox screen, just to make sure there's no danger of anything *unexpected* happening to you." She checked her watch again and shrugged. "You've been out for a while. They should be back with the results any time now. Soon as they are, we can get this party started."

A moment later — so soon I swear Vondie must have orchestrated it — there was a tap at the door. They'd hung me with my back to it so, when anyone came in or out, I'd have the fear of anticipating their identity and purpose to add to the humiliation they were already putting me through. A nastily sophisticated little touch.

Vondie threw me a triumphant glance as she rose to meet the new arrival. I didn't see who it was. Male, by the tonal frequency of the voice. Harried — shocked, even. I let my body droop slightly, like I was really hurting until I heard the door close again. Not much acting involved.

I expected Vondie to regain her seat for a leisurely read, but she stayed behind me at first, so all I heard was the rapid flick of turning pages.

"You've been a bad girl, Charlie," she said at last, apparent pleasure in her tone. "According to the lab boys, you have Vicodin in your system. Something hurts, huh?"

This time when it came, her touch — in the deep scar at the back of my left thigh — was a sharp jab. My leg buckled and I swung precariously, gulping down the pain with enough air to swallow the noises I was desperate not to make.

By the time I'd staggered upright enough to have my feet and my breath back under me, she was seated again, watching.

"Not enough of it for you to be addicted," she went on, as though there'd been no interruption. "But we could soon change that."

She smiled at my frozen expression for a moment, milking it, then dipped her eyes back to the lab report. She'd almost scanned right to the bottom of the page when she stopped abruptly.

I saw her shoulders stiffen, the paper quiver as her fingers did the same. My gut tightened the same way, like we had some kind of visceral connection.

She looked up again, eyes glinting. "So, tell me, Charlie," she said softly. "Who's the father?"

THIRTY-TWO

"What?"

I jolted like she'd hit me with that damned TASER again. The single word was torn out of my throat as the implications rushed in through the shattered hole. "You're bluffing," I said, and couldn't keep the shake out of my voice.

She has to be bluffing. I can't be! No way! Can I . . . ?

She watched me flounder for a moment, head on one side. "You had no idea, did you?" She smiled thinly. "Well, in that case, let me be the first to congratulate you, Charlie. You think you'll get to keep it?"

"You're bluffing," I said again. *Better. No wobble this time.*

"It's too early for you to be showing any signs, but give it another few weeks and those hormone changes will be kicking right in. You won't be able to ignore them. The mood swings, the nausea, the cramps and the cravings. Before you know it, you'll blow up like a goddamn whale."

She rose, taking care to smooth down her skirt, emphasizing her slender figure, and gave me another malicious smile.

"I assume that bastard Meyer is the lucky guy," she said. "Seeing as you're listed as cohabiting. Unless you've been fucking your new boss on the side, just to hedge your bets. Parker's a cutie, isn't he?"

I clamped my mouth shut and said nothing, but she didn't need to be a mind reader to see the slur of wild emotion tumbling behind my eyes.

"Shame you're gonna lose that flat stomach you've worked so hard on but, hey, you won't have much else to do in the slammer other than work out." She smirked. "That and try to prevent some big butch gang of lady truckers from raping you in the showers. Still, that'll be nothing new to you, huh?"

That punched me out of shock, brought me scrabbling back to the surface, relit the fire. "You sound like you've been there, Vondie," I threw back at her. "Miss it?"

"It's *Vonda*," she growled. She took a breath, got a grip. "So he really doesn't know?" she murmured. "Pity. We could have used that."

I tried a laugh that came out more as a gasp. "You have no idea what you'll be letting yourself in for, if you try hitting Sean with this. . . ."

"Screw what he'll do to *me,*" Vondie dismissed. "What's he going to do to *you?* Consider a hypothetical for a moment. Even supposing by some miracle you get out of this, what happens to your precious so-called career now?"

She waved a careless hand towards the manila file that was still lying on the floor next to her chair. "Can't go risking your life every day, being a bullet catcher, when you've got a kid, Charlie."

"I —"

"And what's Meyer's reaction *really* going to be, huh?" She tapped her fingers against her lips. "Is he still going to be so keen on you when you're just the little wifey at home with the squalling brat? Right now, you think you're *somebody,* huh? Working for Armstrong's outfit in New York — and what about Parker? God, the ink's not dry on your green card yet."

She shook her head, as if bemused by the turn of events. "What happens when you don't have that anymore? When you spend your days up to your neck in unwashed diapers and puke? Is Meyer still going to even *want* you — holding him down? Holding him back?"

She smiled again, warming to her theme. "Being able to blow some guy away at sixty feet isn't exactly the kind of skill that will impress the local neighborhood PTA. And there isn't much else you're good for, is there, Charlie? Of course," she added, her expression turning sly, "there's nothing says you have to keep it." She nodded towards the surgical tray, towards the loaded syringes. "We could do you a favor there."

"You bitch," I said, ragged, losing it as the rage fizzed the edges of my vision. "You utter fucking *bitch* . . ."

Vondie laughed out loud. "Oh, Charlie, your mother would be so shocked — what a potty mouth!" she said, her voice rich with delight. "Speaking of mothers, I seem to remember from our file on Meyer that *his* ma comes from a long line of good Irish Catholics. He may not go to Mass every Sunday, but I'll bet it's gonna go *way* against the grain, finding out you've aborted his kid."

"He won't." *Because I won't. Because I can't. . . .*

"Find out?" Vondie shook her head in synthetic disappointment, making tutting noises. "Oh Charlie, keeping those kind of

515

secrets will kill any relationship stone dead," she said with mocking sadness. "You know that."

She stepped to the trolley and picked up one of the syringes out of the surgical tray. She held it against the light and tapped it with her fingernail, as if checking for air bubbles. The liquid inside was a dull yellow. I'd no idea what it was, only that I didn't want it inside me. Or inside anything I might have inside me, either.

"Speaking of secrets, time to get you to spill yours, I think. Of course, there are a few side effects to this stuff I probably ought to warn you about," she said, gloating openly now. This wasn't work to her. "Birth defects, that kind of thing, but let's not allow little things like that to worry us."

She'd moved closer, unable to resist it as she taunted. She was within a couple of meters now, leaning forwards, shoving that smug smiling face into mine.

"I warned you what would happen if you hurt my mother, Vondie," I said almost under my breath. I thrashed impotently against the restraints, an apparently useless gesture that allowed me to get the feel of them and made noise, so she had to come nearer still to catch my words.

Come on, a little closer. Just a little closer . . .

"Well, that's *nothing* to what I'd do if I thought you were going to hurt my child," I muttered. "Past having your own are you? You dried-up old hag —"

She took that last step, offense coloring her face as she caught the gist.

I bounced up, bunched the muscles in my arms to jerk my feet clean off the floor, scissored my legs and lashed out.

I tried to tell myself later that it was never intended to be a killing blow. That I wanted to cause enough pain to incapacitate her, no more. So I aimed for her face, for the nose I'd already broken once, intending to add insult as well as further injury. But at the last moment she jerked upright and so I gathered a little more momentum before I struck, a little lower than I'd anticipated. Or so I tried to tell myself.

My foot landed hard, side on across her throat. Above my own bellow of effort and pain and rage, I swear I heard the quiet pop as her larynx collapsed.

Vondie dropped the syringe and fell backwards, windmilling her arms. She crashed into her own chair, which tangled her legs and tripped her. Her shoe skated on the manila folder she'd so carelessly dropped, then her back hit the far wall and she slithered down it, clutching at her throat and gasping, eyes wide with shock.

"Top five percent, huh, *bitch?*" I said, breathing hard. "Like I said — real slack year."

Instinct had her battling to rise, clawing for purchase on the smooth face of the blocks. I strained against the cuffs that held me, but I knew they weren't going to give way. There was nothing I could do but dangle there, helpless, and wait for her either to die or to kill me.

Whichever came first.

Vondie made it upright by no more than sheer bloody willpower. She lurched for the trolley again, grabbed another syringe without caring which, and came for me.

I twisted wildly, kicking out. No technique involved now, just anything I could think of to stop her getting that damned needle into me.

And in the back of my mind was the deep, sick sense of panic that it wasn't just me she was trying to hurt.

As she lunged, I jumped again, managed to get both feet up and punched them out into her stomach. The blow sent her reeling backwards. She hit the trolley containing the drugs she'd been intending to use on me, overturning it in a clatter of steel on concrete and shattered glass, and fell amid the ruins, gasping her last breath.

I waited, but she didn't get up again. She'd been dead from the moment I'd crushed her throat. She just hadn't known it.

It took me a minute or so to get my feet back under me, by which time my arms were shaking. Everything was shaking. I was colder than I could ever remember and weary to the marrow of my bones.

Another death on your conscience, Fox. Now what?

I hung like that for a while. I had no way to mark the passing of time, so I don't know how long. It felt like forever, but in reality was probably no more than a quarter of an hour. Long enough. More than long enough for me to think a lot about life — the one I'd just taken and the one that might have just begun.

The sound of the door opening behind me made me start. I braced, but knew I didn't have the energy to mount another defensive attack. I heard footsteps come in, two sets, which faltered as the new arrivals took in the scene of my destruction. It was only a momentary pause.

Terry O'Loughlin moved delicately in front of me, eyes flicking to Vondie's body. The other person with her turned out to be the young security guard who'd put the restraints on me and my mother out in the lobby.

"Ohmigod," he kept saying, trying both to look, and not to look, at my body and at Vondie while he did so. "Is she, like, *dead?*"

So elegant in life, Vondie was awkward and ungainly in death, limbs sprawling, her skirt riding up, revealing a surprisingly utilitarian pair of white cotton knickers.

"I bloody hope so," I said. I met Terry's eyes, saw the shock in them, but anger, too. I hoped it was pointed at somebody else, or my chances had not just improved. "Either cut me loose or shoot me, Terry," I said tiredly, "because if you're not going to let me down, shooting me would be preferable to what Collingwood will do when he finds this."

She stepped forwards. "I had no part in this, Charlie," she said, fierce to the point of tears as she fumbled with the restraints. "Please believe me."

"I do," I said.

My arms dropped abruptly and I discovered I'd been entirely right about one thing. Being strung up was nasty but, for the moment, being let down seemed worse. My knees went and, if Terry hadn't arrested my descent, I would have fallen. The blood pounded back into my whitened fingers, making the nails pulse as though I'd plunged both hands into boiling water. I tried to cradle my arms to my body, but all they did was flop like a pair of drowning fish. The young security guard fumbled out of his jacket and draped it round my shoulders. His face was past scarlet and heading for a shade of purple.

I tried to smile my thanks but my eyes kept sliding past him, wouldn't focus.

"Go and tell them we've found her," Terry said to him. "Tell them to hurry!" He all but ran out of the room.

And, by the sound of it, straight into a fist.

All we heard was the contact of something hard meeting something softer by comparison, the explosive whump of air being knocked out of the guard's lungs, and the solid thud as he hit the ground.

Terry started, but before she could do more than half-rise, the door was pushed open again and Collingwood came in. He was carrying a standard-issue Glock 9mm with the lazy facility of someone completely at home with a firearm, and the dead-eyed stare of someone who thinks nothing of using it.

He took in the scene almost instantly. My

incapacity. Terry, crouched with her arms protectively around my shoulders. And Vondie's body. He moved towards her as though his legs were taking him of their own volition, against his better judgment. Silently, he stood over his dead agent, as if to confirm she was really gone. But there was nothing in his rumpled face. No pain, no sorrow, no anger.

I skimmed my own eyes over the corpse with something close to regret. Regret that I hadn't grabbed the opportunity to take the gun off her hip the moment I'd got loose. As soon as the thought had formed, I dismissed it. I wouldn't be able to hold the damn thing straight yet, anyway. My arms were burning with pins and needles, so I wanted to rub them to ease the violent scuttering under my skin, but I couldn't bear the touch.

Collingwood turned towards us, the gun still held casually at his side, the fingers of his free hand twitching.

"You shouldn't have done that," he said softly. "That was a mistake you'll pay for."

"For God's sake," Terry said, her voice cracking. "She was *torturing* Charlie!"

"Desperate times call for desperate measures," Collingwood said, certainty ringing through his voice like struck crystal.

Desperate measures. Was that all you were doing, Vondie? Trying to break me? Is that why you told me I was pregnant? Even though . . .

"What 'desperate times'?" Terry demanded.

"Whether you want to believe it or not, Ms. O'Loughlin, we are at war. The enemies of our country plot against us constantly," Collingwood said. "We must, ah, use every means at our disposal to combat that threat."

"And that includes torturing innocent women?" Terry threw at him, the anger almost, but not quite, subjugating her fear. She rose, shoulders stiff. "I must have missed the day they taught *that* class at law school."

"Sacrifices have to be made," Collingwood said blankly. "Collateral damage."

Collateral damage. Is that how Vondie thought of me? She was going to pump me full of drugs, knowing what they'd do to an unborn child. Was that just collateral damage, or was she simply having a good time?

"Is that all Dr. Lee was to you?" she asked. "And his wife? And Charlie, her parents, Sean? Me?" She stepped forwards, looked him straight in the eye. "What about me, Mr. Collingwood? Am I just collateral

523

damage, too?"

He stared back and I saw his shoulders drop a fraction. For a second, I thought she might actually have got through to him.

"Yes," he said. He bent his elbow to bring the Glock up, pointing straight at her. "Move back a little farther, if you don't mind, Ms. O'Loughlin. I really would hate to have to kill you unless it was entirely necessary."

"Yes, I'd hate that, too," said a voice from the doorway, and Sean slid into view fast and smooth. Like Collingwood, he too had a Glock, but he was holding it at shoulder height, right hand supported by left, finger inside the guard and already taking up the first stage of the trigger, which acted as the safety. The gun was a hairsbreadth from firing, but Sean's voice was steady, relaxed, showing no strain.

His eyes darted sideways, just once, but I knew he'd taken in the whole thing in that single rapid survey. Knew he'd seen what they'd done to me, could fill in most of the rest.

But not all of it, Sean.

For the first time since he'd entered the room, Collingwood's face showed a hint of unease. He glanced at Terry, not letting the muzzle of his own gun deviate. He gave a kind of sad smile and looked back at Sean.

"You pull that trigger, son, chances are I'll fire anyhow."

Sean shook his head and smiled politely. "Two through the mouth will take out your brain stem," he said. "The only thing you'll do is die. Quickly."

"You Special Forces boys are all the same — all show," Collingwood said. "Had a sniper in Afghanistan who swore the same thing to me. Tried it on a rebel who was holding a ten-year-old girl hostage. Bastard still blew her brains out as he dropped."

"Perhaps your sniper wasn't as good as he thought he was."

Sean was good enough, I knew. He always had been. And if they'd matched off hand-to-hand, he was good enough to break Collingwood's neck before the older guy had a chance to spit.

"Perhaps he wasn't," Collingwood said. "Either way, somehow I don't think you'll risk it, son. Not today. So, I'll give you three seconds to put that gun down before I shoot the lady lawyer here. One."

Sean's Glock stayed up and on target. So did Collingwood's. It was Terry who'd begun to tremble. Sean didn't waver.

What kind of a father will he make?

"Two."

Sean shifted slightly. Collingwood wouldn't have been human if he hadn't let his gaze slide sideways to check the movement. As if they'd planned it, Terry O'Loughlin leapt forwards, her right foot swinging, and kicked him in the balls like she was hoping for nothing better than to see them reappear as lumps in his throat.

Collingwood's reactions were nowhere near as good as Sean's had been under the same circumstances. The government man didn't even get to twitch before the blow landed. He certainly didn't get the chance to take a shot of his own before Sean was on him, twisting the gun out of his nerveless fingers.

Collingwood folded up slowly, mouth working without producing sound other than a slow exhalation, like the last gasp of a deflating rubber dingy. Sean watched him go down and turned away.

"I have to hand it to you, Terry," he said as he came past her, "you've got one hell of a set of legs on you."

"Mm," she said, breathless, her voice almost remote. "I played soccer in college."

"Yeah, and I'll bet you were a striker." He bent in front of me, fingers under my chin to tip my head back, checking the size of my pupils. "What did they give you, Charlie?" he asked, and if he seemed cold and detached, I knew that was the only way he could deal with this.

"They stuck me with something to put me out after they cattle-prodded me," I said. My throat felt raw like I'd been screaming. I nodded towards the smashed contents of the trolley. "Vondie was after payback as much as info, I think, but she didn't get a chance to add anything else to the mix."

He brushed my chin with gentle fingers, brought my focus back. "Good," he said softly, and smiled at me.

I nearly told him right then. Nearly let it burst out of me, but the words just lodged in my throat.

"What?" Sean said quickly, but behind us Collingwood got enough of his breath back to begin to groan.

"It'll keep," I said, dredging up a smile of my own from reserves I didn't know I had.

It'll keep until I know for certain.

We heard footsteps outside the door. Sean turned, braced, shielding my body with his own, but it was my father who came in. On the outside, he looked as together as always, even his tie was perfectly knotted. But inside was a different story. He saw Collingwood stirring limply on the floor, then caught sight of Vondie's body and froze. It was the sight of him, more than of Sean, that snapped me back to reality.

I struggled for my feet, had to claw my way up the wall to make it. "How the hell did you both get in?"

"Terry," Sean said shortly, but his eyes were on my father. "Turns out there *was* a back way, after all."

Terry had found my clothes. They must have been stashed somewhere close but I hadn't seen them. She handed them over, flushed, looking miserable. I needed help to get into them again. My father had seen me naked more times than either of us could count, but he still kept his back turned while Terry and I struggled.

Going to need practice dressing someone else — someone helpless — aren't you, Fox?

I shut it out, yanked on my shirt with enough force to split a seam at the back of the arm, then let Terry nudge my fat fingers aside to button it.

"Did you get hold of Parker?" I asked Sean.

"We tried — believe me," he said with feeling. "It went to voice mail every time. I've left him half a dozen messages."

"Voice mail?"

"Yeah. I'm hoping that means he's in flight." He had moved up alongside my father and there was something strangely similar about the way both of them stood and gazed down at Collingwood while he got himself back together.

"Where's Elizabeth?" my father demanded, in a quiet arctic tone I didn't quite recognize, even from him.

Collingwood looked up, eyed the pair of them. "My guys'll have taken her somewhere nice and, ah, *safe,*" he said. "How long she stays that way depends on you. You let me go and maybe she might come out of this in one piece."

Sean stepped forwards and hit him in the face, a casual downward left that nevertheless had all his weight and muscle behind it, delivered so fast it seemed no more than a trick of the light. One moment the government man was half-sitting, propped on an elbow. The next, his head jerked back and bounced off the wall behind him. He rode it as best he could, brought a hand up and tested the inside of his lip.

He smiled for the first time, a full-blown grin.

"Is that the best you've got, Meyer?" he said, spitting out a bubble of blood. He reached up and tugged at his hair, and a section of it covering his crown came loose and dropped into his lap. Underneath the toupee, the top of his head was completely bald. The ugly scar tissue shone in reddened blotches like a crude patchwork quilt.

"I was an intel man working with the Afghanis," he said. "Got ambushed by a group still loyal to the Taliban. They had me three days — *three days* — and I didn't tell them a thing, Meyer. Think you've got three days to work on me now?"

THIRTY-THREE

"I don't need three days."

My father's voice was utterly calm. Even the underlying tension that normally characterized his speech, gave it its distinctive clip, was gone. His face was a mask. I recognized the sight and sound of him, but not the man beneath.

"Richard —"

"I know more about the human body, its strengths and weaknesses, than you will learn in a lifetime," he said, cutting Sean off with a faint little half smile.

"And you think you can hurt me more than a tribe of Afghanis with bayonets and a fire pit?" Collingwood threw at him.

"Hurting you would be barbaric and pointless. The body's memory for pain is generally poor," my father said disdainfully. "No doubt you can recall the emotions attached to the pain you experienced when you were tortured, Mr. Collingwood, rather than the actual pain itself." He let his gaze settle softly onto the government man. "I have no intention of causing you any more pain than is absolutely necessary."

He walked across to the fallen trolley, ignoring Vondie's body as though she'd never existed. He picked up one of the pairs of latex gloves and pulled them on with practiced ease, turning back to his "patient" with something approaching a smooth bedside manner.

"No pain, huh?" Collingwood said, almost with a snort. "You haven't grasped this whole interrogation idea, have you, Doc?"

"It is a new experience for me, I admit," my father murmured. "Of course, if you continue to refuse to release my wife, unharmed, I do intend to cause you irreversible physical damage."

Beside me, Terry took in a gasp of air.

"You might prefer not to see this, Ms. O'Loughlin," my father said politely, glancing in her direction. "Your colleague was injured just outside. He was unconscious and I placed him into the recovery position, but it might be as well to check on him, if you wouldn't mind?"

Terry nodded, a little dazed, and stumbled out. Without her support, I had to lean heavily on the nearest wall for balance. It was just the aftereffects of the TASER hit and the drug they'd given me, I told myself, but I had to forcefully bring to mind what had been done to me in this room, on Collingwood's orders. What they'd been prepared to do to me, regardless of the consequences. And what they might also have been doing, out of sight, to my mother.

My torso felt shaky, my gut churning. I had a vision of my internal organs already parting and shifting like a giant puzzle, repositioning themselves to accommodate the growth of a child.

It's a lie! It has to be a lie.

My father turned to Sean. "I'm going to need his shirt off," he said. "And a very sharp knife."

Sean holstered the Glock and dragged Collingwood upright. The government man tried to resist, but Sean danced him face first into the block work and held him there with unforgiving fingers digging in to the pressure points at the back of his scrawny neck.

He bent close to Collingwood's ear. "I'll rip it off you if I have to. Your choice."

Collingwood's struggles continued and Sean roughly loosened the cheap tie, then grabbed the back of the collar and yanked. The buttons popped and scattered. I could

533

only watch, the way Vondie must have watched while Buzz-cut and the pickup driver stripped the clothes off me.

Collingwood had a lot of body hair. It covered his chest and back like a thick black pelt, showing glimpses of skinny white flesh beneath. I could see his ribs flexing as his breathing quickened, but his nerve still held. There were more scars there, the crisscross of old lash marks where he'd been beaten till he bled. My father froze at the sight of them. Even Sean paused, sucked in a quiet breath.

"Think you can, ah, *match* that?" Collingwood asked over his shoulder, pride hot and strong. "You're a *civilized* man. That was done to me by savages."

"All men are savages under the skin, Mr. Collingwood," my father said, icy in his control now. "Your agent, and her associate, terrorized my wife in her own home. They threatened to beat and rape her — on, I have no doubt, your orders. Did they also stand over Miranda Lee while she slipped into unconsciousness? That tends to take the shine off one's sense of decency and fair play."

Sean caught sight of the restraints hanging from the ceiling and, just for a second, a stillness came over him that I recognized as rage.

He rammed his elbow into Collingwood's kidneys, hard enough to blind him, and swung him away from the wall. By the time the older man had got his breath back, Sean had cuffed his hands over his head and had stepped back, leaving him to sway there. Collingwood's back was towards me and, cowardly, I was glad I couldn't see his face.

Sean reached into his own trouser pocket and pulled out a folding lock knife with a wicked four-inch blade, snapped it open and presented it, handle first, to my father.

My father's face showed nothing other than concentration as he moved round so he could meet Collingwood's eyes, holding the knife up so it was in plain sight as he examined the blade.

"Not quite the edge I'm accustomed to, but I'm sure it will suffice," he said. He looked up. "As you so rightly pointed out, Mr. Collingwood, we don't have three days. I want my wife, and you're going to tell me where she is. If you don't, I will insert the blade of this knife between various of your vertebrae, severing your spinal cord at that point. The longer you refuse to talk, the higher I will go. I have been a surgeon for more than thirty years and, however hard you've tried to ruin my reputation, the fact remains that I am highly skilled in these matters."

My eyes snapped to Sean's and I saw the shock there, but the respect, too. It sickened me. I took a step forwards, stumbled and would have fallen if Sean hadn't grabbed me, propped me back upright against the nearest wall.

My God. We can't let him do this.

I can.

I slumped, pressing an arm across my belly like I was shielding it from witnessing any of this. I imagined a minute fetus sucking cells out of my brain, building itself out of my DNA, somehow absorbing the imprint of everything I'd seen and done. I shut my eyes.

"Here," Sean said. "You look like you could use these."

I opened my eyes again, to see he was holding my bottle of Vicodin in his outstretched palm. You were not supposed to take it with alcohol, I remembered sharply, or if you were operating heavy machinery, or had liver disease. Or if you were pregnant.

And if Vondie *wasn't* lying . . .

"No," I said, shaking my head. "I'm fine."

My father had circled behind Collingwood, who tried to twist with him but the restraints brought him up short. He was starting to sweat.

My father stopped directly behind him and laid his gloved fingers very carefully on the man's lower spine, right around his belt line. I saw the quiver of reaction, quickly stilled.

"Injuries to the lumbar or sacral region of the spinal canal usually result in decreased control of the legs, hips and anus," my father said, matter-of-fact, as though he was delivering a lecture to a group of his medical students. "There is also the likelihood of bowel, bladder and sexual dysfunction."

Collingwood let out a shaky laugh. "You can't do this, Doc," he said, and I wondered if it was us or himself he was trying to convince. "Meyer there, or your little girl, now, they've got the look. I've seen enough killers in my time to know. But you? You're a doctor — sworn to *uphold* life, not to destroy it."

"Quite so," my father agreed easily. "Just as I imagine that *you*, Mr. Collingwood, have sworn to serve and protect your country. It's the interpretation of that oath that makes the difference, wouldn't you say? If," he added, without waiting for a reply, "by sacrificing your health, your mobility, I retrieve my wife, unhurt, then the end will have justified the means."

They were the same words Collingwood himself had used to Terry, back in the lobby. He couldn't possibly have known that, of course. Just fate running one of those odd parallels.

My father walked his fingers slowly a little farther up Collingwood's back. The government man was thin enough that the ridges of his vertebrae stood out like the plates of a prehistoric stegosaurus, just as easily defined.

"Damage to the thoracic spine results in paraplegia," my father went on. "You're likely to retain control of your hands but not your abdominal muscles, so you will not only be confined to a wheelchair and catheterized, but you will have to be strapped in like a rag doll."

"Pretty pictures you're painting, Doc," Collingwood said. He was sweating badly now, and even he heard the desperate edge, the false bravado, in his tone. But he had guts, I'll give him that. "I can't say I approve, but you have, ah, a certain style."

"How's this for a 'pretty picture,' Mr. Collingwood?" my father snapped, his face tight and white across his bones. "Spending your days tied to a wheelchair, shitting into a bag, pissing into a tube, and never having another hard-on for the rest of your life."

My mouth dropped open, I know it did. My father was cold and clinical and there were times when I would have sworn he had ice in his veins, but I'd never heard him stoop to crudeness. Never heard him really swear, or lose his temper, or make an off-color remark. That shocked me more than the violence of what he was proposing.

It must have taken Collingwood aback, too. He was silent as my father's fingers walked higher still, to somewhere up above his shoulder blades. "Cervical injuries are the most debilitating," my father went on, toneless again now, his outburst forgotten. "They normally result in what is known as full or partial tetraplegia — complete paralysis. C-7 — here — is the last point at which you can still expect to live any kind of independent existence. You may have some control over your arms, but your hands and fingers will be compromised."

"The Afghanis beat the soles of my feet, flayed the skin off my back, broke both my arms, my hands, and my left leg in three places," Collingwood said, like he was clinging on to the conviction that whatever was about to happen now would not — could not — be worse. "They left me to die in the mountains."

"Yes," my father said distantly, "but you didn't die. And you must have known that, should you survive, there was every chance of recovery." He moved slower now, counting off each rise. "C-6 means you'll entirely lose the use of your hands. C-5 and C-4 — you might perhaps be able to move your shoulders and biceps, getting weaker, naturally. At C-3 you lose diaphragm function. You'll need a ventilator to breathe."

His fingers were almost at the back of Collingwood's neck now, delicate, light.

"I don't think you need to know about anything higher — the atlas and axis. You'd be dead. And I have no intention of letting you take the easy way out." He leaned closer, so he could almost whisper in Collingwood's ear. "Not like your people gave poor Jeremy Lee the easy way out. But that was after his spine had collapsed over a period of months, causing chronic pain as well as a gradual paralysis. Do you consider it ironic, Mr. Collingwood, that the same fate is going to befall you?"

He stepped back, seemed to shake himself, glanced at Sean's expressionless face but carefully avoided mine. "The incision itself will be excruciating — albeit briefly," he said. "You might want to hold his legs."

"Wait a minute —" Collingwood sounded

breathless, but that could just have been from the way he was hanging. He twisted again, struggling now. Sean anchored his legs while I stood as a helpless bystander, unable to stop the sudden runaway plunge of thoughts inside my head.

Hey, Mummy, what did you and Daddy and Grandpa do in the war?

"You don't have a minute," my father said. He steadied the tip of the knife against the skin covering Collingwood's spine. "You have participated in the deaths of two people of whom I was extremely fond. You have ruined my career, ordered the torture of my daughter, and now you are holding my wife. Say good-bye to your legs, Mr. Collingwood."

His hand slid forwards and the blade penetrated, sending a vivid viscous spill of scarlet across the pallid skin.

Collingwood shrieked. His body voided, but still the overwhelming stench in that room was sweat and blood and fear. Sean let go and staggered back as if, right up to that point, he'd believed my father was bluffing. A part of me had believed it, too.

Collingwood's knees buckled, so he was hanging entirely from his arms. I saw his spine flex, saw the ripple of vertebrae as he collapsed, then realized that he was still moving his feet. Still capable of doing so.

My own legs refused to keep me upright and I slid, very slowly, to the base of the wall.

"The next cut," my father said, unconcerned, mopping away some of the ooze with Collingwood's own tattered shirt, "will be for real."

"She's in the lab!" Collingwood almost screamed it. "In the research lab. Second level. They haven't touched her. They're waiting for my orders. They haven't touched her! Please! You have to believe me."

My father paused, stepped back. His expression was carefully blank, but I saw the throb of veins pulsing at his temple and could only feel some minor relief that this was having an effect on him after all.

But not enough to make him stop.

"Why?" It was Sean who spoke, recovered enough for his tone to be as dispassionate as my father's. "Why should we believe that a man who held out for three days against Afghani tribesmen would give us the truth so easily?"

"I am!" Collingwood yelped. "I am. I swear to God. Jesus. Why would I lie?"

"Because you know what would happen if she's already dead?" Sean said, arms folded, head tilted slightly. "Why did you arrange a trap for us here, Collingwood? Not to arrest us, certainly. You tried misinformation, blackmail, threats, but they didn't work, did they?"

He moved round in front of the government man, ducked so he could be sure of eye contact. "Richard loves his wife — enough to ruin himself for her. You counted on that. But you didn't count on the fact that Charlie loves her parents too much to allow them to go down without a fight." He straightened, looked down at the bowed head without emotion. "If you'd done your homework, you would have known you had to take out Charlie — and me — right at the start, instead of leaving us until last. And you're foolishly still hoping you can come out of this on top, aren't you? So, is Elizabeth alive or not?"

Collingwood lifted his head, pulled his lips back as much in a snarl as a smile. He'd bitten his tongue and the blood stained his teeth.

"I don't know. Could be," he said, panting. "We were waiting to see what we could get out of the girl before we killed the old lady. Hell, we were going to kill the whole fucking bunch of you, anyway. Medical research lab is always working with bodies. What's a few more?"

My father had moved in again, to lean over his shoulder. I couldn't see exactly where he had his hands, but from the set of his shoulders, I could guess.

"Don't," I said, finding my voice. It came up rusty. "Please don't. We have what we need. We have the information. He's finished. It's over. You cross the line and there's no coming back. Please, don't do this to him — to yourself."

My father twisted, flicking his eyes back to meet mine. Same color, same shape. Same blood between us, binding us together. What else had I sucked out from his genes? What would I, in my turn, pass on?

"Do you hear that, Mr. Collingwood?" he said softly. "My own daughter thinks I've become a monster. Well, at least you have the satisfaction of knowing that, whatever I am, you helped create me."

His arm, his hand, slid forwards. Collingwood threw his head back and his body jerked, horror and utter disbelief in his eyes in the split second before they rolled back in his head and he fainted.

My father carefully withdrew the knife and wiped the blade clean. He neatly folded it up and handed it back to Sean with an absent nod, like he'd just borrowed a handkerchief or a pen. He peeled off the gloves and dropped them on the floor. They were bloodied to the wrists.

"You may as well let him down," he said, straightening his cuffs. "He won't be going anywhere."

THIRTY-FOUR

In the corridor outside, Terry O'Loughlin was sitting next to the groggy security guard. She had both hands pressed over her ears and her eyes tight shut and she jumped when I staggered over and touched her shoulder.

"Is it . . . over?" she said, pale as winter. "Is he dead?"

"Yes, it's over," I said. "And no, he isn't."

But maybe he'll wish he was.

My father paused and looked down at her. "Whereabouts on the second level is the research lab?" he said, and the clipped note was back with a vengeance.

She gathered those lethal legs underneath her and pushed to her feet. "I'll show you," she said, doggedly undaunted.

"Just tell us, Terry, and we'll find it," Sean said, his voice quiet. He jerked his head. "What started in there isn't over."

Her jaw hardened, just a little. "And I

546

helped start it," she said. "So I won't shy away from seeing it end."

Sean stared at her a moment longer, then nodded like she'd passed some kind of test. His eyes flicked to me. "And are *you* up to this, Charlie?" A challenge there, too.

No.

"I'll be fine," I said, knowing he'd sense the lie but have no choice other than to run with it. And even as I spoke, Vondie's words came back to me, cruel and bitter as a blade.

Keeping those kind of secrets will kill any relationship stone dead. You know that.

Sean moved in close, crowding me. "You're suffering, Charlie," he said tightly. "Do you think I can't see it? If the damned Vicodin will help you get through this, just take it and don't be so bloody stubborn."

"I —." I stepped back, still trembling but gaining steadily. "I'm fine," I repeated.

He handed me the Glock he'd taken from Collingwood, watched me close my fist around it. I didn't expect that a man of Collingwood's experience would carry a weapon unready, but I brushed my index finger over the loaded chamber indicator anyway, just to be sure, dropped the magazine out to verify a full load, slapped it home again, and returned his stare, defiant. "Let's just get this done."

"All right." He stepped back, his face shut down. "Okay, Terry, lead the way."

She took us up a utility stairwell to the next floor, through a maze of corridors that all looked the same and went on for miles, past labs and huge soulless open-plan office spaces. The place had the sterile smell of air conditioning over new carpet and old sweat, laced with the thin pine scent of industrial cleaning fluid.

We moved as quietly as we could, Sean ahead, Terry directing him, my father behind her, seeming almost unaware of his immediate surroundings, me covering our rear, my limbs returning to me with every stride.

Working weekends was obviously not company policy at Storax. We encountered nobody, saw nothing except the empty cubes of office drones, containing cluttered desks and dead computer monitors. Did these people have any idea what the company that employed them had been working on? If the check arrived each month, did they care?

Terry halted. "The lab's up ahead," she said, keeping her voice low. "Through the next set of doors. On your left."

"Good," Sean said. "What's the layout?"

Terry shrugged helplessly. "I don't know," she said. "I've never had cause to go in there

548

before. Maybe if I had . . ." She broke off, frowning.

"You've done more than enough, Terry," Sean said. He smiled. It was the kind of smile that, when he directed it at me, had a tendency to make me go a little stupid. It seemed to have much the same effect on Terry. "You'd best stay here. I doubt they'll let you close enough to punt their bollocks into their throats, in any case."

"Excuse me?"

"He means you probably won't get a chance to kick them in the balls," I supplied as I came past her.

"No, I guess not," she said, looking faintly embarrassed. "But I'll stay close. I reckon, when this is over, you might just need a good lawyer. And I have a feeling I'll be making a career move."

I glanced at my father. "You should stay here, too," I said abruptly. "We can't protect you when we go in there. Trying may get us all killed."

"I don't expect you to protect me, Charlotte. I expect you to do your job," my father said, coldly imperious.

I stared at him blankly for a moment before I saw the underlying thread of panic.

If you don't save her now, how can I live with my part in this?

Was this acceptance at last? If so, why did it feel like it had all come too little, too late? And why did I feel he'd turned into someone whose approval was the last thing I wanted.

He nodded to Sean, a stiff jerk of the head. Sean nodded back. Then we were moving forwards, the pair of us, strides matching. I'd seen Sean kill and it hadn't affected the way I felt about him. But seeing my father primed to do the same had sickened me to the soul. Ironic that it was probably a mirror image of how he felt about me.

I shut it out, shoved it down deep, and did the only thing I knew how to do well — prepared to kill two strangers without even knowing their names.

We went through the doors into the research lab totally in sync. Low left, and high right, angled so we were covering each other's back.

As soon as we were through the door, we saw them. Buzz-cut and the limping pickup driver. I had the Glock up and sighted instantly, but the picture presented meant I did not fire. Neither of us did.

The lab was mostly white, lined with cupboards and workbenches, with half a dozen clearly delineated workstations. No clutter. Just mundane, like a particularly large kitchen that happens to have no appliances. It smelled of something sharp and acidic that I couldn't place.

My mother was perched on one of the high stools that were slotted into each workstation. It had been dragged out into the center of the tiled floor and she sat very upright, with her knees together and, from the awkward set of her shoulders, her hands bound behind her back.

The man I'd christened Buzz-cut was standing to her right, which made him mine. He had a large-caliber silvered semi-automatic with the hammer back and the muzzle jammed into my mother's ear, where it wasn't going to come off target easily.

As soon as we'd come in, my mother's eyes flew to mine and stayed there. She was terrified, but I saw the relief creep into them at the sight of us — at the sight of me. The situation was hopeless, impossible, but she saw us and for some reason I didn't think I'd ever be able to fathom, it gave her hope.

The pickup driver was far right, splitting our field of fire. Sean's Glock seemed to lock onto him of its own accord. The pickup driver also held a Glock. Without hesitation, he pointed it right back.

"Looks like we have a standoff," Sean

said. "Are you prepared to die here, gentle-men?"

"If we have to," Buzz-cut said calmly.

"You must see this is not a winnable situation," I said evenly. "From either side. You shoot, we shoot. People will die. What's the point?"

He shrugged. "Surrender is not an option," he said, and I saw the fierce pride in him. He skimmed eyes over me that were cold and flat. "You should know that ma'am."

So, he'd been a soldier, recognized like for like.

"O-kay, so, what happens now?" I said, allowing a hint of impatience to show. "We all wait here till we die of old age?"

Buzz-cut didn't answer. Time bunched up around us, slow and heavy, as we waited for the first nerves to fail.

Then, suddenly, the door behind us punched open. Sean and I darted sideways, ready to meet a new threat, but it didn't take a fraction of a second to know we were outgunned.

The six-man team that entered were dressed in SWAT black, armed with Heckler & Koch MP5 submachine guns, utterly focused, and completely multilateral when it came to taking sides. They pointed weap-

552

ons at all of us.

I tuned out the yell of commands to give ourselves up and get down on the ground, and kept the sights of the Glock lined up steady on Buzz-cut's face. Until he lowered his weapon, I was damned if I was going to lower mine.

The pickup driver was the first to fold. But then, I suppose he had the freshest memory of what it meant to be shot. He came off target, letting the barrel rise as he brought both hands up. Very slowly, using only his finger and thumb, he laid the gun on the ground. When he straightened, his hands were already linked behind his head.

As soon as the pickup driver surrendered his gun, Sean snapped his aim across to Buzz-cut, nearly giving the two guys who were covering him heart failure. If they'd been any less well trained, less experienced, they probably would have taken him out right there and then.

The shouting died away. They must have known they were wasting their breath. I wondered how long it would be before the shooting started.

Then I heard more footsteps slightly behind me, to my right. Two sets. Not the harsh dull clatter of boots on tile, but the lighter tread of good shoes with leather soles. I didn't take my eyes away from Buzz-cut, even when I saw the way he stiffened at the new arrivals.

"Sean, Charlie," Parker Armstrong said in a calm and reasonable voice. "Please lower your weapons."

The surprise was such that, for a moment, neither of us moved.

"In case it's escaped your attention, Parker," I said, without turning, talking through gritted teeth to avoid moving my jaw and unsettling my aim, "the guy over there has a gun to the head of a hostage."

I had to think of her in those terms. Depersonalize it. It was the only way I could function.

"It hadn't," Parker said, and his voice was dry now, "but I need you to trust me on this."

There came a silence into which I swear I could hear the beat of my own heart.

"If he pulls the trigger," Sean said in that pleasantly lethal tone I knew so well, "I will kill him, regardless."

"And if you don't, I'll kill him for you," Parker said, diamond hard and just as polished. "But it won't come to that. We *will* work this out. Stand down, both of you."

Sean let out his breath on a long hiss, then relaxed out of a shooter's stance. With a feeling of hollow regret, I did the same. The nearest man in black held out his hand for the Glock. I stared him down and kept it in my hand, letting it hang alongside my leg with my finger outside the guard. He saw the blood in my eye, shrugged, and didn't make an issue of it.

Across the room, my mother's lids fluttered closed, like she was praying. I couldn't bear to watch, glanced towards Parker instead and saw my boss was back in his usual sober-suited office attire. He looked tired, the lines on his face more deeply etched than when I'd last seen him in the rest stop south of Boston, only days ago.

He acknowledged our capitulation with no more than the twitch of his facial muscles, but a little of the tension went out of his shoulders. He'd staked his reputation on being able to control us, I realized, and more besides.

Parker threw a look to the man who was standing silently alongside him. *I've played my part. Now you play yours.*

The other man was older, someone I'd never seen before, with a silver mustache and cold, cold eyes. He, too, was wearing a somber suit, with a bland tie and spit-polished shoes, but he was military through to his bones. He accepted Parker's unspoken challenge without a flicker, and lifted his chin, letting his voice carry over to Buzz-cut.

"You too, son," he said, low and slow like tires on a gravel road. "Stand down, now."

Buzz-cut braced, like he had to force himself not to come to attention.

"Sir, I am acting under direct orders from Mr. Collingwood —"

"Mr. Collingwood is no longer . . . fit for duty," the man said, slicing him off. He let his eyes trail briefly over me and there was nothing in them. It was like being gazed at by a snake. "He has been relieved."

A faint flush appeared across Buzz-cut's cheeks. "I'm sorry, sir, but my orders still stand. Mr. Collingwood was very clear on that."

You had to admire his guts, if nothing else. Six men pointing guns at him and he never flinched, never wavered. Easy to see why Collingwood had chosen this man to do his dirty work.

My mother's eyes were still closed. As I watched, a single tear broke loose from the confines of her right eye and trickled slowly down her cheek.

"Son," the man with the gray mustache said, with ominous quiet that was more ef-fective than any parade-ground bark, "you know who I am, don't you?"

Buzz-cut paled visibly. "Yessir!" he said. And still he didn't lift the gun away from my mother's head.

I caught a slight movement behind Parker. My father and Terry O'Loughlin had moved into the doorway of the lab. They would have been told to stay back, I knew, but could no more obey that command than voluntarily stop breathing. The man with the mustache ignored them both.

"I don't know what Mr. Collingwood told you, son," he said. He took a step forwards, speaking each word clearly, so there would be no mistakes, "but I can tell you, right now, that you have been involved in an unsanctioned operation. Do you understand what that means?"

"Sir?"

For the first time, his gun lightened a fraction. To my left, one of the SWAT team rolled his shoulders a little and settled more fully into the stock of his own weapon.

The man with the mustache sighed, took another step. "Mr. Collingwood took it upon himself to encourage Storax to investigate the side effects of one of their drugs without withdrawing it from testing. In order to do this, he lied, falsified his reports, and misused the resources placed at his

557

disposal by the federal government. He may even have believed he was doing the right thing, but in truth he was off the books — off the goddamn planet, if I'm any judge," he said, temper finally cracking through like a whip. "And I will tell you now that I intend to deal with his transgressions most . . . severely. He may have convinced you he was a patriot but in reality, son, he was a traitor. A traitor," he went on, beating the message home with measured strokes, "who has brought disgrace to his country and his office . . . and to the people who placed their trust in him."

Uncertainty reamed Buzz-cut's features. His eyes skimmed over the man with the silver mustache, the SWAT team, calculating the odds. It can't have taken him long to work out that resistance was, indeed, futile. I cursed him from inside my head, spitting soundless screams, as if I could compel him to yield by will alone.

But still he held.

The silence stretched, gossamer threads that sparked and snapped under the artificial lights. My eyes locked onto my mother's face, the flutter of her eyelids as God knows what thoughts careered through her mind. If she died here, now, then everything we'd been through — everything we'd done —

would have been for nothing.

"What we have to decide here, son," the man with the mustache went on, halfway across the narrow gulf that separated them now, "is just where your loyalties lie. Did you trust Mr. Collingwood's word implicitly, or did you actively collaborate with him to develop a bioweapon using a company that's foreign-owned, operating on U.S. soil? The stand you're making here leads me to believe you knew all the risks. This is the last stand of a desperate man, son, not a patriot."

"Sir! I am a patriot, sir!" Buzz-cut rapped out, voice close to breaking.

"Well, in that case, son," the man murmured, "you'd best prove it to me."

He took a final step, bringing him within a meter of Buzz-cut. He held out his hand, palm up. After a long, agonizing two seconds, Buzz-cut withdrew the gun from my mother's skull and let the hammer down slowly. He reversed his hold and handed the piece over to the man with the mustache, grip first in smartly formal presentation.

I heard a collective exhalation, the quiet gush of relief from the SWAT team as they realized that today was not their day to kill or die.

The man with the mustache handed off the gun to one of his men, who crabbed forwards to take it. Another yanked Buzz-cut's wrists behind him and tightened the PlastiCuffs in place.

Buzz-cut stood, head down, gaze turned inwards, as if replaying all the things he'd done without question, on Collingwood's say-so. More than he could justify, if his misery was anything to go by. More than he could bear. When he lifted his head, his eyes were glistening.

My mother opened her own eyes, very slowly, the shock blatant in them. Sean elbowed his way through the mill of black and brought out the same pocketknife my father had used to torture Collingwood. He sliced through the ties binding her wrists.

With nothing to hold them, her arms flopped forwards and, when she climbed down from the stool, her legs folded under her. Sean tucked an arm behind her knees and lifted her without apparent effort. She clung to him and let the tears fall freely now. When I fell in alongside she grabbed my hand with icy fingers, paper skin over fragile bones, and wouldn't let go.

As Sean carried my mother past the man with the mustache, he reached out and put a hand on Sean's arm. The touch was light, the way it can be when it's backed by limitless strength and power.

"You and Miss Fox wouldn't be thinking of taking off again, would you, Mr. Meyer?" he said, making it both a threat and a polite inquiry, all at the same time.

Sean paused just long enough to make his lack of intimidation felt. "No," he said.

The man nodded. "Good, because this time you *would* have the full weight of the U.S. government tracking you down," he said. "I believe we have some things to discuss. I trust you'll make yourself available."

Sean bridled but kept it in check. "Yes sir," he said, in the same blankly neutral tone that skated thinly along the borders of insubordination.

"I'm sure that you will," the man with the mustache said. His gaze shifted onto my father, who'd come forwards, unable to hold back any longer. "This whole thing has been a goddamned mess," he added in that careful way of his, eyes moving to me now. "It's going to take some cleaning up."

"I'm sure we can work something out," I said, injecting just as much steel into my own voice.

I thought I saw a wisp of a smile skim across the older man's face, but it didn't trouble his eyes.

"Oh, I'm sure we can," he said.

THIRTY-FIVE

"Here," Terry O'Loughlin said, "drink this."

She handed me a cone of water from the cooler in the room she'd coaxed us into after the man with the mustache and his team had departed.

I took what I was offered, grateful, realizing as I did so that I still had Collingwood's Glock in my hand. For a moment I struggled to recall quite how it had got there. *Still punchy.*

Out of habit, I jammed the gun between my thigh and the chair cushion, keeping it within reach, and took a sip of water. It was cold enough to feel the glassy slide of it right down the inside of my ribs, clutching at my heart as it went.

My mother had been clamped to my father's side ever since Sean had put her down. My father had snatched her close, splaying his hands across her back and burrowing his face into her hair, like he was trying to take the very essence of her into himself. Proof of life.

I heard sobbing, but I couldn't have said for certain which of them it emanated from.

I desperately wanted to reach for Sean in the same way but I knew, if I did so, I was likely to break into pieces and it would all come spilling out. And I couldn't bring myself to do that in front of Parker, in front of my parents. Even in front of Sean. So I shrugged off the hand he put on my shoulder, throwing a quick *later* smile in response to his frown of concern.

Vondie was lying, I told myself again as I pulled away. *No way can it be true. We've always been so careful. . . .*

Terry had quietly taken charge, shepherding us gently into what looked like a staff break room nearby, where there were low chairs and tables and the watercooler.

Beside me, Sean sat leaning forwards with his forearms resting on his thighs, shoulders hunched, staring low into nothing.

Pure exhaustion sucked the blood out of my veins. Adrenaline, as I knew full well, was a single-minded taskmaster, strident and brutal. As it dissipated, I felt my system overload by way of retribution. A vicious headache — I told myself it was from the TASER or the drugs — had started hammering at the base of my skull. The more attention I paid to my body, the more I found there wasn't a part of it that didn't ache, from my neck and shoulders to the soles of my feet. It was another jolt to remember why.

It had been a long time since I'd killed somebody that way — up close and personal. That part of it didn't get any easier with practice.

"I won't ask if you're all right," Parker said, hitching the crease of his suit trousers as he sat down opposite. If it wasn't for those watchful eyes, you'd have thought him urbane, unthreatening. "Because I can see you're not — any of you."

"No," Sean said, and he was looking at me while he said it.

My mind was drifting. I pulled it back on track with effort. "Parker, what the hell are you doing here?" I said. I jerked my head in a vague gesture to indicate the direction in which the man with the silver mustache and his burly entourage had departed. "And who *was* that guy?"

Parker glanced at Sean, then let his gaze shift to Terry, still hovering by the water-cooler. "As soon as it became clear that Collingwood wasn't on the level, I began trying to go over his head," he said. He let out a slow breath. "Not easy. Nobody likes to hear there's something rotten at the core of their own organization, and the kind of agency Collingwood is a part of, well, they like to hear it even less."

"But you convinced them," Sean said, and it wasn't a question. It was praise.

Parker took a drink of water, ducked his head in acknowledgment. "Collingwood's immediate superior was stalling, so I had to fight my way farther up the food chain. Epps — the guy you just saw — let me just say you don't get much higher without being voted into office."

"So, he has the power to make all this . . . go away?" I said faintly. I scrubbed a tired hand over my face, but the image of Vondie's crumpled body and Collingwood's damaged spine was imprinted on my retinas. I glanced at my father. He and my mother were sitting thigh-to-thigh on the sofa to Sean's left, not quite listening, but not quite oblivious to the conversation going on around them, either.

Parker nodded. "Once I laid it all out for Epps, he took immediate action. Guy at his level wants something done, it gets done. We were already in the air with a full HRT — Hostage Rescue Team," he elaborated for Terry's and my parents' benefit, "when

Sean's messages came through."

Out of the corner of my eye, I saw my father straighten, very slowly.

No. Oh no.

Sean must have seen it, too.

"You did what you had to, Richard," he said, speaking fast. "We had no way of knowing how close Parker was when we went back in."

"But if we'd only waited a little longer," my father said, swallowing the bitterness that threatened to spill out over his words, "I wouldn't have had to do any of it, wouldn't you agree?"

"Twenty-twenty hindsight," Sean said with quiet vehemence. "We didn't know, and couldn't afford to wait."

My mother reached out and threaded her fingers through her husband's. Her gaze was fixed on his face, which was still pale and shiny from the aftermath, anxious at his obvious distress. He glanced sideways at her and flinched away from the absolute trust he saw there, like it burned him.

Because he no longer trusted himself.

"I've always prided myself on being a rational man — one who doesn't let my emotions rule me," he said in that remote voice. "I know you sometimes find me cold, Charlotte. I am required by my profession to be clinical, but I have never considered myself to be without compassion."

He broke off, swallowed again. "But I realize now that what I did back there . . . in that room, was utterly indefensible in human terms. I can offer no justification for it."

"They would have killed her," Terry said suddenly, conviction in her voice. "I think Collingwood would have killed all of us."

"Perhaps," my father said, dismissive, like maybe she was humoring him. "But he didn't get the chance, so we'll never know for certain." He looked up, met my eyes and I saw the violent slur of emotions washing behind his own. "I honestly do not know how you live with yourself, Charlotte. Doing what you do. Knowing what you can do. Why do you think I worked so hard to save that man after we were ambushed in Boston — in spite of what he'd done? So my own daughter wouldn't have another death on her hands, on her conscience." He took a breath to shore up his voice enough to go on.

"But now I have to live with the fact that while I was in that room, torturing another human being, I had no doubts whatsoever about what I was doing. None. And I should have done, don't you think?"

And with that, my cold, detached and rational father put his face in his hands and wept like a child.

EPILOGUE

A month after we got back from Texas, I sat alone in the lofty apartment in Manhattan, staring at a small white box on the coffee table in front of me. I'd faced loaded guns with less trepidation, but that small white box scared the shit out of me.

I'd gone ten blocks out of my way to visit a pharmacy I'd never been to before on the edge of Chinatown. I loitered at the back of the store until the checkout came free, so I could snatch up my purchase and rush it through, hardly breaking stride. Guilty as a teenage kid buying their first pack of condoms.

The irony of that comparison wasn't lost on me. I'd already worked out that the only time Sean and I had been too careless — in too much of an all-fired hurry — to think about such basic precautions, had been that time in the hotel in Boston. That one time.

But sometimes, I knew, one time was all it took.

I knew I'd been putting off finding out for certain if Vondie had been lying when she'd read out the results of that all-encompassing blood test with such sly conviction. That's the secret of a good interrogator, after all, to inject a writhing, squirming sense of self-doubt into the subject. To catch you off balance and batter you down, and to strike while the soft skin over the jugular is exposed.

She'd stripped away my bravery down to bone-level fear and I'd responded in the only way I knew. I'd killed her.

So, what kind of mother would I make?

I thought of my own parents and, somehow, knowing they'd been in the room next to ours, had heard with mortifying clarity what might turn out to have been the conception of their grandchild, made it all the worse.

Surprisingly, perhaps, I'd been in regular contact with my mother since I'd got back. She seemed to have emerged from the events of the previous month with a kind of serene calm, rediscovering an inner core to herself that had been long buried.

"I just feel lucky to be alive," she told me frankly, during one of the chatty transatlantic calls I'd grown, strangely, to enjoy. "It's so easy to waste the time we have, don't you think?"

I wished my father had responded with the same composure but, as my mother had come out into the light, so he'd withdrawn, like the little figures on an ornamental clock. He'd taken a leave of absence from his surgical work at home, my mother told me, was considering early retirement. I didn't get my father's take on it directly. He never seemed available to come to the phone.

The mysterious Mr. Epps, meanwhile — true to his word — had done some considerable cleaning up on our behalf. In return for complete silence on the subject of the whole Storax affair and Collingwood's involvement in it, Epps had seen to it that Vondie's death, and what had been done to Collingwood, was swept under the carpet. My only thought was that it must be one huge carpet — with a bloody big lump in the middle of it.

Collingwood, so I was told, had suffered a partial paralysis of his right leg, and other areas of impaired function. I didn't inquire as to the details. It was not quite enough to put him in a wheelchair, as my father had so eloquently outlined, but it did mean he had to rely heavily on a cane to take the daily half hour of exercise that was all his current incarceration allowed. I doubt I'll ever know if my father spared him the full cut by chance or choice, but I'm inclined towards the latter.

Epps magicked away the charges arising from my father's enforced visit to the brothel in Bushwick. The Boston hospital suddenly clammed up on the subject of Jeremy Lee's accelerated demise. We were not even questioned over the shooting of Don Kaminski during the roadside ambush Vondie had organized just outside Norwood. But, on the downside, Miranda Lee's death remained officially a suicide.

Storax announced a delay in the launch of their new treatment for osteoporosis. Manufacturing inconsistencies were cited as the main reason.

There wasn't much even Epps could do about the news reports that had already gone out regarding my father, or the opinions that had been formed from his own damning statement on TV, which I'd seen at the gym with Nick that day. It seemed a long time ago. But without any ongoing charges to propel the story forwards, it was already old news.

Now, too restless to sit, I jumped up,

stuffed my hands into my trouser pockets and paced to the window.

It was edging towards November, early evening. A wet day, where a sneaky wind had surfed between the skyscrapers to tug at hats and umbrellas down at street level. It had driven the rain down the back of my bike jacket and penetrated the fingers of my gloves as I'd ridden the Buell home through traffic. And I hadn't cared.

I loved my job. More than that, it fitted me, gave me a unique sense of place, of belonging. I didn't have to explain to these people who I was, or excuse what I could do. They already knew and they accepted me in spite or maybe because of it.

I thought back to the conversation I'd had with Madeleine when Sean and I had gone to Cheshire to retrieve my mother, and I realized that I could finally tell her yes, at last, I had the respect for which I'd been searching.

And maybe it was better not to think about the price.

When we'd got back from Houston, Parker had put me straight back into the field without hesitation, even before I'd passed the Stress Under Fire course in Minneapolis. I'd returned from that the week before, to find Sean on assignment in Mexico City.

He'd be gone another week, maybe two.

More than long enough to formulate a way to tell him . . . whatever I needed to.

I turned away from the sliding pattern of rain on the outside of the glass and looked across the room to where that damned white box lay, taunting me. Even buying the bloody pregnancy home testing kit was a form of defeat, I considered. It gave credence to Vondie's invention. Somewhere in the back of my mind I heard her laughing at me still.

But I was late. Nothing unusual in that. My body clock had always been skewed and the slightest stress or trauma tended to knock it off its stride. Taking a hit from a TASER, an armful of dope, a life — it was enough to put a crimp in anyone's day. But it meant I could no longer pretend this might not be a real possibility.

I took a deep breath, snatched up the box as I passed the coffee table and locked myself in the bathroom, even though I was on my own in the apartment.

I had to read the instructions three times before they sank in, followed them to the letter, and set the plastic stick on the vanity, next to the Tag watch Sean had given me. The packaging on the kit boasted 99 percent accurate results in less than a minute.

Sixty seconds, and then you'll know. . . .

I sat on the edge of the bathtub with my arms wrapped round my body as if to ward off pain, and stared at the second hand as it made its stately sweep.

And, quite unbidden, an image of Ella came into my mind. The little girl whose mother's life I'd failed to protect in a frozen New Hampshire forest the winter before. Four-year-old Ella had sneaked under my skin and made off with my heart when I wasn't looking. I'd nearly died trying to save her mother. I'd been fully prepared to do so in order to save the child.

But to do it, I'd had to let the monster out. The cold-blooded monster inside me that could kill without pause or pity. She'd glimpsed it, and been so terrified I'd been ordered to sever all contact with her, permanently. I'd missed her, I realized, more than I'd allowed myself to admit.

And, riding in on the back of that revelation came a bubbling excitement, a dreadful kind of secret joy, that the kind of love I'd felt for that child, and set aside, might be mine again.

Thirty seconds. Come on, come on!

I thought of my father. Would he forgive me, finally, if I presented him with a grandchild — a grandson, to make up for the disappointment of a daughter in the first place? We'd had brief moments of connection along the way, but the greatest of them had been the one that had ultimately driven us furthest apart.

Now, he couldn't even bring himself to speak to me. Did he look at me and see what he'd become, I wondered. Did he blame me for that?

Forty-five seconds. Did that damn watch stop?

I wavered. The fear drenched me in a cold wash. A child. How the hell could I bring up a child to know right from wrong, when I spent each working day with a gun on my hip and had a body count in double figures? How could I be trusted, if I was tired, sleep-deprived, pushed beyond endurance, not to snap and do something even I would find abominable?

And, disregarding Vondie's gleefully dismal predictions, how would Sean *really* react to the news he was going to be a father?

It won't happen. False alarm. She was lying. It'll be fine. . . .

I checked my watch again, to find my minute was up, reached for the plastic stick with hands that were slick and not quite steady. For some time after that, I stared dumbly at the indicator, reread the instructions even though I knew there was no room for doubt about the result. It was indisputably, definitely, positive.

So, Vondie hadn't been lying after all.

ABOUT THE AUTHOR

Zoë Sharp is the author of Barry Award finalist *First Drop* as well as *Second Shot*. She spent most of her childhood living aboard a catamaran on the northwest coast of England. She opted out of mainstream education at the age of twelve and wrote her first novel when she was fifteen. Zoë went through a variety of jobs in her teenage years, before becoming a freelance photojournalist in 1988. She lives with her husband in Cumbria, England, where she is hard at work on her next novel. Visit her at www.zoesharp.com.

The employees of Thorndike Press hope you have enjoyed this Large Print book. All our Thorndike, Wheeler, and Kennebec Large Print titles are designed for easy reading, and all our books are made to last. Other Thorndike Press Large Print books are available at your library, through selected bookstores, or directly from us.

For information about titles, please call:
   (800) 223-1244

or visit our Web site at:
   http://gale.cengage.com/thorndike

To share your comments, please write:
   Publisher
   Thorndike Press
   295 Kennedy Memorial Drive
   Waterville, ME 04901